P9-DCO-707

BRANDED BY A KISS

"You are so beautiful, my cheating lady," Deron breathed, his voice husky. And then, almost roughly, he pulled her against him. Slowly, in contrast to his hard embrace, he bent his head and let his lips brush hers softly.

Meredith felt her eyes close, felt the incredibly soft sensation of his mouth tracing hers. She felt his hands stroking her hair, her face, and the room whirled as she surrendered to his kiss.

All at once he pulled away from her, his eyes blazing down as they swept her face and focused on her mouth. "And now," he murmured, "you are mine, My Lady. And I will not have you forget that you belong to me. . . ."

THE BEST IN HISTORICAL ROMANCES

TIME-KEPT PROMISES   (2422, $3.95)
by Constance O'Day Flannery
Sean O'Mara froze when he saw his wife Christina standing before him. She had vanished and the news had been written about in all of the papers—he had even been charged with her murder! But now he had living proof of his innocence, and Sean was not about to let her get away. No matter that the woman was claiming to be someone named Kristine; she still caused his blood to boil.

PASSION'S PRISONER   (2573, $3.95)
by Casey Stewart
When Cassandra Lansing put on men's clothing and entered the Rawlings saloon she didn't expect to lose anything—in fact she was sure that she would win back her prized horse Rapscallion that her grandfather lost in a card game. She almost got a smug satisfaction at the thought of fooling the gamblers into believing that she was a man. But once she caught a glimpse of the virile Josh Rawlings, Cassandra wanted to be the woman in his embrace!

ANGEL HEART   (2426, $3.95)
by Victoria Thompson
Ever since Angelica's father died, Harlan Snyder had been angling to get his hands on her ranch, the Diamond R. And now, just when she had an important government contract to fulfill, she couldn't find a single cowhand to hire—all because of Snyder's threats. It was only a matter of time before the legendary gunfighter Kid Collins turned up on her doorstep, badly wounded. Angelica assessed his firmly muscled physique and stared into his startling blue eyes. Beneath all that blood and dirt he was the handsomest man she had ever seen, and the one person who could help beat Snyder at his own game.

Available wherever paperbacks are sold, or order direct from the Publisher. Send cover price plus 50¢ per copy for mailing and handling to Zebra Books, Dept. 3208, 475 Park Avenue South, New York, N.Y. 10016. Residents of New York, New Jersey and Pennsylvania must include sales tax. DO NOT SEND CASH.

SWEET LIES

MIRANDA NORTH

ZEBRA BOOKS
KENSINGTON PUBLISHING CORP.

ZEBRA BOOKS

are published by

Kensington Publishing Corp.
475 Park Avenue South
New York, NY 10016

First printing: November, 1990

Printed in the United States of America

Prologue

London, 1784

"Gabriel's done what?" asked Deron Redvers, Duke of Raceford, in disbelief. Above the roar of the crowd at Boodles, London's most notorious gambling establishment, he could barely make out what the man standing before him was saying.

The man looked askance at the duke, taking in the narrowed eyes, the lowered black brows, the set of the square jaw. Dash it, if Raceford didn't look actually furious! This was new. Usually the green eyes were hooded by lazy lids, the face a mask of polite boredom, except when a wager was being made.

Raceford was twenty-eight and had the world at his feet — and didn't seem to care. He was black-haired and handsome as the devil, rich and titled, as yet unmarried. And wild to a fault, always ready for any adventure, showing no signs of settling down to being the respectable peer of the realm or to taking his seat in the House of Lords.

And since he'd come back from America, Raceford had seemed to care for nothing but gambling, horses, and women, with never a serious thought in his head.

Except that, at this moment, he looked dashed seri-

5

ous.

"Our friend, Gabriel, has challenged that sniveling twit, Lord Hamilton Bidwell, to a duel over the Lady Vivienne. St. James Park . . . midnight. Though I can't see why Gabe's done it. She's thrown him over for some rich count nearly twice her age, you know, and her being married to some filthy rich Scottish goat besides. Really quite—"

The Duke of Raceford didn't wait to hear the rest. He was already elbowing his way through the crowd of gamblers in the smoke-filled room, heading toward the front entrance near the huge bow window that overlooked St. James Street.

Raceford peered once out the window and saw a hansom cab waiting at the curb, its driver asleep on his perch. He threw his jacket around his shoulders before plunging through the door into the street outside.

"You there, wake up," he shouted at the man.

The driver awoke with a jump and started to get down from his perch.

"Don't bother. I'm going to borrow—" Raceford thought a moment, then reached in his pocket and withdrew a bag of coins—his winnings from that night—and tossed them up to the driver. "Better yet, I'm going to buy this horse," he finished as he started to unhitch the animal from the hansom.

In a moment the horse was free, and in one fluid movement Raceford had swung up on top of the beast, kicked its sides once, and shot off down the street like a bolt, taking the shortest route he knew to St. James Park.

As he rode, he mentally kicked himself for having lost track of Gabriel for even an instant. His joy earlier that evening at seeing his boyhood friend after nearly a year apart was soon dashed when he realized Gabriel was in the grip of the blue devils over a woman. Why, he hadn't even been able to distract Gabriel with a few hands of faro—a strange circumstance indeed, when he and Gabe had spent their lives competing against each other in the most cutthroat fashion.

Only the brandy bottle had been able to distract Gabriel this night, it seemed. And so with a sigh, Raceford had sat down at the tables alone.

And then had begun to win hand after hand of faro—a not too unusual occurrence. He loved winning. It was a passion stronger than the wager itself. But tonight his passion had cost him. He had lost track of Gabriel. He'd just cleared his winnings from the table and looked over to where his friend had been sitting. Gabriel had disappeared.

Raceford dug his heels into the horse's sides and spurred the animal on. "Damn the Lady Vivienne!" Though he'd never met the woman, her reputation certainly preceded her—a fickle pursuer of pleasures, beautiful, but with a heart that held no conscience. He'd felt a tinge of worry when he heard of Gabriel's liaison with her. Gabriel was an open, fun-loving soul, far too innocent and idealistic for the heartless and accomplished Lady Vivienne.

How foolish of his friend to fight a duel over the woman's reputation. No doubt, Lord Hamilton had indiscreetly mentioned her rumored liaison with the count. And with the drinking Gabriel had been doing, the duel between them had been inevitable. It was obvious Gabriel was still in love with her . . . enough to duel over her.

Dear God, what if he was too late? The thought made Raceford spur his horse on even harder. He was

7

afraid of what he might find—Gabriel, a man condemned for murder, or worse yet, dead. He had to hurry. His friend's life depended on it.

Quickly, making a decision, he turned his mount into an alley, one that led to the street that passed along the north side of the park. It was a chance, but if Gabriel was fighting a duel, he and his opponent would have appointed a place easily identifiable for the both of them.

Raceford shot through the alley on the horse and pushed out onto the street. Beyond the park's open iron gates, he saw what he was looking for—the fountain that marked the north entrance. Quickly, he urged his horse in its direction.

Then he saw the glimmer of a sword and heard Gabriel's shouted taunts to his opponent. His guess had been correct. Raceford sped toward the fountain and reined his horse to a halt before swinging down and drawing his own sword.

Gabriel and Lord Hamilton were panting and drenched with sweat from their efforts, but neither ceased their assault on the other. Raceford felt helpless. He'd hoped to arrive before the duel had begun, to talk them out of it. But to intervene now would mean dishonor to Gabriel, and to distract either opponent could mean death for one or the other. He looked around and saw two onlookers, seconds to the duel, passing a bottle of port between them. It was apparent both Lord Hamilton and Gabriel had been well into their cups when they decided to duel.

Then Raceford turned his attention to his friend. His hand tightened on the hilt of his sword as Lord Hamilton lunged and rent the material of Gabriel's shirt with the point of his sword. Gabriel was an accomplished swordsman, but Raceford wondered if his kindhearted friend had the nerve to fight this duel to the death. And all he could do was watch, every muscle in his body tense, as Gabriel retreated momentarily, slightly shaken by the close call. Then his friend made a counter lunge, thrashing the air wildly with his sword. Metal rang as the two men's swords connected above their heads and held, both men vying for control, grunting and tensely staring each other in the eye. He saw Gabriel gather his strength and shove Lord Hamilton away, sending him sprawling on the ground on his back. Gabriel leaped to stand above his opponent and pinned him to the ground with his sword, the point making a threatening dent in the skin of Lord Hamilton's neck.

Hamilton panted up at Gabriel. "A fine duel, Justice, but it doesn't change the fact that the Lady Vivienne has thrown you over for the count."

Raceford could see the immediate tightening of Gabriel's hold on the sword as he applied pressure to the point of his blade. Lord Hamilton winced but didn't give up. "You're a fool, Justice, like so many others regarding the Lady Vivienne."

Then Raceford spoke up. "Hell's gate, Gabe, he's right. Killing Hamilton won't bring her back. She's gone."

Gabriel paused. He was listening at least. "Stay out of this, Race."

"And where will you be when he's dead? In prison? Don't give the Lady Vivienne that satisfaction," Raceford persisted.

Gabriel glared at Hamilton but didn't release his hold.

"And don't give this reprobate the satisfaction of goading you into killing him. He's a wretch and a drunken sot. Why waste your time with his opinion of

9

the Lady Vivienne? You're above all that, Gabe, and you know it."

Time seemed to stretch infinitely as Gabriel considered this last remark, then he relaxed his hold on his sword and flicked its point safely, but still with a hint of threat, away from Lord Hamilton's neck. "You're right, Race. He's not worth it." And quietly he added, "And neither is she."

Hamilton breathed a sigh a relief and picked himself up from the ground, sword still in hand.

Raceford stepped between the two men. "Both of you, sheath your swords." And when they complied, he turned to Gabriel. "Now what do you say? Let's get out of here."

But before Gabriel could answer, Raceford heard Hamilton's sword sliding from its sheath behind him. He pushed Gabriel aside and, withdrawing his own weapon, whirled on the man.

Hamilton's voice dripped with venom as he took his stance of attack. "I'll show you who's a wretch and a drunken sot." And with that, he lunged at Raceford.

Hamilton was no match, Raceford knew, drunk or stone-sober. The simpleton's attack was a complete irritation. With an almost bored sigh, he raised his sword, brought it down with a ringing blow against his opponent's weapon, and held it there, forcing Hamilton around until his back was to the fountain. Then with a slight push, he sent the drunken lord feet over head over the ledge of the fountain and into its pool.

"There will be no more dueling this evening, gentlemen," Raceford stated with a note of finality that even the furious Hamilton heeded. Raceford threw his arm around Gabriel's shoulder and led him off in search of the horse he'd bought earlier that evening. Gabriel leaned heavily on Raceford as he took unsteady steps alongside him. The brandy was catching up to him.

When Raceford looked at Gabriel again, he saw the pain in his friend's eyes had retreated and been replaced by anger. "Damn her!" Gabriel shouted at no one in particular. "How dare she treat me this way! It's true, Race, she's thrown me over for money. I saw her and the count at the opera house in Covent Garden night before last. And tonight . . ." his voice trembled, "I nearly killed a man on account of her. My God, what was I thinking of? Well, that's it. No more. *I'm* through with *her!* She's forgotten."

Raceford said nothing.

Gabriel threw up his arms. "I mean it, Race. I've already forgotten her. And to prove it . . ." He reached inside his shirt and pulled a chain from beneath it. A locket dangled from the loop of gold. Gabriel grasped it in his hand and yanked it from around his neck, tossing it on the ground and stepping on it with his booted foot.

Gabriel stood smiling at his friend, weaving slightly from drink.

Raceford laughed and started to move on. "Come on. You're soused. In the morning, you'll be mooning over her all over again."

Gabriel stopped. "I will not. I refuse to moon over the likes of her. She's everything everyone's been telling me. And it's time I admitted it. She's the heartless vixen she's rumored to be." He leaned heavily on Raceford. "I've even been thinking of going to the country for a while. What do you think?"

"An excellent idea."

Gabriel stopped and the smile faded from his face. "She has violet eyes, you know."

They'd reached the horses and Raceford was untying the reins, listening to his friend's drunken ramblings with half an ear. "Nonsense," he said, throwing the leather straps across the back of the horse. "No one's eyes are purple."

"I didn't say purple. I said violet . . . the most alluring shade of violet you've ever seen."

"You've got to get ahold of yourself, Gabe."

Gabriel nodded and brushed back the dark golden curls that hung about his face. Raceford looked at his friend's boyish features, at the dark brown eyes that held both relief that the duel was over and defeat at the hand of the Lady Vivienne.

He and Gabriel had been friends since childhood, and Raceford had always protected the younger man as if he were his brother. It hurt to see his friend in such pain, and he despised the Lady Vivienne for what she'd done to Gabe. As a player himself, he believed there were strict rules to the game of hearts. If you wanted a discreet affair, you picked an experienced, like-minded partner . . . not an innocent like Gabriel.

Raceford continued. "No woman is worth throwing your life away for in a duel—especially not a woman like her. How could you have fallen in love with such a heartless jade?"

"If you'd met her, you'd know that the last thing she appears to be is heartless."

"If I met her," growled Race threateningly, "I'd see her pay for what she's done to you. Someone ought to teach the woman a lesson."

Gabriel shot his friend an uncertain look. "What do you mean, teach her a lesson?"

"I've half a mind to teach the jade what it feels like to have a broken heart. Then perhaps she wouldn't be so fast to toy with others."

"Vivienne does not toy with others. She's not like that. Damnit!"

"And I thought you'd forgotten her. Don't you want to see her as unhappy as she's made you?"

"Well, y—yes," he stammered doubtfully. "I'd give twenty golden guineas to the man who could teach Vivienne what it feels like to have a broken heart," he finished with bravado.

Raceford smiled. "Done. Just tell me where to find the lady."

Gabriel stared in shock at his friend for a moment, a secret thought beginning to form. "You're on," he said. "You will find her in Paris."

Gabriel guided the horse through the gates and slowed to a trot. He finally allowed himself the laugh he'd been stifling since Race had proposed the wager. What an actor he was! And he laughed again. At last he had Race in a bet his friend couldn't possibly win. And why? Not because the Lady Vivienne was cruel and heartless, fickle and unfaithful, but because she would be nowhere near Paris and nowhere near Raceford to succumb to his charms. She would be in the country with him, and in his arms the whole time.

How desperate he'd been to be alone with Vivienne, but it seemed every move they made was the talk of the town. And the talk was getting quite serious. Vivienne had been afraid that the rumors would get back to her husband and ruin her reputation. And they'd both intensely wanted to spend time with each other. So, together they had started the rumor of their supposed break with each other. Gabriel himself had been responsible for the tittle-tattle about Vivienne and the count.

And it had worked. The rumor mills had been positively abuzz with the word that the Lady Vivienne had thrown over the Honorable Gabriel Michael Justice. Now no one would suspect that they were together.

Still, did he have to have been so convincing with Raceford? Hadn't staging the duel and lying about his reasons for retreating to the country been sufficient? But he'd sworn to Vivienne not to tell anyone. And a vow was a vow . . . and one made to the woman he loved was unbreakable. It had been hard to lie to Raceford, but now he was glad it happened that way. He could hardly wait to see his friend's face when he learned that he'd at last lost a wager to Gabriel, an occurrence that happened rarely. And he allowed himself one last hearty laugh.

There was just one last bit of business to conclude — the matter of paying off Hamilton for his role in the duel that they'd staged. The fop would gouge him for more money for the dunking Raceford had given him, but it was the imbecile's own fault for challenging Race. Nevertheless, it would be worth the extra pound or two it would cost him, for Hamilton had asked no questions, just greedily accepted his offer.

Once Hamilton was paid off, Gabriel's part of the plan would be complete. The rest would be up to his dear Vivienne. And, of course, to the Comtesse Genvieve. He smiled again as he wondered what Raceford would make of the "Lady Vivienne" he was going to meet in Paris.

Raceford turned his horse back to St. James Park. When he arrived at the fountain, he jumped off his mount, then scanned the ground, looking for the locket his friend had discarded. He saw the gleam of the golden trinket and bent to pick it up. He struck a light and held the miniature up to the wavering flame.

So this was the Lady Vivienne Winter.

She was as beautiful as she was rumored to be, raven-haired with piercing violet eyes, Raceford noted, accentuated with sensual brows, full red lips, and a creamy complexion in a heart-shaped face. The artist had given her a penetrating expression, with the tilt of her head and the directness of her gaze, an expression that told Raceford this woman understood her power over men. No wonder Gabriel had fallen so hard.

He grasped the locket in his hand and sat down on the fountain's ledge, thinking for a moment, then opened his palm to look at the miniature again to memorize the woman's features. Her knowing eyes peered up at him.

So this was the enemy.

Chapter One

It was just coming on four-thirty of an April morning in 1784, when a second-story window on Helston Grange slid quietly upwards, in a most furtive fashion. The world was still dark at that hour, and not a sound came from the slumbering red brick house; all of the occupants, save one, were still asleep.

A slim figure leaned out the window for a moment, listening for any telltale noises from the kitchens below. But only the slight rustle of the wind met her ears. Not even the kitchen maid was up yet to stir the coals; not even the birds were singing at this hour.

Satisfied that she would not be observed, Meredith Westin swung a leg over the windowsill, a leg that would have scandalized her aunt and her staid cousin, Louisa, had they seen it. For the leg was clad in a pair of dun-colored breeches and booted to the knee with black leather riding boots. Straddling the window in a most unladylike way, she pitched a cloth bundle over the roof of the greenhouse below, where it landed on the grass with the barest of thuds.

An observer might have believed that the girl was eloping or perhaps running away. But no young man waited impatiently on the lawn beneath. And the bundle was hardly large enough to be supplies for a flight from home.

Though many was the time Meredith had wished she might actually run away. The trouble was, she didn't have the money to do it or any place in the world to go. As hated as it was, Helston Grange was the only home she had.

Athletically, with a grace that spoke of well-used muscles, Meredith put one booted toe in the gap between the red bricks and climbed down a few feet of wall to the sloping greenhouse roof, with a confidence that came from having done this many times before. Again she paused to listen before making her way down the roof to its lowest edge. Then she let herself over the edge, hanging full length for a moment by her hands before dropping on the ground below and hitting it with a practiced roll.

Quickly, she bent to pick up her bundle, and unrolling it, threw a long black cloak over her shoulders against the early-morning chill, then disposed the rest of the bundle under her arm. She ran across the kitchen garden and back lawns to the gate in the gray stone wall and, unlatching it, let herself quietly out. She smiled as she pulled the gate closed behind her. It moved silently on its hinges, thanks to the fact that Meredith herself kept it well oiled.

Beyond the gates were rolling hills and fields, with an edging of well-tended woods in the distance. The fields belonged to Squire Abernathy, whose passion was fox-hunting. He kept a well-stocked stable of horseflesh and a kennel full of hounds. And though most of the horses were in his stables, a few would be out to pasture, far out of sight of either the Grange or Abernathy Hall.

Meredith trotted rapidly along, knowing the way even in the dark. The outlying paddocks were her goal, and as she ran she hoped that today the sweet black mare called Devil's Daughter would still be out to grass.

When she reached the paddock with its small stone barn, hidden from view by the rolling hills that enclosed it on all sides, the first light was just touching the world, turning the grass from black to gray and shapes of things around her to ghostly outlines. As if at a signal, a blackbird gave voice to song from the copse that edged the paddock, though the shadows in the woods were still black.

Meredith reached the fence and, in the growing light, saw that the small herd of horses was not far down the fence to her left. Quickly, she climbed the rails and landed inside the paddock, walking down toward the horses, making a soft chirruping sound and holding out her hand.

One dark shape detached itself from the rest and came trotting toward her with a whicker, knowing full well that the hand Meredith held outstretched in offering contained sugar.

As Devil's Daughter, dark as night with a white star on her forehead, lipped the sugar from Meredith's palm, the young woman patted the mare's neck and spoke softly to her. Out of the bundle came an old and worn bridle, one that had been discarded when the headstall was broken. Meredith had mended it herself. Devil's Daughter stood patiently as she was bridled, knowing that more sugar would be forthcoming in a moment. In a trice the bridle was over the mare's head, and Meredith led the horse to the paddock fence. Leaving her bundle near the fence, she climbed the rails and swung herself astride the mare's back.

Soon they were out of the gate, Meredith careful to latch it behind her. She'd be in trouble enough if

Squire ever learned she occasionally borrowed one of his horses for an early morning ride . . . but she couldn't begin to imagine the consequences if she ever carelessly let the rest of them escape.

She turned the mare toward the woods, where she was most unlikely to be seen by an early-morning passerby or farmer's wagon going to market. Though if she were seen, it was unlikely that she'd be recognized. She was slender enough to pass for a lad, and the cloak concealed any feminine curves. Her hair, raven-black waves that reached her waist, was twisted up beneath a shapeless cloth cap. And her hands, slender and white and a dead giveaway, were encased in leather gauntlets. No one would connect the young lad astride the mare with the demure poor relation who lived in Helston Grange. No one would believe that mouse of a girl, who never had a word to say for herself, would be dressed bold as any gypsy in boy's breeches and out committing horse theft before sunrise.

Well, not exactly theft. Simply, Meredith told herself, a bit of unauthorized borrowing.

Though she wondered if the squire would see it that way. And she bit back a moment's giggle at the thought of how scandalized Aunt Phoebe would be if she were ever caught.

Once well into the woods, Meredith struck a path and put her heels to the mare, who responded at once, breaking into a gallop. As the light grew, the horse and rider fairly flew through the woods, and Meredith laughed aloud, feeling free and happy at this only bit of amusement and defiance her life permitted her.

The path climbed steadily through the woods, making for the summit of one of the hills. When she reached the top the woods ended, and Meredith reined in the mare at the edge of the woods to take a few moments to drink in the view spread beneath her.

The sun was just now rising over the edge of England, and everywhere around her the woods were filled with birdsong greeting the dawn. To Meredith, it was the most beautiful hour of the day, one she hated to miss. The April green of the Thames valley below her was at its freshest, the hills soft and lovely in the growing light. Above the hills, towering white clouds were tinged with gold and apricot, and a line of glimmering yellow fire hemmed the world.

Just below in a fold of the land, a sleepy village stood beside the wide flat banks of the river. The houses, many of them thatched, were built of gray stone, and above the roofs the spire of the church was outlined with dawnlight. Henley-on-Thames. Nothing had changed in Henley for centuries, and nothing was ever likely to change it, Meredith considered.

From where she sat, she could see the roof of Helston Grange. It was a rambling, red-brick Tudor manor house, not of a great size. Before it, long lawns sloped to the river, where swans floated in timeless peace. Ivy covered Helston's walls, and old roses with thick canes overgrew the low walls that meandered to the river. It was a place filled with serene peace, a lovely and civilized spot in the green garden that was England.

And as dull as ditchwater.

As were its inhabitants. Since Meredith had been left an orphan at the age of fifteen, she'd come as companion to her Aunt Phoebe. Aunt Phoebe was widowed and had a daughter, Louisa, who was two years Meredith's senior. Aunt Phoebe was overbearing, a natural manager who believed she knew the best for everyone and enforced her dictates with a will of iron.

One of her axioms was that those not fortunate enough to be born with an annuity must earn their keep; hence Meredith had been put to work from the moment she stepped through Helston's front door. The fact that she was a relation did not save her from being treated as a poor one.

Phoebe Travers was a stupid, obstinate, garrulous, and self-righteous soul, and her treatment of Meredith stemmed perhaps not a little from jealousy. For while anyone could see that the fifteen-year-old Meredith, though slender as a wand, promised to be a fetching beauty when she reached womanhood, with that abundant black hair and those winsome blue eyes, not the same could be said of Louisa. Poor Louisa had inherited her mother's unfortunate tendency to stoutness, along with a head of mousy-brown hair, a rather sallow complexion, and features that could, with kindness, be called plain. And Louisa was neither clever nor accomplished, to offset her looks, but instead possessed a rather phlegmatic and incurious nature. She was docile and rather stupid, not having any of the spirit that distinguished her cousin, Meredith . . . a spirit that, from the first, Phoebe had done her best to extinguish in Meredith. It simply was not suitable in one who would be forced by virtue of being a penniless orphan to earn her keep.

So, rather sourly, Phoebe had set out to make the best of her daughter and the worst of her niece. Meredith was not to speak unless she was spoken to; she was to keep her eyes cast down and have no opinions; she was to devote herself to good works and to the study of being serviceable to others.

And she was to forget the unfortunate ideas that her unconventional upbringing had given her.

Often Phoebe had almost despaired of making the

22

girl biddable; but it wasn't to be wondered at, she opined, when her wild, gambling rake of a father— Phoebe hardly believed she could have such a brother—had dragged the child all over England to horse fairs, having treated her more like a son than a daughter once Meredith's mother had died.

Though it was just as well Meredith's mother had died, after all. It had scandalized Phoebe when her brother, Thomas, had brought home his bride, a poor Irishwoman with nothing to her name and doubtless no morals whatsoever. How else had she caught a man so far above her than by . . . snaring him with her charms, not to put too fine a point on it? It was actually rumored he'd met her at some horse fair or another, where she'd been selling hot pies. The very idea of having such a sister-in-law made Phoebe shudder to this day. Yes, in Phoebe's opinion, it was best that the woman with her earthy, uncouth brogue had died. And really better for the girl in the end that her brother had passed on as well. For he'd been addicted to gambling, and to horses, and to exposing the child to a most unsuitable life.

Seven years had passed since Meredith had come to Helston Grange. Now Louisa was twenty-four and still unmarried, and Meredith was twenty-two. And there were days when Meredith considered she might well go mad if something didn't happen.

But at last, today was different than the string of days that had gone before. At last, today, something was happening.

Yes, a great event was happening in Hensley, of all places. Perhaps the dullest village in England, Meredith thought, and the last place a person in their right mind would want to come and visit.

So why on earth was her cousin, Vivienne, coming

today?

And after ignoring their existence for so many years?

The sun climbed the sky in a blaze of gold glory, and reluctantly, Meredith turned her horse. She'd been out overlong already; usually she only dared a swift gallop and was back in the paddock before full sunrise. But today her cousin's visit was much on her mind, and she'd lost track of the time.

As she touched her heels to the mare's flanks and sent her at a hand-gallop back down the trail through the woods, she thought of Vivienne with resentment, not a little tinged with envy.

Vivienne's mother had also been her aunt, the eldest sister of her father and Phoebe. And a famous beauty, so it was said. Gorgeous enough to catch the eye of a man far above her station. She'd married a wealthy Scots baron, who was as much above her touch as Meredith's mother was beneath her father. And she'd severed her connection with her family, evidently having her head much turned by the new and illustrious place she occupied in the world.

It was ironic that her cousin, Vivienne, was only a year older than Meredith. Being so close in age, in other families the girls might have been close friends as well.

But Meredith had only laid eyes on Vivienne once, in a disastrous visit she and her father had made to the baronet's mansion when she was eight. It was a year after her mother's death, and Meredith felt shy from the first of the grand surroundings and the haughty family who dressed so extravagantly and spoke in such a refined manner. It did not help that Vivienne told her during the course of the visit that her father was no better than a beggar, as he'd come to ask for money to pay off his many gambling debts; the humiliation had been deep.

From the first, Meredith had not liked Vivienne. Maybe it was because the two children were very much alike in looks. Both had silky black curls and eyes of two startling shades, of blue, in Meredith's case, and violet, in Vivienne's case. Though Meredith was the younger, she was half a head taller than her cousin and the slimmer of the two. Otherwise, with the unformed features of childhood, they might have been sisters.

Though you could always tell them apart by their dress.

The first time Meredith had seen Vivienne, she'd thought her dressed like a princess, all in a gown of white lace with a deep violet velvet sash and hair ribbons that matched her eyes. Meredith, on the other hand, wore a mended tarlatan wool that was too short at the ankles.

Vivienne's parents treated her like a princess, and it told on her temperament. By the age of nine, she was utterly spoilt, throwing fits of temper when she did not get her way, and lording it over every other child—or indeed servant—she encountered.

That first evening they'd ended in a spat, rolling on the floor and trying to snatch each other's hair out. Meredith smiled at the memory, for she'd been the one to launch herself at her hateful cousin when Vivienne had called her father a beggar.

And since that short visit, she'd never set eyes on Vivienne again. When her father had died, both her aunts had come to the funeral, but there had been no offer from the wealthy branch of the family to take her in. It was all settled. She was to go with Phoebe and learn to be "useful."

Not to her Aunt Isabella's and cousin Vivienne's, where she might have learned to like luxury too much for one who was, after all, doomed to poverty.

She often wondered if it might have been different if her mother had not been an Irish peasant. If that was why her rich relations wouldn't have her in their house . . .

She emerged from the woods then, slowing the mare to a walk as she approached the paddock gate. It was full daylight as she swung the gate open, and she hurriedly dismounted and was unbuckling the bridle when a low laugh startled her.

"And just what," said a masculine voice, "do you think you're doin'?"

She gave a small gasp and turned, finding one of Squire Abernathy's grooms standing in the door to the barn and looking at her.

John, his name was, she recalled, turning beet-red as his bold dark eyes traveled down her frame, taking in the close-fitting breeches. Hastily, she tugged the cloak closed, but it was too late. He'd seen what she was wearing . . . and he'd obviously seen her on the horse as well.

John was young, with a swarthy, coarsely good-looking face, dark blond hair, and a thickset, strongly muscled body. Meredith knew who he was, as she knew everyone in Hensley, though she'd never spoken to him before. He had a crudely knowing grin, a swagger to his walk that Meredith did not like. He looked as if he thought he owned the earth.

"It's Miss Meredith, isn't it?" he grinned, sauntering toward her. "And decked out like a boy. Taking one of Squire's horses for a ride, too. He'll be right angry when he hears, for Daughter's the apple of his eye."

He stopped a bare foot from her, smiling in what

26

seemed a very wicked way to Meredith, who could feel her heart hammering in her chest.

"I—John, please, don't tell him," she said, finding her voice at last. "I meant no harm. It's the first time I've ever—it's just that Aunt has no riding horses, and I missed—Aunt will be so angry if she finds out," she finished.

"Aye, but not as angry as Squire," he agreed amiably enough, his dark eyes dancing. "You looked right . . . nice in them breeches, Miss Meredith. Mayhap I won't tell after all. That is, if you'll make it worth my while not to."

Meredith's heart sank. She had hardly any money, her aunt considered her keep enough compensation for the chores she did. But she saw that somehow she'd have to find a way to pay John to keep his silence. At least he could be bribed not to tell.

"How much do you want?" she said, bravely enough.

"How much? You insult a man like me to think I'd be takin' money from a lass . . . and from a lass as pretty as you. No, I had somethin' else in mind."

His grin was back, and Meredith was puzzled. What could he want if not money? "What do you mean?" she said.

"I'll not tell if you'll give us a kiss, lass."

A kiss! Meredith stared at him in amazement, taking in the faint shadow of beard on his jaw, the corduroys splattered with mud, the bold dark eyes.

"Never!" she gasped, affronted. To think she'd kiss a man she barely knew!

"So a stablelad's not good enough for you, eh?" he said, frowning. "Well, I'd best be goin'. 'Tis my duty to tell Squire his mare's bein' overridden, and I'm sure he'll be callin' on your aunt . . . ." He turned and

27

started to walk away.

"John . . . wait!"

Meredith watched in despair as he walked back toward her, looking cocksure and knowing. But what else could she do? If he told, she'd be in all kinds of trouble. Her aunt would see to it her life wasn't worth living. And what harm would a kiss do? It was to be hoped no one would ever know.

"I will let you kiss me . . . once," she said firmly.

John needed no further invitation. His arms went round her, and she was pulled close to his sturdy chest. He smelled, not unpleasantly, of horses. He looked down at her and smiled.

"Did anyone ever tell ye you're the prettiest lass in these parts?" he asked huskily, and bent his head to hers.

The kiss was short but passionate enough. His lips moved over hers possessively and Meredith pushed him away, flustered. It had felt strange indeed to be held so by a man she barely knew, and his kiss had brought a peculiar heat to her.

"That's . . . enough," she said, shaken and rather embarrassed. "I—you promise now you won't tell?"

"Aye. And maybe, if you liked that, you'll come again? I'll not say a word that you're ridin', as long as I may claim a kiss each time for my silence."

The gall he had!

Meredith turned and ran away, her cheeks hot, snatching her bundle where it lay near the fence. As she ran down the hill toward the Grange, his laughter came down the wind after her.

"Nothing . . . but *nothing* interesting will ever happen to me." Meredith, elbows on the windowsill, stared gloomily out at the drizzling rain and felt she could only smile if an earthquake were about to swallow Helston Grange and all its inhabitants—herself included. The fair morning had turned overcast once again, and it had rained every day for a week. The park was flooded, and a less cheerful vista would have been difficult to imagine. "And I will never *go* anywhere interesting, either, for that matter," she added with a ring of finality.

John's kiss that morning had put her in a black humor. Her rides were over, that was for certain, for if she went there again, he'd no doubt be waiting for her and take her appearance as encouragement. He'd put a stop to the one pleasure she'd had.

"Nothing interesting?" A detestably cheerful voice came from behind her, filled with scornful disbelief at her words. "You can say that, with the Lady Vivienne comin' to visit and all? And stop leanin' on your elbows, miss, or they'll be as wrinkled as your Aunt Phoebe's!"

This brought Meredith up off her elbows and away from the less-than-riveting prospect of her window. Jane, the maid, was briskly shaking out gowns from the wardrobe and laying them across the bed. From her smooth brown hair to her rosy cheeks to her neat gray dress, Jane radiated good cheer. Though she was officially Miss Louisa's maid, she and Meredith were good friends, and when she had a spare moment, Jane came to "do" for Miss Meredith, as she did not consider it fitting for the young woman to be treated like a servant.

"You call Vivienne's visit something interesting?" Meredith demanded sourly. "It is bad enough to listen to Aunt all day, recounting my shortcomings and rhapsodizing over Vivienne—but all the perfection that is Vivienne, actually here, in the flesh? I ask you, how can I be expected to bear it?" Meredith flopped back dramatically on the bed, running distracted fingers through her thick black hair until it had a wild look.

"At least we'll get a show of what's all the rage in fashion, I expect," Jane said placidly. "And something to talk about this winter. I've never known a lady to cause more talk than she does, and the Lord knows we could use something to talk about, for naught ever does happen here."

It was true that Vivienne's visit would give them plenty to talk of, servants and gentry alike. Talk had always followed the Lady Vivienne Winter like the tail does a comet . . . at least, since she was old enough to turn every man's head, from stableboy to statesman. In fact, Meredith thought with a dispirited sigh, Vivienne *was* very like a comet, all sparkles and blazing fire, giving off streams of glamour wherever she went. All the fashionable world followed her progress from one escapade to the next with indecent excitement. What fuel for gossip she'd provided when she'd married one of the richest peers in Scotland—and a man old enough to be her grandfather. And then proceeded to live apart from him for a good portion of the year. Tales of her behavior since her marriage, whether founded in fact or not, were everyone's favorite near-scandal.

"Henley. You are right, Jane, there has never been a place quieter this side of the churchyard," Meredith said, thinking of the daily walk from Helston Grange to the vicarage and back. One day both a farm cart and a pony trap had passed them within ten minutes, and Aunt Phoebe held forth that night at dinner that it was a scandal how crowded the roads

30

were becoming.

"Aye, 'tis hard to imagine the Lady Vivienne wanting to come to Henley. She must be in hiding from some rake, no doubt, who won't give her a moment's rest for he's mad with passion for her. Or maybe she's shattered her nerves dancing with dukes 'til all hours, I shouldn't wonder, and she's decided to come here to repair her complexion."

"And to think she's my cousin." Meredith gave a rebellious kick of a foot at the thought.

"Yes, strange to think she's so rich, while you haven't a penny to bless yourself with," Jane remarked. "Odd, the ways of the world, ain't they?"

"Not simply rich, but a famous beauty to boot," Meredith grumbled.

"Why, you're every bit as pretty, I'd wager."

Meredith sat up and pushed the colt's mane of hair out of her eyes. "When we were small, they did say we looked alike. I believe it made her quite wild. But I doubt there will be much comparison between us now, with her decked out in silks and dripping with jewels, while I have to wear *that!*" She scowled at the dress Jane was holding up for her inspection, a dull day dress of brown stuff, without even a ribbon to soften its severe lines. Aunt Phoebe had very strict notions that companions should have only "serviceable" dresses.

"This'll be fine for tea when Vivienne arrives, I think, for we've got to save the blue for evening and the tarlatan had that mended tear. No, life ain't fair, miss, and the sooner you learn that, the happier you'll be. Besides, it ain't all roses for Vivienne, I'd be willin' to bet! Look at the man she married! Lord Winter is eighty if he's a day and never leaves that castle of his in Scotland. If you think Helston Grange is dull, you ought to try it up on those bleak moors with a pack of dour Scotsmen on every side. Real wild men, I hear tell."

"But Vivienne simply leaves him in his castle and he doesn't mind, you know that. It's as if she wasn't even married to him. She hardly ever sees him. And look at my prospects for marriage. At least Lord Winter is rich, while Augustus—"

Meredith gave a little shudder at the thought of Augustus Sett, the curate, who'd been calling for months and clearly expected to marry her. The only men she'd encountered were the curate and now the groom, John. One was as boring as could be, the other crude and cocksure. But what was she to do about Augustus? Though she'd avoided being alone with him, she knew she couldn't put him off much longer. His complacency at her answer was hard enough to bear, but Aunt Phoebe also expected she'd consent to the match. And what choice did she have, really?

Jane looked uncomfortable at this outburst and was for once at a loss for one of her cheerful homilies. "Well, I admit he is stout and a trifle boring, but he's a kind man and you could do worse."

Meredith flopped back on the bed with a groan. "Oh, please. Imagine how you'd feel if you had to marry Augustus! But Aunt won't feed me forever. She reminds me every day I'm living on her charity, until I'm almost distracted."

"Well, maybe with this visit your fortunes will change. You know that gypsy dame we visited at the fair last year said you'd see the world. Maybe Vivienne's remembered she has a cousin at last and means to do something about it."

"I doubt it," Meredith said glumly. "For a more selfish creature never breathed. Besides, the one time she met me, she hated me." Meredith looked out the window. It was raining harder than ever. "In all this rain, maybe she'll not come."

Jane clucked. "And don't tell me you wouldn't be disappointed if it were so. Aren't you curious about her?"

Meredith smiled. "Well, yes, I admit that I am. But I'm more curious about why she is coming here. I don't trust her. I am sure she has some reason for coming, for Vivienne never did anything that wasn't for her own benefit."

As Meredith dressed, her thoughts wandered from her cousin to the scene that morning with John.

Her first kiss. And sad to say, with a man whom she didn't even like. She wondered how many times Vivienne had kissed a man — and more. She thought of all the handsome men her cousin must know, of all the fascinating experiences she must have had out in the glamorous world.

With a sigh, she finished pinning her hair back in the severe knot her aunt decreed she must wear and looked at her reflection in the glass. Dull brown merino dress, plain hair. Pretty blue eyes and a slender figure, to be sure, but she looked like a governess. Even if she ever chanced to meet a duke, her dress guaranteed she'd never be noticed.

Not for the first time, she wondered bitterly at the fate that had made one cousin so poor and the other so rich. And then she left her room to go downstairs and await the arrival of Vivienne.

"And so, Vicar, it is most fortuitous that dear Vivienne should favor us with a visit just at this moment, for as I am sure you are aware, my darling

Louisa is nearly of an age to make her debut in Society—though I sob to think it! How can I be so old? . . ." There was the merest of pauses, but long enough, Meredith thought.

"Never, never think it, Mrs. Travers! You are the soul of youth!" the vicar protested, as expected.

Aunt Phoebe favored him with a coquettish smile, then went on in a piercing voice Meredith was sure could be heard in the stables, "Yes, dearest Louisa is due soon for her coming-out ball, and the influence of a titled lady such as Vivienne—Lady Vivienne I suppose would be more fitting, though I cannot think of the darling child by such a formal title when I have known her since she was in pinafores!—will be *most* gratifying at such a time, and—Louisa! Do *not* slouch, child! How many times have I told you that a lady's carriage speaks volumes about her?"

A moment's fierce glare at her hapless daughter, Louisa, who did have an unfortunate tendency to slouch, and Aunt Phoebe turned back to the vicar, a gracious expression replacing the frightening one. She went on without seeming to pause for breath. "And of course, dear vicar, I am charmed that you could be here to welcome Lady Vivienne, for we must show our sophisticated guest that although we are rural here, we are not *entirely* rustics and can boast a man of letters in our midst. And I am glad you were able to come, also, Mr. Sett."

From her seat in the corner, Meredith looked at Augustus through her lashes with distaste. Why did he have to be here? But she knew well that her aunt would not have missed the chance to show off her distinguished guest to the neighborhood.

Evidently her look was not veiled enough, for the portly figure standing at the mantelpiece detached himself from her aunt's side and made his way toward her.

Oh Lord—Augustus! Meredith dropped her head and pretended to be absorbed in her embroidery—Aunt Phoebe insisted that idle hands were the Devil's playground—but she heard his heavy tread on the carpet and the fruity clearing of his throat.

"Ah . . . I say, good afternoon, Miss Westin."

She was forced to look up in time to see him, with some difficulty in such a tight coat, making a gallant bow to her.

She inclined her head, saying coolly, "Mr. Sett," and dropped her eyes again to her sewing. But she knew it was no use. Augustus simply didn't take hints. In fact, if she only knew it, he thought her coolness was evidence of her demure, reserved manners. He also thought her shyness—the way she answered his remarks in monosyllables—evidence of what a wonderfully meek and quiet curate's wife she would make. In short, the more she tried to discourage him, the more he believed her to be perfect.

I ought to do something really shocking to drive him away, Meredith thought desperately. *Maybe curse, or drink six glasses of wine the next time he's at dinner . . .*

"It is most pleasant to see you, Miss Westin, on this festive occasion," Augustus said. "I feel quite privileged to be admitted to the family circle when you welcome back such an illustrious member. But then, for some time I have felt, if I may be so bold, almost a part of the family."

He gave her a speaking look. *Or maybe,* Meredith thought wildly, thinking of John, *I ought to somehow let Augustus catch John kissing me!*

"I see you are industriously employed as always, Miss Westin, and not letting a visit of a member of the

35

fashionable world turn you from useful pursuits. May I?" He indicated the chair next to hers, and when she nodded, Augustus lowered his bulk into it. Meredith glanced uncertainly at the spindly gilt legs and wondered if they would bear his weight. She had a vivid mental image of Augustus crashing to the ground amid a splintered chair and then rolling about, unable to get up . . . .

She forced her attention back to what he was saying, in order to stifle a laugh.

"And so the neighborhood is in a ferment, breathlessly expecting the Lady Vivienne's gracious visit. Indeed, there has been talk of little else this past week. But may I be so bold as to say that though her beauty may be as distant and dazzling as the sun, I do not expect she will eclipse the lesser constellations that shine in Helston Grange."

He beamed at her, his round red face slightly moist, and Meredith simply stared at him, unable to decipher what he was talking about. Then she realized he was complimenting her.

She was saved from replying by an imperious call from across the room. "Meredith! I have forgotten my lorgnette! I shall not be able to see a stitch of what Vivienne is wearing without it. Fetch it at once, child!"

Meredith put aside her sewing and rose, for once profoundly grateful for her aunt's demands. "Please excuse me, Mr. Sett. My aunt requires my service. Nay, pray do not rise for my sake," she added, for he was struggling to heave himself to his feet.

She left the room and made her way to her aunt's bedroom. Upstairs, the carpeted halls were silent, the only sound that of Meredith's slippers and the patter of rain on the windows. Lorgnette in hand, she paused for a moment by one of the deep embrasures, pushing aside the maroon velvet drapes. Outside the rain was still pouring down.

She heard the rattle of coach wheels on gravel. Meredith peered through the mist, able to hear the coach before she could see it. And then there it was. Black paint glistening in the rain, four matched bays with black stockings flashing along, a gold crest shining on the door as the Winter equipage rolled to a flourishing halt before Helston Grange's front steps.

Two liveried footmen descended, and the coachman climbed down. The coach door was opened, steps were set in place, and a maid swathed in a gray cloak and a black bonnet climbed down the steps. She carried a large leather traveling case importantly, inside would be the famous Winter jewels. A small white dog shot down the steps, barking shrilly, and was seized by the maid.

There was a moment's glimpse of scarlet cloak and a black hat with sweeping crimson plumes, an enormous sable muff, figure as bright as the day was dull. And then the umbrellas unfurled, obscuring the figure.

Vivienne had arrived at last.

Chapter Two

Meredith caught up her skirts and hurried down the stairs. She reached the drawing room door just as Vivienne entered from the hall, Aunt Phoebe following close behind her, and taking the lorgnette from her hand.

"Darlings! How divine to be here at last!"

The vicar and Augustus rose as Vivienne swept into the room, and Louisa managed an awkward curtsy. Meredith, watching from the doorway, sighed. Vivienne was even prettier than she remembered.

She wore a crimson traveling suit with a short jacket open over a crimson silk dress, which was caught beneath her breasts with a black velvet ribbon tied in a wide bow. Above the bodice, delicate handmade lace foamed. Deceptively simple, the ensemble was cut and draped by the hand of a master. The dress clung to Vivienne's full curves and was trimmed with yards of black braid. She held a rakish hat in her hand, and against her black shining ringlets, her skin was as white as clouds. The chill had brought a bloom to her cheeks, and her full lips were as red as her dress.

But it was Vivienne's face that caught and held the attention. Gorgeous was really the only adequate word. She had spectacular eyes of an unearthly shade of brilliant violet, fringed by the longest lashes Meredith had ever seen under arching dark brows. She was vividly beautiful.

"*Dear* Aunt Phoebe! How absolutely marvelous you are looking! You haven't changed, not a single bit! In fact, I would swear you are looking younger, if that is possible. How simply wonderful of you to have me here for a visit. How I do miss my family and wish that I could spend more time here. But Lord Winter is terribly selfish and hates to have me away from his side. I am afraid that is what happens when a woman marries; her time is no longer hers to call her own. But this *cannot* be Louisa! My dear, you have become a young lady! And how blooming you look!"

With a swoop and a rustle, Louisa was briefly enfolded in Vivienne's embrace, but Meredith noticed that the rosebud cheek came no closer than a foot to Louisa's more sallow one. Vivienne, Meredith reflected, was all syrupy sweetness. What could she be after, to put on such a show of gracious affection? Not only that, but she had accomplished the impossible, silencing Aunt Phoebe for a full two minutes!

"Vivienne dearest, allow me to extend the warmest of welcomes to you on your visit to Helston Grange!" Aunt Phoebe trumpeted, gaining her voice. "It is simply too charming of you to honor us with a visit. I know how demanding the fashionable world can be. Why, it was not so long ago that I myself was subject to those very demands. . . ."

"Yes, it has been simply *too* exhausting, Aunt, and that is why it is divine to be here in the peace of the country. I—"

But having recovered her voice, Aunt Phoebe was not so easily silenced. "My dear Lady Vivienne, allow me to present two distinguished guests. This is our dear Vicar, Vicar Andrews, and his curate, Mr. Augustus Sett. The Lady Vivienne Winter."

The two men were bowing over Vivienne's hand and making fulsome compliments when at last Vivienne turned, looked up, and caught sight of Meredith standing in the doorway. For a moment, it was as if the two of them were alone in the room. Vivienne's eyes widened, her gaze sweeping Meredith from head to toe with a most avid look.

"And *there* is Cousin Meredith!" she exclaimed, a delighted smile stretching those perfect lips. Vivienne didn't come forward, however, but just watched Meredith as she walked into the room. The smile never reached her eyes, which seemed to be devouring Meredith with the most considering of looks.

"How lovely to see you again, Meredith. How often I have remembered fondly those hours we spent playing together in childhood. Tell me, have you still such a taste for strawberries?"

Meredith found herself enveloped in Vivienne's embrace, and this time, the rosy cheek was pressed fondly against her own, silky smooth with powder. Vivienne smelled like a garden of blossoms, roses and lilies, the most expensive of scents.

Meredith backed off and saw that Vivienne's eyes were twinkling. How condescending of her to remember a taste of Meredith's . . . and how like her to mention the strawberries. As a child, Meredith had been disgraced for raiding the strawberry plants in the hothouse and eating every one.

"Cousin Vivienne. Welcome to Henley," she said, then added with a twinkle of her own, "Strawberries are still my favorite. And tell me, are you still partial to hair ribbons?"

Vivienne laughed aloud. Her own disgrace had

come a scant week later, when she'd been caught filching hair ribbons from a shop in town. "I see you remember me far too well. But what I remember the best was how everyone used to swear we were alike enough to be sisters. I wonder, do we still look so similar?"

Vivienne slipped her arm through Meredith's and pulled her across the carpet to the pier glass over the mantel. She stopped, and together they stared at their reflections, fascinated.

It was true. For all that Meredith was dull in brown, her hair smooth against her head, and Vivienne sparkled in crimson silk and a profusion of ringlets, they were much alike still. Meredith was almost a head taller and much more slender than Vivienne, who had rounded, voluptuous curves. Vivienne's face was heart-shaped, with a full Cupid's bow mouth, a short retroussé nose, and full rounded cheeks, while Meredith's features were more delicately sculpted, with a straight patrician nose, a wide, generous mouth, and high cheekbones that curved above a square jaw. But for all that, they could have been sisters.

Almost the same were the eyes except for the color, dark blue and violet, slightly tilted, large and beautiful under well-marked brows. And the black hair that shone like a raven's wing was identical. Though when they stood next to each other, none would have mistaken the tall and slender Meredith for the shorter and plumper Vivienne, the overall resemblance was striking.

"Well. We *do* look like sisters after all, do we not?" Vivienne laughed and seemed much delighted by the fact.

Behind them, Aunt Phoebe was frowning at this unwarranted friendliness between a nothing like Meredith and a great lady like Vivienne. She had plans of her own for Vivienne's visit, and those definitely did not include Meredith. She intended that Vivienne would be captivated by her own Louisa's gentle manners and refined ways, and that the two would become inseparable during Vivienne's stay at the Grange.

"Meredith! Do go and see what on earth has happened to the tea. Vivienne dearest, do please come and sit down! You must be fatigued with your journey, and in all this rain, too! Some tea will refresh you. I declare, this part of the country is never at its best in the spring. Take this seat near the fire, and take the chill off. Perhaps you'd like to repair to your rooms and rest for a bit?"

Meredith sighed as Vivienne was seated with great ceremony near the fire, and she dutifully left the drawing room. The door swung shut behind her, cutting off the conversation. Dispiritedly, she trailed down the passage toward the kitchens. Despite herself, she was fascinated with her cousin. Oh, to be like Vivienne! she thought. To have such magnificent clothes, such unprecedented freedom! Imagine being able to pick up and go wherever you pleased, whenever the mood took you! To know brilliant, intelligent people . . . people in politics, the arts. To wear jewels and attend the opera, the latest plays. It would be worth a dull husband, especially one who gave you the freedom Vivienne had. For all her talk of how her husband kept her close, Meredith was sure it wasn't true. Too often she'd read Vivienne's name in the London society papers. She was hardly ever in Scotland.

As she entered the hot kitchen and waited for someone to notice her, her mind wandered. Imagine *being*

Vivienne, she thought. Waking up as late as you pleased, then sitting up in a vast bed in a frilly bed-jacket, idly sorting through the morning's post—love letters, invitations—while sipping your morning chocolate. Then a brisk ride in the park on the most gorgeous of high-stepping grays, while the feathers on your hat blew in the wind and handsome men made eyes at you and admired your horsemanship. Then perhaps a luncheon, then a nap, then the task of choosing a glamorous ballgown and the right jewels. The evening? Perhaps the opera, or a ball . . .

"Miss Meredith, you tell your aunt that tea's on its way out. It would have been done sooner had that stupid, clumsy Martha not spilt the kettle on the fire and half put it out," Cook said. "I'm near distracted! There's scones and cucumber sandwiches and a lobster salad. Now run on, Miss Meredith, do, before she comes in here and rips me up with her tongue."

Meredith backed out of the doorway and started down the hall. She could hear the murmur of voices in the drawing room as she approached, and Meredith sighed again. In a week perhaps, the excitement of Vivienne's visit would be over, and life would return to its boring routine. Walking her aunt's dogs in the morning and evening, reading to her aunt in the afternoons, enduring calls from Augustus, and church twice on Sundays. And so she would grow old. Either buried here at the Grange, her aunt's unpaid slave, or married to Augustus, a life of good works ahead of her. At least, she reflected, if she married, she would have children to love. . . .

But oh, how she wanted *something* to happen to her first! An adventure, or the chance to fall in love with a handsome and perhaps wicked man! To travel, and to see more of the world than just Henley.

Back in the drawing room, everyone was grouped around Vivienne, vying for her attention. Phoebe and Louisa were seated on either side of her, and the men in chairs across from her. Meredith murmured to her aunt than tea was on its way, but Phoebe barely glanced at her. As she sat in a straight-backed chair near the edge of the group, she realized that this must be how it was for Vivienne all the time. In the center of a group, everyone hanging on her every word, staring at her.

". . . and so, I simply felt I *had* to get away, before I just dropped one night and crumpled on the pavement! What with having to appear at so many social functions—for the sake of my dear husband, of course—and then all that endless travel between Scotland and London! Lord Winter's ill health keeps him in Scotland, but he has so many interests and connections in London, which he entrusts me with. Lah, it was most exhausting. The last time I was in Scotland, my Lord told me quite bluntly that I was looking pinched, and I answered as frankly that I had need of a long rest. Somewhere quite away from it all. To regain my strength. My doctor despairs of me ever reaching thirty if I keep up this pace. And so I came here because—"

"But my dearest Vivienne!" Aunt Phoebe was quite overcome. "This is the *very* place for you to rest and regain your strength! Say not another word. You are welcome to remain here as long as you wish! How gratified I am that you thought of us!"

"Oh, but Aunt dear," said Vivienne with a trace of wistfulness, "would that I could stay here in this haven of peace. But my indifferent health will not permit it." Meredith thought cynically that she'd never seen anyone who looked more vibrantly, robustly healthy than

44

Vivienne. "I am afraid my doctor ordered me to leave England altogether," she went on, waving a graceful hand toward the long windows, where it appeared that someone was pouring a bucket of water down them. "He insists the climate is too damp for me. Another English summer will see me in my grave, he told me, and I must believe him. We must be guided by those wiser than ourselves, must we not, Vicar?"

The amazing eyes looked confidingly at the vicar for a moment, and that worthy man reddened and hastened to agree. "Indeed we must, Lady Vivienne, and it is refreshing to see that a young person like yourself is guided by her elders."

"Oh, I do depend on my elders, Vicar. No, dear Aunt, much as I would love to stay here in the bosom of my family, I must leave England. But of course, I quail at the thought of traveling alone. If only Lord Winter's health would permit . . . but alas. It cannot be. So I came to beg a favor from you. I am going to Paris for a stay of some months. I shall be staying with an old friend of mine, the Comtesse Genvieve d'Anguillame. But I am afraid the comtesse has many social obligations I shall want to shun. I shall need someone to spend the quiet hours with . . . a companion. So I have come to ask you, Aunt, if you could spare—"

The tea arrived. There was a procession of servants into the room, a laying of trays, an uncovering of cloths, a rattle of cups and plates. Meredith saw that Aunt Phoebe was smiling alternately at Louisa and Vivienne, as if she could not believe her good luck.

Paris! Meredith felt a bitter stab at her heart. Louisa to go to France, and she to stay here for another rainy, dull summer! It seemed unbearable to her all of a sudden. Wildly, she resolved that she would leave Henley somehow. Apply perhaps for a post as governess to a family emigrating to the New World. Oh, dull Louisa had all the luck, and she wouldn't even be able to appreciate it!

Louisa's hand was shaking as she poured out, and Meredith accepted a cup with a puddle of slop in the saucer. At last everyone had a cup, and as plates were being passed, Aunt Phoebe trilled.

"Paris! How lovely! And the climate is sure to restore you. Say no more. I could not be happier. It will be such an opportunity for Louisa, to be in the company of a fashionable lady like yourself and to travel. So broadening. Of course, my dearest Vivienne, I can spare you my daughter. Anything to accommodate you."

Vivienne set down her translucent teacup and looked Phoebe directly in the eye. "Oh, but Aunt, you mistake me. I mean to be very quiet when I am there. It will be of no advantage to Louisa to live so retired with me, seeing no one. Why, it is her coming-out year! I myself spoke to Lady Willingham, my good friend, about having a presentation ball for Louisa, to see her out properly. No, I could never dream of taking Louisa away from such an important year of her life. But since the two of you will be so busy in London this year, I thought that perhaps—"

And Meredith watched as those violet eyes, so like her own, swept the assembly and fixed on their target.

"I thought that perhaps you could spare me Meredith."

Chapter Three

Meredith felt the blood drain from her face. There was a distinct rattle of cup on saucer as she set her teacup down, very carefully. The room seemed suddenly to fade to gray, everything misty except for a pair of violet cat's eyes holding hers.

"Meredith!" cried Aunt Phoebe in affronted tones.

"Meredith," agreed Vivienne, turning to Aunt Phoebe with a soothing smile. "As I mentioned, my dear friend, Lady Willingham, intends to give a ball for Louisa, and of course Louisa will be presented at Court. I have spoken to so many of my good friends to be sure Louisa is invited *everywhere*. So sad that my own indifferent health prevents me from showing Louisa to the town while I am away, but then, I have told my dressmaker and hairdresser to be at her disposal while I'm gone . . . and of course, since I won't be using it, you will stay at the townhouse. I would feel so much safer if I knew it were not standing empty while I am buried in the country."

Aunt Phoebe sat back slowly, and Meredith nearly laughed at the expression on her face. She could almost hear the points being ticked off in her head: a ball at Lady Willingham's, presentation at Court, invitations from Vivienne's fashionable set; Louisa's so-

47

cial success was assured.

And the townhouse. A huge structure in the midst of London's fashionable West End, it would have been impossible to obtain an address as good. Occupying it would set the seal on Louisa's season, and its address would assure any parties held there would be a success.

Aunt Phoebe smiled.

"How very generous of you, Vivienne. Naturally, you are right. It *would* have been difficult for Louisa to miss her season. We shall enjoy using the townhouse. And of course I can spare Meredith if you're sure she is the companion you want. She's rather quiet, but skilled with a needle and reads aloud beautifully. Since you won't be going into society, she is perhaps the correct choice. She is quite used to the country."

Vivienne's smile was triumphant. She turned back to Meredith. "But then, she hasn't said yes. I have so wanted to do something for Meredith, since we are cousins after all, and it occurred to me she might like a chance to travel. But perhaps I'm wrong. Do say yes, Meredith. I would like it above all things if you came to Paris with me."

Meredith looked at her cousin, her previous shock fading into slight suspicion. As far back as Meredith could remember, her cousin had shown her nothing short of scorn. It was obvious Vivienne wanted something—perhaps even needed something—and oddly, a thing that only Meredith could give her . . . or she wouldn't have gone to such lengths to solicit Aunt Phoebe's permission to take her to Paris. But even more puzzling to Meredith was the fact that Vivienne traveled all the time, in company of a maid, a dresser, a small army of servants. She was never alone, and she was going to stay with an old friend.

48

Why on earth would she want me along?

Meredith stared at Vivienne. How intense her cousin's eyes were just now! As if she were willing Meredith to say yes.

And of course, she would say yes. How could she not? Free of Aunt Phoebe for even just a short time. And in Paris with the notorious Lady Vivienne Winter. She may not have liked Vivienne much, but she had to admit she was fascinated with her lifestyle. She'd be a fool to refuse such an exciting adventure, no matter what their differences had been in the past.

And why did everyone persist in saying that they were staying in the country? They were going to Paris!

All these thoughts passed through her head in a flash, and slowly, she became aware that everyone was staring at her. For once, she was the center of attention. Her eyes swept the company and fell on Augustus Sett. He was gaping at her like a beached fish, looking absolutely stunned.

Color flooded back into her face and Meredith spoke with a calm she hardly felt. "Yes, Cousin Vivienne. I gladly accept your invitation to accompany you to Paris." No sense in letting Vivienne think she was eager to go, at least not until she knew what her cousin had planned.

Meredith smiled sweetly at Vivienne, who laughed—a laugh that held a hint of relief, Meredith noticed. Why, her cousin had actually been afraid she would refuse. What an interesting afternoon this had turned out to be after all. And she supposed, it would get more interesting once she and Vivienne had a chance to talk alone.

Then Meredith raised an innocent eyebrow and asked, "When do we leave?"

49

"Now," said Vivienne, shutting the door firmly behind her, "we can talk. I think I should tell you right away, Meredith, that I lied. I have no intention of going to Paris."

Meredith watched Vivienne, who sank down into an easy chair and bent to pull off her gleaming black boots. They were in what Aunt Phoebe called the "Rose Room," presumably because of the garish cabbage roses on the wallpaper and the pink counterpane on the bed. There were also paintings of roses on the wall, but it was a pretty enough room. The mahogany furniture was a ruby dark contrast to all the pink, and Meredith liked the moss-green carpet. Outside, the rain was pouring down the windows and veiling the world in gray.

Meredith seated herself calmly in an armchair opposite her cousin. A wave of disappointment washed over her, and she couldn't help the dismay in her voice. "You lied? You're not going to Paris? Then what on earth was the purpose of that charade downstairs?"

Meredith felt as if her stays were a vise cutting off her breathing. She was getting angry. How dare Vivienne tell her she was going to Paris, and then turn around and say it was a lie? And she had the gall to smile!

Vivienne leaned back, putting her hands behind her head, elbows akimbo, and wiggled her stockinged toes. "You heard me correctly. I am not going to Paris. But what an apt word you have chosen. Charade. It describes exactly what I have in mind. No, I am not going to Paris, but you needn't worry. You are."

"I am?"

"And you must. Everything depends upon it."

Meredith was completely puzzled. "I hardly understand why I *must* go to Paris and why *you* are not."

"You *must* go to Paris *because* I am not." Vivienne wiggled her toes again and laughed at some joke that escaped Meredith entirely.

"You are infuriating, Vivienne, and you know it. I've known since you arrived that you were plotting something. You've never come to Helston Grange willingly that I can remember. And suddenly you're here out of the blue, offering Louisa a season in London that had Aunt Phoebe practically drooling in her teacup. *And* you've asked me, of all people, to go to Paris. Why me?"

Vivienne looked affronted. "Can't I do something nice for my country cousin without being accused of some ulterior motive?"

Meredith gave Vivienne a pointed look that told her cousin her patience was growing thin.

"Meredith, you were always such a clever girl. I'm surprised you haven't figured it out for yourself."

Meredith gave an exasperated groan. "Well, forgive me for being so dense. Now tell me at once or I won't go to Paris, and I mean it." She sat back, all determination. Really, Vivienne's dramatics could be maddening.

But before her cousin could answer, there was a knock on the door. Meredith could only stare at her cousin, while Vivienne smiled at her mockingly.

"Come in," Vivienne called, and Jane came bustling in.

Jane glanced at Meredith, then planted herself in front of Vivienne and made a sketch of a curtsy. "Afternoon, My Lady. My name is Jane, and Madam sent me up to help you unpack. I imagine you

51

brought your own maid, but if I can assist her or you in any way, you have only to ask."

"Are you a lady's maid?" came the lazy inquiry from Vivienne. She was looking Jane over from head to toe, very much the way she had Meredith when she first saw her downstairs.

"I am that, My Lady. I do for Miss Louisa."

"I see. And has Meredith told you she is going to Paris?"

"No, My Lady, seeing as how I just saw her now. But if I may say so, My Lady, it's the talk of the servants' hall already, so I knew."

Vivienne laughed lightly. "So hard to keep secrets from servants. I wonder why we even bother to try. Do you know all of Meredith's secrets, Jane?"

Meredith could stand no more. "Cousin Vivienne," she broke in, "I hardly think the secrets Jane and I keep matter. Just now, I am most anxious to continue our discussion!"

"Then I'll take my leave . . . if you don't mind?" asked Jane, curtsying.

"But I think the secrets you and Jane keep matter very much indeed. It so happens my own maid has a headache and is lying down—provoking creature! She says traveling doesn't agree with her. And I do so much of it, I begin to wonder if I should dismiss her. I certainly can't expect her to go to Paris. Jane, stay, for I shall need you to unpack my bags after all."

Jane threw a look at Meredith, who tightened her lips. It was obvious Vivienne was enjoying this little game.

The look wasn't lost on Vivienne. "I see Meredith's opinion matters very much to you, Jane. Tell me, are you especially loyal to her, or are you just as loyal to . . . Miss Louisa, for instance?"

"Oh, I'd lay down my life for Miss Meredith, that I would. When our Willie needed a position, Miss Meredith saw to it he was taken on as an under-groom in the stables here. He's a good lad, is Willie, but the job would've been out of his reach if it wasn't for Miss Meredith's good word."

"Still hanging out in the stables, I see, Meredith. Well. Then if keeping a secret would help her, you'd keep it, would you, Jane?"

"I would." Jane nodded vigorously and looked pugnaciously at Vivienne, as if daring the young woman to make her say another word.

"This has gone far enough!" Meredith burst out. "Stop talking in riddles, Vivienne! Tell me what you mean by saying I am going to Paris and you are not."

Jane stared open-mouthed at Meredith, then at Vivienne, who smiled beautifully at her cousin.

"Meredith, I promise I'll tell you in just a moment. But before I tell you what I'm up to, I have to demonstrate something to you or you'll never believe me. Now, as I recall, you used to be quite adventurous. I hope it's not all been taken out of you by Aunt Phoebe and you'll hear me out."

Meredith realized it was futile to protest. Vivienne was in control of the situation, as always. "Oh, very well. We'll do it your way. At least I haven't been bored for the past few minutes, and I thank you for that."

"That's the Meredith I remember. Now, Jane, open that red leather trunk. I believe you'll find a violet dress in there, wrapped in tissue. Get it out. And Meredith, take off your dress."

"But—" Meredith began.

"You said you'd bear with me. Must you argue every step of the way?"

Shaking her head, Meredith began unbuttoning the many tiny pearl buttons down the front of her dress. She was stepping out of it when she heard a delicious rustling.

She turned to see Jane holding up the loveliest creation of a dress she'd ever seen. Midnight-violet tulle, with yards of diaphanous silver netting that drifted around it like moonmist, and was caught here and there by clusters of velvet violets and silver ribbons.

"Jane, put the gown on Meredith."

Reverently, Jane dropped the shimmery creation over Meredith's head. Meredith was facing away from the mirror and started to turn to see, but—

"Wait!" commanded Vivienne. "Let down her hair, Jane."

Meredith felt Jane's deft fingers pulling out her hairpins and fluffing the loosened waves as they fell on her shoulders.

"Now you can look," came Vivienne's voice. Meredith turned, hardly daring to move, and confronted a vision. Clouds of violet and silver, dark and brilliant as moonlight and midnight. Blue-black hair on white shoulders. The dress almost fit her; she was just a bit taller and slimmer than Vivienne. The dress made her someone else, someone she'd never seen before.

Not Vivienne. She didn't have Vivienne's high coloring, her reckless look. She didn't have her dashing features—the pointed chin, high cheekbones, small nose, and sensual mouth.

Instead, she was delicate, a dream. Long slender neck, oval cheeks, soft wide mouth. But the eyes were the same.

She gasped. "My eyes! They look purple!"

Vivienne laughed. "It's the dress, and the dim light. If you lean close to the mirror, you'll see they're still blue. But from farther away they pick up the color of the dress. Nice effect, isn't it? It's why I so often wear violet. Try moving around a bit."

Meredith hesitated, then giving Jane a conspiratory look and a smile, she took one step and then another as she crossed the room. She felt like a cloud drifting through a summer sky. The dress floated around her like a whisper. She threw back her shoulders, lifted her chin, and moved to the opposite side of the room near the window.

"Don't look at your feet," coached Vivienne. "And take smaller sliding steps. Let the dress sway slightly from side to side, but not too much. Perfect. Now stop and turn. Not too fast. Give the back of the dress a slight kick. There. Now walk back this way as if you're passing through a crowded ballroom. There are people all around you."

Meredith obeyed, smiling and nodding at imaginary guests, assuming the role Vivienne had assigned her with zeal.

"Very good," Vivienne encouraged. "There's the Duke of Boredom and the Count of Wit. The count is devastatingly handsome, don't you think?"

Meredith lowered her eyes, smiling ever so slightly, and coyly brought a hand to her throat as she passed by the imagined count, then shook back her curls flirtatiously and moved on, chin high.

"Superb!" cheered Vivienne.

Jane clapped her hands. "Oh, Miss Meredith!"

Meredith turned her attention to Jane and struck a pose for her benefit. She curtsied deep and low, then rose and took one of Jane's hands. "Lady Jane, what a pleasure to see you again. So kind of you to invite me to the ball. But how is your dear husband? Not suffering from the chill, I hope? The weather's been dreadful lately, has it not?"

Jane giggled and stuck her nose up in the air. "Raaather."

And then both Jane and Meredith were laughing and hugging each other until Vivienne spoke up.

"Now I see that what I hoped is true. In the right clothes—and with a bit of coaching—anyone who saw your black hair and blue eyes would believe you were me . . . if they were told you were."

"Believe I was you?" echoed Meredith.

"Yes. That's what I want of you, cousin. I want you to go to Paris as me . . . as the Lady Vivienne Winter. No one knows me there. They will all believe it."

"Me . . . go to Paris . . . as you?" Meredith thought with a superstitious shiver how just an hour ago, she'd been wishing she could somehow *be* Vivienne. . . .

She shook her head a little uncertainly. "No. I couldn't. It . . . would never work. I wouldn't know what to do or how to act. Jane, please help me out of this dress." She turned so the maid could unfasten the dress. "Vivienne, you must be mad. It's one thing to dress up and play make-believe in one's own bedroom, but—"

"If I didn't have every confidence you could do it, Meredith, I wouldn't have asked. Besides, I can teach you all that you will need to know. I wouldn't dream of sending you to Paris unprepared." She looked at Meredith and her eyes sparkled. "And just think of the places you'll go—the opera, the parties—and the people you will meet. You'll have my entire wardrobe at your disposal, and you'll be staying in what could modestly be called a palace. And you won't be alone. Jane will be with you."

"Me!" squeaked Jane.

"If Meredith is posing as me, someone will have to

56

play Meredith," Vivienne said, as if it were all perfectly obvious.

"Oh, miss," said Jane, sinking into a chair and looking at Meredith with a mystified expression.

"Really, Meredith, can Helston Grange compare with Paris? If you stay here, you'll positively rot. Won't you do me this one small favor?"

It was just like Vivienne to think of this as a favor. Meredith pulled one sleeve of the dress from her shoulder and looked at her cousin. "This is more than just a favor you're asking," she said with an incredulous laugh.

"Then I am prepared to make it entirely worth your while. I'm willing to give you whatever you think is necessary to leave Helston Grange . . . forever. I think it a fair exchange."

Meredith stopped and considered this.

"Heaven knows, I've got the money. And things can't be all that pleasant with Aunt Phoebe hovering over you all the time. . . ."

What an understatement, thought Meredith. And damn Vivienne for knowing just what strings to pull. Meredith looked to Jane for help.

"I'll go if you go, miss," was Jane's eager reply. "I ain't never been to Paris."

Meredith let out a defeated sigh. She did want—more than anything—to leave Helston Grange and Aunt Phoebe forever. And Vivienne had said no one knew her in Paris. What could possibly go wrong? Even if she wasn't completely successful at playing Vivienne, would anyone really know the difference?

She hoped she wouldn't regret it, but she turned and confronted Vivienne. If she was going to do this, there was still one last thing she wanted to know.

"And while I am in Paris pretending to be you,

where will you be?"

Vivienne smiled a triumphant cat smile. "Then you'll do it?"

"Where will you be?" Meredith repeated with emphasis.

Vivienne laughed lightly and flopped into the armchair opposite Jane. "I? Meredith, I didn't think you were *quite* such a child. I can see we will have work to do before anyone will believe you are me. They might be fooled by your looks, but no one would believe I could be so naive. Where will I be while you are taking Paris by storm in my name? With my lover, of course!"

Chapter Four

The news of Vivienne's impending arrival was already causing much talk in Paris.

The afternoon sun came filtering through heavy brocaded draperies, causing the man lounging on the sofa to groan and shield his eyes. The room around him was blindingly lavish, filled with soft draperies in rich materials and colors, thin gilt-covered furniture, marble statues on pedestals, and enormous pastoral paintings covering the walls and ceiling. He was a figure as elegant as the room. Silver-blond locks fell about his head in careful disarray, and his tall frame was clothed in the most incomparable of Oriental brocade dressing gowns, in shades of dark green and maroon.

The door opened, and a footman in white wig and gold-laced livery came in.

"A caller to see you, Viscomte. The Comtesse d'Anguillame."

With a lazy wave of his hand, the young man ordered, "Show her in at once." But he sat up straighter, and there was a spark of interest in his previously languid eyes.

A woman entered, a vision as fresh and ornate as anything in Paris. The sunlight turned her red hair to flame, and she was resplendent in an emerald silk overdress open over a petticoat of copper satin. She narrowed lovely sherry-colored eyes at the young man rising and bowing over her extended hand to kiss it.

"Really, Nicki, you are a disgrace," she said. "It is three o'clock in the afternoon, and you are not even dressed yet. I despair of you. Another night spent prowling through the sewers of Paris, or was it gambling again?"

He smiled down at her, magnificently handsome. He had sky-blue eyes under dark brows, a tempting mouth that curved in appreciation at the sight of her. "But my dearest Genvieve, the sewers of Paris are so amusing. There one can find pleasures not available elsewhere."

She walked to the sideboard and poured herself a glass of wine, then turned. "Expensive pleasures, Nicki."

"I can afford it," he smiled, casting a meaning glance around the spectacular room.

She raised a flame-colored brow. "Indeed? That is not what I hear."

His dark brows drew together in a thunderous scowl. "Where did you hear? Who told you?" he demanded.

She shrugged. "I hear many things. One is that your wild ways have caused your father to write you out of his will and leave his fortune to your younger brother, who is more dutiful. I know the estate and title are entailed to you as eldest, but you have already borrowed many times over the value of your estate. And it is not even yours yet. And now Charlot will get all the money, and you will get nothing. You are a poor man, Nicholas St. Antoine, and can no longer afford your expensive pursuits."

"How many know this, Ginny? Is it the talk of Paris?" He sounded desperate.

"Do not excite yourself, Nicki. It is not common knowledge to the world yet . . . and may not become so until your father dies. I myself will say nothing. Your tailor will still make for you the clothes you look so enchanting in. . . ." Her eyes caressed him, taking in his matchless looks. "And your wine merchant will still bow and scrape to you. But eventually—"

"Eventually I will be ruined." There was a despairing note of finality in his voice.

"Not necessarily." She crossed the room and sat beside him, running one white hand down the lapel of his dressing gown. "You could do what so many others have done in your position. You could marry."

Hope leapt into his sky-blue eyes, and he looked down at her warmly. "I could marry *you*, Ginny. Say you'll change your mind. You have enough for both of us. . . ."

She laughed, a tinkling sound. "But how romantic! You will marry me for my money! I am afraid not, my beautiful one. For one thing, we both spend like Midas, and my widow's portion could not keep us in opulence in Paris."

"Damn it, Ginny, you know you are rich enough to buy and sell a sultan!"

"Do not pout because I do not take you up on your oh-so-loving proposal, Nicki my darling. Besides . . . a man like you would be far too easy to fall in love with. And you do not have it in you to be faithful to one woman. You are a rake, my friend. Have you not told me of lying with everyone from your chambermaid to the queen herself?"

"But you always demand an account of my every seduction!"

"Only to keep myself reminded that I have no wish to be another in a string of conquests . . . but we stray from the point. You need a rich wife, Nicki. You are young and exceptionally handsome. The world still believes you to be the heir to Valmy. Before it learns otherwise, marry an heiress."

"But . . . my habits are well-known. Most mothers wouldn't allow me within ten feet of their virginal daughters."

"I did not say marry a Parisian girl. A country heiress, perhaps, or—" She opened her reticule and took out a folded page of a society paper. "Here, read this."

" 'The Lady Vivienne Winter, wife of Lord Chalmers Anthony Winter of Scotland, arrives in Paris next week for a visit with the Comtesse Genvieve d'Anguillame,' " he read aloud. Then he looked up, quizzical. "An Englishwoman? But she is married."

"Married to a man as ancient as he is rich . . . well into his eighties. He is bedridden, in ill health, and they are childless. The bulk of his fortune goes to her on his death. Not his estates, but his money. And what difference does that make? You cannot afford to maintain more estates. It is gold you need. She has enough to make you rich for the rest of your life if you marry her when she is a widow."

"But she is not a widow!"

"Precisely. This can only work to your advantage. When she is widowed, with her fortune and her looks, she will be besieged by suitors. But if you win her heart before she is widowed—and it will be soon, my friend, for her husband is very ill—you will perhaps be able to keep it. You are able to make women fall in love with you very easily, I believe."

"How do you know so much about her?"

"Didn't you read that she is coming to visit me? Vivienne is an old friend of mine. And she is very, very beautiful. But you must act at once. Already, another man has been inquiring about her and asking me for an introduction. Even now you will have competition, and he is almost as handsome as you are."

If not just as handsome, she thought, thinking of the black-haired duke who had so lately called on her. His green eyes were enough to make a woman weak in the knees, and besides, there was something quite reckless in his smile. Indeed, if she were not already madly in love with the man who sat across from her . . . if she did not already have plans to win his love . . . she might have lost her heart to Raceford.

Instead, she had promised him an introduction to the Lady Vivienne when she arrived, after ascertaining to her relief that he'd never met the lady in question while in England. For if he had . . . She shuddered at the thought, relieved.

And it wasn't true that the *mamans* of Paris would let Nicki nowhere near their daughters. They were a practical lot, and he was the heir to a fine old title. In fact, it had been from one of these mothers, a neighbor of Nicki's father, that she'd learned about Nicki's troubles. The mother had not cared that he'd have no money, for "there is the title," she'd explained, "and my Suzette has enough money to maintain the estates and more besides."

This Suzette was an exceptionally lovely child, and very, very rich. And Ginny had no intention of letting Nicki be caught by another. No, she needed time to make him fall in love with her, for less than his undying love she'd not settle for.

So let him pursue a pretend Vivienne, one whom he would think was rich and safely married . . .

"So, I seduce her?" Nicki said, smiling.

"Imbecile. Of course not. She is trying hard to distract herself from a loveless life, and all she finds is those who offer her *affaires*. No. She must believe that between the two of you is a deathless love, fraught with romance. You must treat her as if she is an unassailable virgin. She must see you as the knight in old times loyal to his lady fair. This way, she will keep you bright in her heart and marry you and no other when her husband dies."

She rose and gave him a grave look. "I suggest you spend the week devising some way to get her attention. First meetings are important. She must see you in a rosy light, believe you are a hero. If you could rescue her from some dire peril . . . then it will be hard to tarnish the picture she has of you, no matter what she may later hear. Besides, you can tell her you were wild in your youth, before true love reformed you. All women love a reformed rake."

"Why are you doing this for me?"

She smiled and paused in the doorway. "Really, Nicki," she said, looking fondly at his silver-blond hair, his gorgeous eyes, "I could not bear to see you ruined. Life would be most dull without you in it, and the unrequited passion we have between us."

"We could requite it."

"We could . . . but first, I think you must win the Lady Winter's heart. And fortune."

And with another dazzling smile, she swept out.

Chapter Five

Meredith leaned forward eagerly, practically pressing her nose against the coach window. The coach rocked and swayed over the rutted roads, but inside all was comfort, from the cushioned leather seats to the fur lap robe spread over her legs. She reached up to adjust the huge hat that sat on her curls, a creation of lavender silk and purple grosgrain ribbons, black ostrich plumes and black dotted netting. Her traveling suit was dove-gray, with sleeves turned back to show lavender insets that were trimmed with black ribands. White point lace, lavender kid gloves, and sapphire earrings surrounded by jet stones completed what she knew was a stunning ensemble.

Across from her sat Jane, reading a book of poetry, a suggestion Vivienne had made to help the woman improve her rustic speech. Jane looked fresh and pretty in a dark blue gown and straw "milkmaid" hat decorated with pink silk roses.

And beside Jane sat Vivienne. Vivienne was modestly attired in a black woolen cloak, beneath which Meredith knew her cousin wore a plain muslin dress, no jewels. And beneath the hood that covered her head, her cousin had forgone her usual elaborate hairstyle and pulled her hair back into a single loose braid that hung nearly to her waist. Vivienne had donned the clothes eagerly, mischievously calling them her "disguise" for the trip to France. And although she was simply dressed, Meredith thought her cousin was no less radiant, perhaps even more so, for they were nearing Meudon, where they were going to meet Gabriel. From Meudon they would separate — Vivienne and Gabriel to their hideaway in the country, and Meredith and Jane on to Reveille, their last stop before Paris.

They'd crossed the channel days ago and were well past Campiegne. As they drew nearer and nearer to Meudon, Meredith couldn't help but notice the excited flush that had risen to Vivienne's cheeks and that her conversation had become far more animated.

"You seem anxious to see Gabriel," Meredith said, looking at her cousin, whose face was pressed nearly as close to the coach's window as hers had been moments ago.

"I am," breathed Vivienne simply, without looking away from the view rushing past them. "And we're almost there!"

The countryside they were traveling through was green with the new growth of spring. The midday rays of the sun fell gently over the land, giving the meadows that rolled aimlessly away from the road a soft, fresh glow. All around were snug gray stone farmhouses, with red tiled roofs where doves nested in the gutters, orchards in deep bloom, legions of lily of the valley and violets growing recklessly everywhere. They passed a woman herding a flock of geese along the dusty road, a sturdy peasant man leading a cow. Now and then, behind the rolling green hills, Meredith caught a glimpse of a gracious château, like a building out of one of the fairy tales she'd read when she was a child.

She shook her head as if she were waking from a dream. "I can hardly believe this is happening—traveling to Paris in the most lavish of coaches, wearing the most expensive of gowns, with trunks and trunks of your clothing strapped to the top. It's incredible . . . a dream come true."

Vivienne laughed. "Dear Cousin Meredith, you act as if you've been crowned queen."

"I feel as if I have!" she laughed in return, and gave her cousin a warm smile. "I know we've had our differences in the past and I know I had my doubts about this little adventure, Vivienne, but I want to thank you for making it possible. Really, it's very generous of you."

Vivienne's glance dropped thoughtfully to the floor of the coach and she shrugged her shoulders, then drew her gaze to the countryside again without replying. In that one quick gesture, Meredith knew that her cousin felt undeserving of the gratitude she'd expressed, and something close to sympathy for Vivienne rose in her heart. Her cousin had more than once in the past month of coaching Meredith in her role as Lady Vivienne shied away from the tentative friendship that was developing between the two of them. As conspirators, they'd come to know each other better, reaching a kind of hesitant, yet mutual respect in the process. But still Vivienne held Meredith at a distance, never getting too close. When Vivienne came too near to letting down the facade that was the Lady Vivienne, she immediately pulled away. Meredith thought that her cousin, for all her bravado and appeal, was afraid she wouldn't like her.

But she did like Vivienne. She may not have approved of her cousin's behavior at times, but grudgingly she had come to like her, and now she wanted to let her know somehow.

"I only hope I don't embarrass you by doing something wrong in Paris. That would be poor payment for all you've done for me," she ventured.

Vivienne was caught off guard. "What do you mean embarrass me? You've worked very hard. It is I who should be embarrassed. It's a very selfish thing I've asked you to do, only that I can be with Gabriel. But then I'm a selfish person, or so everyone tells me."

"Well, I don't think you're selfish at all. You're very kind, and I only wanted you to know I appreciate your help in making all this possible."

Vivienne looked up, obviously embarrassed by being complimented. Then she laughed and changed the subject. "But you'll be cursing me before the summer's over, I can guarantee it! All those dreadful parties and afternoons entertaining the most boring companions you could imagine. You'll be wishing for your quiet country life *and* Aunt Phoebe before you know it. But I nearly forgot!" Vivienne opened her reticule and pulled out a sheet of paper. "Last night I compiled a list of some of my travel anecdotes."

Meredith groaned.

Vivienne handed her the piece of paper. "Stop groaning. You'll be thankful some evening when you're left in the company of a really dreadfully boring duke and you have positively nothing in common to talk about."

Meredith took the piece of paper and began to

look it over. After the previous month of vigorous coaching from Vivienne, on everything from dancing and dining to how to walk, sit, stand, curtsy, flirt, sneeze, *and* cough, her cousin had pronounced her ready for Paris, and Meredith had thought her lessons complete. But Vivienne had thought otherwise. Each day of their journey to Paris had been filled with Meredith poring over lists that Vivienne had compiled for her—lists of what seemed to Meredith to be of hundreds of acquaintances, their titles, and their association with her cousin; family trees; places she'd been; past flirtations. Meredith's personal traveling case was near to overflowing with these lists. And Vivienne, without notice, would pop up with a question relating to the lists in the middle of a conversation about something else. Very annoying at times, but Meredith knew it was necessary if she was going to carry off this charade.

It seemed there was no detail of her cousin's life that had been left out—with the possible exception of Vivienne's liaison with Gabriel Michael Justice. And of all the information given her, this was the one area that Meredith was most interested in.

About Gabriel, Vivienne had been exceptionally secretive. Any questions Meredith had asked about him had been completely disregarded by Vivienne, the subject immediately changed. All Meredith knew about him was that he was her cousin's lover, just as Vivienne had confessed her first day at Helston Grange. But she'd said no more of him.

But at the same time, her cousin had spoken openly and kindly of her husband, Lord Winter. When Vivienne told of her relationship with her husband, she had shown Meredith a miniature of

Lord Winter. The handsome old man's face had made Meredith feel somehow guilty. She wanted to know more of why Vivienne would go to such lengths to be with Gabriel, but she didn't know where to start. And time was running out. They would soon arrive in Meudon, some time before nightfall, and Vivienne would leave them to make the journey to Paris on their own.

Meredith folded the piece of paper in her hands in half and regarded her cousin carefully before speaking. "I don't mean to intrude, and up to this point I've respected your privacy, but it would help to know a few things."

"What do you want to know?" Vivienne asked, turning her attention to Meredith.

"You've spoken lovingly of Lord Winter all along. . . ."

"Lord Winter has been very good to me."

"Then tell me, Vivienne, how can you betray him so?"

Vivienne looked stunned for a moment, but said nothing.

"I'm not passing judgment. I only ask as a friend," Meredith persisted.

Vivienne bit her lower lip. "I've told absolutely no one about this."

"Your secret is safe with me." Meredith waited for her cousin to reply, but she could tell Vivienne was struggling. "You're in love with Gabriel, aren't you?" she offered.

Her cousin nodded her head and sighed. "I never set out to fall in love. Oh, it's true I am known far and wide as a flirt . . . but that is all I have been until now. As you know, I am fond of my husband,

and I promised him I would bear no bastard to the Winter name. So though sometimes my flirtations have included some hot stroking and I've tumbled to a few kisses, that was all I had done. Until I met Gabriel."

"Why was he different?" Meredith asked curiously.

"Gabriel? Because he's like the archangel of his namesake. Oh, Meredith, you should see him! Dark golden hair and brown eyes the color of Scotch whiskey. I've never seen a more handsome man. From the moment I first met him in society, he had the most unsettling effect on me. It was as if nothing else existed except we two. As if I had already known him for a long time."

"What's he like?"

"He can make me laugh. He's wild and funny and daring. We can talk for hours about anything and everything. But haven't you ever been in love, Meredith?"

Meredith shook her head.

"Love. Meredith, when you are in love, you'll find the world is well lost, and nothing . . . nothing else matters except being with your lover. That is why I would risk everything to have this time with him."

Meredith ran a gloved hand across the lap robe, wondering. Vivienne looked so soft, almost glowing, when she talked of Gabriel. Would she ever know love? No feelings like the ones Vivienne described had ever happened to her.

Vivienne shifted in her seat. "I was mad to be with him. wanted to run off, leave for America, can you imagine? But he was worried about my reputation. He told me we had only to be patient, that my husband could not live forever, that someday we would

71

be married and together." A shadow crossed Vivienne's face. "I hate to seem to wish for my husband's death, and indeed, I do not! He is very old and has lived a long and full life. One day, he will die. But I can't wait that long to have Gabriel to myself."

"So . . . how did you decide on this plan?"

"Gabriel felt we should break it off, stop seeing each other. What we felt for each other could not be hidden, and tongues were beginning to wag. He was worried lest my reputation be ruined. I was wild with despair at the thought of parting from him! Though he assured me he would love me forever, I was so afraid he would forget me! He is so handsome that other women are always after him. Here. I always keep this close to my heart."

Vivienne drew off a locket and opened it, handing it to Meredith. It was a portrait of an exceptionally handsome young man, Meredith saw, with a dimpled white smile that could have charmed birds from trees. He had a lighthearted, open look, and Meredith could imagine that women were drawn to him. She handed it back to Vivienne, pondering her last words. The very confident Vivienne—insecure? Jealous? It was a side of her cousin she'd never expected. It seemed that this thing called love could turn everything upside down.

"He is handsome indeed."

"When he said we had to stay away from each other, I had to admit that I could see no real way to be with him. I had so many obligations, and when I am away from my husband's side, everything I do is written of in the society papers. If he were constantly my escort, it would not take long for Lord Winter to find out. And believe me when I say there is nothing

I want to avoid more than hurting my husband. He has been very kind to me."

Vivienne fell silent for a moment, then continued with a ragged sigh.

"He's even suggested I look for my next husband in Paris. My lord husband is ill and he knows he will die soon, and he wants to make sure I am well cared for in that event. He understands the predicament of a young wife with an elderly husband."

"And that's what makes this all so difficult for you?" Meredith ventured.

"Meredith, I have to be discreet for his sake, but I want so desperately to be with Gabriel. I wailed to Gabriel one day, 'How I wish there could be two of me! One to do my duty, the other to be at your side.'" Vivienne's tilted eyes fixed on Meredith. "It was then that I thought of you. Remember when we were small, how we were always taken for sisters?"

Meredith nodded. "Some things never change."

"It was just then that I received an invitation from Ginny to come to Paris. I was in Scotland, positively pining for Gabriel and fretting with worry over whether he truly meant to put me aside. My lord husband was most concerned about me. He said I was pale and growing thin. And he brought in some doctor to examine me. This doctor prescribed a stay out of England, and Winter himself suggested I visit Ginny. I wasn't sure about my plan of passing you off as me, so I came to Helston Grange, hoping against hope you hadn't changed too much or married. When I saw you, I knew it would work."

"And did Gabriel agree to this plan?"

She smiled. "By then, he was as desperate as I was at our separation, and willing to agree to anything. I pointed out that we could stay near Paris, within call if you needed me. He was only too ready to agree. But he was still fearful for my reputation if we left the country at the same time. So he spread it about to his friends and at his club that I had broken it off with him — and broken his heart. He had one friend he wanted to tell, but I insisted. No one could know our secret if we were going to succeed."

"And Jane's part in all this?"

"My dear Meredith. If you are supposed to be in Paris, then you'd better be there. My husband will read of your activities — in my name — in the society papers, and believe I am enjoying myself. So will your aunt, I imagine. And beside my name must be that of my companion, my cousin Meredith. Besides, I do not trust servants. It's a blessing we have Jane to take with us and not some talkative maid." She threw Jane a warm smile.

Jane sighed, looking up from her book of poetry. " 'All days are nights to see till I see thee. And nights bright days when dreams do show thee me.' It's beautiful, ain't it, Miss Meredith? Though I ain't quite sure what he means."

"I know exactly what he means. I feel the same way about Gabriel. But, Jane, you must say isn't, not 'ain't'," Vivienne corrected. "And you must start calling Meredith 'Vivienne'." Vivienne gave Jane's hand a reassuring pat when she saw the girl's hurt expression.

"I'm going to ruin everything, I just know it!" Jane wailed.

Meredith leaned forward. "Nonsense. You'll do just fine. Everyone speaks French and they'll hardly notice an 'ain't' or two. They'll think you have a charmingly quirky accent. Besides, I'll be there to help you."

"Dear God!" Vivienne nearly screamed.

"What is it?" asked Meredith. Vivienne looked as if she'd seen a ghost.

"I nearly forgot. Oh, this will never do. We can't have gotten this far only to have to turn back. How stupid of me!"

"What is it?" Meredith asked again.

"It's known that I can speak French passably well. Everyone will expect you to be able to do the same. Meredith, you're still fluent in French, aren't you? Please don't tell me you've gone rusty or that you've completely forgotten the language," Vivienne said in a panic.

"No, I'm still fluent. Aunt Phoebe had me tutor Louisa when I was not fetching and carrying for her." But then she added, with panic rising in her own voice, "However, I do need help from time to time. Please tell me Ginny can speak English."

"Flawlessly."

The three of them let out a collective sigh of relief. They looked at each other and then started laughing at their needless panic.

"Thank heavens! I was beginning to get nervous," breathed Meredith. "I'm sure there will be things we have overlooked, but if Jane and I put our heads together, I'm confident we'll muddle through. Right, Jane?"

"Right, Miss M—Cousin Vivienne. And my name *isn't* Jane. It's Meredith," Jane said, sticking her nose in the air in mock indignation.

"Forgive me, dear Cousin Meredith."

"You are forgiven, Cousin Vivienne." The two of

them giggled between them.

"Enough of this diversion," demanded Vivienne, like a schoolmaster commanding the attention of his pupils. "Meredith, the history of Castle Winter."

Meredith groaned. "You're relentless, Vivienne. If I haven't learned all this by now, I'll never know it."

"The history of Castle Winter," Vivienne persisted, a slight smile curving her lips.

"There is a ghost that walks the battlements of the castle whenever a member of the family is about to die. . . ."

An hour later, a weary Meredith, her head stuffed with facts, leaned back in her seat, grateful that the lessons had ended and for the ensuing silence in the coach. Jane had gone back to reading her poetry, and Vivienne kept a watchful eye out the window of the coach.

Meredith thought perhaps she'd take a nap. Meudon couldn't be too much farther and it would be nice to rest before they arrived, especially after the merciless paces Vivienne had put her through. But just as she closed her eyes, the coach lurched around a corner, and a small shriek emerged from Vivienne.

"Meudon! We're here!"

Meredith looked out the window and glimpsed the sleepy little village. The rays of the westering sun were casting a slanted light over Meudon, and there was a haunting quality in the bloom of purple twilight falling over the woods and meadows in the distant east.

Meudon gave her the feeling of going home, a day's work done. To one side of the dusty road that wound through the village sat a large brick farmhouse with a monumental stone gateway, and behind it were rolling meadows where cattle grazed. The other side of the road was bounded by several thatched cottages and a small country church, its steeple tinted red in the sun. And nestled among huge weeping willows, the wheel of a mill could be seen churning up the water of the river that ran past, sparkling gold and red in the late afternoon light. A line of village girls in bright skirts, kerchiefs on their heads, carried their washing back from the mill, waving and shouting greetings to them as their coach rolled by in the direction of the gateway.

Once through the gates, another shriek came from Vivienne.

"Gabriel!"

Beneath the deepening shade of an elm in the front yard of the farmhouse sat another coach. As their vehicle approached, Meredith saw the figure of a man step out of it, his golden hair glinting as he ran to greet them.

Vivienne barely waited for the coach to stop before she flung open the door, swept out, and threw herself into Gabriel's arms.

When Jane and Meredith stepped from the coach, they found the two lovers embracing each other. Tears were running down Vivienne's cheeks as she clung to Gabriel and he held her tenderly, kissing her hair and whispering reassurances to her. Meredith watched as Gabriel pulled away and then gently pressed his lips to Vivienne's.

It was obvious to Meredith that the two were indeed very much in love. Never before had she seen such shining expressions on the faces of two people as they gazed into each other's eyes. Even though her head told her that what Vivienne was doing was wrong, her heart wanted her cousin to have this happiness with Gabriel.

When at last the two lovers parted, Vivienne turned to Meredith and Jane. "Gabriel, I should like to introduce you to my cousin, Miss Meredith Westin, and her companion, Miss Jane Stikely."

He bowed slightly in acknowledgment, then stepped forward to take both of Meredith's hands in his. "Miss Meredith, thank you for doing this for us. You don't know how much this means to both of us. We are forever in your debt." And then with a winsome smile and a laugh, he held her hands out and looked her up and down. "You really are close enough in looks to be sisters. I didn't think it possible for anyone to rival my Vivienne in beauty."

Meredith blushed at the compliment, and Vivienne stepped forward. There was a look very close to jealousy in her cousin's eyes as Vivienne looped her arm through Gabriel's and ever so gently pulled him away. If she knew her cousin, poor Gabriel would catch the devil for his innocent compliment later!

"Gabriel, we must go if we are to reach our destination by nightfall," Vivienne said.

"And we must be on our way, too. We still have two or three hours on the road before we reach Reveille. Then on to Paris!" Meredith announced, stepping forward and giving Vivienne a generous hug. "Be happy, Vivienne. And don't worry about Jane and me. We'll be fine."

"If you have any trouble, you need only send a message to me in St. Denis in care of Monsieur Anton Laujon. Gabriel tells me we'll be staying in the most lovely little farmhouse there. And you, Meredith, must try to have fun." Vivienne returned her hug and then turned to Gabriel. "Are you ready, my love?"

"More than ready." He put his arm around her and together they ran to their coach. Vivienne shouted back to her, "Good-bye and good luck, Meredith! Remember, there's a whole new world waiting for you in Paris!"

And then the lovers were inside the coach, and the vehicle rolled past them along the drive through the gateway, Vivienne waving from the window.

Meredith waved back and then turned to Jane. "Are you ready, Jane?"

"Oh, miss, if the truth be told, with Miss Vivienne gone, I'm a bit frightened."

"Me, too," confided Meredith. "But I suppose that's to be expected, isn't it?"

Jane nodded reluctantly and followed Meredith back into the coach.

As they left Meudon behind, Meredith was deep in thought. Was she mad to be doing this? To think they could possibly succeed with such a wild plan?

But then she thought of Augustus Sett, Aunt Phoebe. Success in Paris meant she would never have to see them again. Vivienne had assured her of it. Oh, she'd be madder to go back to Helston Grange now. There was nothing for her there, nothing but drudgery and miserable boredom until she grew old. . . . And then she smiled, taking heart in Vivienne's parting words to her.

Out there, if she only had the courage to seize it, waited a whole new world.

A cloaked and masked figure sat his horse on a hill

that overlooked the road below. The sun was just now setting and the man watched the coach, a shadow in the twilight, as it approached. His hand briefly touched the pistol at his hip, where his saber usually hung.

"That's it, sir," one of his men said, pointing in its direction. "We spotted it a quarter of an hour ago, just a few miles past Meudon. We rode like the devil to get here."

"And you're certain it's the Winter coach?"

"The Winter crest, big as day, on the door."

"Perfect," the masked man whispered to himself, and a smile spread across his lips. Then he turned to his companions, six masked men on horseback, pistols at the ready on each man's hip. "Gentlemen, prepare yourselves, and do mind your manners, for tonight we make the acquaintance of a lady . . . the Lady Vivienne Winter."

Meredith heard the sound of hooves pounding on the road, then a shout and a wild neigh. All at once the driver was yelling, and the coach took off with a great sway that pitched Jane almost in Meredith's lap.

"What is it?" Jane cried. "Are the horses running away?"

Meredith, frightened by the wild swaying of the coach as it bounced over the ruts, tried to lean forward to look out the window. But only a deep twilight met her eyes, the countryside veiled in falling night. "I don't know," she gasped. "I can't see a thing. If he doesn't slow the horses, we'll turn over or break a wheel!"

"Ohh!" Jane wailed. "Why doesn't he stop them. We'll be killed for certain!"

There was a loud report—almost a boom—that silenced them. There was another report, then a shout.

"My God," gasped Meredith. "The horses haven't run away. That's a gun! We're being held up by highwaymen!"

For a long moment, the two women stared into each other's terrified eyes. The shots must have had the desired effect, for they felt the wild ride of the coach slowing, slowing to a trot, then a walk.

The coach ground to a halt.

Jane was across the gap and plunking down next to Meredith, closest to the door. "Oh, miss, if there was only somewhere for you to hide! I'll protect you from them. . . . Here, give me that foot-warming brick! When they open the door, I'll bash them!"

Meredith clung hard to Jane. "You'll do no such thing! You'll do nothing brave or foolish, take no risks!" she swallowed, trying to sound calmer than she felt. "It is well known that Vivienne is rich, and look at the coach we're in. Holdups like this are common on English roads as well as on French ones. It's never happened to us before because we never had anything worth taking. All they want is our money and jewels. Don't say a word! Let me do the talking, and do whatever they say."

Outside, they could hear rough shouts and curses, could feel the coach rock as the driver and postilions climbed down.

Meredith braced herself.

The door swung open.

Against the night she saw a shape blacker than the gray hills. Broad shoulders, tall, cloaked. And the fading light showed clearly enough the gleam of a gun barrel leveled at her heart.

"Good evening, My Lady. You will do me the courtesy to climb out? You will not be harmed if you do as I say."

The voice was deep, and Meredith thought she heard a ripple of laughter in it. But it was a commanding voice as well, and she had no thought other than to obey it. She nodded frigidly, and was gathering her skirts in her gloved hands as she stood, when she froze.

He had spoken English!

A gauntleted hand was extended to her. "Come, we cannot waste time. The moments fleet past. I will help you if you are too unsteady to manage the descent."

Meredith raised her chin. "You are English!" she said accusingly.

A deep laugh was her answer. "I claim that honor. Your passion for jewels is well known, My Lady. Worth a trip across the channel, I thought. But we can tarry no longer."

Two strong hands reached up and grasped her waist in an iron grip. Meredith gasped as she was lifted from her feet and swung out of the coach into the night. He handled her as if she were no heavier than a feather pillow, and she was set breathless on her feet.

She found herself staring up into a pair of compelling eyes under dark peaked brows. Long, wicked eyes gleamed at her above a dark scarf that covered the rest of his face. He was a full head and shoulders taller than she was, and her fascinated gaze was drawn to his midnight hair, black as her own, that swept back from his forehead and fell in gypsylike disarray to his shoulders. The dim light of early evening showed her the one golden hoop gleaming in his ear. He looked every inch a gypsy, with high cheekbones she could see above the scarf.

"Lovely," he murmured.

With a start, his voice made her realize he was only a few inches away from her, and those breathtakingly strong hands were still clasping her waist. She caught her breath and started to back away, but the insistent hands smoothed the curve of her waist and moved slightly upward before she broke free.

"Small enough to span with my hands," he said in a low murmur for her ears alone. "And if we were alone, My Lady, I would take my time in discovering the shape of the rest of you."

Meredith felt the color flood her cheeks, felt her heart begin to race, but couldn't look away from those reckless eyes. It was as if he'd cast a spell on her from the moment he'd touched her, from the moment she'd found herself looking up at this tall, dark-cloaked stranger.

He stepped back and put gauntleted fists on his hips. Again she heard the laugh in his deep voice. "And now, My Lady, your money or your virtue is, I believe, the proper sentiment for the situation we find ourselves in."

At last Meredith could tear her gaze from his mocking one. She saw that around them was a small band of masked men, who were tying her postilions and coachman and gagging them. Only Jane and she were left free.

"J—Meredith," she caught herself. "My jewel case and my reticule with the money in it. Give it to the man."

She kept her eyes cast down, not daring to look at him again, and peeled her gloves off shaking hands. She wore rings and a bracelet. In a moment she had them off, then began to struggle with her brooch and the jeweled clips that held back the veil on her hat. But she left on her earrings, hoping her hair would conceal them.

At last she was done. Again raising her chin, glad that the fallen veil half shrouded her frightened face, she held out a remarkably steady hand with a glittering pile in it.

"Here. Take them."

His touch, fingers against her bare palm, was like a shock. Then the jewels were gone and she closed her palm, suddenly cold.

His head bent as he examined the open jewel case, tossed her jewels in it, opened the money purse, and ran the coins through his gloves.

He looked up again and she was held by his eyes. "Not enough, I am afraid."

Meredith found her voice. "Not enough? It is a small fortune in jewels, and all I have!"

"But jewels can be sold for only a fraction of their value, and the money you have here will barely pay the expenses of our trip across the channel. However, I think I can remedy the problem. You are rich, and your husband would pay a small fortune in ransom to have you returned to him unharmed."

"Ransom?" The word came out in a cracked whisper.

"Ransom indeed. Are the men tied?"

Nods answered him from the masked men around them. Meredith could see there were six cloaked shapes.

"Then bring the horses. Carry the men into the woods and help the maid here into the coach. You, My Lady, will ride with me."

"Don't separate me from my mistress, you knave! If I'm going in the coach, then she is, too, you serpent-hearted blackguard! You—"

With a silencing gesture, Meredith shushed Jane and stepped forward as the men spread out to carry out his orders. "You cannot mean this. Please, I beg you, let us go! If it's money you want, I'll see that you get it. Let us go and meet me in two days' time, and I'll bring any sum you like. Only don't—"

"Meet you, so you can see me swing from the gallows? I think not. But we haven't time to stand and argue the point. Someone might come and spoil the game."

The dark shape of a tall horse was led alongside them, and Meredith took a despairing, running step toward Jane, who was being marched, struggling, toward the coach. Strong iron hands seized her around the waist, and she struggled wildly against the grip that pinned her. And then she felt herself being lifted through the air to land with a jolt astride the tall horse.

He was up behind her, and she was being held firmly by hands that were bands of steel. She struggled again and heard him laugh behind her. His boots touched the dark horse's flanks, and they were galloping into the deepening night.

Meredith felt her hair uncoiling and streaming in the wind. She could feel his thighs hard against hers, surrounding her in a way that was embarrassingly intimate. His arms clasped just below her breasts where he held the reins, and to avoid pressing against his hands, she had no choice but to lean back into his broad, strong chest.

Again she heard his laughter in her ear, felt him bend his head so his warm breath caressed her neck. "Don't fear anything, Vivienne, for with me you are always safe."

Vivienne! He did know who she was—or wasn't!

As the hooves of the horses pounded down the road like the devil's troops, Meredith lifted her head so her black hair streamed out and mingled with the hair of the gypsy whose arms she was clasped in. And strangely, as they rode wildly into the night, she realized something: Gypsy or not, she did feel safe in his arms.

Chapter Six

Hooves pounded on hard-packed dirt as the small band of horses galloped through the night. In the darkness, lit only by a fitful moon and a scattered handful of stars, she could only see treetops and the deep black shapes of pines. The road seemed to follow a riven path through the rolling hills, diving into dells, sheltered on each side by steep banks. Now and again she glimpsed lights in the distance, but knew this little band of riders would be hard to spot in this deep-cloven, hidden road.

Meredith thought frantically, trying to devise some plan of escape, wondering what the highwayman had in store for her. Finally, the horses slowed their pace and turned into a narrow track that wound up a steep hill. In the distance, Meredith saw the dark outline of a peaked roof against the night, but no lights showed.

The horses slowed to a walk as they approached the dark building. A door opened, spilling yellow lamplight and red firelight into the courtyard, and Meredith's captor halted his tall horse and leaped down. Meredith looked uncertainly at the stout man standing in the doorway holding a lantern, wondering if an appeal for help would do any good. Surely not. This was the highwayman's place, their safe haven from a hostile world.

She tried hard to memorize what she could of the house. It was of weathered red brick, timbered by great black beams, with small leaded windows that were, for the most part, shuttered closed against the light. The two-story house had two deep wings that surrounded the courtyard and steeply sloping roofs. There was a jumble of low-roofed buildings near the back—stables and barns and sheds. But in the weak light, she could see there was little remarkable about it. It was like a hundred other farms they'd passed.

Hands closed on her waist once again and she was swung off the back of the horse, but this time not onto her feet. His arm came up under her knees, the other supported her back, and she realized he meant to carry her inside.

She kicked. "Put me down. I can walk!" she hissed.

"And deny myself the pleasure of holding you in my arms again?" he said.

She looked up at him uncertainly, marveling at his strength. He carried her as if she weighed nothing, and Meredith knew that struggling was useless.

They gained the doorway and Meredith had no more than a glimpse of the red-faced older man, holding the lantern, who threw them a startled glance as they passed. Her captor strode through the passageway and took the stairs two at a time. Behind her, she heard the others stomp inside, the door slam, and crude voices calling for ale and food.

She could see they were in a rough farmhouse, with walls of white plaster and thick dark beams low on the ceiling. The floors were uneven, the furniture old and massive, and there were bunches of onions and dried sausages hanging from the rafters. A great cask of wine and another of ale were glimpsed as they passed the door to the kitchens, where a delicious smell of cooking wafted out. As they gained the upper hall, they passed a number of stout oak doors, all shut.

"Where are we?" she demanded, beginning to really worry about what might befall her. She was alone in a strange farmhouse miles from anywhere. She no longer felt that irrational sense of safety she had on the ride. "And what's to become of my companion?"

He reached a door and kicked it open. "I'll go see to her now. Don't worry. I won't leave her with the men. I'll see to it that she has a room to herself, supper, and a good fire. We don't intend to harm either of you, but to treat you as guests. I told you that you are safe with me."

He set her down and for a moment towered over her, black scarf, black hair. In the light from the fire his eyes were shadowed and dark and she couldn't see their color — or their expression. Then he turned on his heel and went out, closing the door behind him. She heard the turn of a key in the lock.

Clasping her hands nervously, Meredith turned to examine the chamber she was locked in. It was a spacious room, with a crackling fire, sturdy oak furniture, thick Turkish carpets covering the wood floors. Drawn up before the fire were worn but comfortable wing chairs with a table between them, and another table with two chairs stood beneath the windows. On that table was a wine bottle and two glasses. Two glasses? So he'd planned to bring her here all along. But the sight that caught and held Meredith's attention was the huge curtained bed that dominated the room. He'd locked her into a bedchamber!

On shaky legs, she crossed to the window and pulled back the drapes. She was on the second floor of a large rambling farmhouse and the drop was a high one—but one that could perhaps be managed if she could get the window open. Bracing her hands against the crosspiece of the window, she pushed, straining. After a moment, she stopped and saw what she'd missed in the dim light.

It was nailed shut.

She turned from the window and looked around. Maybe a weapon. Perhaps she could hit him over the head when he came in, then escape out the door. Crossing to the fireplace, she gave a grim smile. The poker hung neatly next to the grate. Picking it up, she went to the side of the door and flattened herself against the wall, listening for a step on the stairs.

But then she thought of his deep humorous voice, his compelling eyes, his easy laugh. Did she really want to hit him? What if she hit him too hard and killed him? She shivered at the thought. And if she did escape the room? She'd have to get past all those men downstairs, find her way outside, steal a horse. She had no idea where she was and she had no money. She could encounter worse dangers alone on the road at night.

The truth was, she didn't really want to hit the highwayman. She wanted to see what happened next.

She lowered the poker and walked across the room to the fireplace, hanging it up again. Then she reached up for a brace of candles and a tinderbox that stood between two pewter tankards on the mantel. In a few moments, the candles were lit.

A stranger stared at her from the mirror over the mantel. A wild-haired stranger with spots of rose blooming in her cheeks and wide, excited eyes. Eyes

90

that were sparkling.

Why, Meredith, you're enjoying yourself! she thought. It was true. She was enjoying this adventure. As Meredith, her life had been dull, dull, dull. As Vivienne, already she was hostage to a highwayman, in danger, in the middle of a story as exciting as any she'd read during those long afternoons at Helston Grange. Escape and miss the next chapter? No thank you.

Meredith saw the reflection in the mirror smiling, and she reached up to disentangle a comb that still held back part of her hair. She pulled the comb through the shining raven waves, then started to coil it to pile in a twist on top of her head, when she heard a key in the lock.

The door opened, and he was there. A tall, broad-shouldered form in a black cloak that reached the heels of his gleaming black boots. He still wore the scarf over his face, and she wondered if he was going to take it off or leave it on so she wouldn't be able to identify him later.

He spoke. "Leave it down. It's seldom I've seen such beautiful hair, and tonight I wish to admire the way it shines in the candlelight."

Meredith considered. "I will—if you will take off your scarf so I may see the man who holds me captive."

His deep laugh sent the lightest shiver down her arms. He closed the door behind him, locked it, and crossed the room to stand before her. "I am yours to command," he said softly, and reached up to untie the scarf and let it drop.

She found herself staring up at the most startlingly handsome man she had ever seen. His face was browned by the sun, with a strong and square jaw and cheekbones that could have graced a gypsy king.

A straight nose above a wide mouth that curved in a wicked smile. A sensual mouth with deep lines bracketing it on either side.

But his eyes! In the candlelight she could see their color. Under dark brows with a slight arch, he had long green eyes with thick black lashes. Emerald eyes.

Meredith felt faint, and she tore her gaze from those compelling eyes to sweep his hair. Black as her own, midnight dark with blue lights, it was tousled by the wind and swept away from his temples to fall onto a strong neck, where it was tied back by a black ribbon.

He smiled down at her and, she felt the room spin.

He reached out, and his hand caught a long strand of her hair and drew it forward. For a moment, he felt its silky texture, and then, his eyes on hers, bent his head and pressed it to that beautiful, wicked mouth in a light kiss. "We are cut from the same cloth, My Lady," he murmured, letting the lock slip through his fingers.

Meredith drew in a breath and stepped backward, astonished and a little frightened by her response to his touch. She'd wanted to lift her own fingers to touch his midnight hair, to sway closer to him. His scent seemed to be everywhere, leather and horses and clean, cold air.

With easy grace, he swept off his cloak and let it fall over a chair. Meredith felt her heart speeding as she watched him. He was dressed in a loose white shirt and black pants that hugged long, muscular legs. His waist was slender, his stomach flat, but his shoulders were wide, the skin of his throat brown and smooth against his open collar. He was like a green-eyed panther, sleek and powerful, and she wondered how she was going to keep her composure, locked alone in a room with this gypsy highwayman who took her breath away.

"And now, My Lady, we know each other. I've looked into your face and you've looked into mine. Names are not necessary, are they? Tonight, as I have said, I am yours to command. We will talk and dine and drink wine. And enjoy this evening that is stolen out of time and is ours alone. Don't fear for yourself or for your virtue. Though I find you more beautiful than I can say, I am not one to force any woman to share my bed. The women I hold in my arms are there because they want to be."

I can imagine, Meredith thought, spellbound. This incredible man must have no end of women tripping over themselves to be held in his arms. There was something about him that went far beyond looks. It was a quiet aura of confidence, a sincerity in those level green eyes, an integrity that was apparent in the way he spoke and moved. He was a man who would make any woman at once feel safe and protected, a gallant cavalier who would shelter his ladylove from the storms of the world.

How had such a man become a highwayman? His speech was cultured, educated, his eyes gleamed with intelligence. But then, there was that little spark of the devil in them that gave Meredith a clue. This man would go his own road and bow to no other.

She shook her head, trying to clear the mist he had created. What was she doing, standing here wondering about him?

She should be wondering about her own fate! But the evening was taking on an increasing sense of unreality. It was as he'd said—a night stolen out of time.

"How is J—I mean, my companion?" she asked. She was going to have to be careful! It would never do to slip up like this. She ought to be used to calling Jane "Meredith" by now. After all, they were almost in Paris! "My companion, Meredith, is very nervous, and I am worried about her." There! At last she'd managed to sound indignant.

He laughed. "Nervous? That is not a word I would choose to describe her. She scorched all of our ears, let me tell you, and fought like a wildcat. She keeps demanding to know if you are all right and threatening me with the direst of fates if I should touch a hair of your head." His eyes lingered on her hair. "So it would seem I am already damned, as I have held your hair in my fingers and touched it to my lips. But it's a price worth paying. I imagine many men have lost their souls to you."

Weakly, Meredith backed to a chair and sat down, willing herself to keep her eyes off his, for he made her too flustered when he spoke in such a caressing tone! She heard him cross to the table by the window, heard the soft sound of a cork being drawn, the pouring of wine into glasses. She stared into the fire and didn't look up at him even when a browned hand descended, holding a cut glass filled to the brim with ruby wine.

"Here, drink this, My Lady. I fear this has unsettled you. After all, it isn't every day you are kidnapped, I imagine."

She shook her head, but the wine didn't go away. "But I insist. We'll share a glass and warm ourselves by the fire while we wait for our meal to be brought up. Then we will dine together. I won't move until you take the wine and drink it."

She had no choice but to take it. Otherwise, those

disturbing long legs sculpted with muscles would stay in front of her gaze, and she would be forced to almost feel the heat of his nearness. She took the glass, and for a moment, his fingertips touched hers. She felt the light contact all the way down to the toes of her riding boots.

Then he was gone, and she heard him take the seat next to her in front of the fire. He leaned forward and tossed another log on the blaze, and she sighed with relief. With him farther away from her, with the fire to safely stare into, she should be able to gather her wits. No man had ever affected her like this — and she wasn't sure she liked it. She took a deep drink of her wine. It steadied her, and after a few more sips, she set her glass down on the table. The sound of pouring told her it was being refilled.

Meredith picked it up and sipped again, moistening a throat that felt far too dry. "And now, sir, perhaps you will tell me what you intend to do with me? Hold me for ransom was, I believe, your plan. But I am expected in Paris by the Comtesse d'Anguillame. I have another suggestion. Why not escort me to Paris? There, we can go immediately to my bankers, and I will obtain whatever sum it is you ask for. That way, your 'ransom' can be accomplished without outcry — and without scandal to my name."

"And your name is such a stranger to scandal?" His voice was a silky whiplash.

Meredith sat up straighter. "I will not listen to insults."

"I mean no insult. It is just that I have heard certain stories about you . . . stories that perhaps I hoped were true. It isn't every day I am locked into a bedchamber with a woman as beautiful as you are."

Meredith faced him with her coldest expression.

She saw that his eyes were intent. "Forget whatever it is that you have heard. Scandal follows the name of any young woman married to a man many times her age. You do not know me, sir. I am a stranger to you."

She hoped her cool words would have some impact. Good heavens, she didn't want this highwayman to believe he was locked in a room with a woman of easy virtue!

He sat back, his eyes still intent. "Fair enough. We will be strangers then, and I will forget anything I have been led to believe about you. Now this plan of yours . . . it has merit. You are clearly an intelligent woman. Much quicker and less risky than holding you in some out-of-the-way place for several weeks while demands were being made and searches for your person begun."

"Name your price. Your price for my freedom," Meredith said.

"One thousand pounds," he said coolly.

A thousand pounds! Meredith's head spun. It was a fortune! She'd been paid twenty-five pounds a year to be Aunt Phoebe's companion. Oh, what would Vivienne say when she discovered such a huge sum of money gone?

But, then, what would she say if Meredith disappeared and there was an outcry all over France? The ransom would have to be paid eventually in any case, and the scandal would cut Vivienne's trip short. Lord Winter would demand her return to Scotland after such a harrowing experience. Meredith guessed that Vivienne would count a mere thousand pounds cheap if it purchased this time with her lover.

"Done," Meredith said coldly.

There was a soft knock on the door, and apprehensively, Meredith looked up. He rose and crossed to the door, saying over his shoulder, "Dinner, My Lady." Then he added, "I would have expected you to drive a harder bargain."

Meredith's gasp of indignation was lost in the opening of the door. The same red-faced man she'd seen in the doorway downstairs came in, carrying a tray filled with covered dishes and another bottle of wine. He stared at her averted face curiously as he placed the tray on the table by the window. In a few moments he was gone, and she again heard the key turn in the lock.

"And now you'll dine with me, My Lady? We can talk and tell each other everything we keep locked up in our hearts, for we are strangers bound together by necessity, and soon we may never see each other again."

Meredith rose and went to the table, where he waited, holding the back of her chair. She sat as he pushed it in, then froze as she felt the lightest of fingers twining in her hair, tracing her neck.

"Yes, we'll dine and talk, My Lady," he murmured, his fingers creating shivers all the way down her spine. "And then—"

"And then?" she whispered, wanting to pull away, not wanting the delicate caress to stop.

"And then, of course, we'll go to bed."

"I . . . stop that!" Meredith gasped, this time jerking away from his searing touch. "How dare you think that I—"

He moved around and sat across from her, leaning back at his ease in the chair. His gaze was amused . . . and something else. The emerald eyes seemed to generate a heat of their own as they moved over her flushed face.

"You mean, how dare I hope that you will wish to share a bed with me? I told you before, My Lady, that I never take an unwilling woman in my arms. But I am hoping that by the end of dinner you will be willing." He paused as Meredith stared at him, aghast.

"You understand, My Lady," he said gently after a moment, "that I intend to seduce you."

Chapter Seven

Meredith felt her heart beating far too fast against her corset. What was she going to do now? Obviously, the man thought she was Vivienne and, as obviously, thought Vivienne would enjoy this stolen tryst.

Vivienne. What would Vivienne do if she didn't want to be . . . *seduced?* Nothing so crude as being mortified, fainting, or shrieking, Meredith was sure. Suddenly, she had a vivid picture of Vivienne, her confidence, her self-assurance. Slowly, she lifted her eyes and met his, then let a tiny smile lift the corners of her lips. She picked up her wineglass and took a sip. If Meredith didn't know what to do, she would let Vivienne take over. It was high time she started playing her role.

The firelight flickered warmly, and the logs crackled and snapped as they settled. It lit the room with a golden glow, filling it with a delicious fragrance. It seemed that applewood logs were being used in the fireplace. There was no question that the cozy room, with its rich beams and merrily burning fireplace, was a romantic setting. And that her captor was himself a considerable figure of romance. What *would* Vivienne do if she were alone with an outrageously handsome man, forced to spend the night with him in the same room — a situation that, with luck, the world would never know about? Somehow, Meredith doubted that Vivienne would keep the man at arm's length for long. She might just decide to join him in that huge — and disconcerting — bed.

She set her wineglass down. "You are very confident of your powers, sir. But you are mistaken in your quarry. I am no dairymaid to be tumbled by a few long looks and pretty words. Alas, I fear you believe my false reputation. Only one thing can . . . *seduce* me, and that is hardly likely to happen in a single evening. And that is love."

"Love." He smiled that heart-shattering smile. "Then you don't believe in love at first sight?"

She smiled back. "If Cupid's arrow can strike so quickly, then let me assure you that it missed me when I first beheld you."

"Then I am the most unfortunate of men, because I fear Eros had an arrow marked for my heart in his quiver."

"Shall we stop this useless fencing with words and eat? I am famished, and poetic phrases aren't likely to make me believe what you say. After all, it is clear you are a rogue of the worst stripe. If you were truly struck by love at the sight of me, is it likely you would be stealing my money?"

He calmly uncovered a dish, revealing a crisply browned chicken surrounded by roast potatoes and vegetables. Meredith suddenly realized she was famished. It seemed hours since she had eaten. He spoke. "Maybe it's a ploy to keep you near me longer so I can make an assault on your heart."

He filled two plates, added bread, and cheese, and replenished their wineglasses. He raised his to her in a silent toast, eyes appraising her. "As you say, let's fence no longer, My Lady. I'd rather talk to you about your life and your feelings. It's hard to believe that inside that seductive exterior beats a heart as chaste as any nun's, and I would learn why your reputation is so black if your soul is so white."

Meredith started her dinner, feeling slightly more confident than she had when he made his intentions clear. He seemed a gentleman, and she felt that he would let her hold him at arm's length if she so desired. And he seemed to believe her Vivienne impersonation.

"My reputation," she began, recalling Vivienne's history. "I married young. In fact, I had never been presented to society. My family was anxious to make a rich match for me, and Lord Winter knew my father. He came to visit. He was an old man, but hale and youthful in figure, still handsome in an imposing way. His first wife had died after years of barrenness, and he was anxious for an heir to the great Winter lands and wealth. He met me and made an offer for me."

"And how did you feel about the prospect of being wedded to a man so many years your senior?"

Meredith shrugged. This part of her story she'd heard from Vivienne's own lips. "It didn't really matter. I'd been raised since birth to expect an arranged match, to have no say in the matter. Lord Winter was kind, and even handsome after a fashion. And so very rich and elevated in position. It was a match I could not have hoped to make, for although my family are gentry, they are far removed from the Winter's milieu. My youth induced him to offer for me — I could bear him heirs. And strangely, we got on very well. You see, I have never been afraid to speak my mind, and Lord Winter, like many men his age, has no patience with meekness. We enjoyed each other's company. Besides . . . my family pointed out that I would be a widow when still young, and, my duty behind me, might marry for love."

"So you had no regrets when you went to your wedding?"

"Not really. You see, I am not a romantic." Meredith allowed herself to smile at him again, and she saw the spark of challenge leap into his eyes. "Well, you may imagine the stir when I was presented to society as Lady Winter. For all his age, he was the most eligible bachelor in England. And then I came . . . the woman who'd made this marriage, a mere girl young enough to be his granddaughter. No one in England believed I would remain faithful. My looks saw to it that I was hated by the women and besieged by the men. How glad I was, when I first went into society, that I was already married and didn't have to choose from among the wolves I found there!"

"So your marriage was happy?"

"After a fashion, for a time. I did not bear an heir, and then illness struck. My husband of two years became bedridden, and there was no longer any question of an heir. But we were fond of each other." Meredith paused. "But tongues are evil. They wagged when I first appeared in society away from my husband's side. I visit him often but it's not enough to still them. Every man who kisses my hand is reputed to be in my bed. Finally, I tired of it and, desiring rest, set out for France. Here, the attitude is more worldly and I can relax among those who do not condemn me. My husband is my friend," she finished simply. "I would not bring shame to the great

102

name of Winter."

For a few moments, he was silent. She looked at him and saw he was thinking about her story. White shirt, long black hair pulled back, dark brows, those wicked eyes. He had a grace about him that took her breath away. While she'd told the story, she'd been lost in it, had almost been Vivienne. But now reality came rushing back at the sight of his dark beauty, at the knowledge that they were alone.

At last he spoke. "It's strange . . . but I believe you. Your eyes are too soft, too luminous with innocence to be the eyes of a dissembler. You don't seem like the haughty Lady Vivienne Winter, but like a lost girl to be protected."

Meredith drew in her breath. Damn! Her impersonation of Vivienne had obviously come up short, and he'd sensed her inexperience. Before he could steer the conversation further into these dangerous waters, she decided to turn the tide.

"And now, my nameless captor, I have told you the story of my life. And in payment I would hear how one who is obviously a gentleman has become a gentleman of the road."

"The answer to that is simple. I am, as you say, born a gentleman. But a third son, without lands, money, or prospects. Life was dull, and I was a perpetual hanger-on at the fringes of society, keeping up an appearance of gentility I could not afford. One night, some friends and I, lit with wine, made a wager. I was . . . known for my prowess with women. My friend bet me that I could not obtain a certain countess' earrings as a token of affection. The lady was most cold to my advances, so I hit on another plan to obtain the earrings. You see, I had no business making that wager. If I wanted to escape debtor's prison, I must win it. So one dark night, I waylaid her coach. It was childishly easy, and those earrings ensured my freedom."

Meredith was intrigued. "But why did you continue?"

"Oh, I didn't, My Lady. That was the last time until now. But I saw you in London and knew that I must find a way to get to know you better. When I heard of your trip to France, I decided the only way to get you alone was to kidnap you."

Meredith felt a shock down her spine. He was lying! He could not have seen her in London — or he'd have known instantly she wasn't Vivienne. Even from afar, they looked different. Only their hair was alike. Why was he lying?

She caught her breath. "I am afraid I don't believe you, sir. Why not tell me the truth? I can hardly think you'd imagine that violence toward my person was the way to my heart."

"But I have told you the truth. It is of the greatest importance to me to win your heart. Let us just say it is a promise I have made myself."

There was a silence as she tried to think of something to say. But no reply came to her. What game was she involved in? All at once she knew he was telling the truth. He was no common highwayman out for her jewels. What secrets were there in Vivienne's life that she had stumbled into? And then he spoke again.

"And how shall we beguile the rest of the evening? For it is too early to go to bed . . . and I have hopes that when we go, it will be together."

"Please, I beg you to stop thinking that I would — "

"But I beg you to give me a chance at my heart's desire. I have an idea. Let's make a wager. Do you

104

play cards, My Lady? I would play a hand with you and have your virtue as the prize, should I win."

"And if I win? What can you offer me that would tempt me to make such a mad wager?"

"Why, your freedom, of course. Should you win, I'll set you on the road to Paris in the morning, unmolested."

Meredith hid a smile. The highwayman could not know that her father had made his living gambling and had not been above cheating when the money was low. She'd learned to cheat at cards while she was still in pinafores, for her father had often played with her to sharpen his skills in the long evenings when he had no money to gamble.

"I agree. The wager shall be made, and I warn you, I expect to win," she said.

"Oh, I doubt it, My Lady. For winning is a passion with me. And with the stakes so dear to my heart, I am afraid that I could not bear to lose tonight. Losing my heart has been enough loss for one evening."

He rose and went to the table before the window. Opening a drawer, he took out a deck of cards and brought them back. "Would you care to examine them? I assure you, they are fair. But see for yourself."

Meredith caught his smile of amusement as she expertly riffled through the deck of cards, running her fingertips along the edges for shavings or cuts. It was as he said. The deck was square. "And what game shall we play?" she asked.

"Faro?" At Meredith's nod, she began to shuffle the cards, turning up the edges at times to see the suits, arranging them without seeming to do so. "A single hand to determine the winner . . . or the best of three?" he asked.

Meredith considered. If they played more than once, he might be able to discern that she was cheating. And besides, he would be the one to deal the second hand, placing her at a disadvantage. "A single hand. I would know my fate as quickly as possible."

The candlelight flickered as she examined her cards. She'd seen to it that she had a superior hand — and that the one he held was going to be difficult to play. She smiled as he cast his first card, secure in the knowledge that she was going to win.

Strange, though. If she won, she'd be free . . . and this adventure would be at an end. She'd never see him again, this fascinating highwayman who said he'd set out to win her heart. Almost, she felt regret. But then she admonished herself. She could not really be so mad as to wish to spend the night with her kidnapper . . . could she?

In the end, it was almost too easy, child's play, to beat him. She watched as his elegant brows drew down over his eyes in a scowl, as his lips tightened as their play progressed. A moment, and she'd be a free woman.

She threw down her last card. "And so it seems that I am the winner," she said, smiling. Yes, her father had taught her all too well. Taught her to cheat at cards — and taught her to be wary of any man who lived his life by gambling. Such a man would break a woman's heart every time.

Like the man across from her. A rogue and a gambler, it was all for the best that she would be away from him in the morning.

He sat back and looked at her, wondering whether to call her on her cheating. It had been obvious to him, for he was veteran of a thousand games and knew every way there was to cheat. Aye, and had used them in a pinch. So, she thought she was free.

"You've won. Or at least, you would be the winner if I chose to overlook the fact that you cheated when you dealt the hands."

He knew! Disconcerted, her eyes flew to his and she found him watching her with a mercilessly mocking expression.

Meredith rose. Moonlight was streaming in through the casements, and the candlelight cast a warm, rosy glow. She walked to the window, disturbed. The wind bent the trees in a restless rhythm outside the window, and cloud shadows scudded across the moon. Behind her, she heard his chair push back, heard his soft footfalls coming across the floor.

"My Lady." The words were a breath behind her, and she was afraid to turn.

His hands were in her hair, the touch gentle, then dropping to her shoulders. She did turn then, taking a step backward.

He stood tall above her, his head bent toward her, his eyes brilliant in the moonlight. He dropped his hands, and a silence reigned, a silence in which they could not look away from each other. She was neither Meredith nor Vivienne now, but a woman who felt a thrill pass between the two of them, a current almost visible in the moonlight.

"Though you say you don't want me, My Lady, your eyes belie your lips," he said softly. "And your lips are what I must claim . . . a single kiss as my forfeit. I would be within my rights to make you play again or claim myself the winner, since you cheated so basely, but I will not force you to become my lover. Instead I will claim only a kiss. A single kiss to seal the bond between us that we both know exists, for you and I are alike, My Lady, both rogues under the skin."

Meredith was breathless, unable to look away, unable to move. His dark skin, so smooth. His scent in her nostrils, male and clean. His eyes on her like a caress.

Gently, his hand came up and touched her cheek, tracing the line of her cheekbone down to her jaw. She felt her lips part as a thrill passed through her whole body at his touch.

"You are so beautiful, my cheating lady," he breathed, his voice husky. And then, almost roughly, he pulled her against him, hands buried in her hair. He held her softness against his hardness for an endless, breathless moment while his eyes devoured her. Then slowly, in contrast to his hard embrace, he bent his head and let his lips brush hers softly.

Meredith felt her eyes close, felt the incredibly soft sensation of his mouth tracing hers. She felt his hands stroking her hair, her face, and the room whirled as she opened her lips under his mouth.

He pulled her up on tiptoe, and she moved her arms until they were around his neck. Oh, how weak she was all of a sudden. How delicious, how wonderful it felt to be held so close to him!

All at once he pulled away from her, and his eyes blazed down as they swept her face and focused on her mouth. "And now," he murmured, "You are mine, My Lady. And I will not have you forget that you belong to me."

She opened her mouth to speak but he crushed her to him. And there was nothing gentle about this kiss. It was a blazing fire of need, his mouth parting hers, his tongue tracing her lips, his hands catching her as her knees buckled and she was too weak to stand. It was a hungry kiss, and they clung together as if they were the first two lovers ever created . . . created for each other. Meredith kissed him back, exploring his mouth, running her hands through his long loosening hair, then over the broad muscles of his shoulders.

All at once he broke away and held her hard against him, and she could feel his heart hammering, hear his ragged breathing, smell the scent of him. Never, never had she felt so warm and belonging, so safe and at one with the world. He held her and held her as if he would never let her go, as if the world could go up in flames around them and never be noticed.

Then he put his hands on her shoulders and gently held her away. His eyes were filled with desire and tenderness as he looked down at her. At last he spoke. "For all that I've claimed you now for my own, I believe you still would not share my bed tonight?"

It took a long, lost moment for Meredith to find her voice. Shyly, she reached up a hand and touched his lean cheek with a tentative finger, drawing it down to brush the corner of his mouth. "I—would not. Not tonight."

He smiled, and turned his head to touch the fingertip with his lips. "Then I must leave you, for otherwise I never will be able to, and you'll have a true scandal to add to all those the world imputes to you. I will go downstairs for a few hours and cool my ardor with a walk under the stars. You go to sleep, and I'll come back late. Don't fear, for I'll sleep on the floor and not disturb you. And in the morning, My Lady, we'll leave for Paris."

"Thank you," Meredith whispered.

"And now I will be given one last kiss, this one not

a forfeit, but one you give me freely as I give you my heart. Don't forget, My Lady, that I have claimed you as my own."

"How could I forget?"

For another long moment, they stared, lost in each other's eyes. Then he bent his head and kissed her again. A third kiss, and different. Not gentle as the first, not passionate as the second, but deeply tender. A long kiss, and filled with what seemed to Meredith like love.

Then he touched her face and turned. She stood, unable to move, as he crossed the room and opened the door. A last glance, and her black-haired lover was gone.

Meredith pressed shaking hands to her burning cheeks, wondering how the world could change so quickly. Not even John, the groom, had kissed her like that, and now everything was different. He was a stranger, a liar, a criminal, and every fiber of her being was shouting that she would follow him to the ends of the earth!

At last she sat down before the fire, pouring herself a glass of wine to calm her nerves. She stared and stared into the flames, unable to still her whirling thoughts, unable to stop seeing him bend his head to hers, clasp her in his strong arms.

Where she felt safe.

And he said he'd claimed her, that she belonged to him. Could a kiss claim her heart so easily?

God help her, but she felt the answer within every cell of her body. She was his. She belonged to a stranger who'd awakened a hunger in her she'd never known existed.

The fire was low when at last a weary Meredith rose and went to the bed. She struggled with the hooks and laces of Vivienne's costume, but at last stepped out of it and folded it over a chair. Then she unlaced her many petticoats until at last only a single pair of lace pantalets and a ribbon-trimmed chemise remained. Shivering, she climbed into the bed and pulled the covers up to her chin.

She didn't expect to sleep, but the excitement of the day and the wine she'd drunk had their effect and she slept. So soundly that she never heard the soft opening of the door, never heard his footsteps as he crossed to the bed.

He stood looking down at her as she lay in the moonlight asleep. She was on her back, one hand under her cheek, and her raven hair was spread in rippling waves across the pillow. Her face was beautiful and innocent, with long lashes that swept her cheeks, a relaxed mouth. The covers had fallen back, and his eyes fell to the gleam of her white shoulders strapped with lace, the hollows of her collarbones, her skin like velvet. Above a beribboned bodice, her breasts curved deliciously, full and enticing. He felt a tightening of desire as he looked at her, the picture of fragile womanhood.

She was not what he'd expected.

Her eyes. In all his life, the Duke of Raceford could not recall such lovely, innocent eyes. Wide with surprise, soft with startlement as she felt his desire, as he kissed her lips.

His gaze fell on her mouth. A lovely mouth . . . but not a mouth that had done much kissing, he was ready to swear. He'd had too much experience with women to be fooled. She was an innocent.

The notorious Lady Vivienne Winter, an innocent?

He would not have recognized her from the miniature Gabe had shown him, but then, that was not surprising. Artists seemed to have but a single idea of feminine beauty, and they all painted their subjects to match it. The portrait had been much more fleshy, not so beguilingly slender, with a small rosebud mouth. Not a wide mouth that begged to be kissed. At least he'd gotten the eyes right, and the hair, black as his own.

All except the color. Vivienne's eyes were blue, just as he'd suspected. Not violet as the miniature portrayed them. The artist had taken poetic license with the color of her eyes as well as with her weight.

But she was a thousand times more beautiful than the portrait. No wonder Gabriel had had his heart broken.

He thought of Gabriel, of his admission he had bedded her. It just wasn't possible. Not when she kissed as though it was the first time a man's lips had ever claimed hers. Not when her eyes were as innocent as a girl's. But why would Gabe lie to him? They were the closest of friends.

Either Gabe was lying, or she was the greatest actress the world had ever known.

No wonder men fell in love with her, if she could become a picture of such sweet and infinitely desirable innocence. She brought out the urge to protect . . . to cherish. He frowned. She had, if everything he'd heard was true, had better men than he for breakfast.

He was going to have to watch his step around the treacherous Lady Vivienne Winter.

Because the truth was, tonight he'd come very close to falling in love with her himself.

And this "innocent" had tried to gain her freedom tonight by cheating at cards as expertly as any hardened rogue.

He turned away at last from the enchanting picture on the bed and, shrugging off his coat and boots, wrapped himself in his cloak and stretched out on the rug in front of the fire. Propping himself on an elbow, he threw a couple of logs on the fire and stared into the flames.

And remembered her kisses. His body seemed to burn as hotly as the fire, and for a wild moment, he almost rose and went to the bed to see, for once and for all, if she was as innocent as she seemed.

Oh yes, he was going to have to watch himself around her, around this woman who could make his blood race in his veins and make him forget the world. Then he smiled.

He had, after all, meant what he said. Someday, he would untie the ribbons at her breasts and make love to every inch of her. Whether or not it had all started as a diversion, he had spoken the truth.

He'd claimed her as his own—and he was a man who kept his word.

Chapter Eight

Sunlight streamed into the room as the curtains were yanked back. Meredith opened her eyes. For a moment, she was disoriented, unable to remember where she was. The bed was warm, the linens deliciously smooth and fresh against her skin. Then she turned her head and saw a tall black-haired man at the window and a pair of green eyes watching her.

She sat up, startled. "Oh!" she breathed, confused.

"It's morning—and a lovely morning, too," he added pointedly, his eyes roving over her hair and then down to rest on her shoulders and breasts.

Meredith gave a startled gasp. She'd forgotten that she'd slept only in her chemise, and she snatched up the covers and held them to her chin.

He smiled at her, a flash of white in his tanned face. In the sunlight, his eyes were emerald. He must have been up for a time, because his hair was damp and neatly pulled back by a ribbon at his neck, and his face showed no trace of whiskers. He looked cool and elegant and handsome, leaning casually against the windowsill.

"Don't worry . . . I'll leave while you dress. I'll go belowstairs and bespeak some breakfast. I could use some coffee to chase the dreams away."

He turned from the window and walked to the door. Her eyes followed his tall figure in a white shirt and black pants, gleaming boots. At the door, he paused. "I'll be about half an hour. Then we'll breakfast and leave. Oh . . . and there's hot water over there near the fire to wash with."

The door closed behind him. Meredith heard the key turn in the lock. Her cheeks started to flame as she remembered the hours last night, unable to forget his searing kisses. But it meant nothing to him, she could see that. He was brisk and businesslike this morning, not a trace of the emotion on his face that had seemed to rock him last night. Well, what had she hoped? To be awakened with a gentle kiss?

Scowling, Meredith tossed the covers aside and got out of bed. That was exactly what she had hoped. She was a fool.

She shivered as she crossed the cold, bare floor to the fireplace. It was burning low, and she tossed some logs on it and leaned cold hands toward it as the flames leapt up. On a table next to the fire was a china ewer and basin, some clean linens, soap, and a mirror. The water gave off wisps of steam.

She washed as thoroughly as she could with the linen, leaving her face for last, lathering it with steaming water and fragrant soap. Then she rinsed, dried, and fetched her clothes so she could dress in front of the mirror. It was going to be difficult to get into everything without help, and she wondered where Jane was. She must be frantic by now. The minute he came back, she'd demand to be taken to Jane.

Doggedly, she struggled with layer after layer of petticoats, lacing them and hooking them in front, then turning them round. She grimaced at the corset but knew she would never get into Vivienne's dress without it. Thank the Lord it laced up the front! Yanking and huffing, she finally had the pinching thing tight, disliking the way it made her breasts jut upward and together to provide cleavage for the front of her ensemble.

The dove-gray folds of the traveling dress were barely crumpled, and she thought again what elegant taste Vivienne had. Colors like gray and lavender were ones she associated with matrons, but set off by the black ribands and cascades of point lace, it was a dashing outfit.

She put on her earrings, then spread out her hair combs and pins. The last way she wanted to look was as if she'd spent a wild night in the arms of the highwayman. No, she wanted to look letter-perfect when she went downstairs.

She combed her hair and subdued it in the severest of French braids, coiling the long rope on the back of her head. Hairpins relentlessly pinned down any errant wisp that had thoughts of escaping. Finally, she set aside her hat and gloves and checked herself in the mirror.

The gray made her look elegant but severe. She looked aloof and untouchable—except for her eyes. They had a softer look this morning, which matched the deep blue of her sapphire earrings. They were eyes that knew what a kiss could mean.

There was a soft rap on the door.

"Come in," she called, and the key turned in the lock.

He entered, carrying a laden tray. With barely a glance at her, he walked to the table by the window and set it down. She heard the clink of china and smelled coffee as he poured. He sat at his ease and she felt unaccountably annoyed. This man had professed to be in love with her just last night!

He was buttering a piece of fresh bread, slicing an apple. She stood, searching for some stinging remark that would shake him out of this pose of indifference. At last he looked up briefly.

"I recommend you eat. We leave soon and I doubt we'll stop again until evening."

"I would like to be taken to my companion," she said coldly, remembering her resolve to seek Jane out and allay her fears.

"You're about to spend the day with her shut up in a coach. As soon as you've eaten, you can see her."

"I won't touch a bite until I know she's all right!"

A shrug was her answer. "Suit yourself."

Meredith stared at him for a long exasperated moment, then all at once, she started to laugh.

He looked up, startled, then smiled, the indifference gone from his eyes. "You know, that's the first time I've seen you laugh. What is it you find so funny?"

Meredith, still smiling, crossed the room and sat across from him, reaching for a cup of coffee. "I'm laughing at myself. How utterly useless it is for me to threaten you with something that will only punish myself. On reflection, I find it is too early for martyrdom or melodrama. I shall take your word that Meredith is fine."

"She is. Still cursing us with a vocabulary I admire, but at least she had the sense to eat her breakfast."

Meredith laughed again. "She has always been one to speak her mind. And so today . . . we will reach Paris?"

"Its outskirts. We'll stop again for the night, and in

the morning, to your bankers."

"Yes . . . to my bankers."

For a moment, their eyes met and held in challenge.

"And then, sir, our business will be concluded."

"And then, My Lady, our business will have just begun. I told you we are destined to know one another better."

He was no longer indifferent. Meredith hid a smile as she finished her breakfast.

He waited while she pinned on her hat and pulled on her gloves, then let her sweep past him out the door and down the stairs. The morning sun was brilliant, and overhead, only a few wisps of white clouds sailed across a fresh blue sky. This morning, the farmhouse was quiet—everywhere except the front yard.

"Every one of you black-hearted wretches will swing from the gallows for this night's work! Where is My Lady? I demand that you produce her at once, and if you've harmed her, poor innocent lamb—"

Meredith rushed out the front door to confront the spectacle of Jane haranguing a sheepish group of men. "I am here! And quite, quite safe!" she called, running down the steps.

"My Lady! Oh, Saints be blessed, you're safe!"

They fell into each other's arms, and Meredith was moved to feel Jane sobbing against her shoulder. She held her for a few moments, then pulled back and searched Jane's face. "Are *you* safe? No one harmed you, or touched you, or—"

Wiping tears away, Jane shook her head. "Safe as houses, My Lady, and even though I hate to admit it, that black-haired devil saw to it I was treated kind. I was fed and locked in a room, but I barely slept a wink worrying what he'd do to you!"

Over Meredith's shoulder, Jane threw a venomous glare, and Meredith had no doubt who it was aimed at.

"As touching as this reunion is, we must be on our way. May I suggest you ladies continue it within the coach, for you'll have all day to recount your adventures to each other," he said behind them.

Meredith turned and threw him a quelling look. "Come, Meredith, let's do as he says. They are taking us to Paris, so you see, we are quite safe after all."

As she climbed into the waiting carriage, he said, "But you know you are always safe with me, My Lady."

The coach door closed behind them. "The rogue!" exclaimed Jane. "As if we could be safe with a highwayman—one who's kidnapping us and robbing us, no less! Now what did you mean, Mere—I mean, Vivienne—when you said they are taking us to Paris?"

As the coach started with a jerk, Meredith told Jane of her bargain with the highwayman to pay the "ransom" herself. "And so, I know Vivienne will be wild when she hears I've given him so much money, but I wager she'd be angrier if the whole country was searching for her and she had to cut her lover's tryst short!"

"You are right, My Lady. I know she'd have your head off at the shoulders if she didn't get to be with her lover! So we must spend another night with that black-haired devil? He didn't harm you?"

Meredith felt the color come into her cheeks and saw Jane's eyes narrow. There was no use lying. She sighed. "Not harm me. He *did* kiss me," she admitted.

Jane's eyes were round. "He did? And you liked it!" she accused. Then she sat back, relenting. "Well, I must admit he's a sight handsomer than any man I ever saw in Henley. Such as a certain Mr. Augustus Sett. I suppose there's no harm in a kiss from a handsome stranger, as long as you don't let it give you any ideas." Jane's gaze suddenly sharpened. "That's *all* he did—kiss you?"

"That's all. He was very much the gentleman. You see, he knew about Vivienne by reputation, and I can't blame him for thinking she might enjoy a chance to spend the night with a highwayman. But when he saw I was serious, he left it at a kiss. And even that, he didn't take by force."

"I see." Jane looked pensive for a time, then smiled. "Well, now that it looks like it will all end well—except for the money and the jewels, of course—I must admit this is fun! Such adventures that Vivienne has!"

"True! More adventures in one night and day than we had in Henley in years!"

They talked for another hour, looking out the windows as they spoke. The French countryside was lovely with spring, fresh green misting the trees, the bushes in near full leaf. Flowers splashed the fields, and they passed horses rolling in the pastures, kicking up their heels and galloping for the intoxication of spring. The countryside was of hills and cultivated fields, and the coach raised a cloud of dust as it rolled down the roads. They passed neat and pretty farmhouses and small streams sparkling in the sunlight, mill wheels turning with flashing drops.

The coach stopped in a flower-laden field for lunch, the women staying inside to eat, enjoying the fresh air that came in through the open window. They shared a bottle of pale cool wine, and when the coach started again, both felt tired. The coach rocked hypnotically and neither had slept much the night before. Pulling the blind to the window, Meredith had a last glimpse of her highwayman riding near the coach, so straight in the saddle he looked as if he'd been born there. For some reason, the sight of him reassured her. She settled back into the soft cushions and was soon asleep.

The coach rode on, raising clouds of dust on the winding roads that went up and down hills and on toward Paris. Raceford had much to think of as he rode along. About how he'd come to be embroiled in all this in the first place—and about how angry the viscomte was likely to be when he learned how his plans had been altered.

It had been just a fortnight ago that he'd visited Ginny with the intention of asking for an introduction to her soon-to-arrive guest. But before he'd broached the subject, she'd asked him what he was doing in Paris, and he'd confessed he'd come because he was bored.

She had laughed and regarded him with narrow, sherry-colored eyes. "But nothing is so easy, *mon ami!*" she'd trilled, patting a straying flame-colored curl into place. "It so happens I have a friend who is desperate for a partner in a most questionable venture! You see, he wishes to win the heart of a certain lady—one of your countrywomen—who arrives in Paris next week. But alas. She is, besides being very beautiful, most wealthy. He is in despair that he will ever catch her eye! And so, he thinks if he can appear to her as a hero, save her from some dire fate, he will have a head start. I suggested that her coach could be held up and that he rescue her from a robbery. Such incidents are regrettably common on the roads to Paris. And *voila!* She will look at him with shining eyes and fall at his feet for being so gallant! He has only one problem: He has no highwayman."

"A countrywoman?" he'd asked, amused and intrigued. Ginny was always up to some such outrageous plan. He'd been right to lay the problem of his boredom before her.

"Why, yes, and you must know her; she is such a famous beauty. And I believe there is no beautiful woman in England you do not know. The Lady Vivienne Winter."

Vivienne Winter! He'd smiled then, wondering at how fate was throwing the very woman he itched to teach a lesson to right in his path.

"I have yet to meet the lady. But I can think of nothing more delightful than to first meet her as a highwayman. They are figures of romance, are they not? It may well make more of an impression on her than the role of rescuer."

"So?" Ginny was clearly delighted that he was thinking of competing for the lady's favors. It would make everything so much more enchantingly interesting. "You will be perfect in the part, *mon ami.* With that black hair you will look most dangerously handsome, a gypsy, and I can speak for women. We love handsome gypsies! Always we fantasize about the stableboy, I confess. So much more virile than those mincing fops we are surrounded with. But come and meet Nicki. Nicholas St. Antoine, Viscount de Valmy. He is your partner in crime and your competitor for the lady's favors."

He had to admit that since he'd agreed to the viscomte's plan, his stay in Paris had been anything but boring.

Near sunset, his eyes scanned the hills for the horsemen he knew would be there. Waiting to see a holdup take place on the road below. Waiting to ride to the rescue.

He wondered whether it would take the viscomte long to figure out that it wasn't any outrider accompanying the coach, but his partner in crime. In a way, he hoped Nicki never tumbled to it at all, for then he'd have the chance to spend another night with her . . .

As the shades of evening fell velvety blue over the countryside, above in the hills, a furious Nicholas St. Antoine lowered the spyglass he'd been holding to his eye and cursed. He sat astride his horse and wondered why he'd been mad enough to let Ginny talk him into this—and here it had gone wrong already. Because there was no holdup on the road below. There was no mistaking the figure riding alongside the coach. It was Raceford, damn his eyes, and far from holding the coach up, he was escorting it! He should have known better than to trust an Englishman. Some rescue this would be, with the lady in no danger whatsoever!

But then, he reflected wryly, Ginny had always been able to twist him round her fingers. When she proposed a plan, somehow it seemed reasonable and logical. He sighed. Well, he'd best get started. Because below in that coach was his prospective future bride. And his financial salvation.

So he'd not let her pass without stopping the coach and seeing what was going on. He turned in the saddle and called to his men to start, and they all put spurs to their horses and cantered down the hill toward the road.

It was almost evening when they woke. Already the sun was dying to a golden glow in the west and twilight was stealing under the trees. They sat up, feeling refreshed.

Meredith twitched back a curtain and saw the evening star burning white in the sky.

"Just think . . . tomorrow we'll be in Paris," she said softly.

"Yes, Paris. Living in a castle and all, and going to balls. I'm right glad you decided to say yes, though I'll admit I'm a mite nervous that we're bound to get caught at it. Don't seem like it can work when someone who knows Vivienne could show up in Paris any time."

Meredith was opening her mouth to speak when suddenly there was a shout from outside, then a shot rang out. Their eyes met in fear as the coach took off, rocking wildly from side to side. It was a repeat of what had happened last night!

Meredith yanked the curtains to one side. She saw the highwayman riding hard alongside the coach, drawing a pistol as he rode. There were more shots, and she gasped as she saw riders converging on them from all sides. Her eyes flew back to the highwayman in time to see him ride off ahead of the coach and vanish from her sight. The night rang with shots, and her heart was in her throat at the thought of his danger. A bullet might find him! After what seemed an eternity, the coach at last ground to a halt.

From what she could see, they were surrounded. Shadowy figures on horseback ringed them. She felt her blood run chill with fear for him. Where was he? Had one of those shots found him?

A deep voice spoke, commanding, in English but accented with French. "So, *monsieur*, it is a standoff. You have us in your sights, we have you in our sights. But there are more of us. If you fight, we will surely win. But if you hand over the Lady unharmed, you are free to go. Consider well before you speak."

She held her breath as she listened for the answer. Oh God . . . please, let it be he that speaks! she thought wildly.

"It seems that you have us at a disadvantage."

Meredith almost crumpled with relief. Her shoulders slumped and tears started. It was him! He was safe!

"Normally, sir," his voice continued, "I would never be so craven as to refuse a fight, no matter what the odds. But I have my men to think of . . . and the ladies as well. I have promised a certain lady that she would be safe with me, and a stray bullet might harm her. Therefore, I will set the lady free if I have your word we are free to go as well."

"You have my word—on the condition that the lady is perfectly unharmed. Produce her at once or you are a dead man."

She heard the grate of boots on gravel, heard the coach door unlock. There he was, his lean dark face already so unaccountably dear, sardonic eyes under black brows, looking every inch a highwayman.

"My Lady," he said gravely, extending a hand to her gracefully, "it seems that you and I must part. For your safety, I must hand you over to these men. Never fear, I know who they are and you'll find they are of your station in life. Come. Let me help you down."

Meredith rose, giving him a single look in which she put her despair and worry for him. She put her hand in his, and with the air of duke, he handed her down into the twilight.

The first thing she saw was a man on a white horse. He was dressed in a suit of dull silver and pale blue, white lace at his throat and cuffs. His hair was silver blond, but his eyebrows were dark over deep-set eyes. He was extremely handsome, impossibly noble, with a long sword at his hip and gray leather boots. He seemed to gleam in the dusk.

With an elegant leap, he was down and striding to them. He stopped in front of her and made a deep and graceful bow, his hair nearly brushing the ground. He straightened and stared at her with eyes she knew would be blue in the sunlight.

"The Lady Vivienne Winter?"

She nodded.

"You are unharmed in any way?"

"I am unharmed."

"Nicholas Phillipe Ambrose St. Antoine, Viscomte de Valmy, at your service. I am pleased to be able to effect your rescue from this dangerous highwayman and apologize that I cannot kill him for insulting you. But I am as unwilling as he is to risk your fair person."

Meredith didn't want to be rescued. She'd never wanted anything so little in her life. But this viscomte would think it most peculiar if she wasn't grateful. She made a deep curtsy. "Your courage and gallantry are most deeply appreciated, Viscomte," she murmured. "I am delighted to discover that chivalry still lives in France."

"And I am delighted to be the knight privileged to

rescue such a fair maiden," he said, staring at her in obvious admiration.

There was a soft snort behind her, and she was aware of the gypsy highwayman at her elbow.

She turned. He was holding out a velvet draw-string bag. "Your jewels and money, My Lady. As long as you are being rescued, let it be a complete triumph."

She held out her hand and he dropped the bag into it. She stared at him, then suddenly reached up and pulled off her earrings. She held them out.

"For your care of me, sir. You have treated me like a lady, and I would thank you by giving you these as a token. I recall that you have a fondness for earrings as mementos."

He took them, closing his fist around them. "I will claim them as a token because they are the color of your eyes and because someday I will return to make good that other claim I have spoken to you about."

"I hope you do," she whispered, startled at her boldness, then turned. "I am ready to leave, Vis-comte."

"My men will mount your coach to guard you, and I will ride alongside as your escort. An inn is only a short ride away, and I would see you safely settled for the night as swiftly as possible."

"Certainly, Viscomte. I thank you."

And so once again, Meredith found herself in the custody of a strange man. One had been bearing her away to unknown danger, the other taking her to a haven of safety.

And yet, she thought, as she let her eyes linger for a last moment on the tall cloaked shape standing by the side of the road, it had been in the wrong one's company she'd felt safe.

The door to the coach closed, and the last thing she saw as it started off, with her gilt-haired protector riding alongside, was the highwayman. He lifted her earrings to his lips, and she saw them sparkle as he kissed them.

And then he was lost to her sight, and Paris was ahead.

Chapter Nine

From the windows of the coach, Meredith could at last see the gates of Paris directly ahead, the beautifully wild woods of the Bois de Boulogne disappearing on her right. She and Jane looked at each other with excitement; Paris was ahead! With the viscomte as escort, they had traveled a short way the previous night and rested at a farmhouse no more than twenty miles from Paris.

As they'd neared the city, the viscomte had climbed into the coach to make the rest of the journey in her company. Travel had been slow that day and it was already late afternoon, the sun slowly starting to sink behind them. But there in the distance beyond the gates she caught her first glimpse of the city of enchantment. It was teeming with life, noisy crowds of people everywhere, in coaches and on foot, huge buildings glimpsed through the trees, the spire of a church rising above it all far away. She was anxious to get inside the gates to see it all up close.

At the gates, a gendarme stepped forward, stopping the coach in its tracks. He leaned inside and asked for their passports. Meredith struggled with the contents of her reticule with shaking hands and finally withdrew the papers. She handed them to the viscomte, who in turn handed them to the guard.

After looking them over, the man grunted in satisfaction, handing the papers back to them. Then with a quick bow, he said in French, "Good evening, Viscomte, and welcome to Paris, *mesdames*. May you find our city to your liking."

She nodded in acknowledgment, and replied in French that she was sure she would like Paris very much. She could barely get the words out. Her excitement at finally having arrived had sent her heart hammering in her chest. And then the gates were flung wide and the carriage lurched forward onto the Avenue des Champs Elysées.

Parks spread out on either side of the wide, tree-lined avenue, full of clipped shrubs, flowers, and fountains, a pavilion here, people everywhere. Peasants in wagons were passing them on either side, leaving the city with their unsold sacks of grain from the daily street markets to make the long trip back to their farms in the surrounding countryside. Children occupied the backs of the wagons on top of the grain, either sleeping or playing games with each other, and their chatter added to the already noisy street. The sound of French filled her ears on all sides like a symphony; such a musical language!

And the smells! Although the street vendors were already packing up their stalls for the day, the aroma of their wares still lingered. Breads and sweets, fruits and flowers, roasted meats all mingled together.

A loud honking sound drew her attention, and she looked out the window to see a young girl herding a noisy flock of Strasbourg geese. The girl smiled and gave Meredith a friendly wave before skipping on past, tending to her waddling charges.

It seemed all wonderfully new to Meredith. She'd

been to London once in her life and remembered the crowded narrow streets packed with the throngs in much the same way, but Paris was different, rustic and urbane at the same time, sprawling and colorful. She didn't know which way to look first, afraid she would miss something.

The viscomte was pointing out the window as he said, "You will find Paris far more freer in its affections than your London."

Meredith looked to where he was pointing. Directly in front of them, a young couple had stopped in the middle of the avenue, the young man bending to kiss the young girl on his arm without a care for the milling crowd or the street traffic around them. Meredith was touched to see such affection so publicly displayed and thought how wonderful it would be to be kissed like that.

"Does this shock you, Lady Winter?"

"No," she answered him honestly. "I find it charming."

He laughed. "Perhaps you will become a true Parisienne before the summer is out and find yourself in the arms of a young gallant on a city street being kissed in such a way. Paris has that effect. When you are not looking, it will sweep you up and carry you off like a lover."

And then a shout from the driver of her coach unfortunately sent the young couple scurrying out of their path, giggling and stealing more kisses as they ran.

"Shocking," giggled Jane.

"I am sure you speak the truth, Viscomte," she said, watching the young couple go past. Then she turned, embarrassed, to the viscomte. "I must seem the gawking tourist to you, but it is such a lovely city, I fear I will miss something."

"But I forgot. This is your first journey to our city. How remiss of me not to point out the sights to you. I will quickly remedy that."

As the coach approached a large square, he pointed ahead. "That is the Place Louis XV, and beyond it is the Tuileries."

The Avenue des Champs Elysées spilled out onto the square, where in its center rose the statue of Louis XV on horseback. Below it, a marionette show had just concluded, the puppeteers busily packing up the stage and their marionettes.

The viscomte raised an eyebrow and sighed. "We have missed the play, I am afraid, but not the hordes."

The coach slowed to accommodate the dispersing playgoers, and she got her first real glimpse of the Parisiennes. The sight amazed her. Poor and rich alike, glitter and grit, silk and wool, elbow to elbow, moved aside to make way for their carriage as they turned toward the Seine.

They traveled along the Jardin des Tuileries, and once again, Meredith found herself nearly pressing her nose against the window of the coach to see the beautiful statues that filled the gardens and then the towering edifice of the Louvre as they sped past. The viscomte played the perfect guide for her and Jane, telling them all about the gardens and the Opera House within. The muddy Seine flowed lazily on her right, along banks bordered by weeping willows whose branches all but brushed the water. The river was spotted with small fishing boats and its banks strung with fishermen, their lines drifting out into the water. And then they were crossing the Pont Royal into the Faubourg St. Germain, where the comtesse lived.

The avenues began to narrow but were nonetheless

beautifully tree-lined and well-cobbled. Here Meredith found the sprawling private homes of Paris aristocracy, each one more impressive than the last. Some were set close to the avenue, while others were set back away from the street, surrounded by walls. Atop some of these homes were odd-looking rods, and she wondered what they were. She wrinkled her brow and then heard the viscomte speak.

"Paratonnerre," he said simply.

The word was unfamiliar to her, when she looked at him and even more puzzled than before, he laughed.

"Lightning rod. A new invention by the American Franklin. They conduct the lightning which travels down those long wires into the ground. They are the rage in Paris, a sign of status. Rather silly-looking things if you ask me. Ah! We are here at last."

Finally the coach turned, and Meredith suppressed a gasp at the splendor of the Palais d'Anguillame and the grounds as she and the viscomte traveled the avenue that led to its front courtyard. The wide lane was several hundred feet long, vaulted in trellis work, with maples trained up either side so as to meet in the middle, and planted on either side, trimly kept rosebushes filling the air with their perfume. Overhead chattering blackbirds and sparrows soared in and out of the branches of the trees. And Meredith was sure she heard the song of a nightingale.

As they approached the end of the avenue, the maples gave way to towering cypresses that fanned out from the avenue in a graceful arc, circling the front courtyard.

Meredith at last caught her first sight of the palais. Set in a garden of cascades and fountains, surrounded by lawns that lay like a great Persian carpet and perched on higher ground, rose the large and sumptuous facade of the palais. The central pavilion, rectangular and square-roofed, rose in soft gray stone, story upon story of windows gracing its facade in long horizontal lines, broken by vertical columns set between them. The lower row of windows was arched and their arches were alive with festooned carving—statues and garlands. On either side two smaller pavilions stood in simple symmetry, jutting slightly forward of the larger, but echoing the same graceful lines.

A fountain in front of the main entrance, its stream of water rising from the center of a wide bronze basin and shooting straight into the air, was surrounded on either side by wide and balustraded steps that swept up to the front doors. The windows were alight with a thousand candles, as it was just now getting dark. The draperies had been pulled, but occasional shadows passed back and forth, giving her proof that yes, indeed, someone actually lived here!

It was utterly imposing, unlike any private residence she had ever seen in England, fit for a cardinal or prince. Vivienne, though she'd never seen the palais, had warned Meredith to expect Ginny to be living in a sumptuous home. But never had Meredith dreamed of this.

And she was going to be staying there!

As they climbed the steps, the double doors opened, and two gorgeous apparitions carrying flambeaux torches hurried down the steps to greet them. They were liveried footmen attired in white powdered wigs, yellow and silver brocade coats, with a profusion of lace at neck and wrists, and knee breeches above white stockings and silver buckled high-heeled shoes. Their waistcoats were turquoise, and as they bowed to her and escorted her and the viscomte up the stairs, she saw they were exceptionally beautiful young men who

134

sported patches on their cheekbones and earrings in their ears.

Beyond the open doors was the front gallery, which could have been transported into reality from a fairy tale. Squares of pink and white marble on the floor, several shimmering crystal chandeliers hanging the length of the vaulted ceiling, gilt mirrors lining the walls, and bouquets of silk flowers in profusion held in sconces. To one side a curving staircase wound its way to the upper apartments.

And coming down the gallery toward them, arms outstretched, was a vision as opulent as the gallery itself.

"My darling, Vivienne! You are here at last!" cried the woman, and Meredith felt herself being folded into a soft and scented embrace. It was Comtesse Genvieve d'Anguillame, known to her intimates as Ginny.

"But let me look at you . . . Is it possible, you are more beautiful than ever?"

Comtesse Genvieve held her back at arm's length, and the two women examined each other for the first time. Meredith saw a simply stunning woman whose age was somewhere in her twenties. Her hair was unpowdered, a deep shade of red, and swept upward into an elaborate confection of a hairstyle that included tiger lilies and leaves on one side. A single curl dropped on a white shoulder. Her face was catlike, pointed, and painted artfully. A pretty face, with narrow sherry-colored eyes that tilted up at the corners, a coral mouth, and a single black star-shaped patch on one creamy cheek.

She would have been striking in any company, but her dress raised her to a spectacle. Marie Antoinette had ensured that fashion had reached heights of elaboration never known before, and obviously Ginny followed fashion. Her dress was a deep orange satin, almost an open overdress that parted down the middle in two halves that did not meet over the bodice or skirt. Underneath was a dress of gold and white brocade that was liberally festooned with tiny gilded rosebuds. The same rosebuds, nestled in white lace, edged the lines where the overdress and underdress met. The neckline was perilously low and square, the sleeves tight until the elbows, where they exploded in a cascade of gold lace. And from the back of her shoulders, a burnt orange satin cape fell to the floor.

She was wearing a gold necklace that Cleopatra might have envied, and the gold fringe of her earrings fell past her jawline. Bracelets set with topaz and sparkling rings completed her ensemble. Vivienne might be used to seeing such opulence, but to Meredith, it was nearly overwhelming.

The comtesse's examination of Meredith complete, she looked quizzically over her shoulder to where Jane and the viscomte waited. "This must be your *cousine*, Meredith Westin, *non?*"

Meredith quickly performed the introductions, as Jane, looking dazzled, remembered how to curtsy. Then Ginny looked at the viscomte.

"But my darling Vivienne, I see you arrive in company with my old friend, Nicki. How has this come to pass?"

"The viscomte has been my guardian angel, Ginny. My coach was held up by highwaymen on the road to Paris, and the viscomte rescued me."

"Alors! You have been robbed? My poor darling, what are His Majesty's soldiers thinking of! The roads have become unsafe for everyone in the last few years! But, Nicki, then I have you to thank for rescuing my

dear Vivienne? How did it come about? You came upon her coach being robbed? But how dramatic!" The comtesse clasped her hands in front of her breasts and regarded them both with sparkling eyes. Meredith looked at the viscomte, and so did not see the slight smile that Ginny gave him, accompanied by a mischievous wink.

"No, I did not come upon the Lady Vivienne as she was being robbed," Nicki said with a scowl, and sent a pointed look toward the comtesse.

Meredith looked from one to the other in confusion. It appeared the viscomte was angry about something, though she couldn't imagine what. Quickly, she added in explanation, "The viscomte rescued me as I was being *kidnapped* by the highwayman."

"Kidnapped!" the comtesse shrieked.

Meredith turned to the viscomte, suddenly wondering, "I meant to ask you, Viscomte, about that. How did you know to stop my coach? I feared that no one knew what fate had overtaken us and I was doomed to remain that man's hostage."

He smiled, more stunning a vision than the comtesse. An archangel, she thought. His silver-blond hair was long and tied by a silver ribbon at his neck. But his straight dark brows and long dark lashes gave him a virile look that was unusual in a blond man. His eyes, as she had guessed, were blue. A striking silvery blue. He had a wide mouth that looked made for mischief, a square jaw, a graceful nose. In his pale blue and silver costume, he looked like a knight out of some old tale, Galahad come to lay his purity and strength at her feet.

His blue eyes clearly approved her now, glowing with warmth as they met hers. Oh, he was a beautiful man! Meredith wondered where Venus was in the heavens, to shower her with two such handsome males in a short time, one dark as the devil, one golden as an angel.

"But your coachmen, of course, Lady Vivienne. They were left tied and gagged in the forest, but one of your men managed to free himself and waved my party down on the road. When I heard what happened, naturally I was quickly able to gather a strong party of men to go after you. It was foolish of that highwayman to stop for the night, for it enabled us to catch up with you."

"Stop for the night!" the comtesse shrieked again. "But my darling Vivienne, do not tell me you have spent the night in company with desperate rogues and murderers! Did they harm you?"

Meredith smiled, deciding it was high time she started acting like Vivienne. "If by that everyone means did the highwayman take liberties with my person, the answer is no. He merely wanted more money than I had, and I struck a bargain with him. We were on the way to my bankers in Paris, where I'd agreed to draw a draft out for him." And then she added, as if she were almost disappointed, "He behaved as a perfect gentleman, I must say."

"You struck a bargain with him? But how brave of you! I would have collapsed in a faint and never thought of anything so clever! But come, my darling, why are we talking in the gallery? We must get you to your room at once! You must be prostrate with exhaustion!"

"She is indeed as brave as she is beautiful," said the viscomte.

Meredith turned to face the golden vision once again, and she couldn't help feeling a slight thrill at the sight of his striking looks. One man had already turned her heart upside down with a kiss. Was she so vulnerable to any handsome man? She'd never suspected herself of being fickle, but she began to understand how Vivienne could be such a flirt if the men in society were this spectacular.

"Once again, I must thank you, Viscomte. Your bravery and carelessness of your own safety have overwhelmed me. I am in your debt, and fear that thanks are too paltry a repayment." As she said this, Meredith looked at him through her lashes, as Vivienne had coached her.

He smiled and took her hand, bending his fair head to kiss it lingeringly. Then straightened and stared into her eyes. "But it was my pleasure . . . and my honor . . . to help you in any way. As repayment, just the chance to look into such beautiful eyes is more than enough. But if I may be so bold, Lady Vivienne, may I claim the privilege of calling on you? As soon as you are rested and recovered, perhaps I could be your guide to the delights of Paris. I would count it as an honor to see you again."

Though she wanted to tell him she would be delighted to have him call on her, Meredith remembered Vivienne's caution not to be too eager at a man's advances. Instead she murmured, with a purr in her voice that her cousin had taught her, "How amusing that would be, Viscomte."

"And now, really, Nicki, I must get her out of this drafty gallery and into a hot bath, then bed." The comtesse clapped her hands, and in a moment, they were surrounded by servants, footmen to light them up the stairs, maids in pretty gray country dresses and starched white aprons to tend to Meredith, a butler to run to the kitchen and order food and drink. Meredith curtsied to the viscomte as he bowed low to her, and they said their farewells.

"Ginny, may I have a word with you privately?" the viscomte asked, before they'd gone three steps.

"You go ahead, darling," the comtesse said to Meredith. "The maids will see to your needs, and I will join you shortly."

In company of the retinue, they climbed the stairs, Jane's arm linked through Meredith's.

Ginny turned to find Nicki scowling. "That expression, my love, does nothing to improve your looks. Now, what is it?"

"Raceford nearly ruined our plan!" he gritted out between clenched teeth. "He stopped her coach a day early and kidnapped her before I could rescue her! He was not supposed to do that!"

"Stop pouting, Nicki. It worked out beautifully despite him. You saved her from even graver peril. She was in the hands of a highwayman, forced to spend the night with him. You are more of a hero to her than if you would have simply stopped him from robbing her, do you not see it?"

He looked away, still pouting.

"Come now, let me see you smile," Ginny teased, running a finger along his jawline. "And you are so rude as not to comment on my performance for Vivienne this evening. Did I not act surprised to hear of her adventure?"

"Yes, you were magnificent, my love."

"But you nearly gave us away yourself with your sour and glaring looks. You must be more careful, Nicki," she added gently, lifting his chin so his eyes met hers.

He nodded reluctantly. "But she did not seem so warm to me, do you think?"

"You were so very handsome and charming tonight.

140

How could she not be enamored of you already? I saw the look in her eyes. There was more than gratitude there."

"But you heard her. It would be 'amusing' for me to call on her."

Ginny smiled softly. "My love, you profess to know so much of women, yet you do not understand their ways. I know Vivienne well, and I know Vivienne is more than amused by you. Do not always be so quick to believe her words. Listen to what her eyes say to you. Trust me, you have already made the first step to winning her heart. You are her hero, her knight in shining armor!"

"Do you think so?"

"I am sure of it, darling."

Nicki gave her a boyish grin as he took her hand and pressed his lips to the underside of her wrist. "We would not have to play such games as this, you and I." His lips moved up her arm to where the lace of her gown fell from her elbows.

Ginny pulled away gently and gave him a playful tap on his cheek. "But it is not I you must marry. So you will play these little games with Vivienne until she falls so desperately in love with you that she cannot refuse your proposal."

Nicki groaned and straightened up. "You are an impossible woman! It would be much simpler for me to marry you. . . ."

"We have already exhausted this subject. Now, you must go, and I must see to my guest or she will think me completely without manners. Trust me in this, Nicki. You will see I am right."

She turned and swept up the stairs, blowing him a kiss.

* * *

"And now, my dear 'Vivienne,' you must tell me everything!"

Ginny sat down on a rose satin divan, an enchantingly pretty picture in a loose robe of pale green silk open over a light yellow bedgown embroidered with violets and green leaves. Her hair was unbound down her back in rich red waves, her feet in yellow satin mules.

Meredith was dressed in a borrowed bedgown and satin robe of pale pink and ivory, for her own clothing had yet to be unpacked. She'd had the most heavenly bath, with three maids in attendance — one to scrub her back, one to manicure her fingernails, and one to mix the most wonderfully smelling perfumes for her water. They'd dried her off and helped her into her bedgown, fussing with her hair and arranging the folds of her gown, as if she were going out in society instead of preparing herself for bed. And then she'd eaten food such as she'd never tasted before — broiled fish with a delicate lemon sauce, brandied carrots, and a sinfully rich raspberry and chocolate torte. Jane had settled in a chamber that was almost as elegant as the one she was in.

She looked around again in wonder. The enormous bedchamber was done in shades of pale pink and frosty blue. Ice-blue watered silk covered the walls, broken up by huge panels framed in gilt, pastoral paintings of soft greens and pastels where nymphs enticed shepherds and cupids hovered above. Carpets in deep shades of rose and blue warmed the white stone floors, and a pink marble mantelpiece surrounded a fireplace that could have roasted a deer. White female statues, naked and graceful, bending toward each other, stood on either side of the fireplace, and gilded china vases held flowers on the mantel. Over the mantel was an enormous mirror that reflected gold and white furniture, delicate and spindly, and candles set in gilt sconces on the walls. A huge bed with dusky-rose coverlets and ice-blue drapes held back by golden cords on the wall at its head completed the room.

It was heaven. And if she'd had any thoughts of returning to Helston Grange, one look at her room banished the idea from her head.

"Where shall I start?" asked Meredith.

"Although I am dying to learn of the abduction, I am also curious about you. Vivienne wrote me that you are some sort of *cousine,* is that not right? But I can see that it is true. With that hair black as night and those blue eyes, there could not be many like you two in the world. But you are very different from Vivienne in temperament, I would guess."

"Was it obvious downstairs—with the viscomte, I mean?" Meredith asked, alarmed that she'd not acted as her cousin might have.

"No, my dear, if you are referring to your performance as Vivienne. You were magnificent! Vivienne has coached you well, and I can see you are an apt pupil. What I meant is that you and Vivienne come from two different worlds, no?"

"That is true. Vivienne comes from the rich side of our family. My father was her mother's younger brother. Vivienne's mother married a very wealthy man and promptly forgot about the rest of her family. My father had only an income enough to keep him a stable. Horses were his first love. He bred them and sold them. My mother died in childbirth, my father of pneumonia. So I was sent to live with his younger sister as a poor relation."

"*Mon Dieu!* Of all fates the worst. And they treated

143

you as a poor relation? What a crime!"

Meredith smiled, wondering what Aunt Phoebe would think if she could see her now. "Yes . . . in fact, I was the paid companion to my aunt. In a small town that never saw a moment's excitement. They believe I am in France as Vivienne's companion while she gets some rest."

Ginny rolled her eyes. "Such rest we should all be having! But this is worse than I thought! A relation . . . put to work! Only the English, so puritanical, would dream of such an outrage! Here in France, the honor of the family would be at stake. And so, when Vivienne came to you with her plan to get away for a time, this seemed not so outrageous to you?"

"At first I never believed it could work. But with Vivienne so close by, I can summon her if anyone who knows her should arrive in Paris. And for me, this is a dream come true. I must confess, I often envied Vivienne her life, her clothes, her freedom. And now to be able to live like her, even for a short time! . . ."

"How old are you?"

"I am twenty-two years."

"Ah! To be so young again! But for marriage, that is not young. I am surprised a girl so lovely as you has not married?"

Meredith made a face. "In Henley, there were few eligible men of my station. Farmers, and two prominent families. Only the curate offered marriage to me. A horrible, fat man, dull and pompous."

Ginny shivered theatrically. "But how simply awful for you! And after this escapade, the prospect of going back will seem more horrid than ever."

"But perhaps I won't have to go back—to Henley, at least. Vivienne has offered me a tidy sum for coming to Paris. Maybe I shall be able to make my own way once I leave—raising horses, I think!" A wistful gleam came into her eyes. "Nothing so grand as all this, but hopefully I'll never have to depend on my relatives again."

"But what will your prospects for marriage be, I wonder? As a woman of independent means, you will not have to marry for convenience, at least," Ginny added pragmatically. "I spent many years in a marriage of convenience myself, and I know how boring it can be. Now that I am a widow, I am freer to amuse myself as I please. In France, these things are more condoned than in England, you understand? But, in any case, we cannot let you leave Paris without something to hold dear to your heart. An *affaire* for love? I will see what I can manage." Ginny regarded her with bright eyes and sat up straight. "But now that we have touched on the subject—men—I can wait no longer but must hear every detail of your abduction and rescuc!"

Meredith began her tale of the shots, the stopping of the coach, the highwayman's proposal to hold her for ransom. It wasn't long before Ginny interrupted.

"But this highwayman . . . what was he like? A great brute of a man, stinking of garlic and gin? I have seen such bandits, with their revolting beards and missing teeth as they go to their hangings. I assure you, to be in the company of one of these for even a moment would have caused me to faint!"

"Oh, no . . . he was nothing like that. He was a gentleman by dress, speech, and action. Tall, with black hair and green eyes. He looked like a gypsy perhaps, for he wore one gold hoop in his ear. But he was dressed elegantly. In a black cloak and white shirt, polished black boots. He rode a beautiful black stallion, the equal of any I have ever seen. And as my father's daughter, I have an eye for horseflesh. Whoever he was, he was no common criminal. I should almost guess he was an aristocrat masquerading as a highwayman, if that were not such an absurd thought."

Ginny clapped her hands together, clearly entranced. "Then he was handsome?" she cried, delighted.

"The most handsome man I had ever seen in my life," Meredith said solemnly.

"More handsome than Nicholas? For every woman in Paris is pursuing that man!"

Meredith smiled. "But I had not seen the viscomte then. It would be hard to choose between them."

"Oh, but you are born under a lucky star, I vow. First the chance to play Vivienne, and then what happens? Kidnapped by a handsome gypsy and rescued by a handsome nobleman! A shame you had to lose your jewels in the process."

"But I didn't," said Meredith softly. "He gave them back to me."

"Oh!" cried Ginny again. "But you are not telling me everything! So you spent the night with this handsome gypsy. What happened? Did you—"

"Perhaps Vivienne would have, but Meredith could not. I am . . . not experienced in love between a man and a woman. If I had been, I would have found this man hard to resist, for all I never knew his name. But . . . he did kiss me."

"You must tell me *everything!*"

Meredith sat back, eyes distant, lost in memories as she recounted the tale of their dinner and game of cards to Ginny. Every detail she could remember, she told. She never wanted to forget that night that was, as he had called it, stolen out of time. At last she was finished, and for a long moment, Ginny said nothing, just looked at her with sparkling eyes.

"But he claimed you! He said you belonged to him? Oh, this is the most romantic tale I have ever heard! And then to be rescued by a man like Nicholas, who is the beloved object of every woman who has ever beheld him. . . . But I have never seen him look at a woman as he looked at you. He was fascinated, I could tell. . . . I wonder if your gypsy will keep his promise and return to claim you? I wonder if he will come for you?"

Meredith sighed. "I have been wondering that myself," she said.

Ginny rose. "Well, tonight you will get some sleep so as to look beautiful tomorrow, no? For I am sure that once you are seen by the aristocracy, you will take Paris by storm. And that takes energy, Meredith. Or . . . Lady Vivienne. Oh, this is such fun! Trust Vivienne to see to it that life is never dull! Sweet dreams!"

With that, she left the room, and Meredith climbed into the great bed and pulled the satin coverlets over her. She blew out the candles in the silver-gilt candelabra on the nightstand and lay there, staring into the dark, wondering what new adventures her stay in Paris would bring.

At last she fell asleep . . . and dreamed. Dreamed of a black-haired lover who stared at her with the greenest eyes, before he bent his head to kiss her softly.

And in the dream, his hands unfastened her dress, and it fell away from her like a sigh. They were both unclothed, his skin like silken fire against hers, and in the dream he was merged as one with her, claiming her as his own with his body, making love to her.

147

The heat of the dream woke her, and she wondered how she could have felt so vividly in a dream what had never happened to her in waking life. And most of all, she wondered if she would ever see her highwayman again.

Oh, she hoped so! Because if she were to have an "adventure," as Ginny termed it, she knew whom she wanted to have it with. Her highwayman. No other man would ever do.

Chapter Ten

"What the hell was the idea of kidnapping her a day early?"

A furious Nicholas St. Antoine rounded on Deron Redvers, his blue eyes blazing. To his anger, Raceford lifted a black brow and looked infuriatingly amused.

They were in Nicki's opulent apartments, and Raceford considered that they perfectly reflected the young man who was their occupant. The hangings of peach and ice-blue and silver complemented his frosty coloring, and the furniture shimmered with silver gilding. Nicki was dressed in a splendid coat of cream and aqua, the latter color matched his eyes. There were diamonds in the lace at his throat and silver buckles on his high-heeled shoes.

Holding aloft his brandy glass and considering its cut crystal against the light of the chandelier, Raceford stated, "I wanted to meet her."

"Wanted to meet her?" Nicholas exploded. "But it nearly ruined my rescue! My party was supposed to come riding along just as you'd held her up and save her from you! You weren't supposed to ride off with her and spend the night!"

"Relax, Nicki. You rescued her in any case, did you not? And I trust she's suitably grateful." The words

149

were dry, the tone indifferent.

"Did you have her?" Nicholas ground out through clenched teeth.

"I did not. I found her most surprisingly unmoved by my advances."

"You made advances!"

"Most assuredly I made advances. And if you were alone for the evening with a woman as adventurous as the Lady Vivienne, you would behave like a monk?"

"That is beside the point. I warn you, Raceford, if you think to cut me out with her—"

"Never fear, Nicki. I am looking for a bride, it's true. But unlike you, I have no particular need for a rich one. I shall choose someone less experienced . . . and definitely less married . . . or have you forgotten about Lord Winter?"

"I haven't forgotten. But the man is ancient and can't last forever. I am simply trying to win her heart before I have too much competition, and rescuing her seemed a good way to begin. But damnit, Raceford, she didn't seem the least bit frightened!"

"She didn't? Then perhaps my advances were not so unwelcome after all. What did you expect me to do, Nicki? Beat her?"

"You didn't have to give her jewels back so she thinks of you as some kind of hero!"

Deron laughed and sipped his brandy. Really, this whole adventure was turning out to be most amusing. He'd arrived in Paris a fortnight earlier, and had begun the round of parties and balls expected of him. But soon it had begun to pall. The French court was more gorgeous than the English one, rising to heights of decadence under those powdered wigs and jewels that had to be experienced to be believed. But in the end . . . still a bore.

One evening he'd been at a dinner at the Comtesse d'Anguillame's palais, and he'd confessed his boredom to Ginny.

She had led him off through her crowded reception rooms, and he'd met the handsome viscomte.

"So . . . you wish to help me in my quest to impress the Lady Vivienne? Why?" Nicholas had asked him, obviously rather suspicious.

"I came to Paris because I was bored, and when I told Ginny that fact, she suggested I participate in this little escapade," he'd said.

"But Nicki . . . he is perfect! She's never met him, and see! He is quite dangerous-looking, *non?* A most desperate mouth, and with that black hair, he could pass for a gypsy any day. She will be terrified."

For a moment, the silver-blond man had regarded him thoughtfully. "Very well. Let him play the part of the highwayman. But I must enjoin you to silence as to your part in this venture. I'd thought to employ one of my servants. . . ."

"You can count on me. I'd not want to pass up the chance to play a criminal," Raceford had said.

It hadn't taken the three of them long to come up with a plan. But Raceford had decided to secretly move the holdup forward a day. A few minutes with Vivienne would not be enough. He wanted to make an impression on her heart, and he was curious about her.

Now he regarded Nicholas with interest. "So tell me, Nicki. Did the rescue have the effect you hoped it would?"

Nicholas frowned. "I'm not sure. I took her that night to Ginny's, and at once they bustled her off to some bedroom, crying over her as if she'd survived the sack of Rome. I called the next day, and she received me most kindly, but its damned hard to tell if you've made an impression or not among spindly chairs and teacups and excruciating politeness! I have higher hopes for the masquerade ball at Versailles later this week. Such affairs are notoriously loose, and I hope to get her alone somewhere and test her gratitude."

"Ah, yes. The masquerade. I'm also attending."

"You are? Who invited you?"

"Ginny's good offices. And she's helping me with my costume."

Nicholas narrowed his blue eyes suspiciously. "Your costume? What are you going as?"

Raceford laughed. "Why, as a highwayman, of course.

And laughed the harder at Nicki's outraged expression. "Now just a damned minute, Raceford! If you think to cut me out with her, I warn you—"

"Nicholas, has no one ever told you that all is fair in love and war? Ginny has told me you intend to behave with her as if you are an angel, so I shall take the opposite tack. We shall see if it's the devil or an angel she prefers. Because it's far too late to make me stop pursuing her, Nicki. You may want her for her money, but I—"

"You what?" growled Nicki irritably, wishing he'd never asked Raceford to help him in the first place. The man was far too personable and had a way with women that was regrettable. It would have been far better to have had some hideously ugly servant be her abductor, rough her up a bit, so that she would have been really scared. Not a man who spoke like a cultured duke and was handsome into the bargain. Really, he'd been a fool not to realize such a rogue was bound to catch a lady's interest.

"But I want her for her body. You see, I believe I

am half mad with desire for the wicked Lady Vivienne, and I shall not rest until I have her in my bed. I give you fair warning."

Nicki took a sip of his brandy and narrowed his eyes, considering. "Very well . . . have a try at her if you wish, my friend. But then, you forget two things: No Englishman has ever beaten a Frenchman in a matter of love . . . and I have never had any trouble in making a woman fall in love with me. I doubt that she will even look at you when I am finished with her."

"And I don't doubt that she will do a great deal more than just look at me," laughed Raceford. "Well, may the best man win!"

"Doubtless me . . . the game is already mine. But go ahead, have your try at her, if you wish to waste your time."

With that, Raceford laughed and raised his glass. "To Vivienne . . . the object of our desires!"

Meredith would have been shocked indeed had she known that the two handsomest men in Paris were drinking a toast to capturing her heart.

Chapter Eleven

"Oh, Meredith—I mean, Vivienne!—you look wonderful!"

"You look equally wonderful, Jane."

Meredith turned from the vision that was herself in the mirror and regarded Jane. "I mean, Meredith."

Both of them laughed. This evening was the masked ball at Versailles, and they were putting the finishing touches on their costumes. As Vivienne's cousin and companion "Meredith," Jane would be included in most of their social activities.

Ginny's dressmaker had been in a frenzy all week getting their costumes ready. Except for two calls from the viscomte, a tour of Paris in his company, rides in the park, and one small dinner party for twenty, Meredith had not been out in society much. Ginny wanted her to make her debut tonight at Versailles to the cream of French society. And no expense had been spared on her costume—or Jane's.

They had at first puzzled over what she could go as. Then Ginny had hit on it. "Lady Vivienne Winter!" she'd cried. "You will go as the Queen of Ice and Snow!"

She was gowned in a dress of frosty white satin, which was sewn over almost every inch with glass

154

crystal beads that caught the light and threw off diamondlike sparkles. A diamond necklace of such magnificence graced her neck that she was almost afraid to leave the palais in it. Her hair was too black to be powdered effectively, so she wore a wig of purest white. It swept upward, crowned by tinkling icicles of glass and silver, the whole dusted with silver glitter. Her wrists were banded by thick diamond bracelets, and at the elbows of her dress, silver lace fell in cascades. Finally, a transparent cloak of shimmering silver tissue fell from the back of her shoulders to sweep the floor.

The white wig dusted with silver made a startling change in her appearance, Meredith considered. Her skin was very white, and in contrast, her dark brows and lashes were striking. Her lips had been barely rouged with pink, and another blush of rouge warmed her cheeks. A tiny black star, strategically placed on one creamy cheekbone, gave her a rakish look. An enormous frosty white lace fan completed her ensemble.

Jane had chosen to go as the Queen of Hearts. She had powdered her curls, and the white locks changed her appearance as much as it did Meredith's. She wore a red silk gown over a white velvet underdress embroidered with pink hearts, and the whole outfit was trimmed with yards of white lace. Her necklace, one of Vivienne's, was of rubies and diamonds. In her hair, pink and red velvet hearts edged with lace were clustered among roses, and on one cheek was a small red heart patch. She carried a red satin fan trimmed with white lace, and skillful application of paint had made her look dangerously pretty.

"My word, My Lady, can you believe the two of us! If this isn't the greatest adventure I've ever been on . . . and tonight, we'll see the King and Queen of France! And dance at Versailles! I really can hardly believe it's all true!"

"Neither can I, but if this is a dream, I hope I don't wake from it."

"Do you reckon the viscomte will be there tonight?"

"He has told me he will."

Jane sighed theatrically. "Lord. If a man who looked like that were courting me the way he's courting you, I'd soon forget my mother raised me to be a virtuous girl!"

"I believe the viscomte has made any number of women forget their virtue."

"But a man has to marry sometime, doesn't he? And if that gorgeous creature were warming my bed at night, I'd forgive him for wanting to share himself a bit. After all, it hardly seems fair that only one woman would be able to enjoy all that!"

Amused, Meredith turned. "Perhaps you should spend some time with the viscomte. I've never heard you talk like this, J—Meredith."

"It must be Paris, My Lady. Was there ever such a city?"

Was there ever such a city? Meredith wondered later as their coach rolled through the night on its way out of the city to Versailles. The river, lit from above by the great palaces with their water stairs. Statues flung in profusion, white against the night. Buildings of gray stone, biscuit-colored stone. Gray roofs and blue roofs, black railings, rows of stately chestnut trees arching gracefully above the wide streets. Notre Dame, so small and perfect, a jewel.

Elegant coaches with twinkling crests on their doors and flamboyant footmen were rolling toward Versailles, through streets crowded with litters and torchbearers, horsemen and foot traffic. Beautiful beyond belief, a city of romantic dreams.

She leaned forward to look out the window as the coach left Paris and its sights behind and drove into the countryside. A silver moon was caught in a net of black branches against a purple sky, and once again, she felt her excitement mount. She was on her way to Versailles to dance in company with the King and Queen of France. Something like this could only happen once in a lifetime.

She glanced across at the insouciant comtesse. Ginny was splendid tonight as Aphrodite, in a white gown draped over one bare shoulder, white wig, and a headdress that framed her catlike face in a golden crown. All over her bare shoulders fell a whisper of transparent gold tissue, and a wide gilded belt circled her narrow waist. The simplicity of the costume in comparison to the overelaborate gowns in fashion was stunning, and Meredith knew she would never have had the courage to appear herself in such a formfitting, revealing costume.

At last they arrived at Versailles, and their coach joined the line of others slowly moving forward to let their gorgeous cargo alight. At the end of the Avenue de Paris stood the Chateau de Versailles, like a river of light. It was huge. Lanterns hung from the trees like stars, and every window of the enormous structure blazed with light, like a bonfire in the distance. From Meredith's seat in the coach, it seemed the chateau stretched into forever. Beyond the towering wrought iron fence that encircled it, there appeared courtyard after courtyard, flanked by separate wings of the chateau, as various in scale, color, and material as anything she'd ever seen. These were staggered until they met at the front entrance. The fence that bounded the grounds was colonnaded with statues, and at its center, the entrance gates flung wide to welcome its guests. Their carriage rolled through the entrance into the paved courtyard beyond. Flambeaux danced everywhere and showed Meredith some two hundred coaches lining the courtyard awaiting entrance, not to mention those behind her coach.

She was awed at the very size of the place, and thought that it was a testament to the power of the great kings of France. Versailles was all arched windows, balustrades, columns stretching to the roof and topped with statues of various classical themes; it was all white stone, light gray stone, biscuit-colored stone, carved pediments and marble staircases.

As the coach rolled forward, Ginny told Meredith and Jane the names of the courtyards they were passing through.

"This is the Cour Royale and beyond the Cour des Ministres, where the Ministers of the Crown are housed. This is the Place d'Armes."

Each name Meredith whispered to herself, as if to commit them to memory. She sighed, thinking this would be something to tell her children on a cozy evening before the fire . . . of her visit to the Chateau de Versailles.

Three avenues converged across the Place d'Armes, and here a vast network of vaulted galleries and spacious courtyards swept the concave of each facade of the building in grand elegance. "This is the Grand Ecurie, where our coach will be kept until we are ready to leave," Ginny announced, preparing to alight from the vehicle.

Meredith looked to Jane, whose eyes were wide and whose mouth nearly hung open to her chest. Laughing at Jane's astonishment, Meredith took her index finger and closed the girl's gaping mouth.

Jane, shaken from her reverie, simply cried out, "I can't help it, Mere—Vivienne. It's too much rich for these poor eyes to take in."

Meredith leaned over and whispered into her ear, "Entirely too much rich for these poor eyes, too. I was just thinking what wonderful stories I could tell my children, but I don't think anyone would believe me."

They laughed together and followed Ginny out of the coach. Hundreds of guests had already arrived and alighted from their coaches. By the torch light, their costumes glittered and sparkled, and their laughter echoed throughout the night, evidence of the gala evening ahead.

They followed the procession of guests through the smaller inner courtyard, the Cour de Marbre, Ginny informed them, lined with potted orange trees and well-lit with sputtering flambeaux. And embedded in the enormity of the rest of the chateau was what seemed like a pretty country house of brick and stone, built around three sides of a quadrangle. The balustrades here were of wrought iron and richly gilded, forming a balcony around the chateau that gave Meredith the impression of golden lace.

This part of the chateau seemed so different from the rest, and at the quizzical look on Meredith's face, Ginny leaned into her and whispered, "It is difficult to think Versailles was at one time a simple little hunting lodge, eh?"

But before Meredith could offer an answer to this

incredible bit of information, she was swept through the entrance gates of Versailles and met a spectacle that exceeded the outside only in its array of color and sound. Inside, she found herself in a huge vaulted chamber. On the opposite wall were three enormous niches that held sculptures. The images of Apollo sat in the central niche, golden bronze, having run his daily course across the sky, resting amid a group of nymphs. And flanking him on either side were his horses being rubbed down by tritons. The walls and ceiling were encrusted with shells, forming a colorful grotto of pink and golden brown. And from somewhere, the sound of music could be heard, its notes echoing in the huge chamber in beautiful harmony.

Meredith whispered to Ginny, "I hear birds."

Ginny laughed. "It is the water organ. It makes the music and the little birds sing. Do not ask me how it works, but it is beautiful, *non?*"

"Very beautiful."

She followed Ginny and the crush of other guests as they made their way through the various chambers and galleries. Meredith hazarded a peek through the windows that lined the gallery they were traveling. Below the gardens of Versailles spread out, lit with torches, stretching as far as the eye could see, symmetrical in their position to each other, yet each one different from the next. There were fountains and statuary, sculpted shrubbery and flowers in profusion. Men scurried below, setting up fireworks that would come later. Meredith shook her head, hardly believing the dream she was living.

Finally, they arrived at the doors to the Salle de Spectacle, where their wraps were taken, their invitations checked.

They paused in the doorway before the glittering throng. Curious faces, white wigs everywhere, turned their way, and for a moment, the level of conversation dropped, then rose again as the newcomers were discussed.

The sight before them was one of fantasy. On every side, costumes each more elaborate than the next were to be seen. Fantastic headdresses towered above painted faces — golden fruit, leaves and flowers, stag's antlers, swan's wings, horns, crowns. Jewels glittered in profusion, and many of the costumes were embroidered with pearls, gems, or sparkling beads. Every face bore a half-mask, often feathered or jeweled, which would be removed at midnight.

The enormous ballroom, which also served as an opera house, was a realm of faerie. Its wooden walls had been painted in varying subtle tones of warm salmon-pink against a background of grey-green, *verd-de-mer*, and richly gilded to resemble marble. In contrast, bright cobalt silk hangings fluttered from the balcony to the floor below. A row of columns graced the upper balcony, breaking into a beautifully frescoed apse above the royal box. And each bay of the colonnade that ran around the elliptical room was backed by a mirror in front of which hung a half chandelier, its other half reflected in the mirror. Meredith counted fourteen great chandeliers hanging from the ceiling, which was a fresco of clouds. The chandeliers' candlelight threw sparkling light from the hundreds of dangling crystal pendants.

Mirrors on every wall reflected the dazzling throng, and the floor was a checkerboard of black and white tiles. The walls were obscured in places with banks of hothouse flowers, like a tropical jungle for guests to hide behind. And yew trees clipped in the shape of pillars with vases on them, set in huge silver tubs, were scattered here and there around the walls. At one end of the ballroom, an enormous fountain arced into silver basins held up by mermaids, and to Meredith's wonder, she saw that wine was flowing from the fountain's jets. Along one wall the buffets, draped in pink velvet fringed in gold, groaned beneath turkeys, boars' heads, fresh salmon, and pâté of trout. Great arched doorways led to balconies above the great formal gardens of Versailles and admitted the warm, perfumed night air. Music from a full orchestra blended with the tinkle of laughter and murmur of voices, and servants as fantastically garbed as the guests rushed here and there bearing trays of champagne glasses.

The comtesse was at once surrounded by a chattering group, and Meredith plucked an icy champagne glass from an offered tray and sipped it to steady her nerves. She smiled at Jane, who was staring round-eyed at the ballroom, and wondered if she herself looked so amazed.

Suddenly, she caught sight of a tall figure walking toward them, dressed in white and silver as she was. The tied-back powdered hair made it hard for her to guess the man's identity, but then she recognized his elegant walk. Nicholas! He reached them and stopped, eyes only for her, then bowed low before her.

"My dear viscomte," she said, extending her hand to be kissed. "What an incredible coincidence that you are all in white and silver, and I am, too!"

He laughed. "You know me so soon in spite of my mask? But I know you as well, I would recognize you anywhere, simply by the way my heart leaps at the sight of you. But this?" He spread his hands wide so they could admire his glittering costume, so like hers, and Meredith heard Jane beside her give a sigh of pure pleasure. "You have no idea what it cost me to bribe the maids to tell me what you were wearing or to obtain samples of the cloth for me. Or the expense from my tailor for such a rush job. But tonight I wanted you to see how well we match when I take you in my arms—to dance with you, of course."

"I believe you have met my cousin, Miss Westin," said Meredith, smiling.

The viscomte at once turned to Jane, who stared for a moment, then remembered to extend a trembling hand to be kissed. "But of course," he murmured as he straightened, not releasing her hand. "The Queen of Hearts. I predict, mademoiselle, that tonight you will steal many hearts. In fact, you would have mine in your keeping had I not first beheld your fair cousin."

At that moment, Ginny turned to Meredith and claimed her to introduce to her crowd of friends. As she turned, Meredith heard Nicholas step a bit closer to Jane and murmur to the dazzled girl, "But of course, my heart is one that is generous and has enough affection for many. Perhaps later you would consent to take a walk in the garden with me and test your powers over my heart?"

Meredith bit off an outraged giggle. Why, he was incorrigible! But what a thrill for Jane. Even though she felt the slightest dart of jealousy at Nicholas' defection, she hoped Jane would take that walk in the gardens with him . . . or perhaps with some other handsome Frenchman she found tonight.

A sudden silence fell, and Meredith turned to see what had caused it. All around, glittering headdresses were bowing low, facing toward the grand entrance doors.

"Their Majesties, the King and Queen of France!" came the ringing call.

Before Meredith sank into a deep curtsy, she caught a glimpse of two shining figures in the doorway who put the rest of the crowd to shame. For a long moment, she held her curtsy, then the rustling around her told her she could rise. In awe, she gazed at the splendid figures in the doorway—Louis XVI and Marie Antoinette, King and Queen of France.

In tribute to his ancestor, Louis XIV, that most glorious monarch France had ever known, the king was dressed as the sun. His suit was all of cloth of gold, and a rayed crown on his head proclaimed his identity. At his side, the queen was dressed as the moon, all in cloth of silver, with a diamond crescent on her forehead. The two figures coruscated in the light of the chandeliers, celestially lavish.

Side by side, they slowly paced down the cleared center of the ballroom, to a wave of deep obeisances. They alone wore no masks. They paused here and there to admire a costume or exchange a word with some great noble, and Meredith had a chance to examine them during their slow progress.

The king, for all his magnificent dress, was not a prepossessing figure of a man. Short and rather dumpy, he had a kindly and somewhat vacant face that could have belonged to a baker rather than a king.

Oh, but the queen! Never had Meredith seen a woman with a more haughty and inviting face, perfect in its delicate Austrian beauty. For all the incredible elaboration of her dress, it did her justice. Meredith imagined that in rags, this woman would still be every inch royal.

Before long, they were approaching the Comtesse d'Anguillame, whom Meredith knew to be a confidante of the queen's. They paused to speak to her, and in a few moments, Ginny turned to Meredith.

"Your Serene Majesties, may I have the honor of presenting a visitor from England? The Lady Vivienne Winter."

Meredith curtsied low again, feeling she might swoon. Here she was, plain Meredith Westin, actually being presented to the King and Queen of France! She held her curtsy for a moment longer than normal, fighting hard for composure.

She straightened, to find the king and queen staring at her. The king spoke first. "From England? But may I be the first to welcome you to our shores. France and England were so long enemies, and now at last exist in amity, madame. In fact, you will find that English things are all the rage in Paris. I admire your costume, madame, and find it a clever play upon your name."

Pleased with his play on words, the king turned to the queen and smiled. Meredith merely murmured how honored she was to meet the king, unable to find anything sufficiently witty to say in the presence of royalty. Marie Antoinette, bored, had turned back to Ginny, and as she talked to her about her gown and the fireworks that were planned for later, she let her large pale blue eyes rest speculatively on Nicholas. Then the king and queen were moving on down the rows of guests, Meredith and her party again dropping into deep reverences.

To have spoken to the King and Queen of France! Meredith's head spun.

Ginny turned to her, pleased. "You have made an impression, Vivienne! It is seldom the king consents to speak to many. He hates these *affaires* and would much rather be tinkering with his clocks or in his woodshop. But of course, Her Majesty lives to dance. She is the most graceful dancer France has ever known, and the king would do anything to please her. So he comes to these balls and dances with not above five ladies in an evening, then retires to the sidelines to watch the queen. Meeting them will set the seal on your social approval. Watch. After tonight, I predict you will be in such demand you will have to fight off invitations!"

A breathless Meredith stood on the sidelines and watched as the dancing began. The king led the queen out alone, for they would dance the first dance together. It was as Ginny had said: The queen was by far the most accomplished dancer Meredith had ever seen. Nervous, she watched every step, hoping that her hours of lessons with Vivienne would be enough. She did not want to disgrace herself—and England! —by being unable to remember the complex dance steps that would be required of her when she danced later on.

The music ended, and Meredith felt her heart begin to race as Nicholas approached her. The ball was about to begin in earnest, and in moments she would be dancing at the Palace of Versailles. Six months ago in Henley, she would never have dreamed that such a thing could ever happen to her.

Nicki joined her, extending a hand to lead her out onto the floor. Other dancers were making their way onto the floor, but Meredith could see many curious glances directed at her. She was unknown to them and this dance would be her first introduction to French society. Oh Lord, she prayed fervently, let me not forget which way to turn, let me not stumble!

The music started. It was a stately dance, a minuet that required mincing steps, precise bows and curtsies to the partner, and no more contact than the lightest of fingertip touches. All around her the room was a glittery swirl of lights and perfume, and as she began the dance, she felt a lightening in her chest. This was one of the dances she had practiced the most. She was letter-perfect in its steps.

At last the dance ended, and Meredith made another deep curtsy to Nicholas. "My dearest Lady Vivienne. It has been my pleasure to dance with you," he murmured. "Please dance with me again?"

"Yes, later in the evening . . ."

"The devil with later! That was no dance. They are playing a waltz, and I would hold you closer than just barely touching your fingertips!"

Before she could protest, Meredith was swept, laughing, into his arms and back out onto the dance floor.

"Nicki, don't you care that you will cause a scandal for me? It is shocking for a woman to dance twice in a row with a man unless they are engaged!"

"Which we would be, if that were possible. Besides, I had to get you away from the hordes that were descending, so as to warn you against some of them. They all want to meet the woman who spoke to the king and queen. But you must not dance with Jacques Larrique, nor the Duc de Nîmes. Both are shocking rakes and bad for a woman's reputation. Whereas I am the worst of all to know, but then, the damage has already been done."

She laughed again, enjoying herself, enjoying the masterful and possessive way her handsome Nicholas was behaving. It was relaxing to be held in Nicki's arms, to see his frost-blue eyes melting with warmth as they looked down at her.

Near the end of the dance he spoke. "I have a simple request, Lady Vivienne," he said softly. "I told you I wanted you to see how well we matched when I took you in my arms. As I dance you past this wall of mirrors, I beg you will turn your head and look."

And she did. She saw his tall form holding hers, both with hair and dress white as ice, the Snow Queen clasped in the arms of the North Wind.

"Thank you, Viscomte, for this dance," she said when at last the music ended.

"But the honor—and the pleasure—was all mine."

And then Meredith was besieged. It seemed everyone in the ballroom wanted to meet her, and the evening took on a sense of unreality, for she knew she would remember none of them, masked as they were. But the masks gave her a courage she might not otherwise have had, and she laughed and sparkled and danced until she was exhausted.

From the sidelines, Nicki and Ginny stood together and watched the dancing. After a moment, Ginny gave Nicki a sidelong glance through her lashes. Really, it was indecent how incredible he looked in white and silver, with his silver-blond hair and black lashes, ice-blue eyes. She ventured the question dearest to her heart.

"So . . . what do you think of her?"

"Hmmm?" Nicki roused himself from a momentary reverie and looked at Ginny. "Oh . . . Vivienne?"

"Yes, Vivienne! I am curious to learn your impression of her."

"Well . . . she's every bit as beautiful as you'd led me to believe, but—"

"But?"

"But really, she seems strangely naive for one purported to be as worldly as she is. Almost as if she were a country mouse, unused to society."

Ginny viewed him with alarm. Really, Meredith was not doing very well at acting if Nicki had seen through her facade so quickly.

"Well, perhaps it is her Englishness. They are more reserved than the French, after all. But in any case, do you not find it refreshing?"

"No, tiresome, actually. I am not used to having to watch my language around a woman. I prefer someone I can speak frankly to, like you, Ginny. Still, I must admit you are a genius, as always. It would not have done to seduce her. I can see you were right to tell me to treat her with respect. A new role for me!"

"So, you don't find her fascinating?"

"As I said, pretty enough. And I don't even find this conversation fascinating. Dance with me, Ginny."

He smiled brilliantly at her and held out his arms, and she allowed herself to be swept into them. They moved well together and were laughing as he swept her past the wall of mirrors.

"I told Vivienne I wore white to match her tonight," he said. "But I'm glad you're wearing it, too. We look like we were made for one another."

"We do fit rather well, don't we, Nicki?"

"And let me compliment you on your costume." His eyes dropped to her shoulders. "I find your bare shoulders most distracting. It's hard to remember I'm supposed to be pursuing someone else when you are so attired."

Playfully, she rapped his arm with her fan. "Don't forget, she is the woman you intend to marry."

His eyes were smoky blue as he looked down at her. "Ah. That must be why she bores me. The thought of a wife has never held much charm for

169

me."

Don't I know it, Nicki, thought Ginny. *And until it does, I'll keep you dangling after a woman you can't marry!* Meredith joined them then, and Nicki tapped her on the arm. "Lady Vivienne, there was a rather elderly woman, English, who came up to me and asked me where you were. It seems she knows you from England and wishes to say hello. The Marchioness of Waterbury."

Disaster! Meredith swallowed, trying to think of what on earth to say. Someone who knew Vivienne, here! What would she do?

She wrinkled her brow as if puzzled. "The Marchioness of Waterbury? I do not recall her. But then, I met so many people in England. If she is elderly, she may well be a friend of my husband's. There were many who came to the wedding whom I only met once. Can you point her out to me?"

Nicholas scanned the ballroom, then pointed at a very elderly woman, all in lavender, who sat on the sidelines clutching a cane. As Meredith watched, she rose with some difficulty and began to cross the ballroom toward them.

She had to get away!

A cool breeze from the open terrace doors caught at her skirts. It was the solution. Saying that she must seek the ladies' retiring chamber, she left her companions. In the boudoir, she freshened her costume and herself. All around her chattering ladies gossiped and recounted the evening's conquests. They all wanted to meet an English noblewoman, and she made ten friends in as many minutes. At last she escaped their thousand questions and slipped away down an almost deserted hallway. Only a couple clasped in each other's embrace behind a palm tree were to be seen, and soon the music led Meredith back to the ballroom.

She was at a side entrance near the sweep of doors that opened onto the balcony, and for a few moments, she stood unnoticed, enjoying the freshness of the night air. To her dismay, she saw that the old marchioness was talking to Nicholas and Ginny, and Meredith knew she couldn't go back into the ballroom. She was turning to walk out onto the balcony when she noticed a gentleman, dressed all in black with a black mask, regarding her. The only relief to the black of his costume was his powdered white hair, pulled back with a black ribbon, and a fall of white lace at his throat. He wore a sword at his side. And he was staring at her steadily.

Meredith decided to flirt a bit with him, for he was obviously interested in her. Snapping open her fan, she raised it to cover the lower half of her face, so that all of her was masked. For a moment, she regarded him steadily, then slowly lowered the fan to reveal a smiling mouth. Then she turned away and headed toward the open doors to the balcony. In any case, she must hide herself outdoors for the time being, until the marchioness gave up on her.

She was out on the terrace before she heard a soft footfall at her side. She stopped and slowly faced him, keeping her eyes lowered. She would raise them slowly to his face, she thought, wondering if behind the mask he was as handsome as he seemed.

"I have come out onto the terrace to be alone, sir," she said.

Her eyes lifted, and then froze. Nestled in the folds of the white lace at his throat was a gem — a sapphire surrounded by beads of jet.

At the moment her eyes met her earring pinned to

a stranger's throat, he spoke. In a voice she would never forget.

"And I have come across France to find you, My Lady, and make good my claim."

Chapter Twelve

Meredith raised her eyes and saw the green ones behind the black mask. It was the highwayman!

"You! What are you doing here?" she gasped, feeling faint with emotions—shock and gladness that he had come back.

His mouth smiled beneath the mask. "But I told you I have come here for you."

Meredith took a swift look around the terrace, seeing that as yet, their conversation was unobserved. She wanted no curious questions from Ginny or Nicholas as to who the black-masked stranger was. "Follow me down the terrace," she murmured, and started to walk off toward the less-crowded shadows.

The terraces were full of strollers enjoying the fresh May evening air, and Meredith meandered toward an area that was more shadowed and deserted of other people. She sat on a wide stone balustrade, fanning herself to dissipate a heat that seemed suddenly too great. Where was he? She scanned the moving figures down the terrace but saw none in black.

Below her, the gardens shimmered, painted colored paper lanterns glowing golden and strung fairylike among the trees. The scent of flowers drifted up from below, and she saw that strollers were gathering in the gardens, waiting for the fireworks that were to begin after the unmasking.

He was standing in the shadow of an open doorway, watching her speculatively. Her white gown glimmered in the night, and he thought almost angrily how lovely she was . . . and how accomplished. Innocent, had he believed her?

Why, the first thing she'd done when she arrived at Versailles had been to catch the eye of the King of France. No shy girl would have the art necessary to catch a king's eye, then hold her own so gracefully, so calmly with him.

An innocent? Look at the way, when she'd felt his eyes . . . what she believed were a stranger's eyes . . . she'd fluttered her fan and lowered it to reveal an inviting smile, like a practiced flirt. Then walked out onto the terrace like any wanton. The wanton she was. Tonight, when she didn't have anything to gain from acting, he'd seen the Lady Vivienne Winter in her true colors, he thought angrily. It would be long before the innocent act, however convincing, would fool him again.

He stepped out of the shadows then and walked down the terrace to where her waiting figure gleamed in the dim night.

There was a sliver of a moon over the great formal gardens below, and the scent of flowers drifted upwards. The perfect night to begin a seduction, he thought.

Meredith saw him coming and drew in a breath,

bracing herself. Glad as she was to see him, she was apprehensive about their encounter. What would he expect? Well, whatever it was, she'd rather face him as herself than as some creature out of a French masque. She reached up and untied her mask, dropping it in her lap.

He reached her and echoed her gesture, tossing his discarded mask onto the balustrade next to her. For a long moment, they just looked at each other. The same gypsy face, long eyes, black brows. His skin was dark against the white wig.

She found her voice first. "Why did you come to this of all places? You were mad to come here! What if you are caught?"

"And who is to unmask me, My Lady, if you do not?"

"Nicholas, for one! The man who rescued me! He would know you in a moment!"

"So . . . it is Nicholas, is it? I take it you were very . . . *grateful* to him for rescuing you from my clutches?"

The implication of his words was not lost on Meredith. She colored, wondering why she had chosen that moment to call the viscomte by his first name. She had never done it to his face. It was just that Ginny so frequently referred to him as Nicki. But she knew what such quick use of a man's first name made her look like. It made her look like a lightskirt.

"I mean the Viscomte de Valmy, of course." She paused, wondering what on earth she could say next. "Naturally, I was grateful to him for rescuing my person and my possessions."

"But what I wish to know is exactly *how* grateful you were, My Lady. If you have forgotten that you belong to me now, then I have not. I will kill him if he has touched you."

The words, spoken so calmly, gave Meredith a chill. Somehow she did not doubt that he was serious. "I have been with the Comtesse d'Anguillame every moment since I arrived in Paris! You may ask her or bribe her servants if you do not believe me! But it is none of your business, sir. And I beg you stop this nonsense about 'belonging' and 'claims.' I belong to no one but myself. A mere kiss does not set the seal of possession upon me."

He stared down at her, a grim smile of triumph touching his lips. So here she was, the Lady Vivienne, revealed as she really was at last! It hadn't taken much provocation to make her show herself. Good. Now it was war, and he need not feel guilty.

He sat down next to her on the balustrade and took possession of her hand. He felt it tremble and smiled, knowing that her response to him that night in the inn, at least, had not been all pretense.

"But you must forgive me, my dear Vivienne," he murmured softly. "You are right that a kiss does not claim you. That is only the hope of my heart speaking. Don't you know I have been mad with love for you since the first time I saw you? I can dream of nothing but your skin, your eyes . . . the way it felt that night you kissed me. Can it be you have forgotten?"

Without waiting for an answer, he bent his head until his lips touched the place where her neck curved into her shoulder. He felt a surge of passion at the touch of her soft skin under his lips. . . . Had he ever felt skin like this, as soft as white velvet? She turned her head toward him, so that he only had to lift his head and he was staring at her, his own mouth inches from hers.

"No, don't . . . Stop," Meredith whispered helplessly, but as always, the highwayman had an effect on her she could not control, making her pulses leap with fire whenever she merely saw him. And when he touched her . . .

"Don't stop?" he whispered.

He was kissing her, gathering her close in his arms, and she was twining her fingers in his hair and kissing him back while thrills of liquid fire shot through her veins.

She was lost in his kiss. Lost to the world, not caring that they were on a balcony of Versailles, that at any moment, someone might come. She could only feel him holding her close, ravishing her lips, and she moaned softly as his mouth left hers. He kissed her face, her eyelids, her neck, his tongue evoking delicious sensations through every inch of her. As he kissed her, he was slowly lowering her backward until she was reclining beneath him on the balustrade.

Above them, the first of the evening's fireworks blossomed in the sky, white stars exploding in a shower of starry lights, followed by a boom.

Her arms wrapped around his neck as his dark head lowered, his mouth on her thrown-back neck, questing lower and lower. Meredith kept her eyes squeezed tight shut, her mind blank to everything except the raging sensations he was awakening in her, the pure sensuality of his body against hers, his open mouth on her skin.

The fireworks lit the heavens above with golden and green and red and white and blue stars, and to Meredith, it almost seemed as if his mouth, their

177

kisses, were creating them. They were a perfect expression of what was happening between the two of them.

Then his mouth found the swelling curves of her breasts, and a shiver took her and she clung to him. All at once, her breasts were aching, begging to be touched, and he seemed to know what she felt, for his hands began to trace her waist and move upward to cup her breasts. His mouth was at the top of her low-cut dress now, his tongue slowly slipping along the lace-trimmed neckline, sometimes darting lower inside the fabric. And then his fingers were sliding the tight dress lower and lower, an achingly tantalizing sensation against her nipples. As they were freed from the lacy ruffles that held them, his tongue touched the tip of one erect pink crest and she moaned again as sensations exploded inside her.

He took her nipple into his mouth, hands exploring the curves of her breasts, pushing them together so he could tease both nipples with his tongue. She arched upward into him, her uncovered breasts exposed to his touch and his mouth, and felt him shift his hands lower. He was pushing her skirts and petticoats upward, his hands on the curves of her calves, bending her knees and placing her high heels on the stone. Higher and higher he pushed her skirts, exposing her stockings, her lacy white garters, until his warm hands were on her bare thighs, smoothly caressing. It was he who moaned softly then as he moved over her, stretching his long legs between hers, his weight pinning her to the stone.

Only lace separated her from the throbbing heat of him, and she felt his muscles, his strength and, for the first time, the full hardness of his manhood as he pressed between her legs. It was so intimate, this feeling, as if he had already possessed her in every sense of the word, as if they were fused into one. His mouth was still at her uncovered breasts, open now, licking her skin with his tongue until she was wet and crying out with desire for him.

At last he raised his head and took her lips again in a hard kiss, and she twisted her hands in his hair, uncaring that they lay on a balustrade, that the drop beneath them could have killed them.

At length, he pulled himself away and stared down at her until she opened her eyes. His dark head was suddenly backlit with a profusion of shooting stars as the evening's display reached its crescendo. He was looking at her with naked desire, and he murmured, "A kiss is not enough to claim you, My Lady. I can see that now." Then he rose, gathering her in his arms, and lifted her from the balustrade. He pressed his lips to hers with an urgency she found impossible to resist.

Meredith was barely aware that he was carrying her away from the balcony, so lost was she in the feel of his mouth on hers, the strength of his arms.

He pushed open the door to one of the private apartments off the balcony. There were no candles blazing; only the moonlight and an occasional flash of the fireworks illuminated the room. She was able to catch fleeting glances of him as he lowered her to her feet and crushed her against him. But in those glimpses, she saw a passion in his eyes that sent heat all through her body. She could see how desperately he desired her, and without shame, she knew she desired him as much.

The darkness only made her more aware of his

scent, the deep, low groans that came from his throat as he pressed her so close she thought they would melt into one being. And the flames of passion he had ignited on the balcony flared out of control.

His urgency became hers as she brazenly moved her lips along the line of his jaw to the base of his neck, pushing his shirt away from the chest that she longed to cover with kisses. Beneath her fingers his shirt slid away from his shoulders, and she ran her hands along the tautness of them, burying her face in his chest, drinking in his male scent, covering him with kisses that burned her lips. How she longed to feel her own bared breasts against that wall of muscle.

And as if he'd read her mind, she felt her gown loosening as he undid each hook. The material slid free of her body in a long, sensual whisper, its trail marked by his kisses along her shoulders to the tops of her breasts and back to her lips. He untied the panniers that hung from her waist and let them drop to the floor with her gown. She moaned and pressed herself to him free of the cumbersome undergarments, longing more than ever to feel his bare skin against hers, but her corset was in the way. She gave an exasperated cry. And then her movements became a frenzy of trembling fingers as she began tugging on the laces of her corset, her mouth crushed hungrily against his, not aware in the least of what her actions meant. When at last the corset hung open, her breath caught in her throat at the anticipation of his touch.

He clasped her to him, and she thought she would die from the sensations that flooded her at the feel of his warm body against hers, hard and powerful, his lips devouring hers.

But how she wanted to feel more.

She arched against him and his lips came down to her breasts, where he teased first one nipple into a rigid peak and then the other. Then his hands were moving along her back to her thighs, loosing the garters that held her stockings. His mouth moved from her breasts to her stomach, and lower to her hips and thighs, as he pushed the stockings down her legs. She grasped his hair in her fingers and pulled him to her. She was lost, utterly lost, unable to think, only to feel what his lips and his hands were doing to her.

Then his mouth was on hers again as he pulled her around, guiding her to the bed, a trail of his own clothing left behind, until at last she was allowed the complete pleasure of his body against hers, flesh so smooth and taut, powerful and intoxicating.

He pulled away from her, and at that moment, the room glowed with light from the fireworks. She heard him gasp as his eyes drank in her nakedness in the momentary light. His hand, soft and warm, ran from her hip to her rib cage, where he cupped one breast tenderly. His eyes met hers, and she was filled with such longing for him, such desire as she had never known before. He brought his mouth down over hers, murmuring, "No, a kiss is not enough to claim a woman as passionate as you, My Lady. If you are to be mine and mine alone, I must claim you completely."

He moved himself over her, pulling her into his arms, his manhood firm between them. His mouth moved to her ear and she heard him whisper, "My Lady, will you be mine forever?" Then his tongue traced the outline of her ear, moving along her neck

181

to her shoulders, sending thrills all through her.

She sighed raggedly and whispered back, pulling him to her as tightly as her trembling arms would allow, "Forever, my highwayman."

His lips sought hers as he entered her. He heard her gasp and felt a slight resistance before he was able to thrust himself fully into her. For a moment, he thought her untried, but as he began to move inside her, the sensations she was evoking in him with her lips, her hands, her legs wrapped tightly around his, banished the impossible thought from his mind, and he was lost, as lost as she was in the rhythm of their bodies moving together.

As he thrust against her, new sensations swept her away. His movements ignited a spark deep within her and she strained against him, moving with him to create a fire she had no knowledge of. He moved his mouth to her breast and took one swollen nipple between his lips, teasing it, rolling it between his tongue and teeth. She moaned with an all-consuming pleasure, and the sound of her moan increased his movements. She felt the spark within her grow into a flame, and the heat of their passion enveloped her as she matched her own rhythm to his. His hands nearly seared her where they clasped her tighter and tighter to him, and she still felt she could not get enough of him. When his mouth found hers, the flame within her burst into a raging fire racing with a blazing fury through her veins, radiating to the very tips of her fingers and toes. She'd never felt such pleasure before, and she cried out.

Her cries quickened his response, as she felt him release his own passion. Soon their rhythm slowed, and the two of them lay in each other's arms entirely spent.

He gathered her to him, kissing her forehead softly, "Now you are mine, My Lady. No other man can claim you. You must remember your promise to me. You are mine forever, Vivienne."

With his words came the reality of what had happened. Heavens! What had she done? She'd given herself like a wanton to this man, writhed beneath him as a woman mad with desire, cried out in her ecstasy without a thought for what was happening. He was a stranger. A highwayman! She didn't even know his name! And then fear filled her. There would be blood on the sheets, undeniable proof of her loss of virginity. If this man discovered it, he would know she was not Vivienne. Fear of discovery now overwhelmed her. How could she have been so foolish!

She turned away from him, her breath catching in her throat. She was trembling all over. "I beg you to go away and leave me alone. I don't know what came over me, but—"

Words were useless after what she had just done. She had to get away from this man, to never see him again. Otherwise, she knew she was lost. He'd know her secret if he looked in her eyes, and he'd brought out feelings she never knew existed. If she was ever alone with him again . . .

She rose. Her knees were quivering so badly she didn't know if she could walk, and her nipples still throbbed painfully. He rose and rushed to her side, pulling her back into his arms.

She pushed him away, avoiding his eyes. "I've got to go downstairs. My friends will miss me. Please, please let me go, I beg you, and do not follow me. I cannot see you anymore—ever again!"

As she turned and began retrieving her costume, he spoke behind her, that familiar ripple of amusement in his voice, "And do you think that after that taste of your charms, My Lady, I will leave you alone? I think not. It isn't finished between us."

She reached for her garments and began dressing as best she could. She wondered how she would ever lace the corset and fix the panniers at her waist again, let alone lift her gown over her head.

He was standing before her in his pants, his shirt hanging loose. He lifted her chin with his finger and looked into her eyes. A puzzled expression came over his face.

She pushed his hand aside and turned to finish dressing without saying a word, her fear growing stronger. *Had he seen her frightened innocence in that glance?* she wondered. She hoped not, or her charade would be over before it had even begun. She had to get out of this room and now. Without a care for her disheveled appearance, she ran to the door and opened it.

"Mark my words, My Lady, it is not over between us," she heard him say. Not daring to look back, Meredith hurried through the door. She found herself in a long and lavish hallway, and from the faint strains of the music, she could tell which room was the ballroom. She couldn't go back inside now. She had to find a place to restore her composure, to repair her costume. She started trying the doors that lined the hallway and soon found one unlocked.

It was a large, deserted chamber, filled with formal furniture and grand paintings on the walls. Some kind of reception room. The walls were hung with red cloth, the floors with thick carpets. It had a glittering chandelier, unlit, but the candles in sconces on the walls and in candelabra on the mantel were burning, and there was a fire in the fireplace. Enough light to see how wanton she looked. And thank God! There was a large mirror hanging on the wall.

Dress rustling, she hurried to the mirror. A stranger stared out at her. A brazen stranger, with lips bruised and swollen-looking, sensually red. Her eyelids were half closed over eyes a sleepy shade of blue velvet, and her cheeks were flushed. Her breasts seemed to strain above her bodice in taunting challenge, begging to be touched and caressed.

A moment's inspection of this sensual stranger told her that her costume needed much repair. She fussed for what seemed a half hour, then inspected herself once more. She smoothed her tousled curls and straightened her bodice, tugging it higher, untwisted her sleeves.

She looked around the room and saw a side table filled with crystal decanters. Crossing to the table, she rapidly poured herself a large glass of brandy and, grimacing, took a gulp of the burning liquid. It was repulsive, but after two sips she found she was somewhat steadied. Then she remembered her mask. She'd left it on the terrace, crumpled beneath them no doubt, as they'd lain full-length clasped in each other's arms.

She grimaced, hot with shame at the memory. Oh, what was it about him that could make her behave that way?

Love. Meredith, when you are in love, you'll find the world is well lost and nothing, nothing else matters except being with your lover. That is why I would risk everything to have this time with him.

Vivienne's words seemed to echo in the room.

Was she in love with the stranger? Or was she only experiencing her first feelings of desire, of sensuality?

She looked around until she found a clock on the mantel. It was after midnight. Good. That meant she'd missed the unmasking and could enter the ballroom without her mask.

Another sip of the nasty brandy, another two or three deep breaths, and she still didn't feel ready. She dared not be gone much longer, or Ginny and the viscomte would think . . . would think . . .

That she'd had a tryst with a lover. The truth.

Meredith hurried down the hall toward the strains of music and stood at last in the doorway of the crowded ballroom. The crowd was glamorous, beautiful faces bared to the light, and squeals and laughter filled the room as the guests discovered the identities of their evening's flirts. Nowhere did she see a figure in black. Maybe he'd left. Pray God he had.

She made her way through the crowds, now all unmasked, until at last she caught sight of Nicholas' glittering white figure and Ginny's slender one next to him. She walked up to them, saw them turn.

"My dear Lady Vivienne! But where have you been? I have been searching simply everywhere for you!" Nicholas' sky-blue eyes looked down at her with concern, his silver-blond hair shining in the candlelight.

"Yes, Nicki has been desolate that he could not find you for so long. He swears it has ruined his evening!" Ginny put in.

"I—I took a walk in the gardens below to get some fresh air. So many people to meet, so many dances, I

186

am afraid I became a little fatigued and craved solitude," she stammered, aware of how lame her excuse sounded. They would think . . .

But Ginny wasn't listening. She was looking over Meredith's shoulder, a wide, delighted smile on her coral lips. "But I hope you are not too fatigued with meeting people, for I have a dear friend that you simply must meet now," she declared.

She saw that Nicholas was suddenly scowling, and she turned to see who was coming, wishing she could just go home and be alone.

It was he.

White hair and black clothes, he advanced on them like a merciless vision from a nightmare. Ginny spread her arms wide in a gesture of welcome, pressing her cheek to his as he bent to her embrace.

She turned. "But my dear Vivienne, here is one of your countrymen. You do not know each other?"

She could only stare, not speak.

"But we have met, briefly," he said, looking into her eyes. "I am afraid, however, that we did not exchange names at the time."

"Then it is my pleasure to make you known to each other. Lady Vivienne Winter, may I present Deron Redvers, the Duke of Raceford?"

He bowed low. "The pleasure," he said, "is all mine."

Duke! She still could only stare, not even return his curtsy. She was dimly aware of Ginny's delighted smile behind her fan, Nicholas' black glower at the both of them. But she could only think of one thing.

How could her gypsy highwayman be a duke?

He took her cold hand and bent to kiss it, then straightened. "It seems that although we do not know

187

each other, we are both peers of the realm of England. Strange that we never were introduced before . . . a lady and a duke." Then he lowered his voice and said for her ears alone, "Cut from the same cloth, My Lady."

Chapter Thirteen

"I wonder what kind of dull time poor Meredith is having in Paris." Vivienne spoke idly, lying on her stomach and toying with a daisy she was plaiting into a chain.

Below her stretched a wide green meadow, dotted with a mist of spring flowers. A small creek bubbled over round stones at the foot of the meadow, and great oaks edged the field with green privacy. The sun shone hotly down on the most perfect of pastoral scenes, and she and Gabriel had the meadow to themselves.

She lay on a wide cloth spread on the new spring grass, the remains of a picnic around her — bottle of wine, a pâté, new bread, cold chicken, and pastries. Gabriel gazed at her with adoring eyes. When she had left behind her life, she'd bequeathed all her grand clothes and jewels to Meredith, and had secretly commissioned a simple wardrobe. And, he reflected, no woman had ever looked more beautiful in simple clothes than she did.

Her long black hair was a dark loose cloud over her shoulders, twined with daisies. He'd made her the daisy chain earlier and thought it a fitting crown for her. She wore a thin white muslin dress trimmed with pale blue ribbons, and her full curves were clearly visible through its light material. No petticoats or corsets, but, by God, not that she needed them. She turned lazy violet eyes on him, half screened with long black lashes, and smiled. He caught his breath. He'd never imagined anyone could have eyes of such an alluring and unusual shade. Wait until Raceford met her. He smiled, wondering how his friend was getting on with their bet.

"So you imagine her as being bored?" he inquired, running questing fingers down her bare arm. In his estimation, if Race had taken up the challenge — and he'd never known Raceford to refuse a challenge — Meredith would be anything but bored at the moment. But he'd not told Vivienne of the bet, in a gentle revenge for her strictures against telling Race their real plans.

"How could she not be? In hateful society, going to those never-ending balls . . . and besides, even though I tried to teach her differently, Meredith is a rather timid soul. I wonder that she had the courage to pretend to be me for this adventure!"

"She didn't sound timid from your description of her," he murmured, letting his fingers move up over a lovely gleaming shoulder.

"But look at how she chose to live her life. As Aunt Phoebe's companion, I ask you! She could have done something else . . . gone off to the New World as she was always saying she would . . . married. But to live with Aunt Phoebe! Why, I'd sooner become a courtesan than stay with that old harridan!"

"If she has the looks to pretend she is you, then indeed I wonder she didn't marry. But I imagine that Ginny is showing her a good time. And in any case, all those hateful balls will be quite new to her. And she has your wardrobe to wear, and jewels. I imagine she is having the time of her life." And the devilish Lord Raceford trying to seduce her, he added silently. Well, he knew that if Race tried, he'd probably succeed. Race's prowess

190

with women was legendary. He only had to give them a single smoldering look from his dark green eyes, and they fell into his arms, ripe for the taking. He doubted a country girl like Meredith would resist Raceford for long.

Vivienne threw him an arch look through her lashes. "It's glad I am she never did marry, otherwise I wouldn't be here with you. If you don't stop looking at me like that—"

"Like what?"

"And touching me like that—"

"Like this?"

"Then I will have to—"

"What is it you will have to do?"

Her eyes melted at the sight of him, all golden strength in the golden sunlight, her own lazy lion, her archangel lover. "Oh, Gabriel, I love you so much!" she breathed, her eyes the color of the violets in the fields.

"And I," his voice was husky, "love you more than I could ever have imagined, my own Vivienne."

For a breathless, wild moment, the two lovers gazed into each other's eyes, each lost in the wonder that their feelings grew more strong with each day they spent in each other's company, with each night they spent in each other's arms.

Then Vivienne rose with a slanting smile down at her lover and dared him, "Catch me if you can!"

She was gone in a froth of white, a barefoot goddess running across a spring meadow for the creek. He caught her when she was ankle-deep in the clear, cool water, so soothing after the hot sun and their hot looks.

He swept her up in arms too strong for her to resist and held her laughing against him for a long moment. Then his eyes gleamed wickedly down at her. "And now, for running away, my love, I must punish you."

"Gabriel!" she cried, as he waded thigh-deep into the sparkling water . . . and dropped her.

She came up, sputtering and laughing, and saw that he was standing laughing down at her. So she dove under and grasped his ankles, knocking him off balance so that he, too, was dunked in the river. Then she surfaced into a sparkling sunlit world and swam away from him while he cursed, laughing, and tried to regain his footing.

When she reached the shallows, she stood, and the sight of her stopped him in his pursuit of her. The thin, wet gown was plastered to her lush curves, transparent enough so that he could see the pink thrust of her nipples, the indentation of her abdomen, the dark triangle at the base of her legs. . . .

"My God . . . Vivienne," he breathed, taking in this dripping young vision who smiled at him so beguilingly.

Then he rose and waded toward her, his own dark pants and white shirt clearly showing every golden muscle, and their eyes locked. This time, she did not run.

When he reached her, he bent his head to kiss her with lips as hot and wet as her own. His hands ran over her slippery curves, and she stood on tiptoe, her arms around his neck, pressing herself tautly against him. She ran her tongue over the clean line of his jaw, then circled his ear with it while her questing hands ran down his belly and found his erect maleness, full with need of her.

"Vivienne . . . I love you," he rasped and, pulling her down, lay her on the soft sand of the river, while the clear shallow water rippled around them and over their flushed skin. He was kissing her as he pulled her dress off, then reveling in the sight of her wet nakedness, his hands exploring every curving inch of her, worshiping her. She was busy herself unbuttoning his shirt, undoing

192

his trousers, and soon their skin, caressed by the river, was pressed together with no barriers.

He lowered his head until he had her nipple in his mouth, and he sucked and licked until she was moaning with need. Her fingers, long used to loving him, were running down his stomach in tickling gestures, until they found his eager manhood and stroked its throbbing length. And his own fingers were parting her legs, gently touching her in the spots he knew would make her ache with need for him, probing the place that would soon receive him.

She lay on her back as he reared over her, feeling the water running over her skin as another caress, wondering why every time with him was hotter and wilder than the last. It was as if their passion were a fire that burned the brighter the more they fed it. She cried out as he slowly slid his length inside her, teasing her by penetrating her so slowly until she thought she could stand no more.

And as she brought her hips up in an arch to meet his, he thrust hard and filled her completely, and soon they were lost in a rhythm as old as time. With every thrust, she felt a building of waves of pleasure, and he was gasping for breath and shuddering with ecstasy the way she was.

At last she felt him explode inside her, just as her own pleasure was pushed over the crest of a peak. They cried out together in purest passion as they felt their release, then gently they rocked together, slowing, until at last their hearts could beat normally again, until they slowly felt all the hot passion in their veins being replaced by warm love.

He carried her up on the bank and wrapped her in his arms, and they lay in the sun and let its hot rays dry them. "I love you, Vivienne. I love you so much it hurts me to think of ever letting you leave my side again."

Above them, the sky was a limitless blue. Larks twittered and sang as they fell, and the only other sounds were their breathing and the slight whisper of leaves in the breeze. It was as if they were together in a new world first created for them alone.

Vivienne turned a face toward him so glowing, so relaxed, and so filled with adoring love that none of her London friends would have known her. "Oh, Gabriel, I love you, too. More than I can even believe. You are the heart of my life . . . my reason for living. I love you."

And then an impish twinkle came into her blue eyes, and she reached out a finger to trace his mouth. Seeing the leap of passion in his eyes, she laughed, "Again . . . so soon? But I am ready for you too, my love. Imagine! Whatever it is Meredith is doing in Paris, I would wager it isn't anything like this!"

And their lips came together in a passionate kiss, which bound them to one another and sealed their love.

Chapter Fourteen

The morning sunlight streamed into the comtesse's breakfast room, and Meredith reached for her cup of coffee, wondering if it would help her aching head. She was alone, having dismissed the waiting servants, alone with her thoughts.

What new disaster would this day bring?

She'd already been kidnapped, rescued, and then behaved like a wanton with a peer of the English realm! Oh, if this was how she was going to enact her charade as Vivienne, her cousin would be lucky if her name wasn't a byword in the streets by the time Meredith was through!

She giggled.

She couldn't help it. Suddenly, she wondered what Vivienne would say if she knew all the things she'd already done in her name. Somehow, Meredith decided her own tenure as Vivienne had probably been more exciting than the real lady's life ever was.

But what about the wanton way she had behaved last night? His touch had made her lose her senses, she had become a different person. It was if she'd dreamed the whole thing. The Meredith who lived in Henley would never have done such a thing, giving herself to a man . . . and in near-public! What had come over her?

A pair of incredible green eyes, that was what. For a few moments, she felt a thrill pass over her as she thought about him. His emerald eyes under dark brows, his bronzed, smooth skin that was fascinating to touch, his black hair, his wide and firm mouth that did such astonishing things to her!

She shivered as she recalled the masterful way he'd taken her in his arms and kissed her. The way he'd lowered his mouth to her neck, then let his lips slide lower to her breasts. Until her breasts were naked beneath the flame of his lips. How strong his hands had felt . . . Most of all, she remembered the wonderful weight of him on top of her, pressed firmly between her legs, rocking her in the fiery rhythm of love. The fireworks exploding outside had been no more thrilling than the ones exploding between them.

How could such a wickedly intimate thing feel so very right? And then she remembered his words. He'd claimed her for his own. She'd been powerless at hearing those words. Whether or not he understood the truth of them, he had claimed her—body and soul—and long before last night.

Deron Redvers was his name. The Duke of Raceford. Good heavens, he was a duke! And she a nobody. Oh, how this charade was complicating matters!

"You are up early!"

Meredith looked up to find Genvieve coming in through the door, looking fresh and pretty in a morning-dress of dusky rose open over a pale green petticoat. She had a lace cap over her curls trimmed with green ribbons and tiny velvet rosebuds, and she looked wide awake. Not like she'd been at a ball until the small hours last night. Ginny sat down and poured herself a cup of coffee from the silver service, then glanced out the window where the morning sun was shining on her formal flower gardens.

A statue of Poseidon surrounded by a bevy of mermaids glinted in the sunlight, the bronze turning green with age. Around the statue, a fountain plashed, and ranks of flame-colored tiger lilies bloomed. A gardener was busy cutting bright snapdragons and delphiniums and placing them in a basket, for every day the abundant blooms inside the house were changed. Graveled paths meandered past shaped hedges and other groups of naked marble statues. A tiny graceful bridge crossed a stream that widened into a small lake, with an island and a Pagoda-shaped pavilion in the center. Far in the distance were the green hedge walls of the maze, in which amorous guests loved to lose themselves.

Meredith sighed. The garden looked so invitingly peaceful . . . and now that Raceford was in Paris, she doubted she would have much peace any longer.

Ginny turned to survey Meredith through acute sherry-colored eyes. "And so . . . last night. You were speechless when I introduced Lord Raceford to you. Pleading you felt faint and had to go. How disappointed Nicki was! But Deron said you'd met before. Obviously, this meeting upset you? You went white as a ghost when he kissed your hand."

Meredith gulped her coffee. She couldn't admit to Ginny what had taken place last night and settled on the lesser shock of the evening. "If I looked upset, there was good reason. It is because until you spoke, I believed Lord Raccford to be a gypsy."

Ginny's brows lifted. "A gypsy? He is dark, I will admit, but —"

"A gypsy who had kidnapped me."

Ginny set down her cup with a small squeal and

clasped her hands together. "It was *he?!*"

Meredith nodded grimly. "It was he who held up my coach, pretending to be a highwayman. But *why* is what I cannot imagine."

"But, *cherie,* this is most exciting!" When Meredith gave her a dry look, the comtesse went on irrepressibly, "But how famous! Deron to abduct you, Nicki to rescue you! Oh, it must have been a jest, a wager, for they know each other."

"They *know* each other?" Meredith was more bewildered than ever, remembering Nicki's cold fury at the roadside when he'd faced Lord Raceford . . . surely not acted! He'd looked ready to put a bullet through his heart. Then all at once she was angry.

"Then I was the target of this little . . . jest? I suppose they found it hilarious to frighten me, then make me believe Nicholas had come to my rescue! But I find it far from funny indeed."

"But, *cherie* . . . you must not take it like that. They were both wild to meet you. Here in France, we'd heard so much of your beauty. And men!" The comtesse gave a little shrug of her pretty shoulders, made a moue. "Who knows why they make these wild wagers among themselves. But I would hazard on Nicki's part, it was because he wanted to gain your favor. By being your gallant rescuer, perhaps he hoped to win your heart!"

"And now that you have told me the truth, do you think that endears him to me?" Meredith asked coldly.

The comtesse smiled at her. "But if I had two such men going to such lengths to win my favors, *cherie,* I would not be insulted. I would be flattered. But in any case, it is not Meredith who needs to feel the insult. It was Vivienne who was the target of their play. Meredith was merely taken along for the ride, so to speak."

Meredith relented. "True. So I suppose I should encourage them next to a duel for my favors?"

Ginny giggled. "No . . . but I think you should spend the next week choosing one of them over the other. They are both as handsome as gods, and I have decided, Meredith, that what you need is a lover. After all, it is only once you will be in Paris . . . not even as yourself, but as another. The only name you can blacken is hers. And Vivienne tells me you have led, up until now, the most boring of lives. No young men, no *affaires*. Well, this is your chance! You have only to choose which one of them appeals to you more." Ginny smiled to herself. She'd seen the look that Meredith had given Raceford last night and did not doubt which of the men the girl would choose. Otherwise, she'd never have suggested such a thing.

Meredith shifted her shoulders uncomfortably and gave voice to the one thing that troubled her about the events of last night. "But shouldn't a woman be pure until she is married?"

"Pah! And so who is it you would be saving yourself for?"

A vision of Augustus Sett rose before Meredith's eyes.

Her expression was not lost on the comtesse. "There! You see? The only man who might marry you is beneath your notice! While here, two of the handsomest men in the civilized world are vying for your favors. Would it be so hard for you to love one of them? I am not speaking, of course, of wantonly giving yourself away, but of love. It comes easier than you think and is no sin."

Easier than she thought. Meredith blushed as she recalled the way she'd wrapped her legs around Raceford last night, running one high heel slowly down a

199

muscled calf . . . the way his mouth had felt on her bared breasts. . . .

The comtesse also saw the blush. "So . . . perhaps Deron has already begun to make you see how easy it would be with the right man?"

"I don't know." Meredith was confused. All her life, she'd been taught these feelings were wrong. But here was Ginny, an experienced woman, telling her they were right. And hadn't it felt right last night? "Have you ever been in love, Ginny?"

Ginny's eyes grew misty, her voice soft. "Oh, yes. Madly and passionately in love. There is one man that I live and breathe for. He is like the sun to me. I adore him."

"And you — you have been intimate with him?" Meredith asked shyly.

Ginny laughed. "No, as of yet I have not been intimate with him."

"Why not?" Meredith was surprised, and at the same time pleased to be having such a frank conversation with another woman. "Surely if you love him —"

"It is just that the time is not yet right. It will be, and then with great joy I shall take him to my bed. But he is a rake, you understand. And I don't wish to be just another conquest for him to tire of in a few short months. I want to wait until he wants me as badly as I want him. Until he loves me. Sometimes, it is not good to give in too soon with a certain type of man."

Ginny's words sent a chill up Meredith's spine. A certain type of man! And was Raceford that type? Could it be that he had merely wanted to bed her . . . that she was "just another conquest"? But Meredith sighed. It didn't matter what *his* intentions were. Such was his power over her once he had her in his arms, that she knew she'd never be able to deny him again if they ever found themselves alone.

"So, it is not enough to love the man. He must love you, too?" she asked, looking at Ginny.

"Pooh . . . love! I have been married, I have had lovers. I have the experience to judge when it is right to hold back, when it is right to surrender. But you! How can you judge when you have no experience . . . when nothing has ever happened . . . when you have not allowed any man to touch you?"

Ginny was right. She was so inexperienced and had already perhaps made a dire mistake. *Caution, Meredith, from now on you will move forward with caution,* she told herself.

"Meredith my darling," said Ginny, "you can learn these things easily, but do not be afraid to let yourself experience them. You will know when the time is right. You will feel it in your heart. And it is time for you to let yourself live life."

"Damn Deron Redvers to hell!" Nicholas St. Antoine savagely downed his brandy and set the glass on the table with a bang.

A tinkling laugh was his answer. The Comtesse d'Anguillame, looking a delicious confection in copper-colored satin with dark green ribbons, regarded him across her reception room. It was early evening and they were alone. She thought that with a scowl he looked most astonishingly virile, and Ginny decided she ought to make him lose his temper more frequently. Tonight he wore black, an unusual change, for generally he attired himself in pastels that sparkled with cloth of gold and silver threads. But the black became him, making him look more startlingly blond, setting off the white lace and diamonds at his throat.

"But what right does he have to try to cut me out?" he demanded angrily.

"The lady does not belong to you yet, Nicki, my darling."

"But he only agreed to help me! Then to spend the night with her in some farmhouse, make advances to her, and then to reveal to her who he really is! She's bound to figure out the rescue was staged!"

"Don't worry, she knows."

"She knows!" He raked distracted fingers through his silver-blond hair.

"I told her." The comtesse's voice was matter-of-fact.

"You told her! Ginny, I warn you—" His dark brows came together in a scowl.

"Don't upset yourself, *mon cher.* As you said, she was bound to figure it out once Raceford revealed he was no highwayman. I thought it would be better for her to hear it from your lips than from his."

"But what shall I tell her?"

Ginny laughed. "Really, Nicki, do you find it so impossible to manage your own *affaires?* Tell her that you heard Raceford make a wager to kidnap her. And that then you decided to rescue her from him."

"But what if he tells her the truth?"

"And do you think she will believe him?"

He crossed the room to stand over her, then gave a dispirited sigh and sat beside her on the couch. "Then I suppose I must seduce her after all. A woman always believes the man who beds her. And I'd better do it before he does. Did you see the way he kissed her hand?"

Ginny gave him a light tap with her fan. "I told you before, imbecile, that is not the way to win her heart! Any number of men try to bed her. You must try to love her. Raceford will, of course, attempt to get her into his bed. Beside such crude tactics, your seduction will be a lover's dance. You must not bed her until she begs you to, and then only succumb because your love for her will not allow you to resist. I tell you, I am a woman, and I know what moves women's hearts."

For a moment, he looked at her, and she thought what a perfectly gorgeous fallen angel he was. Then he said softly, "I know you are a woman, Ginny."

He let his gaze roam over her flame-colored hair, her tip-tilted eyes, the perfect mouth with its black patch at one corner. She glittered in the firelight, sophisticated, desirable.

"I tire of pursuing this black-haired wench, in any case. When compared to you . . . Ginny, if I did not need the money and if I thought you would relent . . . Money is such a tiresome thing. I feel like a tradesman, pursuing it. And to be forced to marry merely for money seems obscene!"

A slim hand on his chest stopped him from leaning toward her. "But I do not relent, my darling Nicki. You know I have a lover. And to call Lady Vivienne a wench! . . . Besides, there are many men who would gladly trade places with you, to have the prospect of marrying such a beautiful and amiable woman."

"All right, then, she is beautiful. But she doesn't have hair the color of fire and skin as white as snow."

"Nicki, you are incorrigible. You always want what is out of reach. I shudder to think how quickly you would tire of a conquest once you'd made it. I believe the chase is all to you."

"Yes . . . well, the chase is amusing, I will admit. But that does not mean I am doomed to be forever fickle. It is just so challenging to try to think of how you will make love to a woman, what words will melt her, make her desire you. These things must be carefully planned. They are not the work of impulse."

"So . . . in Lady Vivienne's case, you must have done some planning. Tell me how you plan to make love to her. What you will say?"

"Don't you ever tire of hearing of my conquests, Ginny?"

She looked at him through lowered lashes. "Never, Nicki. It allows me to imagine how it would be. Oh, you are a dangerous man. One much better for me to hold at arm's length. But tell me, what will you say to her?"

For a moment, his eyes caressed her, and when he spoke, his words sent a shiver down her spine.

"I will say, 'I have been hoping for this chance to be alone with you. I know it is too soon for me to tell you the effect you have on my heart. But I cannot stop myself from speaking, no more than I can stop myself from staring at you. I believe it is your eyes; they are eyes that I could easily drown in. I have never seen eyes that glorious shade of amber before. . . .' "

Chapter Fifteen

" . . . I cannot stop myself from speaking, no more than I can stop myself from staring at you. I believe it is your eyes; they are eyes that I could easily drown in. I have never seen eyes that glorious shade of blue before. . . ."

Meredith tightened her gloves on the reins of the small open cabriolet she was driving and slowed the gray horse to a walk. She couldn't concentrate on driving with the things Nicholas St. Antoine was saying in her ear.

She turned to face him and saw that his sky-blue eyes were adoring, beseeching. "Viscomte, please. I barely know you. . . ."

"I know. I know it is far too soon for me to make my feelings known, and I do not ask that you answer me in any way. That would be too much to hope for, and I know a lady like yourself is not so easy to win merely by words. All I ask is that you let me treat you with the greatest possible respect. That you allow me to be your friend. I apologize for speaking so precipitately. Will you — can you — forgive me?"

He was absolutely impossible to resist, Meredith thought. And he was certainly handsome. The sunlight made a glinting silver halo of his hair, and he was resplendent today in a suit of ice-lavender silk and white lace. White stockings molded his powerful calves, and there were silver buckles on his high-heeled shoes. He said he wanted to treat her with respect, to be her friend. Was there anything wrong with that? It was certainly more comfortable than the ways of that black-haired devil.

"But of course, I forgive you, Viscomte. I hope we shall be friends, for I have too few of them in Paris."

He laughed, a deep and comfortable sound. "But I predict that soon many will be storming your doors protesting friendship. Now that I have won your forgiveness so easily for baring my heart to you, I must beg it in advance on another matter."

Meredith sat up straighter, touching her wide straw hat covered with red roses, wondering what it was he meant. They were rolling down the cobblestoned Place de la Concorde, and ahead were the spreading, statue-haunted gardens of the Tuileries. Above, chestnut trees spread their new-green leaves, and all Paris seemed to be rejoicing on this perfect May afternoon. Had there ever been a lovelier city? she wondered. She would never tire of seeing its sights.

"I have a confession to make to you."

Curious, Meredith stole a glance at his handsome profile. "I am sure on our short acquaintance, you can have nothing to confess," she protested.

"But I do. It has been a dramatic acquaintance, has it not, Lady Vivienne? The night I rescued you . . . I could scarcely believe in your beauty when you first stepped into my sight. But I did not tell you everything. I already knew the highwayman. Raceford was a friend of mine, damn his black heart!"

"You knew him?"

"Yes . . . and all Paris had been talking of your

visit. You were reputed to be so beautiful. Well, Raceford swore to some of us one night that he would be the first to . . . make a conquest of you. We scoffed at him, but he said he would get a pair of your earrings to prove it."

Her earrings! This was sounding too much like the tale Raceford had told her himself!

"Well, when Raceford and I were alone, I asked him how he expected to accomplish your seduction so quickly. After all, you would be staying with the comtesse, well chaperoned. He would never get you alone, I pointed out. 'I know,' he said, smiling at me. 'So I plan to waylay her before she ever gets to Paris. And if she will not succumb to my charms, then I will have the earrings anyway.' You can imagine that I was horrified, but I hid my feelings and asked him when he planned to stop your coach. He named the night . . . but when I found you, I learned also that he'd lied. He'd stopped your coach a day earlier, I would guess to prevent me from interfering if I had such designs. Well, when I saw you—when I was struck to the heart by your eyes—I was furious. I almost shot him on the spot. And if you hadn't said you were unharmed—"

"Yes," Meredith managed. It all fell into place! His manufactured tale about the earrings, Nicholas' fury when he saw Raceford. He'd been telling her half-truths all along.

"But that's why I was so dismayed when I saw you give him your earrings, Lady Vivienne. I know you only meant it as thanks to a bandit you believed had returned your jewels and money, but now—" He shook his head. "He will doubtless show them all around town, and everyone will believe you gave them to him for another reason. If you have jewelry that matches them, I would not wear it. And it would not do to be seen too much in his company. If you are always with me, in the end, no one may believe him."

The rogue! she thought furiously. Meaning to parade her earrings all over town as an exhibit of her lost virtue!

"I will gladly spend time in your company, Viscomte . . . and avoid his," she said firmly. "I am grateful to you for telling me this. Ginny . . . the comtesse . . . told me already that you knew each other, and so I thought you were in on the whole escapade. But this greatly relieves my mind."

"Thought I was in on it!" he said indignantly. "Nothing would induce me to bring shame to your person. As I have already told you, I wish only to be your friend. And perhaps someday, when I have earned it, something dearer to your heart."

Meredith turned the horses, heading back toward Ginny's residence. She placed a gloved hand lightly on his arm, and for a moment, he covered it with his own. His hand was warm through the fabric, and she was conscious of the muscles of his shoulders and thighs, so close to her own.

Her response startled her. Was she a wanton, to be drawn to two men? But she examined her feelings, compared her responses. Though Nicholas did make her heart beat faster, he didn't cause the headlong racing of her pulses that Deron did. And all the time he held her hand and looked into her eyes, she was still herself. A little giddy and light-headed perhaps, but still Meredith, with the world still firmly in place around her. Oh, was she so lost that when a man treated her with respect, she kept her head, but let one ravish her like she was a slave-maiden he'd bought and paid for, and she lost all sense of propriety?

"Thank you, Viscomte," she murmured, then extracted her hand from underneath his.

"There is no need to thank me. But if there were one thanks I desire, it would be to ask a favor of you."

She stole another glance at him. "Name it."

"It would be to call you by your first name . . . and to hear you call me by mine."

She considered. Then she remembered Ginny telling her it was time to live life. This man had promised to respect her and was courting her as gently as if she were precious spun glass. Perhaps a touch of intimacy wouldn't hurt. And besides, it was Vivienne who was letting him be so familiar, not Meredith.

She bestowed a dazzling smile on him. "Yes . . . you may call me Vivienne."

He took her gloved hand and bent his head to kiss it, and she felt his lips burning her even through the fabric. "Vivienne," he said softly, then raised his head, keeping possession of her hand.

"I want to hear you say it. I want to watch your lips when they say my name."

She turned her head and looked full at him, then slowly let her mouth form his name. "Nicholas." She paused, then breathed, "Nicki."

"Never has my name sounded so sweet."

They drove on in silence for a time, until a crowd began to block their road ahead.

"Pull the cabriolet over here!" he shouted suddenly, waving to the side of the avenue. "There is something you must see!"

She guided the horses to a halt at the side of the street and looked to where the viscomte was pointing. In the center of a large park, a huge crowd had gathered around the strangest sight Meredith had ever seen.

"What is it?" she asked Nicholas incredulously. But

instead of an answer, he grabbed her hand and nearly dragged her out of the cabriolet, racing with her to join the throng of Parisiennes. He stopped at a street vendor long enough to buy them both ices, then pressed on, pushing his way to the front of the crowd with Meredith in tow.

She squeezed between Nicholas and a rather stout man who gave her a scowl at being elbowed. She asked his pardon sheepishly, then looked up. From the center of the crowd rose a circular platform flung with fluttering silk, and from this was suspended a huge balloon, larger than an elephant, she imagined. The balloon was of the brightest blue silk, festooned around its doorknob shape with pink velvet and gold tassels. A large scrolled *M* in gold braid was stitched to its silk sides, and it bobbed from side to side in the light breeze that blew across the park. The balloon floated above a gondola that was tethered to the platform, and inside the basket were a cock, a goat, and a squawking duck. A man, gaily dressed for the occasion, stood beside the balloon, gesturing widely to the crowd, making a speech.

"Montgolfier and his balloon," Nicholas said, taking a lick of his ice. "I saw it last year at Versailles. And what a sight it is! Just wait until they release it. It will fly above the city like a bird!"

Meredith looked up again, anticipating the event. She listened to Montgolfier, who was now challenging anyone in the crowd to take a ride in his balloon. Men ribbed each other, daring one another to take the challenge. But there were no takers, and Meredith could hardly blame them. The gondola was barely large enough for the animals, let alone a man, and to think this invention could float through the air!

Nicholas teased her. "What? No sense of adventure,

Lady Vivienne? To be the first to see the city from the air?"

She laughed, shaking her head. "No thank you. But what about you? Or are you too frightened?"

"Perhaps I will," he said, testing the challenge, and made as if he would mount the platform. Then he stopped, hands on his hips, a look of mock fear on his face. "You had better stop me or I will think you do not care for my safety."

Meredith pulled him back, giggling. "Don't be ridiculous, Viscomte. If you go off in this contraption, there will be no one to show me the way back home," she teased. "And then I will be lost in the city."

He feigned a hurt look. "So now I know. You care only for yourself and how you will get back to Ginny's, and nothing for me. You women are so very cruel."

She looped her arm through his and gave it a friendly squeeze. "Of course, if you were gone, there would be no one to amuse me, so I must protect my interests."

"Flirt," he said, wrinkling his nose at her, and then he turned to watch the spectacle.

Montgolfier was talking to the crowd again, then moved to the tethers that held the balloon in place. With a flourish, he raised a knife in one hand, displaying it to the crowd, then cut the ropes.

Suddenly, there was a loud hiss and a huge puff of smoke. Meredith uttered a cry of alarm and backed away from the platform along with the others. Then she watched with delight as the balloon lifted, swaying to one side, its silky sides billowing and fluttering, the fragile gondola and its cargo dragging along behind it. Finally, the balloon righted itself and began to rise, slowly, a steady hissing and more smoke belching from over the gondola. A cheer rose from the gathering as the monstrosity floated off across the park, an entourage of children running after it on the ground. It was the most amazing sight she'd ever seen, and she almost wished she had volunteered for the flight. How wonderful to fly like a bird above Paris! It was something she would be long in forgetting.

Nicholas drew her attention away from the disappearing balloon. He was dabbing at a bit of ice at the corner of her mouth. He looked into her eyes and smiled warmly.

"You are so beautiful with wonder in your eyes and a smile on your lips, Lady Vivienne. I should think to bring you to such events more often," Nicholas murmured, pocketing his handkerchief.

She smiled in return. "You are a very special friend, Viscomte. I shall never forget you or this afternoon," she said with genuine feeling, then realized the importance of what she'd just said. Nicholas was her friend, and though he was handsome enough to send thrills through her, she could think of him in no other way.

Then Nicholas' eyes were alight with new mischief. "But the afternoon has just started. And there is far more to see. Who knows what magic we can find. Come!"

And together they ran, laughing, back to the cabriolet and climbed in.

"Viscomte! Oh, Viscomte!"

They turned from their mutual absorption in each other to see a small carriage stopped near theirs, its elderly occupant hailing them vigorously. Meredith's heart sank. It was the Marchioness of Waterbury!

Since the night at Versailles, she'd not seen the marchioness again, doubtless because the old woman didn't go out into society as much as a younger crowd did. But she'd lived with the dread of knowing that an

212

acquaintance of Vivienne's was in Paris, and that at any moment, the game could be up. Every time she'd entered a room or a theater, she'd paused in the shadows and scanned the crowd for the old woman. And now the worst had happened. She was trapped in a coach at Nicholas' side, with nowhere to escape.

Maybe her looks were close enough to Vivienne's to pass, especially if the woman's old eyesight was poor?

But the marchioness' first words dispelled this hope.

"Viscomte! I am glad to see you. I still have not been able to see Lady Vivienne anywhere. Did you give her my message that I was in town? I'd expected her to call on me, as I do not get out much."

Nicki's face registered astonishment. He glanced at Meredith, who suddenly had an inspiration. "But, Marchioness, this is—"

"Meredith Westin," Meredith broke in smoothly. "How charming to meet you, Marchioness."

The look Nicki was now giving her was even more astonished than the one a moment earlier. "Vivienne—"

The marchioness gave Meredith a regal inclination of the head. "So nice to meet you, Miss Westin. Now, Viscomte, you tell that child, Vivienne, that if she does not call on me, I shall be most upset. I am at home on Tuesday afternoons." And with another majestic nod of her plumed bonnet, the marchioness signaled her driver to start the carriage.

Meredith let out a sigh of relief and found Nicki regarding her quizzically.

"Meredith Westin?" he questioned.

"Nicholas, the woman is the most dreadful social climber! I have never met her, but I've been warned about her! One meeting and she'll be clinging to my skirts for the rest of my time in Paris. You marked that she did not even know who I was. And she had the gall to pretend to be an intimate friend of mine!"

Nicki still looked baffled. "A marchioness, a social climber? I can hardly credit it. Still, you are right. She did not know who you were. Ah well, my dear Vivienne, I'll do my best to keep you out of her way."

As they drove on, Meredith wondered if she should send word to Vivienne to come to Paris. But after further consideration, it hardly seemed necessary. She'd handled the situation. If she saw the woman, she'd think she was Meredith Westin, not Vivienne Winter. And as for her Tuesdays at home, perhaps if Vivienne were rude enough never to come, the marchioness would give up on her.

Another pair of eyes watched the straw hat festooned with red roses as the coach started down the avenue again. Raceford sat astride his great stallion. He'd been following them all day, not even sure himself why he was doing such a thing. He'd come over to the palais hoping to be able to call on her and had arrived only in time to see her driving off with Nicki. And instead of leaving, he'd ridden after them.

It was making his blood boil to see them together. She wore a scarlet riding habit with a tight jacket, and with those black curls, she looked wonderful in red. There were roses in her cheeks to rival those of her hat, and her lips were as red as her jacket. He'd bet that she smelled as sweet as any rose, thinking of the way the memory of her fragrance had haunted him. When Nicki covered her hand with his, he'd been furiously jealous. But he was relieved to see that at least they were exchanging no kisses. They were behaving with perfect propriety.

As they drove into an area of the city thronged by street vendors, he had a sudden inspiration. He spurred his horse down a side street ahead of their carriage, past coopers and tinsmiths, milk sellers and oyster vendors, to a flower stall. There, he leaped off his horse and pulled out his money.

"Four dozen red roses," he said. The fat man behind the stall was delighted and hastened to gather up the extravagant bouquet. Raceford took a piece of paper from his pocket and scrawled a note. "Put this with it — and see that coach driving toward us? Deliver these flowers and this note to the woman in the hat with the red roses on it."

"Yes, sir!" cried the vendor, scrambling to do his bidding.

He retreated across the street and stopped his horse in the shadow of a gateway's arch. He watched as the coach came down the road at a walking pace and the fat man entered the street, almost dwarfed by the brilliant bouquet, waving at the coach. He watched as the vendor presented the bouquet to Vivienne, as she found the note and read it. Then she asked the man a question, and he pointed across the street to where Raceford sat his stallion.

He smiled at her and raised a hand.

She looked startled. Nicki was scowling blackly. At last she bent her head to the roses and breathed in their scent. Then she gave him a tiny nod as Nicki started the coach.

Meredith didn't dare to look back to where Raceford was, but she tucked the note inside her sleeve, to Nicki's evident anger. It had read: "More beautiful than a rose, my wild lady Angel, I miss you every moment. Have mercy on me and let me see you. R."

"He had the gall to send you flowers when you were with me!" Nicki said.

"Oh, Nicki . . . don't be angry. It's only flowers.

215

You sent me those lovely lilies and violets and white roses only yesterday."

"And what did the note say?"

"That, my dear, is none of your business. But you know I have been spending all my time with you — and not with Raceford."

At that, he brightened, and soon they were laughing together again as they drove toward home.

They reached the great wide avenue before the comtesse's residence, and she turned the cabriolet up toward the sweeping drive. As she halted the horse and a liveried groom ran down to take its head, he was leaping from the seat beside her to stand beneath her on the ground.

"Allow me, my Vivienne, to help you alight," he said, smiling up at her.

"I am not 'your Vivienne' yet," she reproved him lightly. "My aunt always told me that allowing a man to use your first name would encourage him to take liberties, and I see she was right."

"I will take no liberties you do not grant me," he said, handing her down. "Vivienne?"

She looked up at him and laughed. "You do amuse me, Nicki. I am so glad you came to my rescue!"

"And tonight . . . you will allow me to escort you to the opera?"

"I will."

"Then I shall count the minutes until then."

She turned to go, but her name from behind her made her turn. "Vivienne?"

"What is it?"

"Say it just once more. Say my name."

She smiled brilliantly at him, then said it. "Nicki."

And she was rewarded by seeing him touch his fingers to his wicked lips and kiss them as if he were

216

catching her words as they floated through the air toward him.

Laughing, Meredith ran up the steps. Nicki, her golden angel.

So different from a certain black-haired devil!

Chapter Sixteen

Inside the house, Raceford stood at the tall pier windows and watched the woman beneath, her arms filled with red roses, select a bloom and affix it to Nicholas' lapel. Then she climbed down and blew a kiss to Nicholas before turning to run inside. With a scowl, he turned from the window and addressed the comtesse.

He'd ridden there from the streets, having giving up following her, with half a mind to demand to see her when she returned home. But Ginny had been there, and he decided it was high time he sought her advice.

"Damn it, Ginny, she's with him every afternoon and every evening."

"Well, my friend, what are you going to do about it?"

"I don't know. She won't see me when I call. What do you suggest? Could you go and get her — not tell her I am here — and then leave the two of us alone? For I must see her alone!"

Ginny rolled her eyes. "Why are men always coming to me to ask how they should pursue their love affairs? It is exasperating!"

He grinned. "I know. If we had any sense, we'd be pursuing you instead."

"Well, that is perfectly true, Raceford. It is rather insulting to be treated as a sister."

"Ginny, you know you are in love with Joffrey."

"Joffrey? Not at all. He merely amuses me."

"Well, in any case, you must tell me how to go on with Vivienne. I'm wild to see her alone. In fact, I'm ready to cause a scandal by kidnapping her again if I can't think of anything else."

"Sit down. Your pacing unnerves me. You are altogether too much like a panther. Let me think of what leverage you can use to cause her to relent."

She watched as Raceford sat down on a sofa, stretching his long legs out in front of him. If she hadn't seen Nicki first, she thought, she'd soon make this one notice her. He was indeed wonderful to look at and had an aura of masculine arrogance that was breathtaking. And that black hair. It made her weak to look at him. He was rather like a savage, she thought, and wondered if his kisses would be as savage as his looks. For a moment she regretted that she would not likely have the chance to kiss him, not when he was in love with Vivienne and she with Nicki. "Hmmm." She tapped a finger on her cheek, pretending to consider. "I do know that, since she is married and has her husband to worry about, she is very protective of her good name. In fact, she left England precisely because there were rumors flying about her and some young man."

Gabriel, Raceford thought, and felt his stomach tighten. Ever since the night of the ball, when he'd taken her in his arms and kissed her, felt her body under his, yielding to him, he'd been doing only one kind of thinking. Thinking with his body. Remembering how silken her skin felt under his mouth, how perfect her breasts were, how abandoned a lover she'd been. And he'd been mad to touch her again.

He'd nearly forgotten why he'd come here in the first place.

Twenty golden guineas, a wager because she'd broken Gabriel's heart. And he'd promised to break her heart in return.

Yes, Gabriel. It burned inside to think that Gabriel had touched that same skin, kissed that sweet mouth—in fact, had done more. Had actually made love to her, as Raceford had done. He'd seen her naked, entered her, rode with her until he'd reached the same ecstasy Raceford knew. In fact, no other woman had him thinking so constantly of making love. But the thought that she'd given herself to Gabriel was intolerable. And to how many others? Was he mad to forget that she'd made love to his best friend and probably to others as well?

No matter how sweet her flesh was, it was well used.

So now he had to get a grip on himself and get back to playing the game. And to play the game, he'd damned well have to see her alone. Otherwise, Nicholas was going to cut him out.

"Her good name? So you think that it's so important to her to protect her reputation?"

"That I do. For a young woman as beautiful as Vivienne, the talk follows her whether she does anything or not. She has to be very careful."

"So if I act as if I know something that would damage her—"

"Doubtless she would see you. Well, I have solved your problem, Raceford. And now the afternoon stretches ahead of us. What do you suggest we do with it?"

He smiled wickedly at her. "Since you say you are not in love with Joffrey, perhaps we could devise some amusement."

He noted the start of color in her cheeks and hoped she'd take him up on his invitation. For he was getting all too entangled with a certain treacherous lady. What he needed was something to divert him, and Ginny would certainly be a delicious diversion.

She lowered her lashes in confusion. "Why, Lord Raceford. You surprise me. I thought you had eyes only for Vivienne."

"There is nothing wrong with my eyes. They are capable of seeing more than one woman at a time."

"It would be most . . . enjoyable my Lord, to dally with you as you suggest. But alas, I am a virtuous woman. And not inclined to become involved with a man who spends all his time devising ways to get another woman into bed."

He stood and came across to her, lifting her chin with a finger. She let her eyes raise only as far as his mouth and saw how firm it was, how sensually shaped. When that mouth began to descend toward hers, she lifted her eyes to his and breathed, "No."

His lips stopped only a fraction of an inch from hers. They were slightly parted, as were hers. She felt an electric thrill go through her as their eyes remained locked.

"You are sure?" he murmured, letting the finger under her chin trace slowly down her neck, across the hollow of her throat, and down her chest to the valley between her breasts.

"I am sure that once started, we would never stop, and that would not be prudent, Raceford," she breathed.

"Most wise of you, assuredly. Still, should you change you mind—?"

"I know where to find you, Lord Raceford."

He moved away from her then, and as she escorted him from the room, she wondered why she had refused him, when just a few moments before she'd been wondering if his kisses were savage and wild. Ah, Nicki, she thought, I love you beyond reason, when for your sake I refuse the handsomest man in France besides you!

Raceford was having similar thoughts. As he left her rooms, he sighed inwardly. It would have been no use in any case, he realized. Yes, Ginny was beautiful and desirable. For a moment, he'd been flooded with heat and the desire to kiss her. But just for a moment. And then the ghost that haunted him had appeared.

Yes, a certain pair of dark blue eyes and a certain mouth he'd kissed had blotted out all desire for other women from him. It was as if she'd bewitched him.

As he left the palais and mounted his stallion, he frowned. Bewitched him. As Gabriel had been bewitched. And now, though he'd been so sure of himself, he was falling into the same trap.

Obsessed with a woman he'd once called a heartless jade. Able to think of no other; not even really wanting to kiss the beautiful comtesse; secretly relieved she'd turned him down. It wasn't a pretty state of affairs.

And if he was serious about teaching her a lesson, he couldn't keep slipping into this weak position. It felt treacherously like he was falling in love with her. And once that happened, he'd be at her mercy.

At least Ginny had given him a line of attack.

She cared about her reputation.

All he had to do was make her believe it was in his power to destroy it.

Chapter Seventeen

The Paris Opera House positively glittered. Meredith thought it looked as delicious as a decorated cake—two stacked tiers of boxes encircling it, all in gold leaf, and magnificent paintings vying with ivory and green brocade drapes swagged with gold tassels. Plush red velvet chairs lined the boxes and the floor below, and the stage was draped majestically in red velvet and fringed in gold. Along the apron, candles flickered, throwing golden arcs of light along the lower edge of the stage curtain. The proscenium that framed the stage was a pandemonium of molded white and gilded plaster in the shapes of leaves and cherubs. And above, thousands of candles blazed in the hanging chandeliers.

The orchestra was tuning up, and a cacophony of arpeggios and an occasional melody mixed with the laughter and talk of the crowd, who were as lavish a spectacle as the House itself or what would later transpire on the stage.

Meredith and her party were there to see the Comedie Italienne perform *Motroco*, a light opera, one which the king had proclaimed the funniest opera he'd ever seen. And from the reports they'd heard that afternoon in Paris, it would not disappoint them. Their footman had stood for nearly four hours in the queue for tickets while they had driven around the city, enjoying the afternoon in the shops and cafes along the Avenue des Champs Elysées, before dressing for the opera.

As Meredith and her party were shown to the comtesse's box, she looked around her in delight. Every day since her arrival in Paris had been filled with one thrill after another, and she secretly thanked Vivienne again for allowing her this mad adventure.

As the viscomte seated her in the front of the box, she noticed he was all attention as he had been the entire afternoon. In the cafes and shops, he'd fed her ices and truffles, as if she were a child, and he'd been very amusing, teasing her with mock proposals. But it wasn't his attention she sought as she made herself comfortable in her seat. To her chagrin, she found herself glancing across the row of boxes and to the floor below, searching not for a pair of blue eyes, but for a pair of green ones, and for dark hair, broad shoulders . . .

"Perhaps you can find who you are looking for with these," teased Ginny, who was being seated with equal grace by her lover, the Duc du Fronde. The comtesse held a pair of opera glasses in her hand and offered them mischievously to Meredith. Meredith gave a startled look to Ginny and then to the duc. He was a huge man who looked as if he could have been comfortable raiding with Genghis Khan's hordes, with his dark eyes and hair, his elegant cheekbones. His intense dark gaze disturbed Meredith when she found it fixed on her, for there was a knowing sophistication in those dark eyes that told her this was a man of the world, well used to power and to reading his adversaries.

Meredith felt herself blush, but she maintained her composure. "I was looking for no one in particular, only admiring the crowd in general," she said offhandedly, but the smile that curved Ginny's lips let her know that the comtesse had not been fooled. Ginny winked at her and said, "If I see something or someone of interest, I will let you know, Vivienne." And she raised the opera glasses to her eyes, the smile now deeply dimpling her cheeks as she scanned the crowd below.

Meredith blanched. Why was she seeking out that devil when Nicki was so attentive? Raceford was a rogue and she would do well to remember it. Were her feelings for him so reckless that even Ginny knew she'd been looking for Raceford? Ginny, so wise in the ways of love.

She suppressed a smile and turned her thoughts to her new friend. She thought Ginny a perfect imp for calling her out, but nevertheless especially magnificent tonight, in cloth-of-gold with champagne-colored lace. A shame that at these formal events one had to powder one's hair, but at least her peach complexion and flame-colored brows were well suited to the colors she wore.

Meredith herself was nearly uncomfortable in the magnificent gown she wore. Supported underneath by stuffed cloth bolsters and an openwork wire cage, its enormous panniers almost didn't fit into the door of their box, so she had to turn sideways to enter. And it was cut so low her breasts were nearly bared. It was a flowered brocade, of dusky blue and white roses, their leaves outlined in gold. White lace over gold lace edged the overdress, open over a petticoat of midnight-blue velvet. Gold roses nestled in blue ribbons were sewn all over the dress. With it, she wore a three-tiered pearl choker, with one long strand that knotted at her breasts, and long dangling pearl earrings. Her white wig was caught at one side by an arrangement of gilded feathers, and she carried a white lace fan with rosettes of blue ribbons dangling from it. She felt an awkward spectacle in a dress that weighed almost as much as she did, but when she looked around the House, she saw that many wore costumes more lavish than her own.

"I have never seen a sight this magnificent," she commented to the viscomte, who was taking a seat next to her. He took her fan and plied it lazily, looked around the House, then meaningfully into her eyes.

"Never, I vow, have I seen one so magnificent, either."

"I mean your Opera House, Nicholas," she smiled.

"And I do *not* mean our Opera House," he countered. "But I am glad to see that you think some of the sights we have here compare favorably with London. Perhaps some day you will consider living here in Paris."

"And why ever," she said, deliberately baiting him, "would I do that?"

He smiled. "Maybe something will convince you that there is more in Paris to love than there is in England," he murmured in her ear, leaning close. She thought that if he persisted, if she'd never met Raceford, he would be easy to fall in love with. Tonight, he wore a midnight-blue velvet coat that deepened the blue of his eyes. For Nicki, there was no need to powder his hair; it was so light, and she much preferred it in its natural state. A sapphire ring graced his hand

226

and a similar stone pinned his lace cravat. Her gaze dropped to the muscles of his legs, enticingly outlined in tight white breeches. As she allowed her eyes to travel upwards, she saw that more than his legs was visible, so tight was the fashion for breeches that season. And in that department, Nicki need fear few rivals.

She blushed when she saw his gaze had followed hers, and he gave her a wicked smile. "But I would be enchanted to satisfy your curiosity, my dear Vivienne. I admit I have curiosities of my own," he murmured, as his gaze in turn dropped to the tops of her breasts, swelling above her low-cut gown.

"Comtesse! At last I find myself in your divine presence."

Meredith saw the duc scowl at the youthful voice, and an exquisite creature entered their box. He couldn't have been more than twenty, wearing a white wig and a startlingly large, dangling topaz earring. He had sharp, foxy features, quite attractive, and a splendid coat of dark golden velvet trimmed lavishly with gold lace and gilt braid. His breeches were spotless white, his high-heeled shoes had golden buckles, and his sword, a useless-looking thing, was elaborately scrolled. It was obvious the young man was unaware of anyone else in the box but Ginny. He looked at her with such mooning eyes.

"Chevalier." Ginny spoke between clenched teeth to the newcomer.

The young gallant bowed low over Ginny's hand and pressed his lips to it, then laid his cheek to it, murmuring, "Like silk, Comtesse. None compare." He placed her hand at his breast and gazed into her eyes. "How I long to hold this hand forever."

"I believe you know the Duc du Fronde. . . ." Ginny interrupted, extricating her hand from the chevalier's fervent grasp. Joffrey inclined his head frostily. "And this is, of course, Nicholas St. Antoine, Viscomte de Valmy. Nicki, this is Artois Delibes, Chevalier de Foucalt."

"But I am most charmed," murmured Artois, without looking once at Nicki or the duc.

Ginny stifled a giggle at Nicki's scowl. "And this, my dear chevalier, is the Lady Vivienne Winter, an Englishwoman come to visit our fair city. She is staying with me."

Artois took Meredith's hand and bent over, kissing it. "A pleasure to meet you. But I had long believed the fairest women were Parisiennes. I see now I shall have to change my opinion and vote for the beauties of Englishwomen. I am utterly slain."

His eyes snapped at hers lasciviously before dropping her hand and turning back to Ginny. He began whispering to the comtesse, and Meredith couldn't help overhearing what he was saying. The duc and Nicki were trying their best to ignore the young man's presence.

Artois whispered, "What a pleasure it is to meet you at last. I must confess I have long admired you from a distance and have hoped to make your acquaintance. Or, if I am fortunate, something closer than mere acquaintance."

"I am afraid, Chevalier, you are too youthful for my tastes."

"Taste. What is that? It is the new experience that lends spice to life, no? And how can we condemn certain forms of pleasure if we have not experienced them? I am considered a marvelous guide to the pleasures of life, Comtesse, despite my lack of years."

Meredith all but blushed at this young man's bold words, but Ginny didn't bat an eye. The comtesse turned briefly to the scowling duc and gave him a look that said he need not get involved. She was perfectly capable of handling such an ardent pursuer.

"I am flattered, Artois, but I have experienced all the pleasures I care to."

"Ah," argued Artois softly. "But a woman as utterly beautiful as you are should not be selfish. She should allow others to adore her. And find out how pleasurable it can be to have someone who is a slave to her pleasure. A slave is a wonderful possession. Let me be your slave, Comtesse."

Meredith was watching the artful skill of Ginny trying to rebuff the chevalier's ardent pursuit, when she found that the Duc du Fronde was at her side. She'd barely spoken to the imposing man all evening, finding his brooding barbaric looks attractive but intimidating.

"And so, My Lady," he said. "You find practices in Paris shocking?"

"A trifle. I never suspected society was so fast."

He smiled, and he had a charming slanted smile. And those breathtaking cheekbones! He was also a huge man, with heavier muscles than most men Meredith had ever seen. She began to see what Ginny saw in him. "Yes . . . here, even one's age does not stop love's pursuit." He nodded at Ginny and the chevalier. "That one will never give up. But of course, the comtesse is a prize of rare beauty. Of that I am well aware. But I am charmed to learn that your sensibilities are slightly shocked by our fast society. For a man yearns, at times, to meet a woman who does not think of flirting night and day, but who could be faithful to one man." Here, his dark eyes rested again on Ginny. She'd been joined by yet two more gallants, who were having a mock duel over which would be the one to hold her fan, and she was laughing.

"Genvieve loves to flirt. It is like breathing to her. But you"—suddenly, his disturbing intense eyes met hers—"are different. More reserved. I find I admire that."

Good heavens . . . the man was flirting with her! She'd long ago realized that in France, it was practically an insult to spend time in the company of someone of the opposite sex and not flirt with the person, but somehow she'd never expected Joffrey to play the game. For one thing, he seemed devoted to Ginny, and also too reserved.

"Why, thank you, Duc," she murmured, casting down her eyes.

"Delightful. A shyness that is refreshing. But I beg you to call me Joffrey. We have spent much time in each other's company, and I would like to get to know you better."

"Joffrey. In that case, you must call me Vivienne."

In reply, he smiled his wolf's smile and, under the cover of her fan, took her hand. His fingers trailed along her palm, rubbing it, sending a little shiver down her spine, to her dismay. Really, was she a wanton to respond so easily to any handsome man?

"Duc. I realize I have left my lady alone for too long."

Meredith looked up to find Nicholas angrily frowning down at where their hands were joined beneath her fan, and she blushed, hastily disengaging her hand. The chevalier was standing with one of the

230

other gallants, whispering in his ear, and both of them were sending Ginny such hot looks it was almost embarrassing.

"Nicki, Joffrey was merely entertaining me. . . ."

"I see. But I think you will find I am all the entertainment you need, my dear Vivienne." The air between the two men fairly crackled.

Below, the Duke of Raceford stood looking up. He'd scowled when he saw the dark head lean closer to hers, having seen perfectly clearly that he'd taken her hand. A wanton was what he was calling her in his mind. First Nicki, and now the intimidating but dashing Joffrey. Nicki no sooner had his back turned than she was letting another man touch her!

Since the night of the costume ball, he hadn't succeeded in seeing her . . . but at every turn, it seemed, Nicholas was at her side. When he'd called, he'd received the cold message that she was "out," and when she was out and he saw her, she was always with Nicki. Well, tonight he meant to have a word with her, and the consequences be damned!

It seemed Nicki was not as oblivious as he seemed, for he took his seat at her side. Raceford could see him glare at Joffrey as he draped a possessive arm behind her bare shoulders and placed a hand over her other hand. Well, damn you, see how it feels, Nicki, when you have to watch her flirt with another!

Joffrey's smile was cool as he rose and went back to Ginny's side, but even from where he stood below, he could see the murderous looks the two men exchanged. And no wonder. She was a prize well worth winning for any man.

He stared angrily up at her white-wigged, lavish figure, feeling an unwilling tug of desire and wondering what on earth had ever made him see her as innocent that first night! She'd played the damsel in distress to perfection, he recalled stormily, even to making him believe her kisses were unskilled, naive.

He frowned. His second encounter with her at Versailles had surely dissipated *that* illusion. Why, he'd had her naked beneath him, her hips pressed tightly against his, her breasts bared to his mouth. . . . He felt a tightening in his loins as he thought of the way she had run her high heel lightly up and down his leg as she'd wrapped herself around him on the balustrade, arching beneath him as if she couldn't get close enough. Inexperienced! That was the trick of a much-used jade if he'd ever had one tried on him! Why, it was almost as if she'd seduced him! When he thought of how passionate her kisses had been, how wet and open her mouth . . .

Abruptly, he turned on his heel and stalked away, unable to bear the sight of her anymore. Damn her! Had the viscomte also felt her writhing beneath him, taken one of those perfect, luscious breasts in his mouth?

The music started with a crashing of chords as he made his way to the lobby. Now he'd have to wait before he saw her . . . and maybe that was good. It would give him time to collect himself.

After all, he was supposed to be making her fall in love with him, wasn't he? To teach her in the end what a broken heart felt like?

He wasn't supposed to be falling in love with her himself.

Meredith dabbed at the tears that threatened to

stream down her cheeks, as she went into another fit of laughter at the ludicrous characters on stage. *Motroco* had been a delight since the curtains had first parted and the silly characters had swept onstage, bringing the sprightly score to life. Affected heroines had sung of their virtue, languorous heroes complained in song but never took action, and cowardly giants boasted and sputtered about.

Just now the charlatan, Motroco, suffering from insomnia, stood alone at center stage, singing an incantation in a deep bass voice. He was going to sacrifice a turkey to the moon in order to relieve his sleeplessness. Meredith held her breath as the charlatan raised his hatchet. The actor on stage, looking fiercely serious at first, yawned, then squeamishly looked away, his deep voice diminishing to a squeak. The music rose in anticipation of the sacrifice, a loud boom of kettle drums and a crash of cymbals, as Motroco finally brought the hatchet down. But the turkey escaped him and, in a flurry of feathers, flew off over the charlatan's head into the wings, releasing a thunderous gale of laughter from the audience. Bewildered and resigned to another night of sleeplessness, Motroco was left on stage as the last chord sounded and the curtain rang down on the first act.

Meredith clasped her hands in front of her. "Oh!" she giggled, truly overcome. It had been splendidly ridiculous. She'd never been to a play in England, much less an opera, and the singing, the costumes, and the stage sets had transported her into a world of complete whimsy.

Nicholas pretended to smother a yawn with her fan, then laughed. "So you are not like the rest of us, bored to tears by the opera, and here only to see and be seen?"

"Nicki!" she pouted. "You cannot mean it! It was very funny! And the music was delightful!"

"But I am afraid I am tone-deaf, my dear Vivienne, and have come here only to allow the ladies to admire me."

"And to admire them," put in Ginny dryly.

He leaned forward, letting his lips curve in a smile. "And now I must ask the question I have been dying to all evening. Do *you* admire me, my dear Vivienne?"

"How could I not?" she said lightly. "For well you know you are the most beautiful man in Paris."

"Only in Paris?" He pretended to be disappointed. "And since you come from England, I am slain."

"Ah, but I shall not tell you what I think of English gentlemen."

"Why not? Would I cry?"

"Cry?" She laughed. "No, but you might become more vain than you already are."

"Your words give me hope," he breathed, running a finger lightly up the inside of her bare arm.

Ginny rose then, plying her fan. "Come, Vivienne. It is too warm in here with these heated gentlemen. I must find the retiring room, while these great dullards fetch us some refreshments. And, of course, I must see and be seen as well. You are absolutely right, Vivienne. The first act was very funny!"

And pointing her retroussé little nose in the air, Ginny took Meredith's arm and swept her out of the box.

Inside the retiring room, no less a spectacle than the House, Meredith flopped down on a long pink velvet fainting couch, glad not to have to sit so straight for a while. Her gown was pinching her, no thanks she was

234

sure to all that Nicholas had fed her that afternoon. She waited while Ginny approached the golden-framed mirrors on the wall and made a fuss about her hair. Everywhere was green marble, gold fixtures, pink silk hangings. And wilted jonquils in porcelain vases were scattered about. The room echoed with the shrieks and giggles of the other women, as fresh patches were applied in more alluring spots, cheeks were rouged and lips reddened, shoulders powdered, perfume dabbed on elbows, and of course, gossip exchanged. Meredith felt almost stifled when Ginny had primped to her heart's content, and she was glad to emerge into the comparatively fresher air.

"And now we must find some swains to make Nicki and Joffrey jealous. It would never do to do anything so tame as to stay by their sides during the entire opera. My dear, it would cause the worst kind of talk!"

So saying, Ginny took her firmly by the elbow and plunged into the crowd, stopped on every side by acquaintances asking to be introduced to Meredith. They were in the midst of one such chattering group when suddenly Meredith's eye fell on a tall figure leaning against the wall and watching them.

Deron Redvers.

He looked magnificent in a coat of dark green that matched his eyes, and alone in that crowd of white heads, his raven hair was unpowdered. It was tied back by an emerald ribbon, and a real emerald winked in the lace at his throat. He wore a white and silver embroidered waistcoat as his only concession to the riotous finery around him. His spectacular long legs were encased in tight fawn trousers, and white stockings hugged his calves. As always, a sword hung at his hip.

235

His brows and gaze were level as they swept her, and his stance said plainly that he was waiting for her.

Meredith felt suddenly faint. "I must—I beg you excuse me, Comtesse, I am feeling faint," she managed.

Ginny turned with an inquiring gaze. "Faint again? Really, Vivienne, I am beginning to be concerned with what can be the cause of all this faintness. . . ."

Ginny's eyes fell on the tall man leaning against the wall, and she added dryly, "Oh, I see. The same as last time."

"Let's go this way," Meredith said desperately, taking Ginny's arm and leading her back down the way they had come. But her ploy was short-lived. A familiar pair of legs were soon planted in her path.

And a familiar deep voice was saying, "Good evening, My Lady."

Ginny let a glimmer of a smile pass over her face before saying, "But I see you two *old* friends have much to discuss! And I must get back to the duc. He will think it most impolite of me to leave him for so long!"

Meredith cast an imploring look at Ginny, but she was already hurrying down the hallway without a backward look.

A firm grip under her elbow, and he was almost dragging her into a deserted alcove off the hallway. Anger surged through her, and she found her voice. She jerked her elbow away from his grasp and blazed up at him, "Let me go! I have nothing—do you understand me—*nothing* to say to you, for you are a devil!"

"But I have something to say to *you*, Vivienne. So I was right. You are angry at me and avoiding me. Just because you let yourself do what you really wanted to do the other night, like all women afterward you must blame the man."

She was truly enraged at this outrageous statement but surprised herself by saying furiously, "Do not call me Vivienne!"

He laughed. "And why not . . . since I already know so much of you"—his eyes dropped to her half-exposed breasts—"so well? But I suppose that after showing me your true nature, you're more anxious than ever to pretend to the proprieties. Very well I will not call you Vivienne."

How dare he say things like that? He was treating her as if she were a whore! But a corner of her mind was glad that he, of all people, would not be calling her by a name not her own.

He stepped closer, fencing her in against the wall. His eyes were so green. He smiled, a smile she remembered too well. "But since I have known you so . . . intimately, it would be ridiculous for me to call you Lady Vivienne Winter, would it not? Besides, I have proved that your name hardly fits you. You are by no means cold. I shall have to think of another name that does fit you. Since I am a devil in your eyes, I will call you Angel."

Angel. Why did it sound so right, coming from his lips?

"Angels have golden hair," she countered.

"Not in my heaven." He let a finger gently tilt her chin up until she was looking at him, then said in a soft voice from which all harshness had fled, "Tell me why you are angry? Is it in truth because once I kissed your lips, I was driven to forgetting where we were, forgetting all else except the desire you were stirring in me? If that is why you are angry, Angel, then it is an unjust anger. Because I believe the same thing happened to you."

Lost. She was lost in those eyes.

And then she remembered why she was angry. Jerking her chin out of his grasp, she said coldly to him, "You are a liar."

A dark brow lifted a fraction. "A liar? But surely that night you could feel the truth of my passions. . . ."

"You lied to me. About who you are. About why you kidnapped me."

"Oh." He stepped back and lounged against the wall across from her, crossing his arms over his chest. Making it clear she was free to go if she wished.

She stayed.

"So you can forgive my passion, but not my lies?"

"You made me believe you were a highwayman . . . told me tales about being a penniless third son . . . and all the time you are as rich as I am, Your *Lordship!*" She practically spat the last word at him, as if it were an epithet.

He said nothing, just watched her.

"And it was all a joke . . . a wager!"

"And you find it intolerable that I would make love to you as part of a joke? But that part, begun in fun, surely turned out to be deadly serious on my part, My Lady Angel. What I feel for you is no joke."

"And the earrings?" she raged. "What about them? Nicki told me how you'd bragged to be the first to *have* me and decided to abduct me so you had your chance! That you'd come back with my earrings as proof. And to think I *gave* them to you! Have you shown them to all of Paris yet?"

"Nicki told you that—and you believed him?" His

eyes were serious, intense.

"Of course I did, for Nicki is not a liar like you are!"

With that, Meredith could stand no more and swept past him, not heeding his call after her, "Angel—!"

The music was starting when she opened the curtains to the box, and she was glad the attention would be nominally on the stage and not on her flushed face or trembling hands. As she sat, Nicki leaned close and whispered, "Where were you? I was frantic with worry."

Why lie, she thought tiredly. Ginny had probably already told him who she'd been with. "I was trying to get away from Raceford," she whispered.

His hand found hers and clasped it. "Next time, I promise I will not leave your side."

Below them, the singing started, but this time, Meredith had no heart for it. She barely listened or saw, seeing instead a pair of green eyes. . . .

At last it came to an end. Their box was filled with visitors as the singers took their bows and had flowers thrown at their feet. Meredith stared into the crowd below, hoping she would not see Deron again on the way out.

And then she heard his voice behind her.

"Ginny, you look dashing. Good evening, Duc. Viscomte. No, I am sorry, Ginny, I cannot stay. I have only come to return something."

He was standing in front of her. She looked up. His face was an unreadable mask. And then he tossed something into her lap.

She looked down. Two sapphire earrings ringed with jet glittered there, and she closed her hands on them.

"I am afraid there has been a misunderstanding,

My Lady. You see, I only kept them because they reminded me of your eyes," he said coldly, then was gone.

Chapter Eighteen

It was a blue Paris evening and the rain fell in veils, running off eaves and out of gargoyle's mouths in downspouts. Muffled to the eyes in a great dark cloak, Jane stood at a side door of the Palais d'Anguillame and looked both ways before descending into the downpour.

She hurried away from the palais and down a narrow path, her dark figure quickly swallowed up by the rain. At last she gained a side tradesman's gate to the palace and stopped with her back against a wall, eyes on the gatekeeper's cottage. But on such an evening the man was inside. Lamplight showed behind lace curtains, and the door was shut.

She walked past the cottage to the gate and quietly unlatched it. The drumming of the rain drowned out the stealthy squeal of hinges, and soon she had it closed behind her and was walking rapidly down the street.

At the end of the avenue a closed carriage waited. The driver touched his whip to his hat as she came up, and a light knock made the coach door open at once. With only a slight hesitation, Jane climbed inside and the door banged behind her. At once, the coach started moving.

"Mistress! You are soaking wet! Thank you for coming out on an evening like this, not fit for even frogs to be outside!" This was delivered in perfect English with a slight trace of a French accent, and Jane let her dripping hood fall back to see who the speaker was.

The single lamp inside the coach showed her a young man of perhaps twenty-four, with an impish smile, deep dimples, and dark copper-colored hair that fell to his shoulders. Under dark brows, he had golden-green eyes that were regarding her with a mixture of mischief and admiration. And he was decidedly handsome.

"Allow me to introduce myself, mistress. Armand Louvain, valet to the Duke of Raceford, at your service!" Though he was seated, he managed a bow.

Jane felt relief wash over her. Ever since she'd agreed to this mad meeting, she'd worried that the duke's servants would be English—and able to detect that her accent was not one a cousin of Vivienne Winter's should have, no matter how poor. What to do about the duke himself she hadn't decided on yet . . . some story, perhaps. But she couldn't go explaining herself to servants. It would make her most suspect.

She reached inside her cloak and produced a folded letter from a dry inner pocket. She held it out, rattling it slightly. "This letter," she began in an accusing tone. "You know I am Miss Meredith Westin, and this letter here says that I must come to hear something that concerns my cousin's good name. So your master the duke must resort to threats?"

Good name! When she had read those words this morning, she had almost fainted. It seemed too good to be true that this masquerade would ever have worked in any case. With a chill, she remembered something Meredith had told her . . . that the duke said he'd seen Vivienne in London and wanted to meet her. All too likely, as the social circle a lady and a duke would move in was small. He must have known at once that Meredith was not Lady Vivienne and, intrigued, perhaps had vowed to get to the bottom of the mystery. It was her anxiety to keep it all quiet that had induced Jane to come to this secret meeting with Raceford.

Armand Louvain smiled at her and the dimples deepened. "Not threats, mistress. His Grace is merely concerned about the lady and, knowing you are close to her, wishes to ask your advice on a most delicate subject."

Jane's heart sank. Oh, he must know! Maybe if she told him the truth . . . begged him to be a gentleman and not reveal their secret. "Very well. I'll do my best. At least I can hear what he has to say, Mr. Louvain."

"Please . . . call me Armand." He sat back and regarded her with what looked to be admiration. Jane had dressed carefully for this meeting, curious about the highwayman-turned-duke and impressed, in spite of herself, that she was going to meet a peer of England. She wore a dark green and gold velvet gown under her dark cloak, and gold ribbons in her light brown curls. "Permit me to say that I find this errand an unexpected pleasure. To escort a lady so lovely. Are you enjoying your stay in Paris?"

Jane felt her heart give a tiny trip at his caressing words. My goodness, she thought, there were handsome men simply falling all about the place in Paris! "I am enjoying it very much. Or at least I was until I got this here . . . this note. And you . . . Armand.

Have you worked for His Lordship long?"

"I have. His Grace hired me years ago on his first trip to Paris. It is all the rage to have a French valet, and I have found that I like England very much. The Duke of Raceford is a man of honor. I think whatever it is he wishes to ask you, you will not find compromising, Mistress Westin." He lifted a corner of the curtain. "But we arrive."

As Jane stepped out of the coach, Armand lifted his cloak over her head to shield her from the rain. She only had a moment to glance at the residence of the Duke of Raceford. It was smaller than the Palais d'Anguillame but no less impressive, located in an older section of the Faubourg St. Germain, nearer the Seine. Her cursory glance showed her an elegant stone edifice, covered in ivy, terraced, and balustraded, with boxes of flowers lining its front. The residence was lit from within, and suddenly the light spilled out onto the front step as a footman flung wide the front doors to admit them.

She and Armand rushed in, and Jane found herself inside a huge gallery of the duke's home. It was warmer inside, and she gladly gave Armand her dripping cloak. Jane looked about, curious to know what kind of man the duke was. The gallery was simply furnished, with a mahogany table, a long mirror above it, and an ormolu clock that chimed the hour from the top of the table. Otherwise, the pristine white gallery walls were only adorned with two paintings on the opposite wall, below which were matching mahogany benches, their cushions needlepoints of the hunt in muted greens and reds. Above her a single chandelier hung and reflected light on the polished parquet floor. At the far end of the gallery, a curving staircase led to the upper apartments.

It was the home of a man, there was no doubt, and an unpretentious one at that, she thought as Armand led her along to an open door where firelight spilled out invitingly.

He turned and bowed. "I must leave you here, mistress. His Grace awaits you inside. But I shall wait most eagerly to escort you back home when your interview is finished." With a last flashing smile, he was gone.

Jane took a deep breath before entering the open door. The duke's apartments were truly magnificent, fit for royalty. The walls were a deep forest-green surrounding large paintings that depicted battle scenes. There were suits of armor polished to a shine, and battle axes, maces, and swords hanging on the walls. The floor, of intricately inlaid parquet, was covered with green, gold, and red carpets in a Persian pattern. On the walls, shelves of books bound in rich leather went from floor to ceiling between the paintings, and she realized this grand apartment was the duke's study. The smell of musty books and a hint of tobacco hung in the air. At one end the fire roared brightly, and before it were two chairs of gleaming chestnut-colored leather. At the other end, a desk scattered with books and papers and a single lamp told her the duke was a serious man. It was a thoroughly masculine and intimidating room. Not one she'd ever have imagined herself entering, to talk privately to a duke, when she was back in a maid's uniform in Henley.

Good heavens, she hoped she could just for a short time talk in the refined accents Meredith had been coaching her in. She was getting better every day, but she tended to slip when she was agitated. She straightened her shoulders and went in.

The Duke of Raceford rose at her entrance, crossing the room to take her hand and usher her to one of two chairs before the fire. Nervously, Jane looked him over. My Lord, but he was a magnificent figure of a man! Tonight he was attired in a dark red velvet smoking jacket, black pants, and a white shirt with the barest hint of lace at the throat.

"Miss Westin. How very kind of you to come . . . and on such a night. Please . . . sit before the fire and warm yourself, and I will pour you a glass of Madeira."

"Your Grace," she managed, sitting down and accepting the glass of wine. And then she simply waited. The less she said, the better. After all, it was he who'd summoned her here.

He sat at his ease in front of the warming, roaring blaze and stretched out long legs. "I shall get right to the point. I know you to be a straightforward woman from our little . . . adventure on the road to Paris, and that you are fiercely loyal to your cousin."

She nodded, not trusting her voice, and stared curiously at his dark, hawklike profile. He turned and gave her a steady look from his green eyes.

"I said in the note that this concerns her good name. A lie, for which I hope you will forgive me, but I could think of no other way to get you here, and I desired to be quite private with you."

Jane felt a wave of relief wash through her, and she took a sip of her wine. So he didn't know! More important than ever that she speak properly in the next minutes.

"Pray go on," she said softly.

"You see, Lady Vivienne has been avoiding me. Understandable, after the incident on the highway. But most painful for me. I have fallen in love with

246

her."

Jane sat up straighter, her eyes flying wide. This man, admitting he loved . . . Meredith!

He saw her shock and nodded. "It all started as a . . . way to help a friend. I know you both believe that it was my idea, but may I assure you it was not. I was asked by someone to play the part of highwayman, and because I was bored, I agreed. I had never met Lady Vivienne, but I had heard so much about her. . . . She was not what I expected."

That's the truest words you ever spoke, Jane thought. "But what—?" she began.

"What does this have to do with you? I am desperate to see her. I want to get to know her the way I should have if she had merely arrived in Paris and I'd met her in the ordinary course of things. I didn't expect to be taken by storm by her, but I swear to you, she had an effect on me I have never felt before. I must see her but she won't see me, and when she is out, Nicholas is always by her side."

"What is it you wish me to do?"

He turned to her and she caught her breath at his eyes. They were as green as spring grass, the greenest she'd ever seen. "Nothing underhanded, I assure you. But I thought perhaps you would know of some place she might be going without that damned Nicholas . . . some place quite public, of course. Some place where I might get to speak to her, perhaps soften her heart toward me. I leave it up to your judgment whether to tell her of tonight's interview."

Jane thought. Well! This was an eye-opener and no mistake! The proud duke, begging for a chance to see Meredith! Her heart was warmed by the romance of it. As long as it was public, what could it hurt?

She came to a decision. "Every morning as long as

it isn't raining, she takes a ride at dawn. In the park. She loves horses. And she plans to attend that horse auction this week. She hasn't a horse of her own here in Paris and I know she wants to buy one." She rose, setting down her wineglass. "And now, Your Grace, I'd better go. For the time being, I won't be telling her of this meeting. And, please, no more notes. If you want to speak to me, call on me in the normal way."

He smiled at her and bent to kiss her hand. Then he rang a small silver bell. "I thank you for your patience in listening to me. And for giving me a chance to mend my fences with Vivienne. I am in your debt, and if I can ever do anything for you, Miss Westin, you have only to ask."

And that might come in handy, thought Jane.

Armand came in, looking a vision indeed.

"Armand, escort Miss Westin home. Miss Westin, my thanks again."

Jane made a deep curtsy—after all, he *was* a duke—and went out with Armand. She stood while Armand draped her cloak around her, felt his hands linger an instant too long on her shoulders.

The rain was heavier than ever when they climbed into the coach, and there was something so intimate and romantic about being closed into such a small space with such a handsome man. Evidently, he felt it, too, for after a few moments, he said softly, "Listen to the rain on the roof. Is it not a lovely sound, mistress?"

"It is," she agreed, watching him.

"Alas, I fear that from now on, rain on the roof will remind me of a pair of honey-brown eyes."

Jane blushed.

"Please . . . don't say such things. . . ."

"You are right, mistress. I am too forward. I realize I am only a valet, while you are a lady of independent means. But may I be permitted to say that I wish we were of equal station, for then I would surely see you again."

"I . . . thank you," Jane stammered. If only he knew! That they were exactly of the same station! For Jane found that there was nothing she'd rather do than see this charming copper-haired man again. For once, she regretted her new role as gentlewoman.

"So, are you finding you like Paris?"

"I am. It's a very beautiful city."

"That's good. I had hoped you might find a fondness for things French. Have you met many French people?"

"Well, I have been going about a bit, to the opera and suchlike. And met quite a few of the comtesse's friends."

He sighed theatrically. "It is as I feared. You must be meeting scores of men. And I imagine they are all pursuing you."

"I wouldn't say that," she countered. "I am a bit shy. I lived quite retired in the country with my aunt, and I'm not really used to all the quick wit that the people here have. They are really above my touch." She wished she could tell him she was a servant just like he was!

"As you are above mine," he said sadly. "Alas. But the men in society must be blind if they are not pursuing you. And such shyness is charming."

"You're not the least shy, are you, Armand?"

He grinned at her. "I have never been accused of it. But, then, something about the rain on the coach roof and being alone in here makes it seem as if we are not mistress and servant, but just a man and a woman."

The look he was giving her was making her feel quite breathless.

"Though I can imagine being your willing servant, now that I have beheld you," he added, and she swallowed.

"I don't think station matters in the least, and I have no wish for servants," she ventured.

"Not even those loyal to you because their heart commands it?"

"I—I don't know what you mean," she stammered.

"Then I wish I could show you," he murmured.

Jane felt her cheeks heating and her heart speeding up as he let his gaze caress her warmly.

"But unfortunately, we arrive," he said regretfully. Too soon, she was alighting from the coach, and he was walking her through the rain up to the dark recess of the side door. There they stopped, the rain shutting them in like a curtain, and she looked up for a long moment at him, her hood falling back.

"I find," he said carefully, "my heart does not recognize differences in station." And with that, he swept her into his arms and kissed her tilted-back lips masterfully.

Her head spun as his lips claimed hers and she opened her mouth beneath his. Their mouths locked, and his tongue was a brand of fire moving inside her mouth. His arms felt wonderful wrapped around her, and she was pressed against every inch of his strong, tall frame. After a few moments, he released a shaken Jane, and with a dimpled grin and a kiss for her hand, he was gone into the rain.

She stared after him, thrills still coursing through her veins at the memory of his kiss.

"Oh Lord," she whispered. "And how do I let him

know I ain't above him at all?"

Deron took a deep sip of his brandy. So, Ginny's suggestion had worked. Just the merest hint that there was a threat to Vivienne's reputation and her companion had come running. And had at once told him where he could find her alone . . . having even promised not to mention tonight's meeting.

It was most peculiar. Why would a woman like Vivienne be so anxious to protect her name when she herself risked it continually by her behavior? She did not live at her husband's side; she was known to keep company with handsome young men; she'd traveled to Paris alone to stay with a fast widow.

Perhaps, he mused, she lived in fear of her husband. But no, surely if that were the case, she'd spend more time at his side. It was hard to figure her out. As it had been since the first day. She just seemed too damned sweet and innocent to be the experienced woman he knew her to be.

For a moment, Raceford wondered what the hell he was doing here, far from home, pursuing a woman with revenge in his heart. He ought to get back to Yorkshire . . . find a wife . . . settle down. Have a family.

A wife. He tried to picture what kind of woman he would marry, thinking of all the eligible girls he'd been presented to over the last few seasons. None particularly had caught his eye. A certain pair of dark blue eyes rose before him, and he had a sudden and disconcerting picture of Vivienne in his bed, waiting for him with welcome, open arms every night . . . as she would if she were his wife.

That vixen, a wife? But the soft blue eyes were not

the eyes of a vixen. . . .

And were she his wife, he'd be able to explore that magnificent body every night, make love to her until he could stand no more and they were both sweetly exhausted . . . and kill any other man who looked at her. Starting with Nicholas.

He looked up, startled from his reverie, as Armand came into the room. "So. She told me what I wanted to know—where I can see Vivienne. You'll have to wake me before dawn tomorrow if it's not raining."

Armand groaned theatrically. "Only the English would rise at such a barbaric hour, Your Grace."

Raceford smiled, realizing that intrigues were such fun that he had no desire to settle down as yet. Not even with a black-haired baggage as a wife. He'd have her again—and without the benefit of clergy, he vowed silently. "But I haven't yet learned everything I wish to know. Such as, in that great pile of a palais, where the lady's bedroom is located. So I have a job for you."

"This begins to sound fun," Armand laughed.

"Indeed. Miss Westin is most attractive. And you are known to have a way with the ladies, so I would appreciate it if you would seduce her and learn where the Lady Vivienne sleeps."

Armand's smile was truly pleased. "My inclinations follow your desire, Your Grace. I found the girl most alluring. Fresh and simple and pretty. I have already managed to kiss her," he said modestly.

Raceford laughed. "I might have known I could count on you if a pretty woman was involved."

"Nothing easier. I shall pursue the girl," Armand said, "until her head spins and she can refuse me nothing. It will be a most pleasurable chore."

252

"May both of us," said the duke, lifting his glass, "have success in love."

"To love," agreed Armand, and gave a devilish grin. "Or at least . . . to a successful seduction!"

Chapter Nineteen

The sun was just rising over a world new-washed by rain, and the Duke of Raceford found he was glad to be up. The chestnut trees were budding lushly green, sending long shadows from their neat rows across the bridle path. The sunrise was pink and golden in the east, the cloudless sky was promising a balmy day, and the air had a freshness that he'd missed of late. He'd spent too many late nights, shut away from the sun, and he remembered fondly how he'd always risen for the sunrise when he was in America. It cheered him that Vivienne, too, seemed to enjoy the mornings enough to rise this early, even though she attended as many late events as he did.

He sat his black stallion at ease, his eye on the bridle path. Before long, a neat bay with black stockings rounded the corner.

It was his Lady Angel.

He watched her approach with appreciation. She was born to the saddle, with a graceful seat and light hands. This morning, she wore a close-fitting habit of dark mulberry and a black hat with violet feathers. Her gloves and boots were black leather, and she made a lovely picture.

He touched his heels to his stallion's flanks and

emerged from the trees where he'd waited, halting in the middle of the path.

She drew rein and stopped her horse, and sat looking at him. "My Lord Duke," she said after a moment.

Meredith couldn't help feeling warmed at the sight of the tall man on the great stallion. His dark hair was tied back, and he wore no hat. He looked magnificent in a fawn-colored coat, with drab breeches and dark brown boots. He smiled at her and she wondered at the way her spirits lifted to see him. He was a challenge, every inch of him. It had been so long. Try as she might, she hadn't been able to dispel him from her thoughts. And since he'd returned her earrings to her at the opera, she had to admit that her heart had softened toward him.

"My Lady Angel. I had hoped to meet you this morning."

"Is that what brings you out at such an early hour?"

"Desperation pure and simple. Since you were never home when I called and in public always had your watchdog at your side, I thought I'd try to encounter you alone at last. I knew the viscomte could never be persuaded to rise at an hour this early."

She smiled and started her horse, allowing him to fall in at her side. "But I thought I have made it quite plain that we have nothing to say to one another, Your Grace."

"And I have come to throw myself on your mercy. To beg you for another chance. If you would grant me but a few moments to plead my case, I swear that if you then ask me to leave I'll go without protest. And stop bothering you if you wish it."

She glanced at him. "Since it seems you offer me a

chance to rid myself of your company, I will listen."

"My Lady. I regret that our association started on such an ill note. I know you believe what you have been told . . . that it was I who instigated your kidnapping. But that is not true. A friend came to me and asked me to play the part of a highwayman in a scheme he was setting in motion. I was bored, and so I agreed. I did not expect to be so taken with you."

"A friend. I see. I suppose you mean to tell me this friend was the viscomte?"

He shrugged. "Believe me or not as you will. But do not be angry in any case. Nicki wanted to meet you and to make an impression on you. He fixed it with me that I should hold up your coach, and then that he would happen along and rescue you. It all began to go wrong when I decided, without his knowledge, to kidnap you a day early."

"And why would you do that?"

"Because I had heard many things about the Lady Vivienne Winter and never met you. I told you before I'd seen you in London, but that was not true. However, you had been lovingly described to me by a friend, so I felt I knew you."

"So many friends," she said scornfully.

"But this one I am sure you know. Gabriel Justice."

Startled, Meredith looked at him and found his black brows cynically lifted, his gaze knowing.

He took in her widening eyes, her fingers tightening convulsively on the reins.

Guilty, thought Raceford.

"Gabriel . . . you know him?" she squeaked, utterly unnerved. Vivienne's lover, God knows what the man had told Raceford!

"My closest friend . . . and confidant," he said smoothly.

256

Meredith swallowed. No wonder Raceford had tried to seduce her that first night and believed he might succeed — and had succeeded at Versailles. In that regard, she'd played Vivienne to the hilt. And no doubt this Gabriel had told him he was Vivienne's lover! Then she remembered something else that dismayed her. Gabriel had told everyone Vivienne had broken his heart. There had been one friend he'd wanted to tell the truth to, but Vivienne hadn't allowed it.

Raceford.

Nervously, she glanced at him. Change the subject, she thought firmly. "So, Duke, you amuse me this morning with stories. The viscomte also tells me stories. And which one should I believe? You have already admitted to a number of lies during our short acquaintance. That you were a poor man. That you had seen me in London. And now you expect me to believe this latest fanciful tale?"

"No, I know that would be too much to hope. All I ask, my Lady Angel, is for a fresh start. When we met, you were angry at me for believing the rumors I heard about you. Justifiably so. And as I got to know you, I found you were nothing like the Lady Vivienne who had been painted so blackly to me. Now I ask you for the same forbearance, though I know I do not deserve it. I regret ever having played the highwayman. I wish we had met in a civilized way when you arrived in Paris, so that I might have begun to pay court to you respectfully. So I beg you for a chance . . . just a chance to speak to you, call on you, dance with you sometimes. Will you grant it?"

Meredith stared straight ahead, her mind whirling. It had been dull since she hadn't been seeing him! Even with Nicki to escort her around, she'd missed

Raceford's cutting remarks, his sardonic eyes, the way he made her feel alive and challenged whenever she was with him! She enjoyed matching wits with him, that was the truth. And now he was begging her for a chance to come back into her life and fill the void he'd left behind. *But caution, Meredith, caution,* she warned herself again. But found no comfort in the warning.

"I must be mad, Your Lordship," she said at last. "But since I do not know if it is you or the viscomte who is lying to me, you may call on me again, and as long as you conduct yourself as a gentleman, you may continue to enjoy my company."

"I am overjoyed. Well, let us speak of more civilized subjects now that we are friends. How are you finding Paris now that you have been here for a time?"

She breathed a sigh of relief at his change in subject and slanted a look at him under the brim of her hat. "The truth?"

"I would always have the truth from you, Lady Angel."

Wincing inside, for well she knew she was deceiving him even as to her name, she schooled her face to blandness. "I do not really love it here. It has been a wonderful experience, of course, seeing the great structures and palaces, meeting the king and queen, but—"

"But?"

"I find it too formal here. Everything is etiquette. And yet, under all the mannered rules and polite ways, the men and women are shockingly loose. They seem to all be having *affaires* and to change partners as often as they change dancing slippers. In a way, I find I am missing England. Perhaps I am just too old-fashioned."

He stared at her, bemused. The wild Vivienne . . . shocked by the Parisiennes' morals? Old-fashioned? It was strange, but he believed he was hearing the real Vivienne speak. But why did she conceal a sweet nature under the manners of a hoyden?

Meredith bit her lip, all at once realizing that was not how Vivienne would speak. Really, in speech she was not doing a very good job of sticking to her role. But, then, when had she? From the beginning, she'd been acting herself more than Vivienne. Oh, really, she made a hopeless actress.

"I find I am enjoying Paris in one sense, My Lady. It gives me the license to act a bit more freely with the lady of my choice than I might be able to in England. For example, to make a bold request."

"But Lady Vivienne!" called a voice. "Always I meet you in the company of such handsome men! You cut me to the quick."

Meredith stifled a groan as they turned to find the chevalier riding toward them. "Oh dear," she whispered. "I am sure he's given up on Ginny and will now turn his attentions to me."

The chevalier reined in his flashy white horse at their sides, and his young eyes devoured Meredith. "But Lady Vivienne, you are looking quite beautiful this morning. Since our last meeting at the opera, I have been mad to meet you again."

"Artois Delibes, Chevalier Foucalt, meet Deron Redvers, the Duke of Raceford. He is English," spoke Meredith, trying to draw the gallant's attention away from her.

"*Madame*, it is your accent I am in love with! And your national *politesse*. So very mysterious. When you speak, my heart quickens." Then the chevalier nominally turned and coldly acknowledged Deron. "My pleasure to be known to you, *monsieur.*"

"I am happy to make your acquaintance, Artois," said Deron, terribly polite, though Meredith could see a little muscle in his jaw working. Could he be jealous of the chevalier's attention?

"Horseback riding is so amusing, is it not? But how charming that we both have a taste for it. I find it stimulating," Artois trilled.

Meredith coughed, trying not to laugh at Raceford's scowling expression. He *was* jealous!

"Perhaps you need someone to be your guide to the delights of our fair city? I would be happy to undertake the task," offered the chevalier.

"Thank you, but I have been here some time and am already familiar with the city."

"Ah, but there are places you will not have seen that only a native can take you to! Private places where a man and a woman can be alone together." The boy's eyes grew dark with meaning, and Meredith shifted in her saddle uncomfortably. Ginny might be able to handle these situations with grace, but she found his persistence impossible.

Raceford's brows drew together. "I do not think I —" he began, but Meredith cut him off, determined to handle the situation herself.

"I graciously decline your offer, Chevalier. I already have an escort," she finished with a nod in Deron's direction.

"We really must leave you. I have only recently remade my acquaintance with this lady and am most anxious to be alone with her," Deron broke in.

The chevalier bowed, looking undaunted. "But of course. And, Lady Vivienne, though you reject my offer today, do not think I have given up. I shall call on you without delay, for I, too, am most anxious to be alone with you." With that parting shot, the chevalier wheeled his horse and cantered gracefully off.

"Oh dear," laughed Meredith. "I am afraid he will never leave me alone. He pursued Ginny for months."

"In that case, I am tempted to leave Paris at once—and take you with me," he added, looking at her.

"Before he rode up, you said you had a request to make."

"Yes, I have a request. A bold one, as I said. That you will remember we have already shared more experiences than most and stop calling me 'Your Lordship.' I detest formality. Would you call me by my name . . . Deron?"

Meredith laughed. First Nicki, now the duke. If she were going to allow one to be so familiar, why not both? But she wouldn't let him win a concession so easily.

"You presume . . . Your Lordship."

"It would please me greatly," he said softly.

She gave him a slanted look through her lashes. "And what would I gain from allowing such familiarity?"

He smiled at her. "A kiss."

She gasped, truly startled. Oh, the rogue! "How can you—?"

"Don't tell me you weren't as shaken as I was by the kisses we shared, My Lady Angel. I have kissed many women in my life, but never have I felt the earth tremble under my feet . . . never have I been so enthralled by anyone's touch. I know it happened for you, for I saw it in your eyes. Like me, you must

261

have been dreaming of those incredible kisses. . . ."

Meredith put her heels to her horse. "I will leave you now . . . and don't follow me!" she said, riding away.

He reined in and watched her go, then called after her, "And may I still call, My Lady Angel?"

She turned in the saddle, feeling a rush of joy at the sight of him. Her heart melted in her chest. How true his words had been. She had been longing every moment for his kiss. *Oh, the devil with caution!* "You may," she called over her shoulder, "Deron!"

His laugh followed her as she cantered away down the green path.

"She is very lovely." The Marquise du Planchet stood on the upper balcony of the palais, looking down at the mulberry-clad figure of Meredith riding up the drive. "I wonder at you, Ginny."

"You wonder at me, Lisette? why?" Genvieve turned and looked curiously at her oldest and closest friend.

"Because you throw her constantly into Nicki's company . . . and I thought you were in love with him yourself. What kind of dangerous game is it you play, *cherie?*"

Ginny laughed and linked arms with her friend, strolling through the honeyed sunlight down the terrace. "But there is no worry at all. Do I look as if I am developing frown lines?"

"But it is madness to allow Nicki to court such a beauty right under your nose! Or perhaps you no longer care for him?"

Ginny smiled, her eyes half closed. "I begin to believe I care for him very much."

"Then—"

"Then do not trouble yourself about it. You see, I have plans for Nicki. And they do not include Lady Vivienne Winter."

"You speak in riddles, my dear Genvieve. Tell me clearly what you mean."

"Well, when I found that Nicki was in danger of losing his inheritance, I knew he would soon see that he was in need of a rich bride."

"And so why did you not accept one of his many proposals?"

"Because Nicki was ready to marry . . . but not to love. He is still young. And more than any man I have known, the chase matters to him. With his looks, women fall at his feet. Conquests are so easy for him. He could only truly fall in love over time . . . with a woman who held back her love from him for years. And when I heard the news about Nicki's need to marry, it was too soon. He did not love me yet."

"So you decided to let him court this one because she is still married? Dangerous, *cherie*. Her husband is very old and could die any day!"

"Yes . . . but I knew that if I turned Nicki loose among the heiresses, he would be married in months. *Mon Dieu,* they have only to look at him to swoon at his feet! And he is of one of the oldest families in France, and still he is believed to be very rich. They would be throwing themselves at him, and my chance would be lost!"

"But Vivienne is a famous beauty. And much sweeter, more girlish than I would have believed. Are you not afraid he will fall in love with her?"

"No, because now the chase has been long enough and he begins to realize he loves me." Ginny smiled, thinking of the glow in his blue eyes whenever he looked at her. Oh yes, he belonged to her now . . . as she had belonged to him for years. "Nicki and I are the best of friends . . . something he has never had with a woman before. We tell each other everything, share all our secrets. How we laugh together. And not a day passes that he does not call on me. He is wildly angry about Joffrey, of course. He was staring at the duc with murder in his eyes just last evening." She sighed. "The Lady Vivienne cannot hope to compete."

"But still—"

"But still, he could never marry her. I know you have kept many secrets for me in the past, Lisette, so I will trust you with one now. That is no titled and wealthy lady. The real Lady Vivienne is in the arms of her lover in a country village near here. No, that is her *cousine,* a plain Miss Westin without a penny to her name."

The marquise gasped. "Ginny, the webs you weave! So when he learns she has no money—!"

"Only to prevent anything dire from happening, in an emergency. Otherwise, he may never know. Yes, I saw at once when Vivienne wrote me of her scheme how perfectly it would serve. Nicki protected from the heiresses, our love given a chance to blossom. It won't be long before I allow him into my bed. And then he will surely want to kill Joffrey." She smiled. "But it will still be some time before I will wish to let Nicki realize he loves me. So until that time . . ." She turned to the marquise and squeezed her arm, "It is most essential that plain Miss Westin continue successfully in this masquerade."

"Besides," she added after a moment, as they passed into the palais, "really, I have grown quite fond of the girl and want her to have some fun before she goes back to a life of drudgery. *Cherie,* did you know that the Duke of Raceford himself pretended to be a highwayman and kidnapped her on her way here. . . ."

"No, really?" gasped the marquise, fascinated. "Tell me everything!"

"It is the most outrageous tale, my love. If either of them were to find out that it is not the Lady Vivienne they are pursuing . . . you will swear to keep secrecy?"

"I shall. For watching this masquerade be enacted will surely enliven a dull season!" vowed the marquise as they went inside the palais, laughing.

Chapter Twenty

The fairgrounds were alive with crowds chattering in French, and all around Meredith there was a holiday feeling. The open-air horse fair, held on the outskirts of Paris, near the Bois de Boulogne, was in full swing, with trading and dealing on every side. The racetrack was being prepared for the races that would take place later that day. Men raked the track and cleared it of debris and rocks, while others were busy erecting the stands that would house the spectators. Makeshift boxes with chairs were being set up, a railing outlining the track and hung with brightly colored cloth fluttered in the wind, and on all sides was a flurry of activity—hammering and hauling, shouts and laughter.

From a group of gossips, Meredith and Jane learned that Marie Antoinette herself might come to watch the races, a well-known passion of the queen. And it was no secret the king disapproved of her presence at the racetrack. She and Jane exchanged giggles from time to time, listening to these rumormongers describe the intrigues of the Court.

A light cover of gray clouds scudding over the sky and a brisk breeze did nothing to dispel the gala feeling. Today throngs came to look over the horses and watch the races. Tomorrow would be the auction.

The fairgrounds were colorful, with tents and pennants cracking in the breeze, and a great barn where the horse auction would take place. It seemed the street shops of Paris had moved to the fairgrounds, for the same delightful smells filled the air with things to coax the appetite: turkey pâté, goose livers, sizzling beef, veal and mutton, bronze-colored whole truffles, bonbons, breads, blood sausages the size of a hangman's noose, deep sea oysters, and the delicious aroma of brewing mocha above it all.

Wine vendors displayed their sparkling vintages—red Bordeaux, Burgundy, and white Calabria—beneath gaily colored tents. And fruit vendors polished apples—sour greens and sweet reds—and washed oranges and pears as big as a man's fist, setting them out with the greatest care to lure passersby into buying. Flower girls walked the grounds, huge baskets dangling from their arms and bursting with an array of flowers, tuberoses, jonquils, jasmine. The combined smells of all these temptations made Meredith's mouth water. She wondered if she would ever be able to leave Paris in the same clothes she had arrived in.

And there were horses everywhere—in blankets, being led across the paddocks, in corrals, being brushed until they shone.

Meredith and Jane strolled with pleasure through the crowds, stopping at the paddocks to watch the horses. Meredith was determined to buy a horse of her own. Something really beautiful. After all, Vivienne had given her an ungodly amount of money to spend, and so far she'd spent very little. She already had an outrageous amount of Vivienne's clothes and jewels, and her hostess and Nicholas never allowed her to spend a penny. But a horse . . .

the kind of horse she'd always dreamed of. For her own.

And then she saw it. A mare with Arabian blood, black-tipped ears turned into toward each other, a dainty dish-shaped face, a soft black nose. A gorgeous dapple-gray, with a white mane and tail tipped with black and four black stockings. She was as sweet a filly as Meredith had ever seen, and excitedly, she watched her being led around the sale ring at a trot, tail tossed high, forelegs flashing.

She walked up to a man leaning on the rail inside and inquired as to the filly's name.

"The gray?" he said, his eyes quickly taking in her rich wine-red riding habit, her sable-trimmed cloak, her air of wealth. "She's named My Heart's Desire, mistress. She'll be sold in the first lot tomorrow morning. Just two years old and a sweeter filly you couldn't ask for. Flashing speed."

"A beauty indeed."

The voice speaking at her elbow startled her, and she turned to find Raceford smiling down at her. "I might have known your eye for horses was unerring. She's the best of the lot. I've had my eye on her myself."

"You aren't thinking of buying her!" she said hotly. "I mean to buy her whatever the cost."

"I am. I decided to have her the moment I saw her."

Was there more to his words than just sparring with her over a horse? "But you already have your stallion. He's gorgeous," she argued.

"Sultan? But he needs a mate. And I've seen none fit to breed him to until I saw the filly here. Come on. Maybe we can find you another horse."

"I tell you, I mean to have that one!" She stood her

268

ground and let her eyes flash at him.

"Well then, we shall just have to see who wins this round, won't we, my dear Angel?" He held out a dark-green arm and smiled. "I will wager you'll not beat me at this. It's time I won a round from you. But though we cross swords in this, will you allow me to escort you around the stalls? For it appears you have lost your companion."

Perplexed, Meredith turned to see Jane cornered by an exceptionally handsome young man whose tied-back hair gleamed a burnished copper. She was leaning against a wall, and he had one hand resting near her shoulder, his tall frame hemming her in. And from Jane's high color and bright eyes, Meredith could plainly see she wasn't exactly objecting to the attentions of the stunning stranger.

"Who is he?" she asked curiously.

"My valet Armand. He met her somehow and has been burning to see her ever since. Threatened me with all kinds of dire fates if I didn't bring him today. He's much taken with her."

"Your valet? Where would she have met your valet?"

He shrugged, then firmly took her arm, leading her off into the crowds. "Does it matter? Maybe at the masked ball at Versailles. I believe Armand attended in costume that night. But come on. The show is about to start in the main barn."

Meredith gave in, allowing herself to be led along by this masterful man. Really, it was ridiculous how her heart lifted whenever she saw him. How she felt light-headed, like it was Christmas morning or like she'd been drinking champagne. Here she was, in a carnival atmosphere, alone with him, with no prospect of interruption, for Nicki had declared he hated

269

the stink of horses and Ginny had shrieked at the idea of such a peasant occupation. So he was hers for the day.

They strolled along through the masses to a large barn looming against the sky, its double doors open. Here in the parade ring, the horses being sold at tomorrow's sale would be paraded one by one and their starting bids announced.

Inside, it was packed to the rafters, all the seats taken, but Raceford used his force of personality and his muscles to find them one place at the rails. Meredith felt hot, so he helped her off with her cloak and hat, and stood behind her while the first horses were led out and around the ring.

His breath tickled her as he leaned close to speak in her ear, and still she could barely hear him over the din. "What about that dun mare? She's a beauty."

Meredith turned her head slightly and felt his breath on her cheek. "She doesn't hold a candle to the dapple-gray and you know it!" She added in an undertone, "Must you stand so close? It is most—"

"Most tantalizing, is it not?" he murmured in her ear. "But I am afraid the crowd is pressing on me and I have no choice in the matter. I'm grateful to the crowd."

"You're a devil, Raceford!"

"And you are an Angel. I thought you promised to call me Deron."

"Not if I have to kiss you every time I do!" she returned.

"Not every time. The first kiss I have yet to claim."

Meredith gripped the rail harder and felt her skin tingle, a warmth flooding through her at the thought of him claiming a kiss. She stared ahead, trying not to feel him so close behind her, trying to concentrate on the horses but seeing nothing.

There was a commotion near the entrance and she turned her head to see a crowd of burly men forcing their way toward the rails with much laughing, cursing, and jostling. She felt the man next to her give her a shove with his shoulder, then from behind her felt Raceford stumble and come up against her.

She was pressed into the rail, with his body firmly against her. Every inch of him was molded tightly to her. She could feel his thighs against the curve of her behind, could feel his chest against her shoulder blades. Two strong arms came down on either side of hers; two browned hands grasped the rail just outside her own hands.

"I shall have to pay these strangers for this service. Delightful, is it not?" He'd bent his head until his lips were brushing her ear, and Meredith felt heat all through her. For a moment she just stood, feeling him pinning her to the rail, his muscles hard against her soft roundness. And then she couldn't help herself. Slightly, she leaned back against him and pressed tighter.

His hands were off the railing and, shockingly, on her hips. And he was molding his own hips close into her backside, pressing himself into her. For just a moment, her cheeks were on fire as she felt the unmistakable thrust of his desire hard against her!

Flustered, she turned, around speedily, only to realize that this position was worse. They stood face to face, with his arms hemming her in on both sides, his lips mere inches from hers, and his manhood hard against her in an even more intimate manner.

"Lord Raceford!" she gasped, and shoved him backward with her gloved hands.

He smiled wickedly at her, a lock of black hair falling over an eyebrow. "Yes?" he inquired.

"You—"

"I apologize. The crowd pushed me into you. Quite inadvertent, but I must say pleasurable." His eyes dared her to say more, twin devils dancing in them. Finally, she couldn't help it. She laughed.

"Oh, you *are* a rogue! No woman is safe with you, I can see that!"

"But I begin to suspect, My Lady Angel, that it is I who am not safe with you," were his quiet words.

Frozen in time for a moment, Meredith could only stare at him. He desired her, that she had unmistakable evidence of, but in his eyes now there was something more. Tenderness.

And in that long moment they stared at each other, Meredith felt the world rock beneath her, felt everything change. Because in that very moment, she realized something.

She loved him. She loved Deron Redvers.

And he was a duke, and she, a nobody.

God help her, what was she going to do?

One corner of his mouth lifted in what might have been a smile. "Maybe it is too crowded in here. Shall we go outside where we can breathe? I find I am having trouble catching my breath."

She nodded, unable to speak. As she walked at his side, her heart seemed to ache with love of him. Hopeless love. If he knew her secret . . . she could never have him. In all too short a time, she would disappear from his life, never see him again.

She loved him and she was going to lose him.

She looked up at him to find he was watching her with a puzzled expression.

"Sad, My Lady Angel?"

"No." She took in a deep sigh. So little time with

him. And she'd wasted so much of it in trying to push him from her. She had to make every moment count. "I would like to go and look at Heart's Desire once more. The horse that as of tomorrow, I shall own."

He smiled. "Nothing easier. Come with me."

For the rest of the day, he acted the gentleman. It was as if the incident in the barn had never happened. She felt easy in his company, relaxed, and as they stopped in a tent to buy some wine to sip, she realized he was, for the first time, treating her without that passionate tension that made it so hard to think straight around him.

"So tell me," she asked as they seated themselves on a bench inside the wine tent, "where did you get your love of horses?"

"From my childhood. I grew up in the wilds of Yorkshire, where there are endless hills and trackless moors, and learning to ride is a necessity if you want to get around. The neighbors are few and far between. But, then, I just loved it from the first. I never felt so happy as when I could be on horseback, out roaming the hills, without a care in the world. A rather rough upbringing for a duke's son."

"Then . . . Yorkshire is where your estate is? May I ask why you are not there? I wouldn't think you could bear to leave it."

He made a wry grimace. "Leave it? I couldn't get its dust off my boots fast enough. I couldn't bear *not* to leave it is closer to the truth."

"But why?" Meredith was genuinely puzzled. She'd always assumed that if you were brought up somewhere, especially on ancestral lands, raised with the expectation that those lands would one day be your own, you would love them as much as life. But evidently that was not the case with Raceford.

He took a sip of his wine. "I love the wild lands, the moors . . . but as I told you, it was riding and walking with the dogs I loved. Hardly a fit occupation for an estate's lord. You see, there is so much work to do there . . . it's endless. For weeks at a time, you're stuck on the farms. And then you must decide local disputes, and sit at the assizes, and go to what seems seven dinners a week with the local gentry. Not to mention hunt balls. All a dead bore. What I like is—"

He paused, looking uncertain.

"What is it?" asked Meredith, delighted that he was being so frank with her.

"What a confession for a duke, eh? That he can't stand duke-ing and wishes he'd been born the second son instead? Indeed, it's a shame that my brother, Geoffrey, isn't the eldest. He was born to be duke. There's nothing he loves better than managing the estate and being the magistrate. He's married, too, and his wife, Anne, is already increasing. Whereas I have given no thought as yet to providing the ducal heir."

"Is he your only brother?"

"No, there are three younger ones. Boys. And two sisters, one older and one younger. My father died some years ago, and my mother is quite frail. Her memory is poor and she needs a nurse at her side at all times. So my older sister, Nell, took over the role of mother to us all, and she still bosses me shamelessly. In her opinion, it's a scandal I haven't married yet."

"But you were about to tell me what you liked," Meredith pointed out gently.

"Was I? Well, what I liked was the New World. I visited there, and there's something about the place

274

that stirs the blood. It's vast, for one thing. I don't know if it has an end to the West! And it's just waiting to be shaped. It's a wonderful land. Just the place to start a horsefarm."

So her duke didn't care about his title. It warmed her a bit inside. But then, he'd spoken of ducal heirs, and he would surely only want a woman of fit station to be their mother.

"How long were you in the New World?" she asked, thinking, *That's where a girl named Meredith Westin often dreamed of starting a new life for herself. What is it like there? Would she like it?*

"Close on a year. It was heaven. I could forget all about being a duke and just be free to explore, have adventures . . . to live! It is quite wild, once you get out of the settled parts. And vast, untamed. There are endless rivers, clear and filled with fish and beaver. The forests are teeming with deer. There are mountains and prairies."

"What are prairies?" she asked.

"They are rather like flat fields that never end. As far as the eye can see, grasslands with flowering grasses and huge herds of buffalo blackening the horizon. They are a wild animal rather like a cow, but twice as large and covered with reddish wool. They have a hump like a camel and wicked short curving horns. The Indians live on their meat, following the herds and living in conical tents made of their skins. You should have seen the sunsets out there! They were breathtaking, filling all the sky with savage purple and red, as violent and wild as the land."

"It sounds wonderful," she breathed, and he looked at her, surprised.

"It sounds wonderful? To a woman whose wardrobe would rival Marie Antoinette's and who spends

275

her time attending balls among the glittering cream of society?"

If you only knew the truth, Meredith thought. "It does. I would love to see it before I die, and I'd gladly trade every gown and jewel I own for the chance."

He smiled at her warmly. "I didn't want to come back, but I had my duty to my family."

But then he turned to her. "But come, Vivienne, tell me. You have the most wonderful seat on a horse I've ever seen and hands like silk. And you love horses as much as I do. Where did you get your love for them?"

Throwing caution to the wind, Meredith decided to tell him the truth. He'd been so open with her that she wanted him to know a little of the real her. And it was unlikely he'd ever learn Vivienne's family history from someone else.

"My father loved horses. I spent my childhood at his side, when I wasn't on the back of a horse. We attended all kinds of sales, from Wales to Ireland, and he taught me the points of fine horseflesh. I was always at my happiest in a stable with my father. He treated me as if I were his son, and I frequently wore breeches until I became a young lady. It was a bitter day when I had to give it all up."

And more bitter still when he died, Meredith thought. But of course she didn't say this aloud, for Vivienne's parents were still living.

"So you prefer to be a tomboy—and I prefer to be a gypsy," he laughed. "I told you we were two of a kind, My Lady Angel. Neither of us respectable enough to carry the titles we do. A pair of rogues, that is what we are."

Meredith laughed, and inside, she had to agree. In

her opinion, Deron Redvers was made for her and she was made for him.

What a shame that she might never be able to tell him, because she was born in another social strata.

His voice interrupted her thoughts. It was soft and hesitant. "Would you care to accompany me to the races?"

She nodded. "That would be delightful."

With all the care of a gentleman, he took her arm and led her out of the tent across the fairgrounds. At the racetrack, he found two seats near the front railing and settled down beside her to watch the parade of horses, their brightly garbed riders waving to the crowd, as they made their way to the starting line.

But Meredith barely noticed the bets being taken around her, the riders taking their marks, or the sound of the pistol shot ringing through the air signaling the beginning of the race. The thunder of the horses hooves as they swept past her and the cheering of the spectators as the horses crossed the finish line seemed not to even reach her ears. She even forgot to look for the queen.

She was watching Deron.

The things he'd told her that afternoon had had a strange effect on her, like that of an artist finishing a portrait. He was more vivid now, more alive and more pleasing to her soul than he had been before. And with this clearer picture had come a rush of emotions she'd never felt before.

Everything else seemed to fade around her, and there was only this man at her side—his scent, his power, his grace emanating from him and infusing her with the most wonderful sense of well-being in his presence. She wished she could suspend the moment forever. Feel this way forever. Everything about him made her love him all the more. His strong hand at rest on his knee, the curve of his jawline, the sweep of his hair. She couldn't help but love him as she watched him from the corner of her eye.

As she watched him through the new eyes of love.

"So, it is my lucky day. To be alone with you. I've been dreaming of it."

Jane glanced up at Armand and thought that just the sight of him had the power to make her heart beat faster. And when he said things like that to her . . .

"How did you know I was going to be here?"

"His Grace told me he was coming here to see Lady Vivienne. Since you are her companion, I hoped you'd be with her. I had to confess to him that I was smitten to get him to let me come along, for a valet doesn't usually accompany his master to social events."

Smitten! She felt her cheeks heat up. "So . . . he was most anxious to be alone with My Lady."

"Yes, I believe he's fallen in love with her. But come along with me. You aren't really interested in horses, are you?"

"No . . ." she said uncertainly.

His arm slipped through hers, and he steered her through the crowds. "I happened to notice a place we can be alone in all this crush. Just past these tents here."

He led the way behind a refreshment tent, to a small green hill that was lush with grass. A line of bushes screened it from the view of passersby, and he held the bushes aside for her.

He shrugged off his jacket and spread it on

the ground for her. "Sit down, and I shan't be a moment."

Jane smiled up at him and watched as he vaulted the bushes effortlessly. The sun was quite hot in this sheltered place, and it was as private as it could be. She felt a thrill in her veins, remembering the masterful way he'd kissed her the night they met.

In a few moments he was back, carrying a bottle and a basket. "Some food and drink. Hot meat pies, cheese and bread, and a chilled bottle of white wine. I can't think of a more pleasant way to spend the afternoon, can you?"

"No," said Jane as he knelt beside her in the grass, setting down the basket.

"But I must confess, I just lied."

"About what?" she asked, thinking that his eyes were as golden green as sunlight through spring leaves.

His hands came up to gently cradle her head. "I can think of a much more pleasant way to spend the afternoon," he said. "Kissing you."

And he bent his head to hers. With Armand's mouth on hers and the sun on her back, Jane soon forgot anything except the magic of his touch. In a few moments they fell together to the grass, twined in each other's arms, and nearly forgot all about the wine.

She was breathless as his hands rose from her waist to cup her breasts, and for a moment, she looked nervously over his shoulder. "Armand! We might be seen!"

"And if we are, I will kill them. Besides, no one is likely to jump over this hedge. We're far from everyone, and they are too busy with their wine." His mouth was nibbling her neck, distracting her so much that she didn't notice he was untying the ribbons at her bodice, slipping them apart. But when she felt his warm hands on her skin as he eased her dress open, she jumped.

"Armand!" she gasped, scandalized.

"Oh, *ma cherie,* you are so beautiful," he said with some difficulty as he finished opening her dress and gazed at her lacy corset.

And then his fingers were working at those lacings, and as she squirmed to get away, he opened her corset and tugged it down, so that her breasts were completely naked to his gaze. *"Mon Dieu,"* he breathed again. "I am in love with you."

That confession left Jane dizzy and melted her resistance, and when his seeking mouth captured her nipple, she could only gasp in pleasure. It wasn't long before that distraction kept her from noticing that his free hand was sliding her skirts upward. When he had her leg bared, his hand came back up and with two hands, he cupped her breasts and pushed them together, running his tongue deep in the valley between them. Just by turning his head, he could flick each nipple until they stood erect and until she was throbbing with desire.

Her own fingers were opening his shirt, wanting to feel his smooth golden skin, which was hot to the touch. And then he kissed her again, and the sounds of the horse fair faded and all they could hear was their own soft cries of pleasure.

Much later, Armand sat up and Jane tugged at her dress. "Well, my darling, much as I hate to say it, we must stop. For such a public place is not where I would pursue events to their final delicious conclusion."

Jane knew Armand was speaking of doing much

more to her than just playing with her breasts and shaping her legs with his hands, and she blushed. He meant making love to her. But where would they ever be alone to do so?

Shocked, she realized she was thinking as if she'd already made up her mind to give herself to him!

He closed his shirt and grinned at her, then spoke as if he read her mind.

"And it is a conclusion I can barely wait for," he said. "Some wine?"

As she sipped the chilled pale wine, hoping it would cool her off, she thought, *And I can hardly wait, either! What a shocking wench I am!*

And how very much fun it all was.

The sun was westering as Meredith, with misty eyes, watched Raceford walk off, beside a tall copper-haired man. At her side, Jane heaved a sigh as deep as her own.

"It was a lovely day, wasn't it, My Lady?" asked Jane wistfully.

"It was lovely." Meredith looked at Jane. "So tell me about Armand."

"Oh, he's wonderful! Everything I ever dreamed about in a man and never thought I'd find. My head's rightly turned. But, you see, he thinks I'm you. And so, out of his reach socially. He doesn't know we're both servants! And I wish I could tell him."

"Well, it won't be long before the need for secrecy . . . at least with him . . . will be over." Meredith sounded as depressed as she felt. "And we'll be going back to England."

"You'll miss him, won't you, Meredith?"

Meredith sighed. "I will." A moment passed, when both women looked glumly at their feet and contemplated the ridiculous mess they were in . . . both in love with men who didn't know who they really were. Then Meredith brightened, and a determined look came over her face.

"Come on. We have someplace to go." She started dragging Jane off toward the paddocks.

"Where?"

Meredith smiled a grim smile. It had been a wonderful day . . . one of the best she'd ever had. Except for in the barn, Deron had behaved toward her like a perfect gentleman. They had laughed together, been easy with one another, been friends. They had each discovered in the other a love and knowledge about horses as deep as their own. Indeed, today had forged new bonds of friendship and companionship between them.

But all was fair, after all, when it was a game you meant to win.

"Where are we going?" said Meredith. "To buy a dapple-gray horse."

Chapter Twenty-one

It was the day of reckoning, and Meredith knew it. Today was the auction . . . the auction she wasn't attending. Because safe in the stable, for a price that was more than the man expected to get, was her new filly, My Heart's Desire. And she knew that Raceford would be furious.

It was a lovely afternoon, and she had decided to avoid any confrontation by accepting Nicholas' invitation for a picnic. Now she, Jane, Ginny, Nicholas, and Joffrey, the Duc du Fronde, all lounged at ease on cloths spread in a flowery meadow. The food was finished; over near the trees edging the field rested the many servants; the meadow sloped down to a river edged with willows and dappled with sunshine. There were daisies in the grass and new green leaves on all the trees. In the distance, the bleat of sheep could be heard in nearby fields and the singing of larks high above in the sky. Not a cloud marred the blue heavens above, and the sunshine felt lovely on Meredith's bare arms. It was perfect peace.

The women all wore country frocks of the type made popular by Marie Antoinette when she played peasant at her mock farm, milking her cows into

Sevres bowls. The fabrics were of the thinnest muslin, almost transparent, clinging to the natural curves beneath, unhampered by petticoats. They wore openwork straw hats much festooned with ribbons and flowers. Ginny was a vision in ice-pink, Jane wore pale yellow with green sprigs and green silk ribbons, and Meredith the palest of blues. All three women wore their hair caught back by ribbons and then cascading naturally down their backs, and looked like girls.

The men were at ease, for once having shed their confining coats in favor of loose white shirts and fawn trousers. They wore boots rather than stockings and shoes, and no one's hair was powdered. There was a delightfully informal, easy feeling to the afternoon, for today etiquette was forgotten. Meredith thought the men looked much more handsome in their casual attire, and especially with unpowdered hair.

Nicholas propped himself up on one elbow. "But your glass is empty, my dear comtesse. Let me pour you more wine," he said.

"Only if I may have strawberries in it again," smiled the comtesse.

"If Ginny needs more wine, I shall get it for her," growled Joffrey, black brows frowning at Nicholas. Meredith smiled. Joffrey certainly was exhibiting signs of jealousy today. He lay at Ginny's elbow, fanning her with her lace fan, giving Nicholas periodic glowers from his dark eyes. But why he should be so jealous, Meredith didn't know. Nicholas had been most attentive to her, hardly leaving her side. She supposed a jealous man could see a threat in anyone.

"But, Duc . . . since it is my picnic, I claim the honor of acting as host," said Nicholas smoothly.

"Yes, Joffrey, don't be tiresome. Nicki is only being polite."

"My apologies," said the duc with his lips, but his eyes still held warning.

"Oh, dear, I wouldn't want such a perfect day to end in anything nasty like a duel," remarked Ginny lightly.

"The perfection has ended," Nicki observed, looking across the meadow.

Meredith looked up to see Raceford striding across the field. But all signs of the duke had vanished. It was as if her highwayman had returned, in his black pants, white shirt, and gleaming black boots. She caught her breath at the sight and thought she never saw him more handsome than when he looked like a dangerous rogue.

"How did he know to find us here?" asked Jane.

"I am afraid I was foolish enough to let them know at the palais where we were going," Meredith said.

"Well! I, for one, am delighted that Raceford honors us with his company. In point of fact, I invited him myself. He is so entertaining," Ginny said brightly. "And such a handsome man," she added, earning another glare from Joffrey.

Meredith watched him cross the meadow with a sinking heart. So she wasn't to escape the dressing-down. Well, she supposed she should know by now that if one crossed swords with Raceford, one had better be prepared to do battle.

He came up to them and stopped, looking down, fists on hips. "What a tranquil scene. Ginny, good afternoon. I thank you for your invitation and regret that I couldn't come earlier. I had some pressing business." One shot from the green eyes at Meredith, and then he was blandly greeting the others. "Nicki, Duc, good afternoon. Lady Vivienne. And Miss Westin . . . a pleasure. I see I was needed to even the numbers of the party. May I?" At Jane's nod, he sat down next to her, as the places at Ginny's and Meredith's elbows were already occupied by Joffrey and Nicholas.

Meredith bent her head as they poured him wine and gave him pâté to nibble on. Her openwork straw hat cast a dappled pattern of light and shadow over her face, and she was grateful for its size. It was covered with white daisies and ice-blue ribbons, and she wore a pale blue and white flowered muslin dress. But after a moment, she realized her cowardice was unnecessary. Raceford seemed to be in a good humor and he was ignoring her, laughing and jesting with Jane.

"And so you enjoyed the horse sale yesterday, Miss Westin?" he was saying, and Jane gave him a bright blush.

"Oh, I did. It was most interesting," she said, clearly embarrassed.

"I know that it was a red-letter day for my valet . . . since he did not have to be bothered with my presence," he said smoothly, and Jane turned even redder.

"Horse sales! Barbaric," exclaimed Nicki. "As long as they are fast and pretty, I do not even wish to know where my horses come from. I cannot imagine going oneself among all the canaille and actually having a hand in purchasing a beast."

"I could not agree more," put in Ginny, with a delicate shudder.

"But some people get a vast amount of enjoyment out of choosing a horse . . . and then purchasing it themselves," said Raceford, with another brief blast from the green eyes for Meredith. "It is a challenge to see if you can outwit those who are competing with you for the same animal."

"But is there not a great deal of cheating that goes on?" asked Jane, giving him back a barb in retaliation.

"There is," he replied. "The trick is to judge who is honest and who is not. You would be astounded at how innocent some of the most flagrant cheaters look." His eyes met Meredith's sardonically.

"A woman must watch out for her own interests," said Meredith virtuously. "And go after what she wants, for otherwise she will be sure to never get anything. Men are so ruthless."

Raceford was about to speak when Ginny roused herself and sent Meredith a smile. "It seems that I have cause to be grateful to you, Vivienne."

Meredith was puzzled. "I do not recall doing you any favors."

"Just the great one of fixing the chevalier's interest. He was constantly at my side until he discovered you; now I no longer receive his unwanted attentions."

Meredith frowned. "I rue the day I met him. He could be a very sweet boy, for all his bold speeches, but he's truly the most persistent thing I've met. Someday his persistence and boldness will get him or someone else in deep trouble. I wish we could interest him in someone else!"

Raceford grinned impishly. "Why, Joffrey, don't you have a niece about his age that we could introduce him to?"

"I hope you are a hand with a sword, Raceford, for even suggesting such a thing. I'd not introduce that loathsome twit to my worst enemy." Joffrey turned to Meredith and smiled. "More wine, Lady Vivienne?"

"Thank you," she murmured. As always, something about the great duc unnerved her . . . especially since that night at the opera when he had taken to flirting with her.

Nicki plucked a daisy and gave it to Meredith.

"Perhaps I will take pity on you," he teased. "I have a friend whose daughter would know how to put this chevalier in his place. And it is your great good fortune that she is exceptionally beautiful. Perhaps I shall bring her with me next time we attend a ball."

"If you would do that, I would have to admit myself in your debt," she said, and noticed Raceford glaring coldly at the viscomte.

"But I think it is amusing to watch the chevalier pursuing you!" protested Ginny. "Far better you than me."

"But the chevalier still has a *tendre* for you, Genvieve," smiled Nicki. "He told me so . . . but hopes to make you jealous by his pursuit of Vivienne."

"He is terribly bold in the way he pursues women. I do not recall ever seeing a man so bold, especially when there are others about," remarked Meredith.

"Then," said Joffrey, "you have not been keeping company with the right sort of man." And he gave her a look from his barbarian's black eyes that fairly smoldered.

"I greatly wonder," said Raceford, glaring at her intently, "what sort of pursuit would be bold enough for you? When I recall your fondness for masked balls . . ."

"What do masked balls have to do with bold pursuit, Raceford?" asked Joffrey irritably.

"A great deal. There, people behave more uninhibitedly because they are masked. But it is hard for me to imagine what a bold pursuit might be in a lady's estimation. One fears to offend their sensibilities. Lady Vivienne, what exactly would be too bold for you?"

Meredith had blushed at the reference to the masked ball. Odious scamp! To provoke her so in public!

"I prefer a gentle and refined courtship," she said firmly. Nicki exchanged a look with Ginny, who nodded imperceptibly.

"Then I shall have to learn to act more gentlemanly. Not to cheat, for example," said Raceford.

The rogue! He'd never let up on the fact that she'd bought the horse out from under his nose . . . nor, to be fair, did she blame him. She'd really behaved rather badly. It was a relief when Nicki proposed a walk a few minutes later.

"If I do not get up and move around," said Nicholas firmly, "I shall fall asleep. And I would not expose the ladies to my snoring. May I walk you to the river, Vivienne?"

Vivienne. Meredith saw one of Raceford's black brows lift lightly at the familiarity, but he didn't turn away from Jane. Feeling slightly nasty, Meredith said, "But that would give me great pleasure, Nicki."

And saw the muscle in Raceford's jaw tighten.

She gave Nicki her hands and allowed him to pull her to her feet. Picking up a white lace parasol, Meredith took his arm and slowly strolled with him through the meadow. The other members of the party were following their lead and leisurely making for the river.

They reached the river and stood for a few moments, enchanted by its sparkling surface and patterns of light and shadow. The banks were grassy, and great willows fluttered their slender leaves above. Mossy logs reclined half in and half out of the water, inviting them to sit.

Nicholas picked another daisy and began plucking the petals one by one and tossing them in the river. "She loves me . . . she loves me not . . ."

He reached the last petal and turned to her with a brilliant smile. "She loves me!" he laughed.

They sat down on a fallen log and Nicki, with a glance to see they were alone, took her hand.

"Could it be true, my dearest Vivienne? Could you ever love me?"

He looked so beautiful, his hair shining silver-gilt in the sun, his blue eyes filled with warmth, that Meredith felt her heart melt.

"I am not sure, Nicki. I know that I have formed a deep affection for you."

He squeezed her hand. "Your words give me hope . . . and have made me the happiest man in France today. Someday, my darling, I will gain the courage to kiss you and perhaps to show you just how warm you can feel toward me. But I will not dare it yet . . . not until you tell me you are sure about what you feel. That perhaps it is warmer than affection."

She smiled at him, and for a long moment, they just gazed at each other, seeing something new and fresh in each other's eyes. Is this how love feels? Nicki . . . he made her feel like she was precious to him, made her feel soft and lovely, feelings that did not shake her inner picture of herself. Not at all like Raceford made her feel.

And of course it was all ridiculous. She was plain Miss Meredith Westin and he was a viscomte, a member of one of the most ancient families in France. He'd doubtless be horrified if he knew who he was really dallying with.

"I do so enjoy your company, Nicholas. It is refreshing to be treated with respect by a man. You are truly a gentleman, ever since the first night I met you, when you rode up like a knight on a white horse to my rescue!"

So, thought Nicholas, *Ginny was right to tell me to court her in a refined way. It is a good thing I did not follow my own inclinations and seduce her. Ginny is a genius. But, then, what did I ever know about women?* And the thought of the Winter millions was vastly comforting.

"If there is ever anything I can do for you, from the smallest request to the greatest imaginable, you have only to ask, Vivienne. I would count it an honor to render you any service."

"I will keep that in mind, Viscomte. And as to your hopes that someday I may feel something warmer than affection . . . I appreciate it that you do not press me. For I am not yet certain how I feel, or what the feelings I do have for you mean."

"Then you feel something for me?" Ardently, he bent his head and kissed her hand, then the inside of her wrist. He raised his head to look at her. "How your pulse is racing! Mine is racing with—I dare to say it—desire. Can it be the same reason yours races? For desire is but the first sign that love sends."

"I do not know what I feel, Nicki," she repeated. But it was a lie. The gloriously gorgeous viscomte certainly did make her feel desire. It was really not wise to be alone with him too long.

"*There* you are!"

Ginny's lilting voice caused Meredith to pull her hand out of Nicholas' and look up to find the four others coming down the bank toward them.

"And now I insist," said Ginny as she came up, "that we trade partners for the walk back. It is *too* boring to flirt with only one man in a day. Nicki darling, you will escort me?"

Nicki leaped to his feet with alacrity and held out his arm. The duc, with a frown, was stepping toward Meredith, but Raceford got there first. He took her arm firmly.

"Since Lady Vivienne and I share a love of horses, I would walk her back. I desire her advice on a certain equine matter."

The duc looked around, but Jane was nowhere to be seen. She'd not accompanied the others on the walk to the river, for she'd caught a glimpse of copper hair at Raceford's carriage and had hung back with the excuse of needing some privacy. Then she'd slipped off to join Armand, much preferring his company to the aristocratic company she found herself in.

"Armand!" she'd laughed, running up to the carriage and waving her beribboned parasol.

"Meredith . . . my foolish girl! And what if your friends see you running off to speak to a groom?"

Armand took her hand and pulled her inside the carriage. It had a light cloth roof that hid them from view. "You are not a groom!" she'd protested.

"I am whatever my master says I am, and today I act as his groom. *Mon Dieu,* but you look lovely," he exclaimed.

She wore a yellow muslin dress with a wide lawn collar, and deep green ribbons fluttered from her hat amid a profusion of daisies and green leaves, all silk, of course.

"Come here," he added hoarsely, and pulled her into his lap.

Jane surrendered herself to his kiss, loving the way his lips moved over hers and the way his arms felt, so tightly wrapped around her. He untied the ribbons under her chin as he kissed her, sliding off her hat without letting his lips ever leave hers.

She felt his hands at her waist, then they slowly and sensually moved upward. Over her dress, he cupped the curve of her breast, still kissing her hungrily, and slid his other hand over her other breast. Soon his hands moved higher, to her ruffled bodice, and caressed the swelling tops of her breasts, easing the fabric down until they were bared almost to the tops of her nipples.

"Have I told you how very much I want you?" he murmured against her lips. He gave the fabric a sudden yank, and her lacy corset was exposed. "Why do women wear so many clothes?" he groaned, pulling at the silken ribbons that laced her corset in the front.

In no time he had it open and was baring her breasts. For a moment he sat back, just drinking in the sight of her, her golden brown curls disheveled, her generous rose-nippled breasts bared to his gaze, her honey-brown eyes half closed, her lips parted. Then he kissed her again, long and deeply, while his warm hands moved over her breasts.

Before long, he was lowering her onto the seat, lying on top of her, letting his questing mouth drop to her breasts. She tilted her head back, gasping under his loving onslaught, and all at once he grinned up at her.

"And what would my master or your haughty *cousine* say now if they came back to find the lady in the arms of the servant?"

"I don't care, Armand. It's what *we* think that matters."

"And what do you think?"

"I think," Jane said deliberately, "that if you do not kiss me again this moment, I shall be most angry."

"Heaven forfend. I would never want to make you angry," he grinned, just before his laughing lips closed over hers.

Back at the riverbank, Meredith steeled herself as she took Raceford's arm and resigned herself to his walking her back to the picnic site. Ah, well. She might have known Raceford would find a way to get her alone and upbraid her for her underhanded tactics.

As they walked off, out of earshot of the others, Meredith said as calmly as she could manage, "So,

I imagine you are angry with me for beating you to the filly and buying her before the sale."

"I should have known, for you have cheated me before. Yet it hardly seems fair that you would not even give me the chance at her."

"But all is fair in love and war, is it not, Duke?"

"And is this love . . . or war?" he inquired silkily.

She shot a glance at him from beneath her hat brim. "Since it cannot be love, I imagine it is war, My Lord."

"But in war, the victor is the one who has won the battle. You did not even give me a chance to fight. Were you so certain you would lose?"

Meredith bristled. "I would not have lost," she grated.

"But, then, we shall never know. Unless, of course, you are willing to give me another chance. Willing to fight and compete fairly."

"After all your deceit with me, I wonder that you can cast aspersions on me for what I did!"

He smiled, and his grip on her arm tightened. "Ah, but then you have been so righteous about my white lies. It seems strange you would allow yourself to sink to a level you profess to despise. It makes you quite a hypocrite, does it not, my beauty?"

Meredith stopped and glared up at him. "I am not a hypocrite!" she flashed.

"Then you will be anxious to allow me a chance to win that horse fairly."

"What do you mean?" she asked suspiciously.

"I propose a fair competition."

"And what kind of competition would be fair?"

He grinned. "I have long admired your horsemanship. What about a race?"

"A race?" Meredith saw the mischievous glint in his eyes. "And if you win . . . you get Heart's Desire. What will I gain if I win?"

"Besides your honesty back? Let's put up our horses against each other. Let's say . . . if you win, Sultan will be yours. You have admired him in the past. And if I win, I will gain My Heart's Desire."

"No."

"Afraid?"

She glared at him. Oh, there was something about the man that made her hackles rise!

"No, I am not afraid!" she spat.

"Then prove it."

She simmered for a moment, then felt her old impulses take over. Heart's Desire was fast . . . maybe fast enough to beat Sultan. And how she itched to teach this man a lesson!

"You're on," she said coldly.

He smiled and took her hand to kiss it lingeringly. "I never doubted your spirit, My Lady Angel. From the first, you were never afraid when I kidnapped you. . . . You have always given me as good as I've given you. I told you we are a match for one another."

His hand clasped hers warmly and she had no wish to withdraw it.

"I recall that you are fond of riding at dawn. Shall we say tomorrow morning at sunrise, then? Here in this meadow? It's long enough."

"Who will be the judge?"

"I think we should be quite alone. The fashionable world would be scandalized if they knew you were doing anything as mad as horse racing. We can tie a ribbon across those trees there and the first to break it will be the victor."

"And I shall be the first," she said, making it a promise.

"Until tomorrow, then, My Lady," he said, "when the winner will take all."

Chapter Twenty-two

Meredith was up while it was still dark the next morning, dressing herself for the race. She had told no one of her plans, not even Jane. She pulled her hair back and tied it at her neck, letting it fall in a long tail that reached her waist. Then she pulled on the narrow breeches and loose white shirt she used to wear on her dawn rides in England. She'd brought them for sentimental reasons, and now she was glad. She'd have no chance of winning at all if she were hampered by full skirts.

She drew on her black boots and wrapped herself in her long black cloak that fell to her heels. Putting the hood over her head, she softly opened the door to her room and looked both ways.

The hallway was deserted, and she slipped like a shade down the grand staircase and through the maze of reception rooms. Not even the kitchens were stirring yet, and she gained a side door without meeting a soul.

The world was still gray when she got outside, and Meredith stopped for a moment, sniffing the air, listening to make sure she heard no one. It was going to be a fine day.

She scampered across the lawns drenched with

dew, avoiding the gravel paths where her boots would grate, until she reached the stables. In moments, she had greeted My Heart's Desire, rubbing her velvety black nose, and saddled and bridled her. She led her out the stable doors and swung herself up astride.

The filly moved like a dream through the gray predawn, and Meredith smiled. How wonderful, to be on a marvelous horse without the bother of petticoats and sidesaddles, skirts and hats! To be riding astride, as a rider should, into a new world, all alone!

Heart's Desire was a wonderful horse, she thought. Her gaits were smooth as glass, effortless. And she was calm, sweet-tempered, with intelligent and fearless eyes. Meredith resolved fiercely she would not lose the race today, not lose this filly she'd already grown to love!

She kept Heart's Desire to a jog-trot to warm her muscles as they crossed fields and small woodlands. She didn't want to wear her out before the race. It was only four miles to the place along the river where they'd picnicked. Just the right distance for a good warm-up for both of them.

The dawn was breaking, a strip of light along the world's edge, with long lines of light falling across the grass and turning the dewdrops to red fire. She topped the rise over the meadow. Everything was green and lovely, the turf smooth and close-cropped, the willows along the river marking its line. And he was there, waiting for her.

He sat at his ease on his great black stallion and watched her as she trotted down the small slope to his side. Meredith saw, with a queer little twist to her heart, that her highwayman was back again.

Gone were the brocaded coats, the knee breeches. Instead, he was dressed just like she was, in a loose white shirt, close black breeches, and tall gleaming boots. Even his raven hair was tied by a black ribbon at his neck, just as hers was. They could have been brother and sister, except for the way they looked at each other.

"Good morning," he said. His eyes dropped to her legs and traveled over them. "I see you came prepared to win."

"I did." Meredith unfastened her cloak and rode to a bush, dropping it over the branches next to another black cloak—his. "And what is the course to be?"

He turned in the saddle and shaded his eyes against the dazzle in the east. Meredith couldn't help but notice the play of muscles in his thighs as he moved, and hastily lifted her eyes to where he was pointing.

"There is a smooth track along the river—a flat two miles. I suggest you ride it to make sure there are no surprises. I already have. See those two trees at the end of the track?" She nodded and noticed the ribbon he'd stretched there as promised. "The first to break the ribbon is the winner. Since we have no judge, we shall just have to hope it is not a nose-to-nose finish, in which case we'll call a draw. Agreed?"

"Agreed," Meredith said briskly, and set off alone to the start of the track. She rode along it slowly, but it was as he'd said, clear and clean. Here and there, it was obvious he'd tossed a branch out of the way. The ground was firm, the course level. There was plenty of room for two horses to gallop side by side. At last she rode back to him.

"It's a good track."

"Then, are you ready, My Lady Angel, to be beaten?"

She flashed him a grin. "You will never beat me, My Demon Lord."

"The terms we agreed on . . . Sultan for My Heart's Desire?"

"Those were the terms. Agreed."

"Good. And now I shall make an honest woman out of you."

"A rogue turning reformer?" It was her turn to laugh.

"Shall we start?" He grinned back at her, a gypsy grin, with confidence sparkling in his leaf-green eyes. The wind took a lock of his black hair and blew it over his brow, and Meredith felt her heart jump.

As they rode to the head of the race course, he said, staring straight ahead but with a slight twitch at the corners of his lips, "Have I told you lately how gorgeous your eyes are? I have been trying to decide whether indigo or cobalt describes them better."

"If you are trying to distract me, it's a feeble attempt," she said.

He sighed. "These modern women! One despairs of them. Their minds are always on practicalities. Perhaps azure is the right word."

"If My Lord is through talking, we have reached the start. Shall we line up? And who is to give the signal to start?"

"I thought of that. I brought this ostrich feather with me. I'll toss it in the air in front of us, and when it strikes the ground, we start. Fair enough?"

"Fair enough. And may the best . . . horse win."

He smiled at her and they carefully aligned their horses, Meredith taking the place closest to the river.

"Ready?"

Tensely, she nodded. He rose in his stirrups and tossed the feather into the air, then sat and gathered his reins. Meredith was almost trembling with anticipation as the morning breeze took the feather and it drifted in a long downward spiral. Heart's Desire felt her excitement and danced slightly.

The feather touched the ground. Meredith drove her heels into the filly's side, and with a thundering start, they were off. All her butterflies were gone as she leaned far forward over the filly's neck, standing in the stirrups, hands thrown ahead. There was only the pounding of hooves, the flashing sunlight, the rhythm of the running muscles, the wind in her hair, and the filly's mane in her face. Beside her and a little behind, Sultan pounded. Oh, Heart's Desire was fast! She was beating the great stallion, she had wings on her feet! Meredith was laughing as the river fled past. She was winning the race!

With a low cry, she urged Heart's Desire on faster, squeezing with her calves, and dared a glance back. Sultan was almost a full length behind them now, and the filly was racing as if she could fly. Meredith's heart was singing, and she laughed into the wind. Just a mile to go and she would have beaten him!

But within a few more strides she heard the pounding of hooves behind her getting louder. She glanced back. Sultan was stretching himself, stretching, his great black legs seeming to eat up ground. Raceford was lying low along his neck, lightly balanced, and urging the stallion on with a low

302

monotone.

"Come on, Desire, come *on*, my beauty, you can do it. Fly, my lovely," Meredith was singing in the filly's ear, and she felt her give a burst of unbelievable speed.

But then he was next to her, the great brute of a stallion, drawing even, and she didn't even look aside, just gave it her everything until she felt her teeth clench and that her heart might burst. But stride by stride, the black was drawing ahead, and she couldn't get an ounce more speed out of Desire . . . They were going to lose. Their own burst of speed had been too early!

The twin trees loomed ahead of them, and Sultan was thundering through them, almost a half length in front of her. Slowly, she sat back, letting Heart's Desire cool her headlong gallop to a hand gallop and then to a canter, finally to a walk.

She'd lost!

The realization struck her with the telling force of a blow. Her beautiful Heart's Desire, lost. The first horse she could call her own. And now she belonged to Raceford!

"I hate you," she said clearly as she rode up to him and past him.

"I wouldn't have expected you to be a poor loser," he remarked, sliding off his horse and tying it.

"You won, fair and square. And I will have Heart's Desire sent to your stable today. Just now, I only want to go home."

Meredith knew she was being unreasonably sulky, but the thought of losing her filly was like a knife in her heart.

"Wait." He ran up to the filly's head and put a hand on the reins, stopping them. "Our business is

303

not finished yet today, my beautiful Angel. There is still something you owe me. Get down."

"I will not! And I owe you nothing else!"

"Must I pull you off that horse, which you ride by my grace now?"

"Just try!" Meredith dared him, and instantly regretted the words. He twisted the reins around a bush and advanced on her. She swung her legs over the side away from him and slid off. Then as rapidly as she could, she started walking away.

"Very well," she called over her shoulder. "Take the horse now. I shall walk home."

"And to see you in those breeches, I would follow you the whole way. It is a most enticing sight. Though I have felt your legs bare beneath my hands, I have never seen them until today. They are a most lovely shape. And might I add, your *derriere* is spectacular. Enough to make a man lose his senses."

Meredith stopped and turned to face him, face burning. She was opening her mouth to speak when he strode up and stopped before her. He let his gaze roam down her shirt to where her breasts tautened the white material, to the narrowness of her waist, then over her thighs.

"And the view from the front is equally delectable. I can't think of a more stimulating way to collect what you still owe me."

"And what is that?" asked Meredith, taking a step backward.

"The kiss you promised me when you called me by my name," he said softly, his eyes on her lips.

Meredith backed up again, eyeing him warily. "I have given you enough for one day!"

"I think not," was the inflexible answer.

304

She sidestepped him, starting to run, but his hand shot out and caught her wrist. Slowly, inexorably, she was drawn toward him, until they were only inches apart. "And now, the kiss, My Lady, that you owe me," he said, and his voice was husky and caressing.

Meredith took one look in his eyes and knew she was lost. Oh, she wanted to kiss him as much as he wanted to kiss her! But the force of her feelings frightened her. Would he see the love she felt written all over her face, feel it in her lips?

His mouth came down on her and his arms came around her, pulling her close. For a moment she resisted, then felt the heat of his lips tracing hers, parting her mouth, opening it. Against her will, her arms slid up around his neck as he gathered her closer and they were locked together in the sweetest of kisses.

The kiss rapidly deepened into searing need on both their parts. His mouth was hard, demanding, and hers was answering him with an abandon she hadn't suspected she had. It had been so long, too long since either had tasted the magical fire there was between them, this delicious passion they yearned for.

His hands dropped from her shoulders and ran over her back, feeling every contour of her through the thin white shirt. And her own hands left his neck and did what she'd wanted to do for so long, feeling his shoulders, the muscles of his arms, his neck, his chest. Then he was cupping her waist, running his palms up her ribs to cradle her breasts, and she arched against him so they pressed against his chest. His fingers found her erect nipples and brushed them, and then his roaming hands were

305

dropping again, this time to the backs of her thighs.

He ran his hands over the roundness of her backside, delighting in the delicious curves, and then suddenly pulled her firmly against him so she could feel the raging hard desire she'd stirred in him throbbing against her.

It brought Meredith to her senses. Her eyes flew open at the hard heat of his manhood against her, at the indecent way his hands were cupping her buttocks and molding her into him.

"Stop it!" she gasped.

"Stop what?" he asked huskily, his hands coming around and running over the fronts of her thighs, the flat of her stomach. His eyes were half closed and blazing with desire. "Why do you continue to fight me?" he murmured, letting his lips drop to her jaw, his warm tongue sliding along her neck. "Why won't you admit that you want me as much as I want you? There is no hiding what you feel for me, but I would like to hear you say it. Tell me you want me. Tell me you burn for me the way I burn for you."

"I'll never tell you!"

"But it doesn't need words. You can feel my desire"—he took her hand and started moving it down his belly, and shocked, she snatched it away—"just as I can feel yours. You are as much on fire for me here"—his thumb caressed her erect nipple—"as you are here . . ." His hand moved lower and slid between her legs, cupping her warmly so that she felt a shock of pleasure, an ache of desire.

"Tell me," he whispered against her lips. "With your mouth."

His hand between her thighs was doing things to Meredith she hadn't ever imagined could be real.

His other hand was unbuttoning her shirt, sliding it open, and his mouth dropped to her breast and he let just the tip of his tongue touch her nipple. She gasped, knowing that if she didn't make him stop what he was doing, right now, *right this very minute*, she was going to fall with him on the grass and let him make love to her.

"Please . . . I asked you to stop!" she panted, pushing him away and standing up straight. Oh, he looked wild, his black hair half unbound and sweeping his shoulders, his shirt open to bare his brown chest — had she done that? — his eyes green as the new grass they stood on. "You have had your kiss."

She backed away from him steadily, her breath coming in uneven jerks, until at last she felt the filly at her back. Clumsily, with shaking hands, she untied the reins and leaped on her back.

She looked down at him, and he watched her without saying a word.

"And you have won the race," she said angrily.

"By fair means. All is fair in love and war, and you yourself told me that this is war, My Lady. At least I have warned you what to expect. I am accustomed to winning."

"You may have won the race fairly," she blazed. "But, My Lord," she warned, putting her heels to the filly's flanks, "You have not won me!"

And she galloped away into the rising morning light, half hoping to hear the pounding of hooves behind her.

But this was one race she won, for when she looked back at the top of the rise, he still stood, just looking after her, letting her go.

Chapter Twenty-three

"Meredith!"

It was another rainy night in Paris and Jane paused, wondering if she'd really heard the hissed word. She peered into the pouring rain, then shrugged and decided it hadn't been anything after all. She had just alighted from the coach in front of the palais, and the hood of her cloak was around her head, muffling the sounds she could hear. She was in a hurry to get inside out of the rain. She'd left a ball at the Marquise du Planchet's early, because she'd hoped against hope Armand would be there. But he wasn't, and she'd had no heart for lighthearted flirtation. She missed Armand.

"Meredith!" A tall figure materialized out of the rain at her side, and she gave a small shriek.

"Quiet! They mustn't know I'm here," whispered Armand. "I came to see you . . . you're my only hope. Can you get me inside?"

"Armand! I can't. They'll see you. Why—"

"I'm wounded, darling, and soaking wet besides."

"Wounded!" Jane stared at him in horror and concern. "How?"

"On secret business of the Duke's. But come, no one must know. Be a good girl and take me inside."

"Follow me," said Jane, coming to a swift decision. Her Armand, wounded and liable to catch pneumonia! "Just don't make a sound."

She opened the door and took a swift look around. No one in sight. He followed her inside and stood dripping on the tiles. "Can you get me up to your room?" he whispered.

"I'll have to. There's nowhere else to hide you."

Laying a finger to her lips, Jane bent to take off her shoes and he followed suit. Soon they were slipping noiselessly up the great curving staircase. When they reached the top gallery, the noise of a door opening caused them to freeze.

Jane pointed, and soon Armand was flattened in an alcove in shadow, and she was pressed in front of him. The slow and shuffling footsteps of an elderly retainer came along the gallery, together with the glow of a single dim candle. He was more concerned with putting one foot in front of the other and didn't look up, though he passed within feet of them. Soon he'd disappeared down the staircase.

"This way," hissed Jane. "Make a dash for it!"

"It was heavenly, being squeezed in there with you," whispered Armand behind her.

"And you wounded!" she reproved.

"Deeper than you know," he replied with a smile in his voice.

After a few twists and turns, they came to the hall where Jane's room was. Armand paused. "How many have rooms on this floor?"

"Just me . . . and the Lady Vivienne. She has the chambers next to mine, but she's still at the marquise's, so she won't hear us."

"That one?" He pointed to a door.

"Yes, that's hers. And this is mine. Come in."

Armand glanced at the closed door they were passing and he smiled. The duke's business was finished. Now he had business of his own.

In a moment, Jane had him hustled inside and the door firmly closed and locked. There was a fire laid in the grate and she stooped to light it, then lit a brace of candles on the mantel. Though her room wasn't as magnificent as Meredith's, it was still beyond her wildest dreams. It was furnished all in peach and yellow, with green and gold carpets on the floor and a golden marble mantel. The bed was hung with shimmering apricot silks lined in spring-green and tossed three-deep with satin pillows and coverlets.

Armand shrugged off his cloak and then helped her with hers. Jane felt a small thrill at the touch of his hands on her shoulders, at the fact that they were alone together in her bedchamber. But then she remembered. "Your wound!"

"First let the fire get going. We're both soaked and we need to warm up. Ah, good . . . you have some brandy. I'll pour us both a glass. We may need it."

Soon a roaring blaze was going, and then she turned to face him, hands on her hips. "And now not another moment. Where are you wounded, Armand?"

His eyes glinted merrily at her in the firelight, gold-green, and she didn't think there looked anything much wrong with him. In fact, he looked like he was enjoying himself immensely.

He put a clenched fist to his breast. "My heart, I am afraid."

"Your heart!" Jane's eyes flew wide, and she searched his dark green shirt for any evidence of blood. There was none. "What do you mean?"

"I told you it happened on secret business of the duke's. When I was first sent here to fetch you. It was then it happened. I am afraid my heart was pierced by love for you."

"Oh!" Jane put a hand to her own heart and sat rather feebly down. "Then . . . it was just a lie? What are you doing here?"

Armand crossed to her swiftly and gracefully knelt at her feet. He captured both of her hands in his. "No lie, my darling. I was truly wounded. My heart ached every moment since I last saw you. I had to see you. I followed you to the ball tonight and thanked the stars when you left early, alone. I knew I had to find any way to see you, be alone with you. And I couldn't stand in the pouring rain with you, letting you get soaked, could I? Besides," he smiled disarmingly, and Jane's heart, already warmed, melted completely, "it was only half a lie. I *am* soaked to the skin, and so are you."

"Say you forgive me?" he added after a moment.

She looked at the deep copper lights in his hair, his handsome face. "I forgive you," she breathed. "But you are mad to come here."

"Mad with love of you. But my darling, you haven't told me yet."

"Told you what?"

"Told me if there is any hope for me at all. If you could ever be wounded by love for me, as I am for you."

Jane stared at him, and everything she felt glowed in her eyes. "I could. I mean, I already am."

He leapt to his feet, eyes shining. "This calls for a toast! I need a shot of brandy to celebrate — and to bolster my courage."

She accepted the glass of brandy from him and sipped, feeling its fire was weak compared to the one already blazing in her veins. "Courage? For what?"

"To—no, I'll ask you later. But wait!" He set his brandy snifter down. "We are both still wet. We've got to get out of these clothes!"

"Armand!" She looked at him standing before her, his eyes twinkling and impish.

"Go on. Take them off," he urged.

"I won't!"

"And I won't catch cold for you," he grinned, starting to unbutton his shirt. "I'm very susceptible to colds."

"Armand!" she gasped again. "Stop that!"

"I won't," he smiled, and his shirt was completely unbuttoned, then off. She could only stare at the lovely lines of him, the wide shoulders, the muscles curving down his arms, the way his flat stomach tapered inward to his pants. . . .

He was unbuttoning his pants!

"Armand, stop that!"

"I have no intention of stopping that. And every intention of stripping your clothes off when I am finished with mine. So you might as well enjoy it."

She knew she would enjoy the sight of a completely nude Armand very much indeed, but it would never do to let him know that. He grinned at her and made a motion as if to pull off his pants, and Jane hid her face in her hands. She wanted to watch, but then, she didn't want him to think she was fast. She would only be persuaded after a *decent* interval.

"Ah." He sighed. "But I can see I must ask you the question I was afraid to ask earlier. You see, I'd planned to compromise you, then afterward you could not refuse me. It is just that you are so far above me in station I could think of no other way. I love you. Will you marry me?"

Jane's head snapped up, her eyes flew wide open. "You—you love me?"

"I do," he said softly and tenderly, love written all over his handsome face. "God help me, first I acted for the duke, but now I act for myself."

"And you want to—to marry me?" She felt the room spin.

"More than anything on earth, my darling. And I will even spend a chaste night in a chair if it will make you happy."

"Oh, Armand . . . no! I mean, yes!" Jane, laughing and half crying, had launched herself across the room at him and thrown her arms around his neck. "I love you, too," she breathed. "And I won't let you spend the night in a chair."

He smiled and bent down to kiss her lips tenderly. "My darling. I am so happy." His smile became wicked. "And now, may I help you with all those hooks?"

Jane turned and, in a happy dream, felt her lover open the back of her dress and help her step out of it. He turned her to face him. "Lovely," he breathed, taking in her lush curves veiled with lace. "You are all I dreamed of." And for a lost time they kissed, until urgency increased their pace, and his fingers were undoing her petticoats and hers were pulling off his trousers.

At last they stood twined in front of the fire, naked, while the rain drummed on the windows. He stepped back to look at her, and shyly, Jane looked at him. The firelight painted his smooth skin bronze, and his copper hair was loose and sweeping his shoulders. His laughing golden-green eyes were full of love.

"I will never forget this night, my darling," he said huskily.

"I never will either," she breathed.

And then he swooped her up and carried her to the big bed, where he dropped her, laughing, among the softness of lace and velvet bed throws and pillows.

"And now," he said, arching a wicked eyebrow at her, "shall we find out what delights marriage holds in store for us?"

"What are you waiting for?" giggled Jane. "I thought you'd never ask!"

And laughing, he joined her in the great bed.

Chapter Twenty-four

Meredith stood at the window of her room and gazed out into the night. A moon was rising above the palais gardens, silvering the night with a heartbreaking magic. Tonight she'd begged off attending a play and then a late supper, pleading a headache.

She needed time to think . . . and she couldn't face Raceford until she'd sorted out her thoughts.

Drawing the sash of her wrapper tighter, she leaned against the sill and sighed. And what exactly *did* she think? Her emotions were in turmoil. Only one thing was clear to her, and that was that she was in love.

Of everything she'd expected when she'd taken on this masquerade as Vivienne, the one thing she hadn't expected was to fall in love. She'd pictured herself as being able to wear lovely clothes and jewels, to see a side of society she'd never seen before, to mingle with the great, to attend wonderful cultural events like plays, concerts. Maybe to learn to flirt lightly as Vivienne did.

But not to fall crashingly in love with a man so far above her he might be the moon and stars.

Restlessly, she walked away from the window and sat down in a chair, watching the bars of moonlight stream over the floor. Her mind went back to yesterday morning in the meadow. Heart's Desire was still in her stable. The only communication she'd had from Raceford was a brief note: *I will come to collect my winnings personally. R.*

R. Raceford. Deron. The duke, she thought dully. *It's only in fairy tales that the great duke marries the milk-maid, Meredith. When he learns who you really are . . .*

She sat up straighter, wondering. He thought she was Vivienne. And his best friend was Gabriel, Vivienne's lover. Even with all the rumors about Vivienne flying, he must be one of the few who had certain knowledge that Vivienne took lovers. And that didn't stop him from pursuing her, did it?

A picture of herself on tiptoe, head arched back, her bared breast being touched by his tongue, came into her mind. Heavens, every time she was with him she acted more and more like he'd expect Vivienne to act. And she'd come damned close to letting him tumble her in that meadow yesterday.

Why hadn't she? Why, indeed? she wondered. She wanted to. Ached to. In fact, burned to. It was only because she wasn't sure if he loved her or not that had held her back. But really, what difference did that make?

If she had a chance of winning him, then it would matter very much indeed. Then she wouldn't want to behave in a way to make him hold her cheaply. But she had to face it. She had no chance with him. No chance at all. He was a duke.

So what on earth did she have to lose by doing what she really wanted to . . . letting him make love to her? She was going to lose him anyway. She might as well have a precious memory or two of him to hold close before he was gone forever.

She set her jaw. That was it, then. She would allow Raceford to carry out his intention to seduce her. And be damned with the consequences!

She smiled in the moonlight, almost able to hear Ginny and Vivienne cheering her. Why, Ginny was all for her having an affair while she was here in Paris . . . and time was getting short. Already a month had flown past. She would have to corner him soon and let him know she'd changed her mind. Tell him she wanted him, like he'd asked her to. Every moment from now on was precious.

She rose, pacing the floor, wondering if it was too late to dress and go to the play. Why waste any more time now that she'd made up her mind? She could let him know tonight. Or perhaps she should send him a note. A *billet-doux*.

Then she sat again. It was already midnight. She'd never dress in time. It would have to wait until tomorrow.

And what would her future be? Meredith tried to push the thought away, but it stayed. Would Raceford make her his mistress once he learned she was not marriageable? Set her up in a house in London?

And when he marries? A cold voice seemed to whisper in her ear. Oh, God . . . Raceford marrying someone else! Her heart froze, and she knew her love for him was so deep she could never share it with another.

She made up her mind. Just this short time, then, and an end. No matter how much it hurt to stop, it would hurt less than to watch him take another woman to wife. An affair she would have. Mistress she'd not be.

And what had she learned from this time of being Vivienne? She smiled, knowing the answer right away. It was so simple. She'd learned not to be afraid.

When her father had died and left her alone in the world, she'd been too young to know what to do. And she'd been afraid. So she'd gone to Aunt Phoebe and been miserable, rather than trying to strike out on her own.

But playacting as Vivienne had given her a new confidence. When people treated you with respect instead of contempt, the effects were contagious. She walked with a new pride now, she knew, head high, not afraid to look anyone in the eye. She could stand up for herself now, be what she wanted to be.

By leaving herself behind and being someone else, she'd found herself.

And found love. Love was bewildering, dizzying. It was an all-encompassing feeling that made life wonderful, each day like a new day in spring. She thought about Nicholas, about the attraction she felt for him. True, he could make the blood sing in her veins with a look, but then he was so incredibly handsome.

But what Nicki made her feel was nothing compared to what Raceford could make her feel. Nicki made her feel desire, but Deron made her feel desire and something more. That was love. It was an emotion that commanded you, made you dream of your beloved, long to be with him. He made you complete, whole.

She thought of the day at the horse fair, when he'd told her about his time in America, his childhood. How close she'd felt to him then. She'd never before had a man talk to her like a friend. Imagine, being his friend! He was so changeable, one moment a devil with a dangerous smile, the next a friend she could talk to as if she'd known him all her life.

With a smile, she thought of that first night at the inn, when she'd believed him to be a gypsy and a highwayman. That hadn't stopped her from being drawn to him, from wanting him to kiss her. She hadn't cared that he was a criminal then, very likely born to hang.

Yes, if he were a highwayman, she'd marry him. But a duke? Born to greatness? She could never be a duke's wife.

Just for one precious moment, she let herself dream that she could marry him. She saw him as her highwayman again, not as a duke, in his plain white shirt and black pants. In her dream, he stood at an altar in a flower-bedecked church, looking so very breathtaking with his long black hair and his green eyes as he turned to her. She wore a simple gown and a white lace veil, and carried a bouquet of white roses. And when they had spoken their vows and were joined in holy matrimony, he swept her into his arms and kissed her . . . When they left the church his great black stallion waited outside, and he set her on it before him. No grand ducal coach but a highwayman's steed, and the arms around her she'd felt safe in from the first.

And then she saw them in a room in an inn, a place very like the room they'd spent that first night, simple but cozy. No grand rooms for her and her highwayman husband. He would take her to the bed. . . .

Meredith smiled and untied her wrapper. She wore a filmy loose nightgown of white, plain except for the lace straps. She climbed into bed, feeling more peaceful, and looked at the moonlight. She could sleep now. Raceford or no Raceford, she'd make her own way, somehow. And somehow, she'd let him know that if he wanted her, she was his to have. He lived alone, and she could spend the evenings at his house without anyone ever knowing, as long as she came back before the night was over.

Her eyes were just closing when a soft noise brought them open. She stared into the dark, wondering if she'd really heard anything and, after a time, decided it was nothing. She was just closing her eyes when it came again . . . the unmistakable sound of the window sliding upward in its sash.

She sat straight up in bed, the covers falling away from her, and stared with horror at the dark shape of a man looming in the window. She opened her mouth to scream, but her throat was closed tight with terror. He leapt down into the room, light and graceful as a cat.

And Meredith recognized something about that leap. In the next moment he spoke, and the deep voice was familiar.

"Don't be alarmed, My Lady. It's me."

"Deron!" she managed, out of a throat that could suddenly speak.

"The same." He sounded amused, and crossed over to stand by the side of her bed, towering above her.

"What are you doing here? And why did you climb in my bedroom window?"

"I've come to collect my prize, My Lady. For winning the race."

"Your prize? But surely you know she's in the stable! You had only to come in the normal way and ask for her . . . . The stablehands have instructions! You know I don't keep horses in my bedroom!"

"It's not the horses in your bedroom I've come for." The ripple of amusement was there again in his voice.

"Then what *have* you come for?"

"I told you I've come to claim my prize, Angel."

Meredith's heart began to beat faster. She could feel the pulse in her throat. "You won the filly . . ."

"I won my heart's desire, My Lady. And I've come to take what's mine," he said.

Chapter Twenty-five

"It is already yours."

Meredith spoke softly into the moonlight, and she heard his soft indrawn breath. He didn't move, so she spoke again.

"There is no need to take what already belongs to you, or to win what you already possess."

"My Angel . . . then why have you fought me if I have already won you?"

"I have not fought you, My Lord, but myself."

Meredith stared at his towering form, silvered by moonlight, and thought how loved he already was. How incredible that he should appear at her bedside tonight of all nights, as if in answer to her wish! And yet, still she felt her heart beating fast, wondering what would come next.

"Then fight your feelings no longer, My Lady."

He moved to the bed and stooped, catching her in his arms. One arm was around her back, the other sliding under her knees. The silken covers slid off her as he picked her up. She was being held against his chest, lifted out of the bed. She put her head against his chest as he strode to the window where the moonlight poured in, and she could feel his heart beating as strongly as her own.

"I would see your face in the moonlight," he said. "Look at me, my love."

Slowly, she raised her face and stared up at him, seeing as if for the first time his features. So handsome . . . so strong! His hawklike nose above a firm and sensual mouth, curved with desire as he searched her face. The sweep of his cheekbones, the square line of his jaw. But most of all, his eyes. Long, beautiful eyes under reckless black brows, eyes that caressed her and made her feel breathless.

"How long I have dreamed of this," he murmured, and bent his head to kiss her.

His lips barely brushed hers, a slow and sensual movement, featherlight, exploring. Softly, he traced the contours of her mouth with his own, sending shivers of delight all though her. Barely touching, his lips moved over hers, and she was lost in the bliss this matchlessly gentle caress was giving her. For an endless time, she was captured in his strong arms, while his lips discovered hers tenderly.

And then she felt his tongue moving slowly over the line of her lips, wetting them, and she couldn't help a small gasp. As her lips opened under his, his tongue came inside her mouth and slowly ran over the inside of her lips. Her hands moved up around his neck as the kiss deepened, its slow eroticism starting to turn to burning fire.

He kissed her until her head spun, his mouth ravishing hers, opening it commandingly. At last he pulled back, and his heated gaze moved over her face.

"To kiss you is beyond any pleasure I had imagined," he breathed. "Untie your ribbons so I may taste the smoothness of your skin."

"Untie my ribbons?" Meredith whispered, feeling

a flush come over her skin at the way he was looking at her. Hesitantly, she dropped her hands from his neck and brought them to the ribbons of her bodice. Silkily, they slid apart at her touch, opening the top of her nightgown.

For a long moment he stared at her, then bent his head so his lips were a trail of fire on her jawline. His mouth was moving down her neck and she couldn't help herself. She let her head fall back, offering him the curve of her neck.

As his mouth moved over her collarbone, her nightgown slipped off her shoulders with the barest of whispers, and she felt the night air on her breasts. She was bent backward in his arms, her hair falling in a river, and slowly, his lips were moving over her breast to claim an erect nipple.

His tongue touched her, sending shivers all through her, and she clutched his neck tighter and arched upward toward him as he took her taut nipple fully into his warm, wet mouth, clinging to him for dear life. He was maddening her, driving her to soft moans, as he explored both of her breasts with his fiery mouth, sending sensations all through her that were pleasure beyond her imaginings.

"I must have you," he murmured huskily. "I can wait no longer to have you naked beneath me, clasped against me."

The room whirled as Meredith was carried to the bed, as they fell on it, entwined as one. Now his hands were cupping her breasts, pressing them together, running over her skin. "So perfect," he said huskily. "So beautiful."

As he kissed her again, Meredith let her hand slide up his chest to part his shirt. Her fingers found the buttons and they flew apart, and she reveled in the hardness of his muscles under the bronze satin of his skin. His own hands were sliding her nightgown downwards, and as his shirt was pulled off, Meredith found herself again experiencing the delicious sensation of having her bare chest pressed skin to skin against his.

It was frighteningly intimate, wonderfully right.

For a long moment he just held her against him, clasping her tightly to him, and she could hear the unevenness of his breathing in her ear. Then he pulled back and looked down at her.

"Let me look at you. Oh, God, you are so perfect. Made for me, as I was for you."

Deron could hardly contain his desire as he stared down at her. Silvered by moonlight, she was perfection indeed. Her dark hair was a soft cloud around her shoulders, falling down her back. Her eyes were wide and soft, filled with love that shone at him, with surrender. Her breasts were the loveliest he had ever seen, high and curving, heartachingly tempting in shape. Taut pink nipples, so sweet in his mouth, set his blood on fire as his gaze roved over her. Her skin was like moonlit velvet, and under her breasts, her rib cage curved down to an indrawn waist before the gentle and tempting flare of her hips. Her legs were long and gorgeously curved. She was like no other woman he had ever seen, a shimmering vision of love and desire, and he knew that after this night, no matter what she might have been in the past, she was now *his*. He would suffer no other to ever touch that satin skin again or kiss her beautiful mouth.

He brought his hands up to her and slowly ran his fingers all over her, as if memorizing her every curve with his touch. Meredith felt him shape her legs, her ankles, the skin over her hips, her waist, her stomach, her breasts, her neck. Then he bent his head and opened her mouth with his own, his tongue thrusting deep inside her. She felt his hand moving up over her knee, then around to the inside of her thigh. His other hand was stroking her breast, his fingers gently teasing her nipple until she gasped under his loving assault.

Boldly, she let her own hands move to his pants, unfastening them, then sliding them down over his lean hips. His skin seemed to be on fire, and she felt the smooth steel of him. In a moment he was as naked as she was, and he moved against her. Long muscled legs and his hard manhood brushed against her, letting her know just how fervently he desired her.

She felt a slight shock as his hand moved up her inner thigh and his fingers brushed the curls at the base of her hips. Ever so lightly, his fingers moved over her curls in a shivering caress that brought a flood of heat to her loins. And then his fingers moved downward, with just the slightest of touches over her center of pleasure, and Meredith jumped, feeling almost a flood of heat all through her.

Firmly, his fingers moved between her legs in a small circle, and Meredith cried out and clung to him while he kissed her, unable to believe the explosions of pleasure rippling through her. Slowly, he slipped his fingers down to where she was hot and wet, sliding them inside her as she arched toward him, wanting his touch, wanting more than he was giving her.

His other hand imprisoned hers and he murmured against her lips, "I want you to know me as I am knowing you. To feel the desire you have inflamed me with." His hand was taking hers downward, until she touched his erect hardness and he was clasping her fingers around him.

Oh, he was large! So hot and smooth and hard! Wonderingly, she ran her hand down the length of his silken shaft and felt him throb beneath her fingers as he groaned in her ear. His own fingers explored her, slipping in and out of her until she, too, was crying out in his ear and her hips were rocking against him, feeling him fill her.

"I want you, my darling. I can wait no longer," he breathed, and his hands were gone from her and Meredith cried out in aching disappointment. But he was on top of her now, and she felt his manhood slide against her, parting her . . . and then, slowly, he slid inside her.

The world seemed to vanish into a burst of stars, and she knew that she was merging into one with her lover.

Deron held his breath as he entered her. Never had he felt such delicious tightness, which caressed every inch of him as he penetrated her fully. He shuddered with delight at the incredible sensation of possessing her, for she was truly made for him alone. Such a wave of pleasure ran through him as he entered her that he had to stop for a time, until he could trust himself to move again. And then slowly, he began to slide in and out of her, as she held him close and began to move with him.

The two lovers were lost in a world that sparkled and moved with sensation and passion, and Meredith cried out as he moved with her, faster and faster, taking her to heights undreamed of. Thrills were shooting through her veins as they quickened together, at last each reaching a peak of unimaginable pleasure. With a cry and a shudder, stars burst inside of Meredith as he exploded inside her with a last masterful thrust, and she heard him cry out in answering pleasure.

Slowly, so slowly, they rocked together, lost in each other, their breath slowing, their skin heated and moist. At last he gathered her close against him and rolled over, disengaging their bodies but not their hearts. His hands were in her hair, stroking her, and he was murmuring words against her ear, love words that thrilled her to hear.

Oh, it had been so right! Nothing in the universe could have been so unimaginably lovely as this joining with him, this surrender to him of her body, her heart, and her soul.

His lips found her forehead. "My darling," he said, "I told you from the first time I saw you that you belonged to me, that I had claimed you. And now I will never let you go. Tonight, making love to you was like it has never been for me . . . like I could never have imagined. You do things to me no other woman on earth could."

Meredith turned and kissed his strong jaw, whispering, "And I have belonged to you since you first claimed me as your own. You captured my heart when you captured me, and I have longed to let you love me the way you did tonight."

His hand traced the curve of her waist, ran over her breast. "I will never get enough of you, my love. I doubt I'll be able to let you spend another night away from me again. You are in my blood, My Lady, and I'll not let you go."

How different it had been this time, she mused dreamily. How tender.

Deron, she thought, looking at him with shining

327

eyes. *I love you and belong to you . . . forever.*

But she was afraid to speak the words aloud. He had not yet told her he loved her.

And besides . . . Meredith believed that love was based on honesty. And there was something she had yet to tell him, this man she loved.

The name of the woman he'd just made love to.

But as she opened her mouth to speak, he caught her to him again and kissed her. And she felt his desire rising hard against her and her own leaping to match it. Instead of speaking, she let him sweep her away again to the new world he'd opened for her tonight.

Yes, tonight was a magic night. The truth could wait, but love could not.

Chapter Twenty-six

It was a week later, and Meredith still had not found the courage to tell Deron who she was. She was being drowned in an ocean of feelings too strong for her, which left her dizzy and unable to think.

Besides, she was frightened.

What would the truth do? Would he be angry? Leave her? Every day she resolved she would tell him, and every day she melted at the sight of him and let herself be carried along by the love that was sweeping them both like a flame.

Not a night had passed that he had not climbed in her bedroom window and loved her until the dawn broke. She thanked heaven above that the French aristocracy, used to late nights, did nothing social until the afternoons. Once he had slipped out her window into the dawn she could turn over and, with a deliciously fulfilled sigh, fall asleep until noon.

And every afternoon, Deron came calling.

How rapidly her heart would beat when she saw him striding into the room, every inch a duke, nothing like the wild lover she gave her nights to. Nicki was beside himself with jealousy that she was spending her afternoons with Raceford, and the only way to pacify him was to spend at least a few evenings with him at the opera or the theater.

Which made Raceford furiously jealous.

Ginny was in her element, delighted at the mad way these two handsome men were pursuing Meredith. She was full of advice and always badgering Meredith to take one or the other into her bed, for "otherwise they will surely kill each other!" She didn't know that Raceford was climbing into the palais window every night.

Only Jane knew the secret, for Meredith had been compelled to tell someone. And to her shock, Jane had told her a lover of her own was spending nights in her room, too!

"And Armand wants to marry me!" Jane wailed.

Meredith had stared at her, surprised and, if the truth be told, envious. Raceford had never mentioned marriage. But then, he believed her to be a married woman. "And what is wrong with that?" Meredith had asked.

"Because he doesn't know who I really am!"

Wincing, Meredith thought ruefully that she and Jane had the same problem. Both taking lovers who hadn't an inkling of whom they were making love to. Oh, it was a mess, and one of these days she really *had* to straighten it out.

It was early afternoon and she stood in the drive, looking mistrustfully at the sky. Large purple and black thunderheads were rolling in, promising to spoil her afternoon ride with Raceford. Every day they rode out together, discovering a fresh delight in conversation, in laughing together, in becoming friends as well as lovers.

She looked up to see him riding up the drive, magnificent as always on Sultan. At her nod, the groom led Heart's Desire to her side but she didn't mount, just allowed herself the pleasure of watching him to her heart's content as he rode toward her.

"Good day, My Lady Angel," he said, smiling down at her in a way that made her heart catch.

"Not such a good day, My Lord Duke," she said, waving at the thunderheads gathering in the sky.

He cocked a brow at her. "And I would never have believed you were fainthearted enough to let a little drop of rain deter you from a ride!"

"Fainthearted? Wretch! It was you I was worried about . . . that you wouldn't want to spoil such a magnificent jacket!"

He was indeed looking handsome in a coat of darkest green that matched his eyes, his black hair pulled back with a dark green ribbon. His fawn breeches molded his powerful legs, and his brown boots were spotlessly polished. He was perfect . . . the Lord Duke. But there were times when she missed her rakish gypsy highwayman.

"The weather matters nothing to me as long as I am with you," he grinned. "And may I say that color becomes you beautifully."

She was wearing a deep blue habit, and there were violet feathers in her hat. She flashed him a smile, secure in his admiration, then fitted a foot in a stirrup and swung herself up. "Then let's be off, and ride into the very teeth of the storm, my reckless Lord."

"As it is your wish, my wild Lady," he said,

laughing.

She rode at his side into the darkening afternoon, her heart alight with love and happiness. Oh, if only every day for the rest of her life, she could ride at Deron's side! She had never known that it takes love to make a person complete. These days, the whole world seemed to glow, and she had only to look at him to be washed over by a wave of joy so warm she could hardly bear it. Just to be at his side was delight, to be in his arms, heaven on earth.

"And so, you went to the opera last night with Nicki," he said, opening today's skirmish. Last night, he'd not said a word to her when he came into her room, just loved her with an urgency that was almost wild with passion. Nicki was a sore point between them indeed.

"I did. It was a terrible performance."

"I could care less about that. My question is, how did the viscomte . . . *perform?*"

"You know I would never allow him to touch me. You know that I belong to you. Why will you not trust me?"

"Because I go mad whenever I even think of another man at your side, that's why. It's not that I don't trust *you*, but Nicholas—! The man has had nearly every woman in Paris! He's a satyr. And most experienced at seduction."

"Trouble your heart no longer, My Lord," she said softly. "For I have been loved by the master of seduction and am now blind to all other men."

"It had best be the truth you speak," he said roughly. "For I detest deception."

The truth you speak. Oh, heavens! And he detested deception! Meredith bit her lips and stole a glance at him, to find he was smiling at her.

"But you give your heart so openly to me, My Lady Angel, that I can find no room to doubt you. I know you are no liar."

Meredith felt almost ill. She wondered if she should tell him now but found she had not the courage. And then a peal of thunder split the heavens.

Raceford looked up. "Ride! This way! We must be out of the trees before the lightning hits!"

They put their heels to their horses and pounded down the green ride, while the long rumble of thunder rolled over them. At last Meredith noticed a break in the trees ahead and saw that they were making for a small clearing.

They gained the glade and Raceford swung himself down just as the first large drops of rain fell from a blackening sky. Meredith was off, too, and they tethered their restive horses to a small bush far from any tall trees.

Meredith pulled off her hat and tilted her face to the warm rain, still falling in large drops spaced far apart. A flash of lightning lit the sky and she turned to find Raceford shrugging off his jacket.

He grinned over at her. "You're right. I have no desire to ruin it, and we're going to be soaked in a moment. Give me yours as well."

She pulled off her jacket and he rolled them up, then put them into one of the horse's saddlebags and closed it. Then he turned to her and took her hand, pulling her into the middle of the glade.

"We'll be safest in the middle away from any trees," he said, and she jumped slightly as a crash of thunder shook the world.

And then the rain came pouring down.

It came in sheets, hard and driving, and in just an instant they were both soaked to the skin. She heard his laugh and looked across to where he was standing, wet shirt transparent against his rippling muscles, black hair plastered to his neck, laughing up into the rain.

How she loved him!

He looked at her and a spark of heat leapt between them. His eyes dropped to her shirt and he smiled, "And now you can see why I took your jacket, My Lady."

Her shirt was clinging wetly to her curves, as transparent as his, and today she wore not even a chemise under it. Then he seized her and pulled her against him, kissing her hard, while the rain pounded down around them.

His mouth was a searing heat on hers, kindling her into a passion that was hotter every time he touched her. Roughly, his hands were pulling her shirt apart, pulling the wet cloth off her, unfastening her skirt as if he could not have it stripped off her fast enough. And she was unbuttoning his shirt just as urgently, opening his pants, kissing his neck, the skin on his collarbone, touching her tongue to his ear.

They stood apart to struggle with pants clinging too tightly to skin, with a skirt dragging in wet heavy folds, with boots that stubbornly clung. Both of them were wild to be together again, naked, and

334

felt the warm rain lashing their bare skin as they flung away their boots.

Meredith drew in her breath at the sight of him naked and proud before her, rain running down his bronzed muscles. Was there ever such a man? His chest was wide, his shoulders broad with muscle, his frame tapering to a vee at his waist. His lean hips and long legs were planted in a masculine stance, and his magnificent manhood rose hard and smooth before him, wet with rain.

She went into his arms, the place where she belonged, and they fell together onto the long wet grass.

The rain was another sensation on her skin, adding a pleasure to their lovemaking as wild as it was erotic. His wet skin slid over her, and he bent his lips to taste the beaded drops that clung to her shoulder, to run his open mouth down her arm. His lips captured her hand, and he took her fingers into his mouth, one by one, sucking and kissing them. She ran her own hand down his wet back over his firmly molded buttocks, marveling at his smooth, sculptured muscles.

Then he was turning her over inexorably, spreading her legs, and she felt her breasts and stomach pressed into the long grass while the rain lashed her back. He ran his strong hands up her legs and over her backside, saying raggedly, "Did I ever tell you that you have the most delectable rear I have ever seen? To look at you drives me mad."

His strong hands were massaging the muscles of her back, her backside, sliding over them wet with rain, and Meredith was shuddering with delight.

She at last could bear it no longer and turned over, pushing him onto his back and pinning him there. "Now let me pleasure you," she whispered.

She ran her hands and mouth over his face, then moved lower to his chest. She wanted to kiss every inch of him until he was hotter for her than he had ever been before. He was delicious, and with abandon, she moved her open mouth, her tongue, over his chest and down his ribs. She felt his stomach jump as her fingers touched his hardness, felt him groan aloud when she began to move her fingers up and down.

And then her fingers were moving lower, to run up and down his legs, to stroke him. Her wet curtain of hair trailed over his stomach as she felt his fingers move between her legs to touch her the way she was touching him. She heard him gasp for breath as she let her hand run down the length of him, filled with wanton desire at his heat and smoothness. She ran her fingers up him, feeling him move convulsively, and then, suddenly, he was pulling away from her, turning her over until she knelt on all fours on the wet grass.

He was gasping with desire as he grasped her hips and she gasped aloud herself as she felt his hard length slide into her. "Oh, love," he groaned as he impaled her to the fullest. She moved back and forth experimentally, feeling a new explosion of pleasure this friction, his control, brought her. His hands grasped her hips and they moved together, rocking, while the rain soaked them and thunder split the heavens. He was mastering her, controlling her, and it was wickedly delicious.

336

Deron knew he had never seen a sight as beautiful as she was as she moved below him, his wild woman, his wanton love. Her back, her slim waist, her enticing behind were beautiful. With a cry, he thrust to fill her as their climax shook them both. Thunder rolled and lightning flashed, and to Deron, it was as if the heavens were echoing the storm of passion that crashed between them.

At last she collapsed in a heap, and they rolled twined together on the wet grass, holding each other tightly. He stroked her wet hair and cheek, murmuring over and over again, "My love . . . my love."

At last the rain slowed and their skin began to chill, so they rose, stopping often to kiss, and dressed. They mounted their horses, both looking wet and rakish, and galloped through the woods to warm their skin again.

When they reached the palais, the sun was breaking through the ragged edge of the clouds and a groom came running out to catch their horses' heads. "My lord . . . my lady! We was worried about you," he said, taking in their soaking wet appearance with round eyes.

"But we were quite all right," said Deron, his eyes a caress for her alone. "My Lady and I were caught up in a storm, and she got quite wet." He grinned devilishly at her as she blushed. "But though we were racked by thunder and lightning, the storm passed. And except for our wet clothes, we are the better for our soaking."

He turned to the groom. "Now take My Lady inside, so she can dry off and not catch cold. I'll ride home to change myself. It's not far. I would have you warm and dry for tonight, My Lady," he said, smiling down at her. "Because I am expecting there will be another storm."

And laughing, he touched his heels to his great black stallion and rode off, her wild lover who had indeed taken her heart by storm.

Chapter Twenty-seven

Meredith scanned the crowd at the theater, look-ing for Raceford, but he was nowhere to be found. She sat in her box, Nicholas at her side, and wished Raceford would hurry and get there. She'd not seen him since their wild afternoon in the rain, and she was aching for him.

Nicki scowled at her, thinking she looked lovely. She wore a gown of black silk, embroidered every-where with little jet beads that caught the light and sparkled darkly. Against the black her skin was glowingly white, and only a spill of gold lace around the off-the-shoulder neckline relieved the blackness, together with a cloth-of-gold petticoat peeking out beneath the glittering beaded skirts. Long fringed gold earrings dangled from under her black curls, and her lips were reddened enticingly.

"Damn it, Vivienne," he said irritably. "This is the first night I've been alone with you in a week!"

She raised delicately arched brows at him. "Such language, Viscomte." He frowned at her, secretly thinking that he'd barely missed being with her, for the whole week he'd been at Ginny's side until Jof-frey had been ready to run him through. But it would never do to let the fabulously wealthy Lady Vivienne know his ardor had cooled somewhat. Besides, it looked as if she'd found a replacement for him in the Duke of Raceford.

"You will get more than language from me if you do not explain your sudden fascination with the Duke of Raceford," he threatened.

"He is a fellow countryman," she said blandly.

"When you have spent so much time with me and led me to hope, now you amuse yourself with another?"

A bit guiltily, Meredith looked at him. He wore a deep copper satin coat over skintight white breeches and was as magnificent as ever. "Nicki, you know I shall ever be fond of you. . . ."

"I had hoped for a great deal warmer feelings than *fondness* from you," he said scornfully. "You might use such a word to describe your feelings for a dog!"

"Nicki . . ." she began, and the curtains behind them parted as someone entered the box.

Meredith looked up to see Raceford, dressed magnificently in pewter velvet and black breeches. A single emerald as green and clear as his eyes pinned the lace at his throat.

Then Ginny's laugh rang out as she and Joffrey came into the box. She dropped Joffrey's arm and came to kiss Nicki on the cheek. "And what has made my darling so sulky?" she asked.

"He will do more than sulk if you persist in kissing him, Genvieve," growled Joffrey.

She straightened. "Goodness! Such tempers tonight! But I must have some champagne to enliven everyone. Joffrey, will you go and fetch it?"

340

Joffrey looked thunderously at Nicki before leaving the box to get the champagne.

Ginny at once sat down next to Nicki, spreading her purple silk skirts wide. "Now, Nicki darling, you must tell me all about it," she said.

Meredith felt a hand under her elbow and was practically dragged to her feet. "You'll walk with me, My Lady?" Raceford asked.

She smiled at him. At last she had him alone! "I will," she said feverishly, feeling heat just from the touch of his fingers.

Once outside he said nothing, just steered her through the crowds. At last he spoke. "Dreadfully boring play, is it not?" he asked, favoring her with a rakish smile.

"Dreadfully," she agreed happily, seeing the envious glances she was getting from the women they passed.

"I vote we construct our own entertainment."

"I would cast a vote in favor, but where, My Lord? I cannot leave the theater without Ginny. . . ."

"Can you not? I imagine she could find her own way home, a grown woman like her . . . but then, I do not propose leaving the theater."

"Indeed? And where is the place we could be alone to construct this entertainment?" she countered.

"Ah . . . then you agree with me that we should be alone to be entertained? But an enterprising man will always find a way," he said smoothly, taking her down a side hall concealed by some red velvet curtains. At the end of the hall was a door.

He opened it, and she saw a winding stair.

"Where does this go?" she asked, curious.

"To the roof, My Lady Angel. I've a mind to look at the stars with you."

She took his arm as she climbed the stairs, her heart singing joyfully just to be with him, to be leaving the boring play behind. In a short time they found another door before them, and as Deron turned the knob, to Meredith's disappointment it was securely locked.

"When you are with a thieving highwayman, My Lady, no door is a bar," he said. Taking a pin from his pocket, he soon had the door open.

Before them stretched a wide, flat roof, surrounded by a waist-high wall all around it. He shut the door behind them and they walked to the wall together.

Above them, a million stars twinkled, remote and beautiful. Below, the lights of the whole city of Paris were spread out in skeins of fairy glitter, dusting the streets and buildings. The night was warm and dark as a velvet cloak, and yet as Meredith leaned on the wall to drink in the sight of the city below, she shivered.

Because he'd come around to stand behind her, his arms around her, his head next to hers.

For a time they simply watched the city, private in their rooftop perch. And then she felt him drop his head and his lips were on her neck, kissing her. Her shoulders were completely bare, the back and bodice of the dress low, and he lifted her hair with his hands as his lips sent heat all through her. He left no inch of her neck untasted, and then his tongue was tracing the shape of her earlobe and even running inside the shell of her ear.

Then his open mouth was on her shoulders, and she gasped as she felt his hands lifting her skirts high above her waist. Under them, she wore only garters and lacy black stockings, and his heated manhood was pressing into her bare backside as he kissed her shoulders and then ran his tongue down her spine.

His hands came around to cup her breasts as he pushed her forward so she was leaning over the wall at the waist, grasping it for balance, almost spilling out of her dress. He yanked at her bodice, and the warm night breeze was on her naked breasts, and below her was the whole city of Paris. His fingers played with her nipples until they were standing erect, and all the time he was thrusting against her bare bottom, making her feel how ragingly he wanted her.

She reached behind her and opened his pants, and in a moment he was sliding smoothly inside her.

He thrust, filling her, as she leaned over the wall and saw Paris dizzyingly below her. For a few moments he thrust into her, and then she gasped in disappointment as he slowly drew himself out.

Eagerly, he turned her around and she ran her hand up and down the tight material of his opened pants in front, feeling the long, hard naked curve of his manhood. And then his hands were at her waist and he lifted her until she was sitting on the wall, her skirts pulled up above her waist, and she was bare to his gaze above her thigh-high garters.

She gasped as he knelt before her, parting her legs wide, and he smiled up at her. "Trust me, my darling Angel, for I am about to take you on a ride you will love."

And with that he leaned forward, his lips meeting her thigh just above her garter, and she felt a shudder go all through her as his lips moved higher and she realized what he meant to do.

Involuntarily, she tried to close her legs, feeling shy and also unbearably excited at the decadent wickedness of it, but his hands forestalled her. Both his hands moved up her legs until they tickled her innermost thighs, and then his mouth was searing hot as it moved upwards, ever upwards. . . .

With a shock, his tongue delicately touched her between her legs at the heart of her womanhood, and she gasped.

With the lightest butterfly of movements, he flicked his tongue softly back and forth across her tiny peak, and she felt a rush of heat and wetness at the utterly delicious sensation of it. For some time, he continued this most delicate of tortures, barely touching her, and then he pressed closer and his tongue caressed her more strongly.

He rose, trailing kisses to her neck, and looked into her eyes expectantly. The smile he gave her warmed her entirely and she smiled back.

He embraced her gently and murmured, "My Lady Angel, we are always in such a passion to have one another, but tonight—"

"Tonight?" she questioned.

"Tonight there is nothing I want more than to look into your eyes and to hold you in my arms as I make love to you."

He pressed his mouth tenderly to hers, and a thousand thrills coursed through her when their lips met. His mood had changed from the hurried passion of moments before, and as if she were as fragile as a flower, he lowered her to the rooftop and braced himself over her, gazing into her eyes with an intensity that made her light-headed. Oh, when he looked at her that way, all else seemed to fade away. She could no longer breathe, as if breathing were unnecessary. There were only his eyes, two beautiful emeralds, as green and peaceful as paradise itself, enveloping her body and soul. And from the embrace of his gaze, she felt nothing could harm them; they were safe, home.

He brushed away a stray strand of hair from her face and kissed her again, never taking his eyes from hers as his lips explored hers lightly. When he pulled away, she asked shyly, "Why do you look at me so?"

He kissed her nose, a soft laugh in his throat. "Because I see the moon and stars reflected in your eyes, and they fill me with such peace and warmth that I cannot bear to even look away for a moment, lest the feeling disappear."

"But they are only my eyes," she laughed.

"Such eyes a man could lose himself in forever, My Lady Angel. And gladly."

He was kissing her again, his tongue exploring her mouth teasingly, his eyes in constant vigil over hers. He lifted her skirts to run his hands along her thighs, then moved over her and entered her again.

She felt the intense pleasure of him as he slid fully inside her, in one unhurried and concentrated movement. Her breath caught in her throat as he set the rhythm of their lovemaking, patient and unending as a heartbeat. Never once did she let her eyes wander from his, for to do so would break the

345

spell that bound them both, as if in their gaze the truth was spoken, and that truth was love. She moved with him and felt the first stirrings of delight at the center of her being, struggling to the surface in want of release. She smiled at him and sighed, and with her sigh came one of his own as he increased his rhythm. And then she was lost in the tide of sensations that took her by surprise and swept her entire body. Together they cried out in ecstasy, their eyes locked in a gaze as deep-felt as the wonders their bodies were experiencing.

With a shuddering gasp his movements slowed, and he finally closed his eyes, pressing his lips to hers in a kiss so strong with emotion that she thought she would cry from the joy of it. She wrapped her arms around his neck and pulled him to her tightly, returning his kiss sentiment for sentiment. Something had happened tonight between them — something unknown, wonderful, and frightening at the same time. In their lovemaking and in that kiss, Meredith felt their fates had intertwined and were now sealed together forever.

It was a long time before either of them could move. They lay with their arms around each other in the shadow of the wall, letting their breathing slow, clasped as close as they could possibly get, in a glorious afterglow of contentment. At long last, they stood and straightened their clothes as best they could, and then clasping hands, they left the roof.

Deron dropped her hand just before they entered the box, but it seemed the others needed only one look at their glowing faces to guess what they'd been doing.

"Goodness!" cried the chevalier, well flushed with champagne. He had arrived shortly after Deron and Meredith had left the box and, from the looks on the others' faces, had been making a nuisance of himself. "It seems that the night is hotter than ever for some!"

Nicki didn't even respond to the chevalier, staring at Meredith with narrowed eyes. "And just where the hell have you been . . . and what have you been doing?" he demanded.

"I think it is perfectly *obvious* what she's been doing," said the chevalier. "Look how red her lips are . . . and that velvety glow in her eyes. But where, that's the question? Maybe you and I can go explore to try to find this trysting place," he said, turning his attentions to Ginny.

Ginny's brows drew together and she frowned at him. "Be quiet, you fickle fool!"

Meredith bit her lip. Damn the chevalier and his brash words! Did he have to draw so much attention to her and Deron? Then she looked to her lover, so calm and undaunted, and suddenly didn't care anymore what anyone thought. Oh, how she loved him and she wanted the whole world to know! "I've been watching the stars," she said dreamily. "It's a beautiful night."

"Indeed?" said Nicki in a tone as frosty as his hair.

"Indeed," said Deron, favoring Meredith with a simmering look.

"It seems," said Nicki coldly, "that you and I have some things to settle between us."

And Meredith looked at him unhappily, thinking that he sounded as if he really meant it!

Perhaps, she reflected, it had not, after all, been terribly tactful to come in glowing with white-hot heat!

Chapter Twenty-eight

Restlessly, Deron strode the confines of his room, a glass of brandy in hand and a scowl on his face. It was time that he did some serious thinking.

He'd been letting events carry him along like a swimmer caught in a riptide. Enjoying loving Vivienne and being loved by her. Taking every day as it came, content to savor the heady feelings that were alight inside him.

What kind of feelings? he thought grimly. Not the ones he'd planned on having, that was for certain. But rather, he was feeling what he'd meant to make her feel. Yes, he'd flown too close to the sun and now his pinions were scorched.

He sat down, one foot on the hearthstones, and decided he'd begin by thinking about Vivienne.

Since the very beginning, she'd confused him. That first night, when he'd abducted her to the inn, and nearly made her pay for her foolish cheating by joining him in bed. Instead, he'd asked for a kiss . . . and had been startled indeed when she kissed as if she'd never kissed a man before.

The Lady Vivienne Winter, an innocent? he'd thought.

Impossible. He knew for a fact that she'd bedded

his friend Gabriel, if not others.

And then later, when he'd stood looking down at her asleep in the moonlight, she'd had the soft defenselessness of a girl, a vulnerable look that had made him want to protect her. He recalled that he'd admonished himself to harden his heart against her, reminding himself that better men than he had fallen prey to her wiles. .

And he had promptly ignored his own warning. He'd found that he liked her company, that being with her was refreshing, as if she were indeed a sweet girl, the kind of girl he'd dreamed of marrying one day. Not a practiced jade who was accomplished at flirting and discreet at conducting her affairs.

Then there was the hot passion she'd made him feel, had shown to him. He remembered that astonishing night on the balcony at Versailles . . . No woman had ever made him feel that way before, so completely out of control, so heedless of everything except her.

From that night on, he had burned for her, ached for her, and been utterly unable to forget her. He supposed it was then that the damnable thing had happened.

That he'd fallen in love with her.

He'd barely been able to stand the sight of her in Nicki's company. The thought that she might be sharing that incredible passion with another man was unbearable. There had been many times when he'd had to restrain himself from yanking her arm and dragging her away from Nicki's side, or leaping on Nicholas and beating him senseless.

She was more changeable than any woman he'd

ever known. From the innocent, vulnerable girl, to the passionate beauty who made him weak with desire, to the companion who raced at his side and knew as much about horseflesh as he did. He'd never met a woman who captured his interest so effortlessly and held it as the weeks passed into months.

He didn't know when she was more beautiful . . . when in full court dress, with diamonds around her lovely neck, or dressed as a boy in breeches and boots. She'd begun to haunt his waking hours as well as his sleep, and he found he couldn't stay away from her no matter how hard he tried.

Also, he found that he was rigorously not letting himself think about his feelings.

And it was worse after the night he climbed into her bedroom window and took what he'd dreamed about since the night at Versailles.

The reality was better than any dream. She was more than he'd ever imagined, an innocent siren who tempted him, teased him, and heated his blood to the fever point.

Since that night, he'd craved her flesh as if she were a drug he was addicted to. He hadn't been able to spend any night away from her side; he'd missed her terribly during the hours he was away from her during the day.

And not once had he thought about his plan, about why he'd become involved with her in the first place. Because if he remembered what he was supposed to be doing, then he'd have to stop being with her, stop loving her, and he didn't know if he could stand that.

The wager. The damnable wager he'd made with

Gabriel.

He tried ticking off all the reasons he should be glad to end it with her.

She was married and saw nothing wrong with cuckolding her husband.

She had made love to his best friend.

She had had other lovers before that.

She was a cheating, lying wench who might never tell him the truth.

His beloved deceiver.

No, he could never lose his heart to a woman who had known so many other men. When he gave his love to a woman, it would be one who loved him alone, not legions of others.

Coldly, he finished off the brandy. In all his thinking, he hadn't thought about the single most important thing.

Did she love him?

She had never once said it. True, her eyes were soft and tender when she looked at him. But she'd never told him she loved him. Of course, he'd not said it either, and she might be waiting for him to say it.

What should his course be now? How could he learn if she loved him or not?

For a start, he would begin to keep his distance from her. He had to get used to living without her, steel his heart against her. And perhaps if he were cool to her, he would see from her reaction how she felt about him.

And then . . . ah, then, if he learned that she loved him, if he saw that she was puzzled and hurt by his coolness . . . then it would be time to carry out the rest of his plan.

Even if it killed him.

Raceford entered the posh gambling club with a scowl on his face. Perhaps the way to get Vivienne out of his mind for the time being was at the tables. Winning had always been his passion, a way to lift his spirits and engage his mind. He ordered a bottle of wine and sat down at one of the tables where play was in progress.

After several hands, he had a considerable pile of winnings in front of him, which was earning him bleak looks from the other gamblers. He played with his usual consummate skill, and yet tonight his heart was not in the game. After another hand, when he realized he was barely paying attention, he rose, collecting his winnings.

Maybe it was just that the gamblers at the table he'd chosen were not very skilled, Raceford reasoned, and he decided to wander among the other tables to observe the play and see if he couldn't spot some experienced gamblers.

And then, among the mostly white powdered heads, he spotted one that gleamed silver blond, and his fists clenched.

Nicki, damn him.

From the first, Nicki had been at Vivienne's side, ardently courting her. And he'd seen the way she'd looked at him on occasion. It was enough to drive a man mad — the recipient of the look mad with desire, the observer mad with jealousy.

It was time he taught the irritating viscomte a lesson. It burned indeed that since he'd given up Vivienne's company, Nicki had been at her side almost every instant. She'd not been long in finding consolation, he thought unreasonably.

He walked up to the table and merely stood, until at last Nicholas looked up.

"A game, Viscomte?" he asked. "High stakes—just between the two of us?"

Nicki tossed his cards negligently on the table. "A game, Raceford, is what it seems we have been playing from the first."

"Yes, but as I recall, you started it—asking me to impersonate a certain gentleman of the road," Deron said, taking the chair opposite Nicholas. The others had vacated the table, leaving the two rivals in possession.

"And as I recall, you at once changed the rules, starting the game with the lady in question a day early."

"Yes . . . but with a prize so worth winning, any tactics are fair, are they not?" Deron started dealing the cards.

"Name the stakes tonight," Nicholas demanded.

"If she belonged to either of us, I would name the lady in question. But she is not ours to wager. So instead I will name what I desire. The chance to fight you—without swords or pistols, but with fists—after the game."

"You English are addicted to barbarous pursuits like boxing," Nicki sneered. "Allow you the chance to mar my elegant face? I think not. And besides, why do you wish to fight over the lady? I believe you have tossed her aside, as the saying goes, leaving the field clear for me."

"I may not be seeing her anymore, but there are still old scores I long to settle with you."

"Come, Raceford. I won't do anything as savage as hitting you in the face. It will have to be rapiers or nothing, if you are really set on fighting me."

"You won't allow the winner the choice of combat?"

Nicki smiled. "Very well. But, then, that means I shall have to be sure to win. What a bore. I generally prefer to take my gambling more lightly, as a sport, not a job."

The men picked up their cards and at once became intently absorbed in their play. It soon became apparent that they were evenly matched in skill; it would be close as to who would win the best of the seven hands they had agreed to play.

As the game went on, they soon attracted a small crowd of onlookers.

"What are the stakes?" one asked.

"These madmen are gambling for the privilege of choosing the weapons in a duel they intend to fight."

"A duel! Mercy!" sang a voice, which, to the men's irritation, proved to belong to the chevalier.

"But this is simply too rich," the chevalier went on. "Could it be the two of you will duel for the honor of the Lady Vivienne?"

Nicki winced. "I believe it is none of your business, Chevalier."

"But I shall have to witness the outcome of this duel, for I have my own interests in the lady. Perhaps I shall be lucky enough to watch the two of you mortally wound each other, and then I shall be able to claim her for myself!" And he laughed a most irritating laugh.

Raceford shot a steely glance at the chevalier, and

the gallant's laughter stopped short.

"But I distract you from your game. Please, resume play, gentlemen," he mumbled contritely.

At the end of the sixth hand, the men were matched evenly in points. The winner would be decided by the last hand. Both of them frowned in concentration, Nicki in his apricot satins and laces, Raceford in his sober pewter velvet.

Nicki threw the last card on the table.

"The hand is mine, and we will duel with rapiers," he said.

Raceford smiled. "I hate to lose, Nicholas . . . whether at cards, with a woman, or in combat. Rest assured that since I have not won the hand, I shall not lose the duel."

"Surely you will fight to the death!" the chevalier goaded.

"We are not. First blood, Raceford?"

"First blood. And since I shall not be able to use my fists on that face, perhaps I shall give you a dueling scar on your cheek."

"Please do. For it will only make me look dangerous and more attractive to the ladies. There are times when I think my appearance is too angelic."

Both men rose, rapiers on their hips, and were followed out of the club by an eager, noisy crowd, led by the chevalier. Soon they were in a secluded corner of a nearby park, where both men stripped off their coats.

The two men faced off, rapiers leveled and winking in the light, their other hands on their hips. They assumed graceful dancer's poses as they considered each other for a long moment.

And then Nicki lunged. Raceford parried his

356

thrust gracefully and brought up his own weapon for a thrust. With a ringing clash, Nicki fended him off and they sprang apart, on guard.

Slowly, they circled each other, Raceford like a wolf, Nicki like a panther. They leapt forward, smiling as they fought, even laughing at times when a particularly good move was made.

There was the dazzle of rapiers, the grace of the men's postures as they danced around each other or struggled to free locked swords. A few long strands of Raceford's hair had come loose, and in a few moments, long silver-blond locks were straggling from the black velvet riband that held them.

Raceford pressed the attack, advancing on Nicki, who was hard put to parry the strokes, so fast were they coming. He leaped on the ledge of a fountain, and then it was his turn to press the attack. Back and forth they went, in a combat as earnest and deadly as any fought to the death. All the suppressed hostility and jealousy of the past weeks was being vented as they dueled. They were as well matched with rapiers as they were at cards, and it seemed to the onlookers that neither would ever gain the advantage.

At last a rapier whickered through the air and met no opposing steel, making a long rent in a white sleeve that immediately bloomed red.

Nicki stepped back, lowering his sword and holding his arm. "First blood, Your Grace. You have bested me." He gave an ironic bow. "Though I believe I won the most important contest tonight. I hate to think of what would have happened if we'd boxed. I never did learn to fight with my fists."

Raceford bowed back. "And now you should have

the surgeon see to that, Nicki."

"Nonsense. It's a flesh wound, no more. Splash some brandy on it, bandage it . . . and give me some wine to drink." Raceford could see that among the younger crowd, Nicki's bravado was much admired.

After he'd had a draught of wine and had his wound disinfected and bandaged, Nicki threw an arm around Raceford's shoulder. "Now that we have fought, can we be friends again?"

"We can. You acquitted yourself honorably, my friend. I believe we go to the same ball tonight?"

"Yes — though I will now be late, on account of having to go home and change my shirt. I will see you there."

Music played and candles cast a soft glow that caught sparks from glittering gems around white throats. The Marquise du Planchet's ball was in full swing, and the tinkle of laughter vied with the swish of full skirts as couples danced beneath chandeliers.

Meredith was miserable.

She wore a gown of sea-foam green encrusted with silver lace, the whole of it open over a daffodil and white brocade petticoat that was embroidered with spring-green leaves. She fanned herself with a silver lace fan, and her hair was piled high and fell in cascades of ringlets on her bared shoulders. An emerald and silver necklace was around her throat, and square-cut emeralds glinted in her ears.

She had caused a sensation when she came into the ball. She had never looked lovelier, and at the

358

moment, she was knee-deep in gallants.

Except that her appearance had made no impression whatsoever on the one man she longed to see more than any other. Raceford.

When she'd come in, she'd seen him looking sumptuous in a dark green coat and had started across the room to him, a wide smile on her face. He'd nodded to her coolly, raised one brow, and turned his back on her.

She'd stood stock-still in the middle of the room as if she'd been slapped.

Now, though she tossed her curls and laughed and flirted with the men around her, her eyes kept turning to where he stood across the room, deep in conversation with a beautiful blond woman. He hadn't left her side all evening. And now, as the orchestra started up the strains of a waltz, Meredith felt her heart sink as Raceford bowed to the blonde and offered his arm. She watched as he escorted her out onto the dance floor, then took her in his arms and circled the room with her.

The blonde's hair was the color of honey under the chandeliers, and she was slim and very pretty. She had a patrician look, delicate features, and an extremely well-bred air. She wore a pale blue gown trimmed with cream lace, gold and pearl jewelry, and Meredith longed to yank her hair out by the roots. She burned as the woman laughed up into Raceford's face, no doubt congratulating herself on having captured the attention of the most handsome man in the ballroom.

Why was he ignoring her?

The last time she'd seen him had been dawn, when he'd lingered in her arms, reluctant to leave, pressing tender kisses on her cheeks and shoulders, until she'd warned him he'd cause a scandal if he tried climbing out of the palais in daylight. And now he was acting as if she didn't exist. She'd done nothing wrong, there had been no quarrel, and yet he was dancing with this awful blonde as if she weren't even in the room, as if he'd never spent the night in her bed.

What on earth could she do?

And Nicki was not even here yet to console her. She turned to the man at her side and gave him an incandescent smile.

"Why, Chevalier," she said, "of course I will dance with you. You honor me by asking."

"The honor—nay, the pleasure, is all mine," he said, and he led her out onto the dance floor.

Perhaps if she were more visible, closer to him, and dancing with another man at that, he'd put an end to this ridiculous charade. He'd always sworn he hated to see her dance with other men, and had stood and glowered at her from the sidelines when courtesy had forced her to accept dances.

Now he didn't even turn his head. He seemed oblivious to the fact that she was on the dance floor. Once, when they passed within a few feet of each other, his eyes passed over her as if she weren't even there, and he bent his head to whisper something in the blonde's ear. At which, Meredith noted with fury, she blushed.

Damn him! she thought passionately. Before the night was over, he'd rue the way he was treating her, the wretch! She'd find a way to make him pay! And she'd find a way to get him alone and demand an explanation—even if she had to drag him bodily out of the ballroom — as soon as he was out of that blonde's clutches . . . for she'd not play the jealous wench in front of another woman.

Pleading exhaustion, she asked the chevalier to lead her from the floor and had him take her into another room, where gambling was taking place. She sat down at a silver loo table, fanning herself. At least here she wouldn't have to see Raceford flirting with another woman! Where was Nicki? she thought impatiently. Raceford had always been wildly jealous of Nicki. Perhaps when she had a blond of her own to flirt with . . .

It was three hands of cards later that Nicholas at last showed up. He was looking beautiful in pink-and-silver brocade, with a black velvet ribbon tying back his silvery blond hair and a black heart-shaped patch on one cheekbone.

"You are late," she murmured.

"Yes, I was detained. Tangling with your friend Raceford."

"Tangling? What do you mean?"

"Just a small matter of a duel, my darling. I shall tell you every detail as we dance."

"A duel? Nicki!"

He stooped to kiss her cheek. "But I see you are occupied, my sweet love," he murmured. "When you have finished your hand, come look for me. I will amuse myself until then."

She stroked his cheek with one hand and threw him a grateful look. Yes, when she entered the ballroom, she'd be tightly pressed to Nicholas' side and would behave as outrageously as possible with him. Maybe then that devil Raceford would take notice!

And what had the duel been over?

Over her?

She stopped in the ladies' boudoir when her hand of cards was finished, to check her appearance. Taking a tiny silver comb from her reticule, she smoothed her hair. Then she put a touch of red on her lips and cheeks, and, on impulse, added a heart-shaped patch to the same cheekbone Nicki's was on, so that they would match. There. She looked dangerously pretty.

And ready to do battle for Lord Raceford's heart.

But when she entered the ballroom, to her dismay, neither of them were in sight.

Chapter Twenty-nine

"And so, Nicki my love, how goes the love affair?" Ginny asked idly as she walked through the Marquise du Planchet's reception rooms, her hand lightly resting on his rose brocade sleeve. She'd only just arrived and was pleased to find Nicki almost immediately.

His dark brows drew together, and he favored her with a long look. "Not as I would hope. The object of my every desire is cold to my advances and never allows me an opportunity to be alone with her."

She smiled and allowed her fingers to squeeze his arm. "Then Lady Vivienne Winter is as cold as her name?"

"Lady Vivienne Winter?" he queried, caressing her with his eyes.

She laughed, feeling a rush of warmth for him. Soon, it would be soon that she would allow him to discover he loved her. "And is that not the lady you are pursuing?"

"For marriage only . . . not for love's sake," he murmured.

"And I believe you are ignorant of love, my darling Nicki. Of desire, you are all too experienced

. . . but love is a stranger to you."

"I would have told you that you were right, not such a long time ago. But now I find my heart is no longer mine to call my own but answers to the whim of another."

"But we were speaking of Lady Vivienne, and—"

"We were not."

"I was! Now, Nicki, you must hear me out. You still must marry a rich woman, must you not?"

"Perhaps. And perhaps my reformed behavior of late has been noticed by my family."

She raised delicate eyebrows at him, really surprised. "It has? Nicki! When did this come to pass?"

He smiled, and allowed his fingers to trail up and down her bare arm. "I visited them and had a frank talk with my father. I reminded him that he was as wild as myself in his youth. And I told him that I intend to marry. And to settle down. I find I tire of endless seductions. They bore me."

"And you told him you intend to marry an Englishwoman? He must have been horrified, even if she is rich!"

"He was not, for I did not tell him I mean to marry an Englishwoman."

"But when he finds out—"

He stopped, and she looked at him, so gorgeously handsome with his silver-blond hair, dark brows, and pink and silver brocade coat. "Ginny, I beg you. I must speak to you alone. I have something I need to tell you."

For a moment she stared at him, and there was a current between them as tingling as lightning. So! Her beautiful boy was at last coming to his senses!

She was about to speak when she caught a glimpse of a figure approaching them over his shoulder.

"And here," she said lightly, regaining her composure, "is the one you must be alone with, *cheri*. But later . . . later perhaps I will listen to what you have to tell me."

"Ginny!" He smiled down at her, joy and hope leaping in his eyes.

She turned. "Ah, my darling Vivienne. How ravishing you are tonight!"

Meredith smiled at the pair of them and returned the compliment. "I've been searching for you everywhere, Nicki. Where did you run to?"

"I did not wander far, my lady," he said rather guiltily, and then charmingly changed the subject. "But have I told you already how exquisite you are?"

She laughed. "Yes, at least a hundred times, Nicki. Though any woman would have a hard time competing with you. You are rather exquisite yourself."

"Yes, not many men dare to wear pink, *non?* They feel they might look *effete* in it."

She gave him a simmering look. "You could never look anything other than masculine, my darling Nicki."

"My dears, I see the duc. How wild he looks to see me with you, Nicki! I simply must go and pacify him!" Ginny cried.

"Do not *pacify* him too much, Genvieve," Nicholas warned, staring after her as she rushed off.

Meredith drew her brows together, puzzled. Why, Nicki was staring after Ginny as if he were in love with her! But how wonderful! What a magnificent couple they would make! And it would make Meredith feel less guilty about her own defection to Raceford.

"You are acting as if you are jealous," she remarked.

"It is a streak in my temperament."

"But the best way to gain someone's attention is to make them jealous in turn. Perhaps if Ginny thought you were enraptured with me—"

And besides, that way I can make Raceford jealous. She'd just seen him enter the ballroom, and he was alone.

"Jealous? But it's you I am jealous of, my darling Vivienne." Nicki turned back to her and took her arm firmly. "Come with me," he said, in no mood to be gainsaid. "There is something between us that is long overdue."

Meredith found herself being almost dragged across the ballroom by the viscomte and out into a hallway. Here, strollers and servants passed back and forth.

"This will not do," he growled.

"But, Nicki, what on earth is it?" she laughed, thinking that if he had been this masterful from the beginning, she would have had a hard time choosing between him and Raceford.

"I want to be alone with you," he said. *"Quite* alone."

She was pulled down the hall and around a corner. Here, in a great tiled hall only dimly lit with candles in sconces, there was no one else in sight. But that still wasn't good enough for Nicki. He tried a couple of doors until he found one that opened.

"In here," he said, and Meredith found herself swept into a library.

"And now what," she asked, a smile playing about her lips, "is this all about?" She had some idea he had dragged her off to ask her about Ginny and was startled by what happened next.

"What it is all about is it is time I kissed you," he said.

Kissed her! Meredith stared at him, eyes wide, taking in his wickedly lovely face, his wide shoulders, his utterly elegant clothes. The black ribbon tying back his pale blond hair was matched by a black patch on one cheek, and to her absolute surprise, Meredith realized she wanted nothing more than to kiss Nicki . . . had always wanted to be kissed by this spectacular male!

What was wrong with her? She loved Raceford!

But she was drawn to Nicki, attracted by his looks and his laughter and his wildness.

"I have tried to treat you with respect, Vivienne, but I find that it is against my nature. I was born to love women, not to respect them. And I have spent too many days being ravished by your lips and eyes to stand this restraint a moment longer. I must kiss you. But only if you want me to. Tell me you want me to kiss you."

Time stood still as Meredith stared into his brilliant blue eyes. Oh, heavens, what was wrong with her? But she was alone with him . . . no one would ever know. . . .

"I want you to kiss me," she breathed.

He stepped forward and tilted her chin up with his fingers. He studied her face for a long moment, then bent his head and let his lips close on hers.

Oh, Lord, Meredith thought, this was a man who knew how to kiss! His kiss was light, elegant, sensual. Not like the passionate claiming that Raceford did, but a symphony of touch, a poem of sensuality. He wasn't touching her anywhere yet except with his lips, and their bodies were apart. Then he captured her hands with his and turned them over, palms up. He dropped his head and let his lips kiss one wrist, then another. Meredith felt a shudder go all through her at this strange caress.

He straightened one of her arms and his lips touched just the inside skin of her elbow. For a moment they burned there, and she felt the barest touch of his tongue. Then he raised his head and his open mouth delicately kissed the swelling curve of her breast above her neckline, then the other one.

He straightened and stared down at her. "Now, kiss me back, Vivienne," he murmured.

Meredith felt as if his lips had branded her everywhere they had touched with fire. She swayed toward him, not able to stop herself, and was caught in his arms. He crushed her against him and his mouth came toward hers.

"A charming picture."

A voice speaking from the doorway penetrated Meredith's mind and she leaped back from Nicholas' arms as if she had been burned.

Raceford stood in the doorway.

"A kiss that was, I hope, worth dying for, Viscomte," he said.

Meredith felt the blood rush to her head, felt her knees grow weak. Raceford had caught her kissing Nicki! And he said he would kill Nicki for it!

His eyes were narrow sparks of green ice, fixed on Nicki, not looking at her.

Nicki gave his most graceful, elegant bow — a slap in the face. "With pleasure, Your Grace. But you have only to name the hour . . . and the weapons. Though I might remind you that the lady is not married to you, nor to me. Thus defending her virtue would not seem to be your place."

"It is my place, for I have claimed the lady as my own. Shall we say dawn tomorrow?"

Meredith at last broke the frozen silence she had been locked in. "But you cannot — you cannot mean to duel!" she cried.

Nicki turned to her casually. "But it is customary when two men are competing for just one woman's favors — and love."

"But you are not competing," she heard herself say. She had to prevent this! She had to stop them from killing one another! And the only possible way she could do that was to speak the truth.

She took a deep breath. "I am sorry, Nicholas, but my heart is already given to Lord Raceford."

One of Nicki's brows lifted. "So? Forgive me if I point out that a moment ago, your heart . . . or at least your lips . . . seemed to have been given to me."

"I was wrong to kiss you," Meredith said between clenched teeth. Oh, this was hard! "It was a moment's temptation . . . curiosity . . . that I should not have given in to."

"I see." He bowed to her, then turned to face Raceford. "Then, since it seems the lady rejects my suit, this business of shooting each other can be dropped?"

369

A curt nod from Raceford was his answer.

"Then I will leave you," said Nicki, strolling to the door, "for it seems you two have much to discuss."

They were alone. For a frozen moment, Meredith could not find anything to say. His eyes were furious.

"Deron . . . please. I am sorry you should have found Nicki and I . . . Deron, we must talk."

"And what is there to talk about?"

She swallowed, fighting for composure. "If you—if you want to cast me off, that is your right. But because of what has existed between us, it is my right to talk to you once more. I have some things to tell you I should have told you long ago. Will you hear me?"

He considered, eyes still blazingly cold. Then he nodded. "I will hear you. When?"

"Tomorrow night?" Meredith ventured. God help her, she was too shaken to speak to him now! All she wanted to do was go home . . . be alone.

"Tomorrow night. Come to my residence at eight."

"I'll be there," whispered a contrite Meredith, and watched forlornly as he strode out of the room.

Deron Redvers stood on his balcony and stared down into the night. Bitterly, he tossed off a glass of brandy, then poured himself another one. He wanted to get drunk. Drunk enough to blot out the sight that was burned into his brain . . . the sight of his Angel in Nicholas St. Antoine's arms!

He was shaken to the depths of his soul by his anger, his fury. How could she—how could she kiss

370

another, after everything that had happened between them!

My God, she was everything he had first believed her, and lately, had stopped believing. She was a slut after all. And he had been fool enough to forget that fact, to — to fall in love with her.

Burning, he thought of Gabriel with a kind of hatred, wondering how he could have forgotten for so long that his friend had made love to her, had tasted all the pleasures that had recently been his. How could he have forgotten himself, allowed this light-skirted, beautiful she-devil to make him love her, ache for her as he never had for any other woman?

Pictures flashed through his mind, pictures of their recent love trysts, when he'd held her in his arms. How his heart had warmed at the very sight of her, how his blood had raced at her lightest touch! She had seemed so untouched, so innocent. When they'd made love that first night at Versailles, her trembling had made it seem as if she were giving herself to him for the first time, as if she'd never known a man before.

When she'd probably known a hundred men!

God, what a fool he was. He loved her, loved her like he'd never dreamed it was possible to love a woman. Now he knew how a woman who fell for some unprincipled rake must feel. The depths of his shame and his sorrow were almost too much for his heart to contain.

He finished off another glass of brandy and poured another, beginning to feel the effects. He would be drunk . . . he would stay drunk until this awful ache of betrayal left him, until he could stand to face the world again.

How empty a world it would be without her.

He wanted to rush to her side, to beg her to love him, to be faithful to him. To demand if all that had passed between them had been a lie, or just a light piece of amusement for her. It could not be — it couldn't be! his heart cried, anguished.

He drank more brandy. When had he forgotten what he had set out to do? When had the tables turned and he fallen in love with her instead of she with him? He'd meant to make her love him . . . and then teach her what it was to be left. But God help him, it was he who was learning the bitter lesson.

But oh, Vivienne, he thought, his eyes glistening with unshed tears, if I ever get the chance, you'll learn what it is to own a broken heart!

Chapter Thirty

Meredith bit her lip nervously as she waited alone in the lavish drawing room at Raceford's residence. Portraits from another time frowned disapprovingly at her; statues gave her basilisk glares. All the talismans of lineage and ancestry seemed to be telling her she had no place here, that she should leave at once. But it had to be her imagination. She'd been in elaborate rooms before this and they had not daunted her so.

She could never remember feeling so jittery, so afraid of what was about to happen. She knew only one thing: It was time to tell Raceford the entire truth.

The truth about who she was . . . and the truth about how she felt about him.

He had never spoken of the future, but his eyes had told her of his feelings. She could not be mistaken. He must care about her, he must!

But how could she start? Oh, she could never bear it if he learned she was just plain Meredith Westin, and then spurned her love. She would always wonder what his reaction would have been before he learned she'd lied to him.

So she would tell him she loved him first. Maybe

that would soften his heart for the second confession.

She wondered what he would think of her tale, wondered if he would think she was mad to have impersonated Vivienne . . . and if Vivienne was terribly wanton to have run off with another man while she was married?

But what did it matter what he thought of Vivienne? What he thought of *her* mattered. How he would scorn her real background, she thought feverishly. First, her birth. Though she was cousin to Vivienne, her mother had been from a social strata far beneath her father, so that Vivienne's family had ignored them. And then her father had been a drunkard and a gambler who had died young of his excesses. She hardly came from stock to be proud of.

He'd seen her only dressed in Vivienne's clothes, in gorgeous gowns that would have leant dash and sparkle to the plainest girl. He'd believed her to be of his station, born to it. What would he think if he'd met her as she really was, Aunt Phoebe's drudge, a downtrodden poor relation? She doubted he'd even have spared her a glance if chance had brought him to Henley and he'd seen the girl dressed in two-year-old drab beige, walking a nasty little dog or fetching her aunt's sewing basket.

The very thought of a grand and handsome duke taking any notice of her as she had been was a ridiculous one indeed. Why, she wouldn't have dared to raise her eyes to him in those days, and if politeness had forced him to speak to her, she would have had no idea what to say back to him. His very station, not to mention his looks, would have overwhelmed her.

What a mouse she had been back then, such a short time ago, she thought with a kind of wonder. So used to keeping quiet, being deferential to Aunt Phoebe, that she had really been on her way to becoming that drab, spiritless creature. That was before she'd had to play Vivienne, fearless, vivacious Vivienne who brimmed with confidence. Thank God Vivienne had come and taken her away from Henley, away from her aunt, away from the life of drudgery she was leading! Even if it all ended badly, with her falling in love with a man there was no hope of marrying . . .

For she did not dare to allow herself to hope.

How her heart ached when she thought of him. She wished they could just be snuggled under the covers of a great bed, miles from everyone, with the rain beating on the windows and the thunder rolling in the distance. She wished they could belong to each other forever. She wished he were really a highwayman and not a duke after all.

She paced up and down the luxurious room, clasping her hands nervously before her. Her thoughts were all of him. She couldn't forget him for a moment; he had become the only important thing in her life. She loved him.

She thought of the night he climbed in her bedroom window. She'd resolved then to be his mistress, at least until he married. Had she the courage for it? To offer herself to him?

Where was he? She dreaded his coming, yet the minutes were dragging. He was making her wait. She crossed to the mirror over the mantel and stared at her reflection. Two hectic spots of color burned in her cheeks, but otherwise she was pale. Her eyes were enormous, dark.

For this one interview, she had scorned being Lady Vivienne. She wanted him to see her as she was—to see Meredith. So she wore a dress of her own, a plain dark blue affair with a high neck and rather narrow skirts. Her hair was simply gathered into a French twist, and she wore no jewels. She wanted him to see the real woman he had loved.

His voice spoke from the doorway. "So I see that this evening you are as sober as a nun. Do you think to convince me of your virtue simply by changing your dress?"

The words were a whiplash of scorn, and she turned to find him leaning in the doorway, his eyes raking her. His dark hair was tumbled across his forehead, and he was casually dressed in a maroon smoking jacket and black pants. As he walked into the room, she suddenly realized with an unpleasant jolt that he was drunk!

"That was not my intention," she managed. "I had a very different reason for dressing as I do, as you will learn in a moment."

"Oh. Entering a convent, are we?" He crossed to a table, poured himself a large glass of brandy, and drank it off, then poured a second glass for her. "I suggest you drink this, madam. This interview will be unpleasant enough as it is without a bracer for your nerves."

He thrust the glass in her hand and Meredith took it, shaken. Raceford was being rude—and he was never rude! God, he must have been more hurt than she had even guessed by the sight of her kissing Nicki! She realized he was very right; she did need a bracer for her nerves. She took a gulp of the brandy and felt it burn its way down.

"I imagine you have come here to try to convince

me of your virtue," he said, and Meredith took a frightened glance at him, seeing that his eyes were bloodshot, his face stubbled. "But I must tell you that in the short time I've known you, I know of three lovers you've taken—myself, Gabriel, and now Nicholas. Your appetites exceed even mine, madam."

Meredith swallowed. Oh, how could she convince him he was the only one she'd ever taken to her bed? Maybe in a few moments, when he knew she was not Vivienne, he would believe her.

"I haven't come to try to convince you of anything, but to tell you some things that I should have told you a long time ago," she said quietly. "If you will just hear me out—"

"I will. And then you will hear me. I suggest we sit." He indicated a sofa, and Meredith went and sat down, still clutching her glass as if it offered a lifeline. "Now, why don't you begin?"

His voice was so icy. She looked down at her hands, wondering how to start. "Whatever you may think to the contrary, Deron, I must tell you the truth. Nicholas means nothing to me. It was wrong of me to kiss him. I told you it was merely curiosity, and I know that is a poor excuse. He'd been courting me so long and—" She stopped, stealing a glance at his face.

"I understand that yours is obviously a curious nature. But I warned you that you belonged to me alone. I do not allow a woman I am in—involved with to dally with other men, no matter how curious she may be."

"And I do belong to you alone!" Meredith cried, deciding it was time to fling caution and pride to the winds.

"Then what the hell were you doing kissing Nicki?" he ground out.

"I—I don't know. But I swear it, Deron. Deron, I've wanted to tell you for a long time now . . . and please, I beg you to believe me. I've been frightened by my feelings . . . frightened by how you might react. Maybe I was trying to deny it when I let Nicki kiss me, I don't honestly know. But—"

"But?"

"I love you."

She stared down at her hands again, then heard him rise and walk restlessly across the room. She looked up to find his back to her, his fists jammed in his pockets. Oh, what was he thinking?

Raceford stared bleakly at the fire. How his heart had leapt when she spoke those words! He'd wanted to catch her to him, to tell her he loved her too. But he was so weak. He'd had to get up before she saw the savage joy in his eyes at her words.

She loved him!

His mouth tightened in a determined line. And was this not the moment he'd been waiting for?

The chance to pay her back in her own coin?

The chance to win the wager.

He turned. She was watching him with such wide eyes, such an anxious expression, that it almost broke his heart. "I am afraid, My Lady, that you have misunderstood our arrangement," he said coldly.

"Our . . . arrangement?" Meredith stammered.

"I never intended that it should include love."

Meredith's indrawn breath of pain was almost more than he could bear and he turned abruptly away, striding up and down the room as he spoke, unable to look at her again.

"You were no more than a challenge to me from the first. An amusement. I wanted to bed you, and I did. But I never loved you. Do you think I could love a woman who gives herself to any man she fancies? When I do love someone, it will be an innocent girl who can give her heart and body to me alone, not a much-used jade who has given her body to many men. I thought with your experience, My Lady, that you understood the rules of the game included desire and its satisfaction. Never love."

Never love. Meredith couldn't help it, she felt tears start in her eyes and spill over her lashes. He had never loved her—never loved her at all! Her throat was so tight she felt she could barely breathe, and there was a burning lump of stone in her chest.

"So it was all just a game to you," she whispered over her tears.

He looked at her then, and never had his heart been so wrenched as the sight of her eyes filled with tears, at the utter misery he saw written on her face. He almost crossed the room to her, but then . . .

"And so now you know what it feels like to suffer for love, My Lady, as you have made so many others suffer before."

"Oh God, Deron . . ." she said, nearly choking, and rose. "I do know what it means to suffer." She started across the room on unsteady legs, toward the door. "God help me, I love you with my whole heart and soul. I—This is the end, then. I will never see you again."

He was across the room and at her side in a few swift strides. "It need not be the end. I enjoyed having you in my bed and would continue to bed you as long as you understand there is no question of love. As a mistress, you are superb."

"No! How dare you speak of such a thing?" She rounded on him, eyes blazing, tears still running down her cheeks.

"So when I treat you like the whore you are, you object, is that it?" he almost shouted.

"I am no whore!" she cried. "You are the only man who has ever—"

His arms caught her by the shoulders and he pulled her to him. "If this is good-bye then, My Lady, I will kiss you once more. Why should I not take what you give so freely to so many?"

Meredith struggled but he was stronger, and his mouth covered hers in a punishing kiss. His hands were bruising her, his lips savage on hers as he ran his fingers up and down her body in an insultingly intimate way. And then he put her from him, staring down at her, chest heaving.

She drew herself up and lifted her chin, letting him see her pain. He was hurt and he wanted to hurt her in return, but he would never shame her. And what was the point, now, of telling him the truth? Telling him she was really Meredith, not Vivienne? For he'd told her he'd never loved her. And if he didn't love Lady Vivienne, how much less likely was he to love a poor girl from a world so far beneath him it was laughable?

"I am sorry that it has to end with such ugliness between us, Deron. I spent the happiest hours of my life with you. You taught me what love is, and I gave my heart and my trust to you. I will remember those times, not this night," she said.

Before he could answer, she turned and ran from the room, down the long echoing hallway to the front door, past the startled servants, out the doors. There was no sound of him coming after her. He was letting her go; it was finished, over.

Raceford stood behind her, shaken, wanting to run after her, forcing himself not to. His whole being ached with loss, with remorse at the sorrow he'd seen in her eyes, the hurt he'd put there.

You taught me what love is, she'd said.

And he'd taught her what it was to lose it.

But God help him, he'd lost it as well.

Chapter Thirty-one

The rain drizzled off the eaves of the palais as Meredith sat staring out the window, chin cupped in her palms, but she didn't see it. She hadn't left her room since yesterday evening, except once to check the post to see if it brought any letters from him. There hadn't been one.

She couldn't stand to go out into Paris society anymore, but of course she had to. Her role as Vivienne demanded it. But last night, unable to subject herself to any further heartbreak, she'd pretended to be ill and begged off her engagement.

It was just that everywhere she went, she saw Raceford. And he looked right through her as if she didn't exist.

All his attention was taken up with the blonde he'd been dancing with that night. Her name was Lady Evangeline Traceforth, and she was of a very good family, one that boasted earls and lords in its ranks. She was innocent, much feted in Paris society, thought by many to be the catch of the season. For though her family was not rich, it was ancient, and she had aristocratic breeding, a sweet temperament, and all the graces and accomplishments a potential duke's wife should have.

Indeed, there was speculation in all quarters that Raceford would marry the Lady Evangeline and at long last settle down. So every night Meredith had to grit her teeth and watch Raceford tamely dance attendance on another. . . .

Another who was so much better suited to marry him than she was.

For after all, her role as Vivienne was just that. A playacting sham. She was plain Meredith Westin, so far beneath the touch of a duke that it was ridiculous to think he'd ever have thought of marrying her.

Really, maybe it was better for him, better for her, that their affair had ended, so that the foolish hopes she'd begun to entertain could be dashed in the dust, where they belonged. He ought to marry a cool English rose of impeccable breeding like the Lady Evangeline.

But it just hurt so much to watch him, night after night, with another woman. And to see his beautiful green eyes meet hers as coolly as if she were a stranger — and not even an attractive stranger at that.

When just so recently, she'd been spending nights in his arms, dying of love for him, overcome by the passion he'd ignited!

Nicki was not much help, for although he was frequently at her side, he was often abstracted, in a deep gloom, and moody. His eyes followed Ginny wherever she went, and Meredith had the depressing realization that neither of the men who'd chased her for so long were in love with her.

Once, only once had something happened that gave her a momentary flare of hope. She'd been at a dinner party, seated a few seats down and across from Raceford, who had the ever-present Lady Evangeline on his elbow. By that time, the world had begun to seem a very bleak place indeed to Meredith, and she'd kept her eyes down for fear of meeting his and sat listlessly toying with her food. On her right, Nicki was about as spirited, barely eating either, not talking, in a brown study.

She'd looked up suddenly, feeling eyes on her, to find Raceford watching her. There was a pained expression in his eyes, as if . . .

As if it hurt him to see her!

For a very long time, neither had been able to look away.

And then Lady Evangeline had placed a white hand on his sleeve, calling his attention to something, and the moment had passed.

It was all she had to comfort herself with in those bleak weeks. That the man she loved more than life itself was perhaps playacting, too, that he found their separation every bit as trying as she did.

But later that evening, when she saw him dancing and laughing with that blond bitch, it all seemed as if she'd imagined it.

For surely, he was a man without a care if she'd ever seen one.

The very next night, he'd finally spoken to her. He'd had to, for politeness sake, as they had found themselves seated next to each other at a sumptuous dinner. He'd spent most of the time talking to the woman on his other side, but at last, he'd turned to her.

For a long moment, he'd just looked at her. Then: "You are looking pale, my Lady Vivienne," he'd said. "Paris does not agree with you?"

"Indeed, it does not. I find it is full of painful

384

memories for me. But you yourself are looking very healthy, Your Grace," she'd added after a moment, thinking it was most damnably true. "Evidently Paris agrees with you."

"Indeed it does. For I have long had it in mind to take a wife, and at last I believe I may have found the right woman." His eyes left hers and focused on the Lady Evangeline, looking a cool beauty in lemon satin and pearls. "Breeding is so important in a wife, do you not agree? After all, I have the lineage of my family and my heirs to consider."

A wife! She'd been frozen with horror. Never did she think she could feel more pain than she'd felt when he'd said he'd never loved her, but now! The thought of him marrying was unbearable! She wanted to get up and leave, but couldn't think of how she could. And his reference to breeding burned her. She'd been so right to know that the fairy tale would never come true, that he'd never overlook her lowly birth.

"But is it possible . . . you are even paler? Have some wine," he'd said.

She'd dared to look him in the eyes then, letting her pain show. "I am ill. I have had some news that makes me sick."

"Then perhaps you should excuse yourself," he'd said coldly. And she had, retreating to the ladies' boudoir, where she'd sobbed her heart out into a handkerchief, insensible to the curious glances of the other women.

Raceford to marry!

Now she sat alone in her bedroom, not even able to cry, for she'd shed so many tears the nights before that she had none left. How she would have the heart to go on with her charade as Vivienne she didn't know. She wanted to leave Paris, leave any place where she would have to smile and laugh. But then, she didn't want to leave the one place where she might see him again. The thought of never seeing him again was too much to bear.

And besides, where would she go? There was nowhere really. She couldn't go back to Aunt Phoebe. Not now. Quickly, she tried to banish the thought of the new problem that was bothering her; she was too upset to think of it now. What could she do indeed? She wasn't Vivienne, and it wouldn't be long before she had to give up her role. Then what? All she could hope was that Vivienne would keep her promise to give her some money to make a new start. Maybe she'd go to the New World, as far away as possible, even if it meant she would never see Deron again. It was really better never to see him again. Her heart might heal faster if she had no hope of seeing him. Not that it would ever heal, she thought forlornly.

Oh, how much she had learned in her time as Vivienne! She had learned the joy of love and the heartbreak it brings. Would she have been better off never knowing love? She shook her head, unable to decide. Though the pain was so great, still, she could not find it in her heart to wish she'd never met him.

She thought of his smile, his sudden laugh, the way he'd talked to her as if she were his equal, his companion. It hadn't just been those magic moments when he'd held her in his arms. It had been so much more. It had been the simple pleasure she'd had in his company, the friendship they'd shared, the way when she was with him she'd never felt alone.

Alone. Well, she was alone now, and she would be for the rest of her days. She had loved . . . and she had lost.

She sighed, turning her head at the sound of the door behind her opening. Jane came in, carrying a tray, and brought it to the table by the window, setting it down.

"You've got to eat something, Meredith," Jane said.

Meredith looked up at the choked tone in Jane's voice. "Jane! You've been crying!" she said.

Jane sat down heavily in a chair across from Meredith and pulled out a rumpled handkerchief. "Yes, I reckon I have," she said glumly, dabbing at fresh tears. "It's Armand. We've quarreled."

"Oh, Jane, what happened?" Meredith sat forward anxiously, for the moment forgetting her own troubles.

Jane sniffed. "I asked him about something he'd once said that puzzled me. He said something about first . . . courting me for the duke's sake. Well, it bothered me, and when I asked him, he told me right enough. He said the duke had told him to seduce me in order that he could find out where your bedroom is in this here big palace."

"Jane!" gasped Meredith. "The—The *duke* did that?" She felt a slow fire burn at this treachery. Oh, it was bad enough that he'd entangled her in his seduction, but Jane, too!

Jane nodded grimly. "Well, I was right angry, Meredith. I stormed at him some, and he lost his temper and asked me didn't I trust him and believe him that he loved me for my own sake. And I said how could I when he set out to seduce me cold-blooded-like, and somehow things got worse and worse and we was both shouting at each other. And Armand, he's proud as the devil, and he stormed out and said he'd love no woman who didn't believe in him, and—" Jane buried her face in her handkerchief and sobbed.

"Oh, Jane! This is too bad!" Meredith leaned forward and stroked Jane's hair, letting her cry for a time. But when Jane's sobs had quieted somewhat, she ventured, "But might he not have meant what he said . . . that he'd come to love you? After all, Jane, he did ask you to marry him. Can you not make it up?"

"I can't!" Jane wailed. "Don't you think I didn't realize that straight off if I'd had time to think? This evening, I kept hoping he'd come to me, but he didn't, so I began to see it was my place to go to him. I'd caused the quarrel by not trusting him, you see. So I went out to the duke's tonight and went in by a back entrance I'd—" Jane colored, but went on, "been in before. It leads straight to his room. I knocked and he called, 'Come in,' and—" Here new tears gathered and spilled over her eyelashes and ran down her cheeks. "Oh, Lord, he was in bed with the under-housemaid, that awful Marie, and they were both naked as the day they were born, she with her head on his chest! Anyone could see what they'd just finished doing! Well, I ran out and he ran after me in a sheet, shouting that he could explain. But I just kept going until I got home, and he had to give up once we were outside on account of he didn't have on anything but a sheet." She paused, and her golden-brown eyes snapped with indignation. "Explain! As if he could *explain* what he'd just done in any way that would make me feel any better!"

"Oh, Jane," Meredith said sadly. "Then it seems it is both of us."

"Yes, it's both of us. Now, Meredith, I guess talking won't mend what's broken, but I came up here to see that you eat, so—"

"Only if you promise to join me," Meredith said firmly. Jane was about to refuse, but she added, "I will divide it up. You've brought too much for the appetite I have, and I won't eat a bite unless you do, too."

Jane nodded, and they both started picking at their food. After a time, Jane said, "It seems strange all that's happened to us since we decided to take part in this mad scheme. I never expected we'd both fall in love and then that we'd both lose them. I almost wish we'd never have done it. I tell you, I don't think I can bear going back to Henley, not for one minute. I don't know what I'm going to do!"

Meredith set down her fork. "Oh, Jane, I don't know either! I don't think I can go back myself. Vivienne promised me some money, to make a start in the New World. Would you like to come with me? I'd feel so much better if we were together."

"The New World! But that's so far from everyone we know, from—"

"Armand?"

"Yes, I suppose so. Somehow I can't believe I'll never see him again, and then I think of him in bed with that Marie and I get so angry I could scream."

"That's the way I feel about Deron. I can't believe it's all over, and yet the things he said to me . . . and he's with that Evangeline every night. Well, think about it, Jane. If you decide you want a new start, I wish you would come with me. We have some time."

But just then the door opened and Ginny came in, agitatedly waving a letter. She shut the door firmly behind her.

"It is a letter from Scotland, with the Winter seal!" she announced dramatically. "It just arrived by a special rider who has half killed his horse to get here. It is addressed to Vivienne, but you'd better open it."

Meredith took the letter with trepidation. What news could merit a special messenger? She'd regularly received letters from Lord Winter, having opened them with Vivienne's permission to skim them quickly before sending them on with an account of her own activities in Paris, so her cousin could answer them in her own hand. But they had all come by regular post, none by special messenger.

With trembling hands she opened the letter, then read its contents. She set it down in her lap and stared straight ahead for a moment, turning pale.

"Well? what is it!" demanded Ginny, hands on hips.

Meredith looked up. "Lord Winter is dead," she said.

Chapter Thirty-two

"Well. And so our adventures are behind us. Meredith, I know you are unhappy to leave Paris, but must you be so positively *gloomy?*" Vivienne sat back against the coach's upholstery and regarded Meredith brightly.

Meredith looked up, surprised. Vivienne had been inconsolable the night before, when they'd met her in an inn on the outskirts of Paris. She had taken the letter with a pale cheek and trembling hand, and read it silently. Then she had sunk into a chair and whispered, "It's true. He is really dead, then."

Gabriel had stood by, offering to comfort her, but Vivienne had looked sadly at him and told him she wanted to be alone to pay her respects to her lord. That night, Meredith had heard her crying in the room next to hers and wondered if she should go in. When she had, she'd found Vivienne most melancholy. "I shall miss him," she'd said. "He was a good friend to me. How glad I am the end was swift! He deserved a release from his suffering. The housekeeper wrote me he knew nothing at the last. She also wrote that the ghost had been seen, three nights running, on the terrace. Ah, well, what can one expect from these country people? They will postpone the funeral until I reach Scotland, but we must travel with all speed." She'd paused. "Meredith, he was a good man," she sighed after a moment. "I will miss him indeed."

This morning, it seemed that Vivienne had mastered her sadness. She'd kissed Gabriel good-bye and told him to meet her in London after the funeral, then climbed into the coach with Jane and Meredith. Now she smiled, with a trace of bitterness. "So you are shocked that this morning I do not seem to be mourning my lord? But I am, Meredith. I will never forget him. But he had a long and happy life, until his illness struck him. He longed for the end; he often told me so himself. And life is for the living."

"Now you will marry Gabriel?" Meredith asked.

"When a year of mourning has passed, I will marry him. He asked me last night. But I don't want to rush things. I don't want to be disrespectful to my late husband's memory."

"How was your time with Gabriel?" asked Meredith curiously. "What did you do down there, so isolated?"

Vivienne's face took on a soft glow of remembrance. "Why, when we were not in each other's arms, we sat in the sun near the stone wall covered in roses or took walks in the green fields. We ate . . . the food was simply wonderful. Shellfish and stews and lamb. We rested a great deal and talked to the village people, sat in the tavern and drank wine. We drove an open buggy into the hills and visited vineyards where wine was made. It was the best time of my life, and not for one moment did I tire of being with Gabriel, nor he with me."

She sighed, staring for a moment out the window, lost in thought. The green hills and valleys of the French countryside rolled by, dappled in sunlight and cloud-shadows. "I shall never forget the evenings in that old bedroom at the inn, both of us looking out the window at the evening star, the village roofs, and the hills beyond. It was so peaceful. But come. Enough about me and Gabriel. You haven't told me why you are so blue, and Jane, too. What happened to the both of you all these months in Paris?"

Meredith hesitated, and Jane spoke up. "You might as well tell her, Meredith, for you know she'll run into him sometime in London. She's bound to."

"Him? Ah." Vivienne sat back, interested. "I begin to see. You had a love affair? With whom?"

Meredith gave up. It was true as Jane said that Vivienne would have to know. Sooner or later she would be confronted by a very confused Raceford. "I did . . . have an affair, as you call it. In truth, I fell in love."

"With whom?" Vivienne demanded again.

"With the Duke of Raceford."

"Raceford!" Vivienne gasped. "You can't mean it! But he's Gabriel's closest friend!"

"I know that—and he has never met you, why I can't imagine."

"So I suppose he came to see you to pay his respects? But this is incredibly interesting! I have heard he is most handsome!"

"He is. And I wouldn't call them respects. He held up my coach on the way to Paris, dressed as a highwayman, and kidnapped me."

"Raceford?" Vivienne looked really shocked this time.

Meredith nodded. "I am not sure exactly what happened, whether it was his idea or Nicki's — Nicholas St. Antoine, Viscomte de Valmy —"

"I know of him, too! Ginny wrote me reams about him, saying he's the handsomest man on the face of the earth! What has *he* to do with all this?"

"Well, all I know is that Raceford was to kidnap me — you, really — so Nicki could rescue me. Nicki wanted to appear a hero in your eyes, so that he might marry you for your fortune when your husband died. I don't know whose idea it really was; they both swore it was the other's. But Raceford kidnapped me a day early and took me to an inn where we spent the night."

"I begin to believe I should have gone to Paris after all! So that is when you became lovers?"

"Not then. He treated me in a gentlemanly fashion. The next day, Nicki rescued me and took me to Ginny's."

Vivienne managed to look skeptical at Meredith's 'not then,' but contained herself. "But he did become your lover?"

"Not right away. He and Nicki were both courting me, and I wasn't sure what I should do. But then, you see, I fell in love with Raceford, so —"

"Both of them courting you! Why, Meredith, and here I thought you were having a very dull time! Well, with all these wonderful things happening to you, why are you so depressed now?"

"It's over between Raceford and me."

"Over? Why on earth? Did you tell him who you really were?"

"No." Meredith hesitated. "He caught me kissing Nicki."

Vivienne laughed, then sobered. "Oh, you poor

dear. And he was quite furious, I imagine. Well, why didn't you make it up with him? A single kiss, after all!"

"Because he believed—he believed I had had other lovers. He thought I was you. He knew all about Gabriel."

"But, you fool, you had only to tell him who you really were to disabuse him of *that* notion!"

"I know . . . but I told him I loved him, and—and he told me he had never loved me at all. That it was just an amusement for him—nothing more."

"I see." Vivienne fell silent, looking sympathetically at Meredith. "Well, it hasn't been much fun for you, has it? I am so grateful, though, for what you've done. In a moment, we'll talk about the future and see how it might be made better. But first I am curious about Jane's long face. Not all in sympathy alone for Meredith?"

The future. Meredith felt a terrible stab at her heart at these words, conscious again of the black cloud that had been hovering over her of late. Oh, whatever was she going to do?

Jane sighed. "Not all, My Lady. I fell in love myself."

"Another lost love?" Vivienne asked gently.

"I'm afraid so. Armand—he was the duke's valet—well, he was told by the duke to seduce me so that he could find out where Meredith slept in the palais."

"Find out where Meredith slept? But how extraordinary!"

"So the duke could climb in her window one night, which he did."

"He did?"

Meredith colored, then nodded.

"But this is positively Byzantine!" Vivienne laughed, clapping her hands together. "Do go on."

"Well, of course I didn't know that Armand had set out to romance me with anything else in mind, and when he told me he loved me and wanted to marry me, I was very happy. But then it all came out, how the duke had set him on me, and we quarreled."

"And you didn't make it up?"

"No, My Lady," Jane said miserably. "On account of there was another woman involved by then."

"I see." Vivienne sighed. "But how terribly romantic and sad it all is. And now what are we going to do with the both of you?"

Meredith swallowed, suddenly nervous. "Well, Vivienne, I had intended to ask you for some money so that I might make a new start somewhere in the world, but—"

"But nothing. If it is money you want, you have only to ask. I shall pay you an annual income for the rest of your days. But I had hoped that you'd decide to stay with me and live. Not as a companion, but as a relative. And Jane will be your maid or companion, of course. I thought that we could see about finding you someone to marry in London."

Jane looked brighter at this plan than she had about running off into the wilds of the New World, but Meredith shook her head.

"I would have liked nothing better than that at one time, Vivienne. But now I am afraid it's not possible. I do want to marry, but, you see, I must marry as soon as I can or not at all."

Vivienne stared. "You mean you are—"

Meredith nodded miserably. "I am carrying Raceford's child," she said.

There was a silence during which Jane and Vivienne looked at her aghast. Then Vivienne said, "You are sure?"

"There can be no doubt. It has been two months since —"

"I see. Well, this is not the end of the world," said Vivienne briskly, taking control. "Other women have been in your situation before. And really, it changes nothing. You simply have to go away for a time. Jane can go with you. Until the child is born. Then we will arrange for a nice family to adopt it, and you can join me in London. No one need ever know."

"I am not giving up my baby."

Meredith set her jaw. Give up Raceford's child, when she loved him more than life itself? Never. She could never do that. When she had known that indeed she was pregnant, she had been fiercely glad. At least, from the wreck of their love, she would have this left. And she would not be alone. But, oh God, how was she going to manage it?

"Meredith, don't be a fool." Vivienne spoke urgently. "There is no place in this world for a woman alone with a child. You'd be an outcast the rest of your days. And think of the child. If it is adopted by some family, your son or daughter will never know shame. But if you keep it, it will know the name of bastard all its life. Can you do that to your child?"

Oh, Vivienne was persuasive! But Meredith had thought of all these things. "I know all that. But if you would pay me a small annual income, I don't see why I can't travel to America and, once there, tell everyone I am a widow. All I ask is enough for myself and my child to live."

"Meredith, it is madness to throw away your life this way!" Vivienne cried. "Besides, a child needs a father!"

"I know that. And my first duty is to marry, if I can. That is why when you are in Scotland, I'm going to Aunt's. There is a man there who might still wish to marry me and provide a name for my child."

"Not Augustus Sett!" Jane gasped, horrified.

"Yes, Augustus," said Meredith with a determined set to her jaw.

"But he's fat and boring! And you can't bear him!"

"He's also kind, and caring, and a good man. And there is much I must bear now if I mean to keep my child. It's the child who must come first, and I mean to marry Augustus and give my child an honest name, if he'll have me."

"Oh, he'll have you!" Jane said warmly. "For he's half mad for you, and that's a fact! But what will he say when you bear him a seven-month's child?"

"That's right, Meredith. You say this is a nice man," put in Vivienne. "Is it right to deceive him so?"

"I do not mean to deceive him—at least, not entirely. I will tell him I am carrying a child. Only, I will say it resulted from one evening with a highwayman who kidnapped me. I owe him that much to salvage his pride. So you see, you needn't worry, Jane. Mr. Sett will likely want nothing to do with me. But I owe it to my child to try. If he does not, then I will take Vivienne up on her offer of an annual income and I will go to America where no one knows me."

Vivienne let out her breath explosively. "Meredith, if I didn't know of old how stubborn you were, I'd try to talk you out of this, but it would just be a waste of breath! I can only hope that time will make you see reason. And of course I will provide you with whatever money you need. But these are mad ideas! Why not do the obvious? Why not appeal to Raceford and tell him the truth?"

"I would have done that if I believed he loved me," Meredith said quietly, hands clenched in her lap. "But Vivienne, even if he had loved me, think of how great the gulf is that exists between us! He is a duke, and I am a nobody!"

"You are not a nobody when you are *my* cousin," Vivienne said warmly.

"But since he does not love me, is it likely he would want to marry me? And I would not wish to force him into a marriage against his will. I am too proud for that, and I love him too much."

"You're hopeless. I shall write Raceford at once. . . ."

"You'll do no such thing!" Meredith said energetically. "You must leave me to manage my affairs myself!"

"I see! As you've made such a bloody mess of them, I should let you make them worse!"

For a moment, the two women stared at each other, incensed. Then Meredith collapsed against the seat. "Oh, Vivienne, I don't want to quarrel with you. You're one of my only friends, and I can't afford to lose any of them in the days to come. You're right; I have made a bloody mess of things. And I'm doing my best to straighten it all out."

The three women relapsed into gloomy silence as

the coach rolled on. None of them spoke, each mourning the man she had lost, each wondering what a new life without those men would be. Paris was miles behind them, and the future lay ahead.

Chapter Thirty-three

The Comtesse d'Anguillame paused in front of a mirror, pretending to check her earrings. It was early evening, and the servants had just lit the candles and were off somewhere else in the palais. The room was peacefully quiet for a change, and the rosy glow of candles and uninterrupted silence gave it a romantic air. And how could she not feel romantic? She and Nicholas were alone in her apartments. He had just arrived to escort her to a dinner party, and this was the only time they might get to spend alone all evening.

She caught his reflection in the mirror, noting his more sober than usual dress. Attired simply in black, he wore a mere suggestion of lace at throat and cuff, and a lapis lazuli as brilliant as his eyes was the only adornment in his cravat. How her Nicki had changed over the summer, and as she eyed his image in the mirror, she approved of the change. Gone was the theatrical clothing he had been so fond of. There stood her sweet Nicki, stripped of all his finery, looking more handsome than she'd ever seen him.

As she gave herself a glance in the mirror, she was glad she'd chosen the dark blue taffeta gown she wore. Her hair was unpowdered and against the deep blue, her flame-colored curls were a brilliant contrast. The folds of her gown shimmered black and midnight-blue in the candlelight, and gave it the appearance of understated elegance equal to Nicki's. She'd been trying on and discarding gowns since the afternoon. Never had it seemed more important to her to look beautiful. And she was at last pleased with her choice. She and Nicki would make a stunning couple at the dinner party tonight.

Made for one another.

She felt her stomach roll nervously at the thought. But what if Nicki couldn't see what to her was so plain. She looked at him again and found him standing a short distance behind her, deep in thought.

She broke the silence. "And so, what you wished for has come to pass. Vivienne's husband is dead . . . and she is a rich widow."

"What I wish for has *not* come to pass." Nicki walked up behind her, and she met his eyes in the mirror. Something in them gave her a momentary thrill.

"What do you mean, Nicki? Vivienne—"

"Hang Vivienne! I don't care if I ever see her again, and I have no intention of marrying her."

"But how foolish of you, Nicki. You need a rich wife."

"Not anymore . . . at least, only one with a moderate income will do. And besides, I have discovered that I really don't give a damn about income. There is something else more important."

"Not give a damn about income! But how peculiar of you!" Ginny laughed. "Nicki, you know as well as I do you could never survive without life's luxuries, away from Paris, anymore than I could."

"I'm not so sure anymore. As I told you, there is one thing so important it casts everything else in the shade."

At last she turned to face him, her gown rustling, and looked up at him. How well-beloved were his sky-blue eyes, dark brows, silver-blond hair! She held her breath, searching his face. "And what is this that is so important?" she breathed after a moment.

"It's love, Ginny."

For a long time they just stared at each other, caught in the magic of the moment, not wanting to shatter its beauty. Then at last he spoke. "I never knew what love was before . . . always I chased women for the fun, the challenge, to stave off boredom. Oh, I liked them very well, was fond of them, or I believe they would not have liked *me* so well." They both smiled, in complete understanding. "But then you set me on this path of pursuing marriage, and I began at last to realize what it would mean to spend my life with one woman. It could be the way it would have been with Lady Vivienne — half a business arrangement, with attraction thrown in — she was very beautiful, indeed. Or it could be something very different. I thought of the woman I spent so much time with, the woman who had become my friend, the woman who knew my heart, who made me laugh. What would it be like to spend the rest of my days with this woman? I wondered."

He paused, still just looking at her, making no move to touch her. "And besides," he went on quietly, "it just so happened that this woman who was my friend was also the most beautiful woman I had

403

ever seen in my life, and the desire I felt for her made everything else I had felt before seem weak. It was then that I realized I was in love with her . . . that I loved her in a way I had not dreamed it was possible to love another person."

"And who is this fortunate woman, Nicki?" she asked softly.

"Ginny, you know that it is you I love. But I tremble now that I have told you because I am afraid you do not love me . . . could never love me . . . as I love you."

Ginny smiled up at him, letting everything she felt at last show in her face. "But I do love you, Nicki. I have loved you from the first."

"Ginny!" he said, looking thunderstruck.

She laughed, feeling the room swing and dazzle with joy around her. "Oh, Nicki, it's true! And don't just stand there! I never thought I would see you not know what to do in a moment of love. Kiss me!"

"Ginny," he said again, and laughed himself. "You're right. I'm as nervous as a boy. I don't know what to do or think!"

But then he seized her in his arms, and there was nothing boyish about his kiss. The two who had waited so long for love found in that kiss that it had been worth waiting for, that indeed they were made for one another.

At last he pulled back and stared down at her face wonderingly. She was radiant, and the sight of her expression caught at his heart. "Ginny, will you marry me?" he asked. "Will you be my wife?"

"Oh, Nicki, I will!" she cried, and to his wonder, he saw tears slide sparkling down her cheeks, tears of joy, and felt a mist in his own eyes.

"Is tomorrow too soon?" he asked eagerly, and they both laughed. "And tonight—at this dinner party—can I tell the whole world?"

"Yes . . . as long as you tell Joffrey first!" she warned.

"Tell him? If I don't kill him," he said darkly.

"Oh, Nicki, you fool," she smiled. "Joffrey was never in truth my lover. He was just a ploy to make you jealous."

"You mean it?" He searched her face and she nodded. "Good," he said, astonishing her. "Because I intend to be the most faithful of husbands, and I want only a faithful wife." And once more, he swept her into his arms and kissed her to seal their love.

Later that evening, after dinner had been served, Nicki and Ginny found a moment to be alone together in the drawing rooms of the Marquise du Planchet. The other guests had broken off into small groups around the room and had left them to themselves.

Nicki looked longingly into Ginny's eyes. "I can hardly wait for this boring affair to end, for then I shall take you in my arms and make sweet love to you all night. But why wait? Let's leave now, my love."

Ginny giggled girlishly. "It would be rude to leave so early . . . and look, there is Raceford! Come, we've got to tell him our news!"

Nicki took Ginny by the arm and steered her across the room to where Raceford was standing alone.

"He should be happier than anyone to hear it," Ginny smiled.

Nicki gave her a wicked look. "Yes, he was mad for Vivienne and challenged me to a duel over her once."

"Nicki! You never told me!"

"It will have to wait for later, and I promise you I'll tell you all," he said with a grin. "How black he looks!"

"He's not been the same since she left. . . . I wonder he doesn't follow her back to England."

"I believe they quarreled before she left," Nicki said blandly.

"The duel? Well, then maybe this news will relieve his mind."

"Maybe . . . Raceford, there you are!" he called as they came up to him.

Deron turned, taking in the radiant smiles of the couple bearing down on him. "Ginny, Nicholas," he said. "You both look indecently happy. Let me guess. Some sensational gossip I've yet to hear?"

"Yes, gossip, Deron," Ginny said happily. "And it's about two of your closest friends!"

"Who?" Deron asked curiously, looking from one to the other.

"Ginny has done me the incredible honor of agreeing to become my wife," Nicholas said.

For a moment, Deron was thunderstruck. "You . . . and Ginny?" he said at last. "But when—"

"Oh, forever," Ginny said, laughing. "I have been in love with him for two years and he's loved me for at least a year, but I didn't let him discover it until tonight."

"Let me discover it?" Nicki protested. "You mean you knew—"

"Women know these things, my darling child," Ginny said, laughing again. "But managing them takes patience. There were times I almost despaired of you!"

"Managing them? You mean I have been managed?"

"Indeed. If you had any idea of what lengths I have gone to, the strings I have pulled, the deceptions I have resorted to to win you, you would be most flattered. But now is not the time to tell you, Nicki—though I promise soon to tell you everything."

"I can see we have a lot to talk about!" Nicholas said, looking amazed. "Though, naturally, I do not intend allowing you to talk for some time to come. We have better things to do. Something that is long, long overdue."

They gazed at each other in delight, both anticipating the night to come, which would be spent in each other's arms.

"But you must both forgive me for not offering my congratulations at once," said Deron. "I was just taken by surprise. I had no idea. . . . But this is wonderful news. It calls for champagne!"

"A superb idea. There goes a servant . . . I'll tell him," said Nicholas, and went off in pursuit of champagne.

For a moment, Deron and Ginny were alone. "I don't wonder you were surprised, Deron. I know you thought Nicki was courting Vivienne."

Deron's mouth tightened into a grim line. "I did."

"But you see, he never really cared for her. I sent him after her myself, on the pretext that he needed a rich wife."

"And why did you just not marry him yourself?"

"Because he didn't love me then. With a man like Nicki, he must realize that the prize he wishes to gain is not so easily obtained before he will value it."

"I see. And you are a prize well worth gaining, Comtesse," he said gallantly. "But then you say he never—"

She smiled. "No, Deron. And I don't believe she ever cared for him, either. I would hazard that once she saw you, she had room for no other in her heart."

"In truth? And I was believing her to be a heartless jade who flirted—and more—with any man."

"How foolish of you, Raceford. Not to see that sweet girl lost her heart to you."

Sweet girl! He'd heard Vivienne called many things, but never that! And this was her closest woman friend speaking. He opened his mouth to task her with it, but at that moment, an ebullient Nicholas arrived with champagne for all of them. They toasted the forthcoming marriage, Nicholas lifting his glass and staring down lovingly at Ginny.

"I tell you, before tonight, my life had no meaning. I never knew what it was to be happy. I am the luckiest man on earth."

Deron raised his glass and drank, and in a few moments, Nicki and Ginny, bubbling with happiness, were swept away by other well-wishers. Their engagement, it seemed, was the event of the season.

Raceford stared after them for a moment, then set down his glass and went to the terrace where he could be alone. He gazed down into the night, thinking of the happiness he had just witnessed.

Nicholas loved Ginny. And he didn't care what she had done before; their love was all that mattered. Ginny was no innocent; she had known other men. And yet Nicholas was happy. Why was he so

408

damnably old-fashioned that what Vivienne had done before was impossible for him to forget?

She'd told him she loved him, and he'd hurt her. For revenge on her past, for the way she'd hurt Gabriel, for kissing Nicholas. For a damnable wager. A wager he'd long since come to regret making.

What if she'd spoken the truth? What if for the first time Vivienne had loved . . . and loved him?

Because God help him, he loved her. He'd been unable to eat, sleep, or find rest since she'd left Paris. Life had become suddenly stale and meaningless, the most glittering parties flat and dull. His heart ached all the time with emptiness, and he found that all he could do was remember.

Remember her laugh, her free and easy ways, the lovely innocent eyes turned to him so trustingly. The morning they'd raced, when she'd looked so right in boots and breeches. The days when she had ridden at his side and they'd talked of everything from life to love to subjects as mundane as shoeing a horse. She always understood him, even at those times when they'd been easy in each other's company without having to speak. She was his equal in every way, the match made for his heart and his soul.

And nights. How he had ached at night to feel her touch again, the touch that could set him afire like no other woman ever had. How could he live without touching her again, without kissing her, without making love to her?

He couldn't.

Suddenly it was clear to him, clear as it had never been before. Love was not something to be called up at will and then put out of one's life. Love was not a pastime where one chose a partner because she fit some ideal. Love was a force, as elemental as thunder and lightning, not to be gainsaid. He loved her, his Lady Angel, and no matter what she had been in the past, it didn't matter. All that mattered was that, of all the people in the world, they'd found each other. And they belonged at each other's side.

She was a widow now, free. But not for long.

"You are going to marry me and no other," he said aloud, and turned to go back inside.

He strode up to Nicholas and Ginny. "I have come to bid you farewell for now, my friends," he said abruptly. "And wish you happy on your marriage. I'm sure we'll see each other before long, and of course, I'll be at the wedding."

"Farewell?" Ginny raised her eyebrows in surprise. "But where are you going, Deron, and in such a rush?"

"I am going to London," he said, smiling at them. "On business that cannot wait."

Chapter Thirty-four

"And so, Meredith, I hope your time in Paris has not turned your head with ideas beyond your station, and you will be able to settle back into your humbler duties as my companion. Really, it was most ill-advised, this trip; I was against it from the first. But Vivienne was so very set on it. I hardly think it suitable that you went gallivanting about in the company of your betters in a city like Paris. Henley is really where a girl like you belongs, and I hope you are still grateful that you have gainful employment here with me. It is so important for a girl without means to learn to be *useful*."

Meredith bent her head and murmured, "Yes, Aunt. I am very sensible of how fortunate I am to have this position."

Aunt Phoebe regarded Meredith for a moment with a stern and admonishing eye, then went on, "Indeed I hope that you mean what you say. Whatever possessed Vivienne to take you with her I cannot imagine. For it was apparent from the society papers that she missed very little in the way of social events and did not at all go into retirement as she said she would. And I was most disturbed to see that your name appeared in these papers as attending these functions as her cousin. Really, Meredith, it was most unsuitable for you to have attended balls and the opera and suchlike. You are a young woman without means, who must be content to earn her keep. Attending the theater is not something you have any right to expect or to get used to. And I repeat, I hope this unseemly experience has not given you ideas beyond your station in life."

"It has not, Aunt," Meredith said, suppressing a bitter stab at her heart. No, indeed, if Aunt Phoebe only knew how roundly she'd been disabused of any pretension to higher social standing! To love a lord and be cast aside by him was a lesson in overreaching herself she wouldn't soon forget.

"Well, then, that is all to the good. I recommend you take up your religious instruction again to see if you can't achieve a *humbler* cast of mind. The curate, Mr. Sett, calls this afternoon. He was most pleased when he learned you had returned from this ill-considered trip to Paris. Now there is a man you could do worse than to encourage, Meredith. He thinks the world of you, and if you can forget this nonsense of going about in society like your betters, I would be confident in stating that you would make an excellent curate's wife. It is just the thing for a young woman like yourself, without means or prospects. You cannot expect to depend on your relatives' charity for the rest of your life. I have my daughter to think of, and as Louisa has had the good fortune to contract an engagement with the Honorable Prentice Oatsworth, I plan to join them in London for a good part of the year after their marriage. A young wife needs her mother's guidance in the sometimes difficult first years of marriage."

412

The poor Honorable Prentice Oatsworth! Meredith thought feelingly, still smarting from her aunt's reference to "charity." Why, she worked harder than most kitchen-maids in her aunt's service and was paid a wage for it! But she was in no position now to be prideful, she thought ruefully.

"I do plan to encourage Mr. Sett, Aunt," she said meekly. "If he is still of a mind to ask me for my hand, I would not refuse him." There! That should give Aunt Phoebe something to think about!

Aunt Phoebe indeed swelled visibly, looking gratified. "Well! Perhaps this trip has taught you something valuable about the world after all, Meredith. I could not be more pleased than to hear that you intend to encourage Mr. Sett. A marriage between the two of you would be most suitable. He is an estimable young man, most sensible." She paused, considering. "In that case, when he calls this afternoon, I will contrive to leave the two of you quite alone. It is possible that your absence may have made him eager, and he may declare himself if given the opportunity. Well, then that is settled. Now fetch the scissors, Meredith. I want you to cut some flowers from the garden, and while you are at it, you may take Chookie for a walk."

"Yes, Aunt," Meredith said obediently, but her heart sank as she went out. Mr. Sett to be alone with her so soon! But, really, what was the use of waiting any longer? Her changing body demanded that she not put off marriage or flight much longer. In another month, she'd not be able to undertake travel nor pretend that the child was slightly premature.

And there had been no letters, no word. Yet how could there be? Raceford didn't even know where she was, much less who she was. If she were really going to marry for the sake of giving the baby a name, she'd better do it soon. And besides, if Augustus were to refuse to marry her, then she had to leave as soon as she could. A sea voyage would not be possible in a few more months. But she dreaded the coming interview. How on earth could she broach the subject of her pregnancy to a man like Augustus? With a heavy heart, she began to cut the flowers, wishing that she had never gone to Paris at all.

That afternoon, a beaming Augustus was ushered into the drawing room by her aunt. "Here she is, Mr. Sett, returned to us quite safely from her foreign travels," trumpeted Aunt Phoebe. Meredith rose and gave Augustus Sett her hand, noticing that he was stouter than ever. "Though she has been going about in society, you will find her quite unchanged and glad to get back to the quiet life here in Henley."

"Miss Westin. How glad I am to welcome you home. These walls . . . and dare I say, those of us who haunt them, have found them bereft of their animating spirit since you have been gone!"

"Thank you, Mr. Sett," said Meredith quietly, over an inner groan. She'd almost forgotten how Augustus talked in periods. Steeling herself, she added, "I am glad to be back in Henley. I, too, found I missed those I had left at home."

"Well." Aunt Phoebe regarded them both with a beaming eye. "I imagine you two young people have much to catch up on, so I shall leave you alone for a half an hour. Perhaps a walk in the garden? It is such a lovely day."

As Aunt Phoebe rustled out of the room, Meredith looked at Augustus. "Would you care to step into the garden, Mr. Sett? The flowers are lovely at this time of year." Oh, Lord, how was she going to tell him she was pregnant?

"If I may be so bold as to say it, Miss Westin, their loveliness must suffer in comparison to yours."

"Thank you, Mr. Sett," she murmured, leading the way into the sunshine of the garden. Hollyhocks and roses bloomed, and sweet peas and daisies made splashes of color along the graveled paths. For a few minutes they walked, Meredith answering questions about her trip to Paris and Augustus telling her of the small events that had happened in Henley during her absence. At last they came to a small white stone bench set under an arched trellis of climbing roses, and Augustus stopped.

"Might we sit here for a moment, Miss Westin? Your aunt has given us leave to be alone for only a half an hour, and the minutes fleet by. And I have something particular I wish to speak to you about."

"Certainly, Mr. Sett," Meredith said, sitting down and busying herself with arranging her skirts so she wouldn't have to look at him. *Oh, Lord, here it comes!* she thought.

"As I have mentioned, this past month the vicar has been speaking to me of his retirement next year. He is feeling his age, and more and more he has entrusted me with the more active duties incumbent on a rector. And this week, he told me he was pleased with the way I had acquitted myself. In short, Miss Westin, he led me to believe that next year I shall be the vicar of Henley."

She stole a glance at him and saw he was visibly puffed with pride. "But that is wonderful news, Mr. Sett. My aunt and I have often spoken of how deserving you are of a place of your own as vicar."

"Yes, well . . . thank you. But this brings me to another subject. Before, I had not dared to speak, much less even hope. As a curate, I was in no position to be thinking of marriage. But as vicar, it is not just feasible but desirable that I take a wife. And, Miss Westin, though I am sensible this may take you by surprise, there is no woman I would sooner have at my side as a life's partner than you. If you will grant me permission, I will ask you if you will do me the honor of becoming my wife."

Meredith swallowed and felt a lump like iron in her stomach. She couldn't do it! She couldn't tell him! But she had to do it. She steeled herself to think of the baby, not of her own humiliation.

Something must have shown in her face, for he leaned forward and said in a concerned voice, "But, Miss Westin, it seems I have distressed you."

She shook her head. Well, she must get it over with. But she found she could not meet his eyes. "Mr. Sett, if I thought it would be fair to you, I would be honored to accept your proposal and become your wife. Had you asked me before I left, I could have accepted without shame. But circumstances that . . . happened in Paris make it impossible that I should be the kind of wife you deserve."

Meredith found that tears were slipping down her cheeks and heard his distressed intake of breath.

"But, Miss Westin, you are crying! And yet your words, mysterious as they are, have made me a happy man, for they give me hope! But what is it that has changed since you went to Paris?"

She took a deep breath and wiped away a tear. "Mr. Sett, this is the most difficult thing I have ever had to tell anyone in my life, and I pray you will respect the confidence I am about to entrust you with. I wish you to understand what it is that stands in the way of our marriage."

"Whatever you tell me, I shall tell no other," he said.

"Very well. When I left for Paris, I was an innocent girl, able to accept any man's proposal of marriage with honor. But on the way to Paris, my coach was held up by a highwayman."

"Miss Westin!" he gasped. "You . . . and Lady Vivienne, too?"

"Lady Vivienne was not with me, for reasons I am not free to divulge. No, I was alone. And this highwayman . . . he took advantage of my unprotected state. He rode away with me and—" she paused, feeling her stomach quake, "And he took my virtue. So you see, I could not come to a marriage as I should, an innocent girl."

He gasped, and she stole a glance at him to see he had turned a deep turkey-cock red, and his mouth was pursed disapprovingly. Oh, well, she thought. It is probably better that I pretend to be a widow after all than marry a man who looks at me as if I were trash.

"But, Mr. Sett, before you speak, I have more to tell you. That night is not over yet. There were . . . results. I will bear a child."

She heard him get up from beside her, heard him walk off a few paces. So this was it, then. He could not even bear to sit next to her. Well, for the sake of her child, she had tried. Her only recourse was to go away somewhere, alone. Tears fell on her clenched hands, and she realized that Augustus was her only chance to give the protection of a name to her unborn child. She could never love him, of course, but for her child's sake, she could have made him a good wife.

"I . . . ahem . . . see. Of course, this is unexpected and changes things. How long were you involved with this . . . criminal?" He spoke with prissy distaste, and Meredith's temper flared momentarily. He spoke as if she'd voluntarily—! And then she almost laughed. Well, after all, she had gone voluntarily to Raceford. For a moment, she'd almost believed her own story.

"Only one night. But long enough to—"

"But, Miss Westin, say no more. This horrible incident is best forgotten, were it not for the fact that there will be . . . results. I . . . ah . . . had always hoped for children, but I am not by any means certain I would be able to give my name to another man's bastard. Forgive my strong language. I am still willing to marry you, under certain conditions."

"Conditions?"

His mouth was prim and he wouldn't meet her eyes. "I feel it would be best if you would go away for a time, somewhere quite remote. Have the child, and we will put it out to nurse and foster. I believe it is best if it is taken from you before you have a chance to see it. And then we can start anew, as if this never happened, and I will give you the protection of my name in marriage, even though you do not come to the marriage bed as pure as a woman should."

"Give up my baby? Are you mad, Mr. Sett? I shall not do such a thing!"

"But have you considered, Miss Westin, that the child is the offspring of a criminal . . . a highwayman? Children inherit their parent's tendencies, and this child will surely be of a moral character that is most undesirable. Can you see raising such a potential rogue in the parish house? I for one would not be able to condone such a thing."

"Mr. Sett . . . and I had believed you to be a Christian, with charitable feelings! Well, this conversation is at an end. I shall not accept your proposal of marriage, for I intend to keep my child, even if I must do it alone!"

"I see," he said stiffly. "Then that is that. May I ask you if your aunt knows?"

"Of course not!" said Meredith indignantly. "And might I remind you that this conversation is in confidence!"

"Yes, and I shall keep it that way, though I believe it is most ill-advised of you to believe you can conceal such a fact for long. May I ask you what you plan to do?"

"Go away, as you suggested, Mr. Sett. To the New World. There I can state that I am a widow and raise my child without shame."

Meredith rose. "And I believe that concludes our conversation. I shall see you to the door."

He rose, too, looking both uncomfortable and disapproving. "I wish you the best, Miss Westin," he said, and followed her out of the garden.

After he was gone, Meredith had to endure Aunt Phoebe, who came bustling at once into the room. "Well? Did he propose?" she demanded.

"No, Aunt. He did not," Meredith lied. If she said he had and she'd turned him down, her aunt would never let her alone. And she could hardly say he had but had rescinded his offer when he learned she was carrying another man's child!

"I see. Well, I imagine it is a bit early to expect him to ask for your hand. You have just arrived

419

back, after all. And besides, Mr. Sett is really a cautious sort of man. Perhaps he will wait until it is official that he will be appointed the next vicar. Still, I will contrive to see that the two of you have time alone whenever he calls. And do your best to encourage him, girl; he is probably shy."

Meredith opened her mouth to tell her aunt he'd probably not be calling, then decided against it. What good would it do? Her aunt would learn the truth soon enough, and she might as well spare herself a little misery. "I am tired, Aunt. I think I will retire for the time being," she said.

When she reached her room, Meredith lay down on the bed, wondering what came next. Vivienne would pay for her passage on a ship to the New World and send her an allowance. But it would be frightening to go all alone. Maybe Jane . . . But Meredith shook her head. Jane had no wish to leave England, and she still hoped to see Armand again. So she'd have to go alone. And book her passage without delay. Time was getting short, and she'd need to be well settled over there before her pregnancy was too advanced.

Dispiritedly, she sighed. Aunt Phoebe would think her mad, of course, but what did she care? She'd never see her vexatious aunt again, and that alone was almost worth the trip to the New World.

But Augustus had been her last hope to give her baby a name. Distasteful as the prospect of marriage to him was, she dreaded the thought of bringing a bastard into the world. Yes, she'd have married Augustus if he'd offered; the child came first.

Wearily, she rose and went to her dresser drawer. Inside her reticule was a heavy purse, and she took it out and counted the bills and coins. Enough gold to pay for her passage and the first few months across the sea in the New World. Well, she'd go tomorrow. And what name should she adopt?

Mrs. Race? Yes, then at least her baby would have a crumb of his father.

But the next morning, when she came down to breakfast, there was a letter waiting beside her place.

A letter from Augustus Sett.

With trembling hands, she opened it. It read:

My dear Miss Westin,

I have reconsidered my hasty words of yesterday. Naturally a mother blanches at the prospect of being separated from her child; I can only admire your refusal in your surely desperate straits.

If you will still have me, I tender my offer of marriage once again and will give your child a name. Perhaps being raised in a religious atmosphere will temper any criminal tendencies the baby might be born with.

I think under the circumstances, we should marry as soon as possible, do you not?

I will call this morning to receive your answer.

Respectfully,

Augustus Sett.

Meredith set the letter down next to her plate and stared ahead. So he'd changed his mind. Only yesterday she'd vowed she would do anything to give her baby a name . . . No matter how distasteful.

But she found she really did not want to marry Augustus. Nothing on earth appealed less to her than the prospect of spending the rest of her life as his wife. And yet . . . She owed it to her child. It was that simple.

"Meredith, what is that letter? Is it from Mr.

421

Sett?"

"It is, Aunt," she said, still staring ahead.

"Well? what does it say, girl?"

"He asks permission to call on me this morning — and to see me alone."

Aunt Phoebe looked triumphant. "He must have changed his mind! Or screwed up his courage to propose! Well, don't just sit there, girl! Make haste! Go and change out of that drab old thing into your best dress. It isn't every day a man comes to ask for your hand in marriage!"

Obediently, Meredith went upstairs and changed into a lavender muslin gown with a white lace collar. She knew what she should do, and yet, how could she accept him? How could she marry him?

She couldn't.

Oh, Raceford . . . if only you knew! she thought, agonized.

She came downstairs to find Augustus waiting for her, his face solemn. Once again, they went into the rose garden and sat on the bench.

"Have you considered my offer?" he asked. "Will you join me in holy matrimony?"

Meredith put her cold hand into his sweaty one. She simply couldn't do it.

"I will marry you, Mr. Sett," she said.

Chapter Thirty-five

Raceford stood on the bow of the small ship, knuckles showing white where they clenched the rail, and stared ahead to where the morning light was dazzling on the white cliffs of Dover. England at last! The morning breeze ruffled his black hair, freeing a strand from the ribbon that tied it back and snapping his cloak behind him, but he didn't notice. The trip had been infernally long, and he could scarcely wait to get his boots on English soil once again.

He'd had nothing to do but think as he'd ridden across France, as the ship had crossed the channel, and it seemed to him he'd learned more in these last twenty-four hours than he had in a lifetime. What did it matter what her past was? Who was he to set himself up as being above any woman? Why, think of his own past, the many women he'd made love to without loving them! She had done less than he had and had never held it against him. And she had taught him what love was.

It didn't matter, in any case. Whatever she had been, she was his now, and he intended to keep her by his side for the rest of her life. She'd have no reason to look aside once he'd made her his own.

And he would never want to look at another woman, he knew that clearly.

Would she be in London? he wondered feverishly. The funeral in Scotland should be ended by now, and she'd have had time to return by now. He'd ride to London as fast as possible and ask for her there at her townhouse. Wherever she was, he meant to find her and tell her . . .

I love you. My Lady Angel, you belong to me!

In a short time after landing, he had hired the fastest horse he could find and was swinging himself up for the long ride to London. He'd be there by tonight if he had to kill three horses under him! Every minute away from her, not knowing if she would have him, if she would forgive him for the lies he'd told her about not loving her, was torture. He set spurs to his mount and galloped away down the long post road from Dover that led to London.

It was dark when at last he gained the outskirts of London. He'd ridden at a killing pace, changing horses twice, but he didn't feel at all tired. He still felt in a fever of impatience to see her, to find her. At last he reached the street where he knew the Winter townhouse to be, some miles down the road. He halted in the courtyard of a small inn and leaped off his horse, tossing the reins to the hostler and striding inside.

In a few moments, he'd galvanized the landlord into giving him a small private chamber, a cold supper, some ale, and some cold water to wash with. As much in a hurry as he was, he didn't want to go to her covered with sweat and reeking of horses. In a few moments, he'd washed and changed into a white shirt and black pants from his saddlebags, and was wolfing down some bread and cheese, washing it down with ale, while he questioned the flustered landlord.

"Do you know Lord and Lady Winter?" he demanded. "They keep a townhouse two miles down this road."

"Oh, aye, indeed I do, sir. Many's the time that their servants have come to the common room here at the inn on their days off. But, Your Grace, Lord Winter is dead."

"I know that. And buried?"

"Buried in Scotland this last week, My Lord."

"And his lady? Is she back in London? Back at the townhouse?"

"I heard tonight that she's just returned today and taken up residence there, My Lord."

The landlord mopped his brow at the gentleman's glittering smile. "Good. Then, my good man, get me a fresh horse with all haste," said the gentleman, tossing him a heavy purse.

In less than ten minutes Raceford was riding down the street again into the night. His watch had told him it was nearly midnight, far too late an hour to go knocking on a lady's door, demanding an audience. But maybe she'd have been out and he'd catch her returning. He had to go there in any case. Wild wolves couldn't have kept him from her door.

At last he reached the imposing front of the residence and, dismounting, tied his horse to a side gate in the wall that surrounded it. Curse the luck, the lights on the ground floor were dimmed, not alight as they would be had they been expecting the return of their mistress. If only he knew which room she slept in! He'd climbed into her bedroom before, and by God, he could do it again!

425

On the thought, he was over the wall with the agility of a cat, prowling through the dark garden. The townhouse was of two stories, with tall regular windows and French doors at the back looking onto the garden. He made his way to the back garden and looked up.

In the widest sweep of windows, there was still light shining. Her rooms? He almost wanted to dare it, but if he was wrong . . .

The lights above began to dim, being put out one by one. As he stared up, head thrown back, his vigil was rewarded. A feminine shape passed before the lit window, with a cascade of hair down her back. It must be Vivienne! The shadow had passed too quickly for him to be sure, but he didn't care. He was going to find out.

He waited as the lights above were dimmed, then extinguished. The second floor was dark. In a few moments, when he was sure no vigilant servant would make a last round of the house, he'd climb up there.

It was easy to find handholds in the wide stones the house was constructed of, and in a few moments, Raceford had taken off his cloak and begun the climb to her window. Carefully but quickly, he climbed upward, making no sound that could be heard from inside. At last he was on the broad stone sill of her window.

He reached out and found the window was open. He gripped the edge and swung it noiselessly outward, then was over the sill and into the room. He parted the curtains and looked to the big bed, where he could dimly make out in the half-light from the windows a woman whose black hair streamed to her waist over her white nightgown, a woman who murmured softly but clearly enough for him to hear, "Gabriel."

She wasn't alone! He stood rooted to the spot for a long moment as her arms reached up and a tall man entered the room and bent to her on the bed. My God! She was with Gabriel—a man he'd once called his closest friend!

A killing rage swept through him and he was almost blinded to everything except the sight of his hated friend kissing the woman he loved. He strode into the room, cursing, "Damn your eyes, Gabriel . . . I'll kill you for this!"

A startled Gabriel looked up only in time to see a furious dark shape bearing down on him. Then a fist connected with his jaw and he went flying backward, stars exploding in his head, and knew no more.

Raceford turned to the shadowy woman who was sitting up on the bed, her dark hair falling in a river all over her shoulders, and grated, "And damn you to hell for this, Vivienne! I should kill you for this . . . but not until I've killed Gabriel!"

A low laugh answered him, rooting him to the spot. A laugh that was unfamiliar to him.

"And who," said a pleasantly husky voice he'd never heard before, "are you?"

"Who are *you?*" he managed, shock running through him.

"But you seem to know that. Vivienne, of course. Who else?"

He peered through the darkness but could make out nothing of her shadowed face. But the voice! It wasn't hers—not Vivienne's! "You aren't Vivienne, or you'd damn well know who I am!" he grated.

A husky laugh was his answer. "It seems we

should have some light on the subject," she said, sounding amused, and leaned to one side. There was a spark of tinder, a flare, and one by one, she lit a brace of candles. As she turned and held them up, he found himself staring into the face of a complete stranger. A very beautiful stranger, to be sure, but a woman he'd never seen before.

"I repeat, madam, who are you?" he demanded, staring at her.

"And I repeat that I am Vivienne Winter," she said, staring equally fascinated at this exceptionally handsome stranger at the foot of her bed.

"You damn well aren't Vivienne Winter, because I've come here to ask her to marry me. Now stop this ridiculous game and tell me where she is! And what the hell was Gabriel doing in here?"

"Gabriel is in here because he and I are going to be married, so it's no use telling me *you* are going to marry me," laughed Vivienne. "But I think light begins to break. You must be Lord Raceford."

"I am. How do you know who I am?"

"Oh dear," Vivienne sighed, her eyes dancing. "It is a long story, and I can't tell it to you with you towering over me so determinedly. I assure you I am Lady Vivienne Winter and no other. But I am quite concerned about Gabriel. Have you killed him?"

It took Raceford a few moments to rouse himself, but then he walked over to where Gabriel lay and stooped to him. He looked up. "No, he's just out cold. Though I imagine he'll have quite a headache when he wakes." He came back to the bedside and frowned down at the woman on the bed.

"I *am* glad that you haven't damaged him. I have just recently lost one husband and wouldn't wish to lose a prospective one so soon. Do sit down, Lord Raceford," she said, waving at a chair next to the bed. "It really is past time we had a talk. Do you know I often thought of writing you a letter?"

He sat, looking bemused. "Writing me a letter? Why the hell would you do that? And who the hell *are* you?"

She laughed again. "Oh, this is *most* amusing! I think I'd better call you Deron and you may call me Vivienne, for in a way, though we've never met before, we've been rather intimately involved. You see, I was actually never in Paris."

"Never in Paris! If you don't begin to talk sense in a moment, I'll—"

"Pray spare me your threats, Deron. I can see by what you did to Gabriel you are a shockingly violent sort of man. If you will listen to me without stopping me, I shall straighten it all out for you."

He nodded. "I'll listen," he said grimly.

"Well, you see, some months ago I—I being, the Lady Vivienne Winter, you understand; it's really who I am . . . I fell in love with your friend, Gabriel."

"And he told me you'd broken his heart!"

"Really, Lord Raceford, you promised not to interrupt! Well, Gabriel and I were madly in love, and my reputation had begun to suffer. Still, we were wild to be together somehow. So he gave it out to everyone that I had broken his heart and it was over between us. Quite the furthest thing from the truth. He wanted to tell *you* the truth, but I wouldn't allow it. I felt we had to be quite secret if our plan was to succeed."

"What plan?"

Vivienne smiled, drew her knees up against her

chest, and clasped her arms around them. "Well, really, Deron, that is *just* what I am trying to tell you, and if you'd just have a little patience—"

"Damn patience!"

Behind them from the floor, Gabriel moaned softly. Vivienne smiled beautifully at Raceford and went on, "But, really, I'd better hurry if hostilities between you and Gabriel are not to break out again when he wakes! Well, as I said, we wanted to go away alone together, and the only way I could think of it working was if I could find someone else to take my place."

"Someone . . . else . . . to take . . . your place?" Raceford said slowly, with a kind of dread.

"Yes. Inspired, wasn't it? I'd never been to Paris, so as long as Ginny knew the secret, my double could just pretend to be me and get into the papers quite often, so my late husband would think I was really there. Of course I was quite close by—with Gabriel—in case of trouble. I must say, it all worked much better than any of us had hoped!"

"Ginny knew?" he said.

"Oh, yes, she had to, because she really knew me, of course. Naturally, the whole thing hinged on finding someone who would pretend to be me, and of course she had to have black hair. She didn't have to look *exactly* like me, but those things about me were well-known, and so—"

"And so you got someone else to pretend to be you in Paris? That wasn't the real Vivienne Winter at all?"

"I am so glad you understand at last. I despaired of your ever listening long enough to get the whole story."

"Then . . . who was she?"

430

Vivienne smiled, delighted. "It *is* perplexing to be in love with a woman—I believe you said you'd come here to marry her even!—and not know who she is! You need have no fear of her birth. She is my cousin. Her name is Meredith Westin."

"Meredith Westin," he repeated, feeling like a man in a dream. "Your cousin."

"That's right. I suppose you want to know all about her. She's an orphan and was doing dreadful servitude to one of our awful aunts as a paid companion, can you imagine! Naturally, it wasn't hard to talk her into this chance at an adventure. She's lived a sheltered life, no suitors except the curate, quite the most innocent, well-bred girl you could ask for. I imagine she must have been quite bowled over by you. Now that I see you, I can readily understand why."

He sat, simply unable to speak. Not Vivienne at all—but someone named Meredith! And an innocent girl! His heart had been right all along to believe in her. He cringed. And he had treated her like a slut! Damn, the things he'd said to her were unforgivable! But, then, she had lied to him. . . .

"Why didn't she tell me that she wasn't you? Not at first, but later, when we fell in love?" he demanded.

"Oh, she was going to, Deron, but she seemed quite brokenhearted. You ought to be able to answer that question yourself. When I asked her, all she would say is the day she went to tell you, you told her that you'd never loved her at all but had just been amusing yourself. Naturally, she couldn't tell you the truth after that."

A groan was her answer. He stood, pacing restlessly back and forth. "Damn it . . . I've made a

431

mess of it all! I've got to see her! Where is she now? In this house? Because she's going to marry me, as soon as possible!"

Vivienne giggled, delighting in this unprecedented scene. "Well, if you mean to marry her, I suggest you hurry. She's not in this house. She went back to my aunt's in Henley-on-Thames. And unless I'm mistaken, she intends to marry the curate this morning."

He rounded on her. "What! Marry the curate? She can't! You're mad! Why would she do such a thing?"

Vivienne shrugged. "I have no idea, except that perhaps now she believes she's a fallen woman. I told you, she's far more virtuous than me, and I don't pretend to understand her! But why don't you ask her yourself? If you ride hard, you should be able to catch her before she gets to the church. Just follow the river road and ask anyone where Henley is."

He stared at her, and then at last started to laugh. She joined him, and for a long moment, they were both helpless with it. "This is the maddest thing I have ever heard of, and I can't believe I've been in the middle of it without even knowing it! But, then, when I think of it, I played my own part—and the first time I met Meredith, *I* was pretending to be someone else! So I suppose I can't blame her for playing her own role!"

He paused, then strode to the bed and stared down at Vivienne, smiling.

"So, at last we meet, Lady Vivienne Winter. I set out to kidnap you once long ago, did she tell you that? You're every bit as beautiful as they told me. And by God, I'd sworn it was impossible, but they are."

"Are what?" she laughed.

"Your eyes. They are violet. Gabriel and I had quite an argument about it once. Well, give my apologies to Gabriel, and tell him I owe him twenty golden guineas, for he's won our wager."

"And what wager was that?"

"I was . . . uh . . . to seduce you, and then break your heart."

"I see. Now that I have seen you, Lord Race-ford—Deron—I find it quite believable that you could seduce any woman you put your mind to seducing."

"And you, any man. Well, tell Gabriel good-bye, for I've an errand that won't wait. But before I go, I'd like to do one thing."

"What's that?" Vivienne stared spellbound up at this tall and exceptionally handsome man with the black hair and killing green eyes.

"I'd like to kiss the real Vivienne Winter," he said and, stooping, took her face in his hands and, for a lingering moment, kissed her thoroughly. At last he released her and grinned wickedly down at her. "After all, you're the woman I've been in love with for so long."

Then he was crossing the room, letting himself down over the windowsill, gone. Vivienne got up and rushed to the window in time to see him drop lightly to the ground. She leaned out, laughing. "Luck, Raceford!" she called.

He grinned up at her and waved. "Farewell, Lady Vivienne! We'll dance at each other's weddings!"

"It's a promise!" she called after him as he disappeared into the night.

She leaned her elbows on the sill and stared

dreamily after him. "Well!" she said aloud. "Imagine *Meredith* getting a man like that! He was quite the most handsome man I've ever seen, except for Gabriel!"

Then a thought came to her and she smiled. "But then," she thought mischievously, "of course, she had to pretend to be *me* to get him!"

Shuffling footsteps behind her made her turn, and Gabriel came up to her, rubbing his head. "Who the hell was that?" he asked. "It sounded like Race!"

"It was, darling. Does your head hurt very much?"

"Not too badly. But what the hell was Race doing here—and why did he hit me?"

Vivienne threw her arms around him and rubbed his temples. "It's a long story, darling, and I promise I'll tell you all about it in the morning. But right now, come to bed. It's not a night for talking tonight . . . but a night for lovers, I believe." And, laughing, she led him to the bed.

Chapter Thirty-six

It was a beautiful English summer morning, and the birds shouted from every treetop. There were only a few clouds in the blue sky, and the day promised to be warm without being too hot. The gentle hills around Henley were softly green as Meredith stood in the drive looking at the peaceful scene around her and waiting for the coach to arrive.

The coach that was taking her to the church as a bride.

She was alone, for she'd asked for a few moments to herself before she left for the church. Aunt Phoebe was driving her mad, and Jane's tears were more than she could stand. It had all happened so fast. . . . She could hardly believe that she was really going to be married this morning, to Augustus Sett.

She wore a simple gown of white muslin, for there had been no time to send for the dressmaker. Aunt Phoebe had leant her some fine old lace that fell simply over her unbound hair as a veil. She wore a wreath of pink and white roses twined on her head and carried a bouquet of summer blossoms in her gloved hands. Pearl earrings and a single-strand pearl necklace were her only jewels, and there was a pink satin sash around her waist. She felt unreal, wondering if she could really go through with it, if there were still time to run away somehow, call it all off.

But she had made her bed, she thought grimly. And she had a lifetime to lie in it.

The sound of coach wheels on gravel made her look up, and the coach stopped. She was really going to marry Augustus! Oh, and he was so unbearably pompous! He'd made it quite clear that he considered he was doing her a great favor by marrying her and giving a name to her baby, and he'd lectured her on the duties of a meek and obedient wife who would look to her husband for guidance in all things. And the thought of sharing a breakfast table with him for the rest of her life, much less a bed—! In the warmth of the summer sunshine, she shivered.

In a few moments, she was sitting down with Jane at her side and Aunt Phoebe across from her, and the coach started with a jerk. For a wild moment, she put her hand on the door, wanting to open it and leap out, and then she sat back. It was too late now in any case. Too late.

"Well, Meredith, I must say you look very nice in spite of this indecent haste for a wedding! Why you had to be married so quickly I cannot imagine. It will start the worst kind of talk—or would have, were it not for the fortunate fact that you were away and so could hardly have been . . . well . . ." For a moment, Aunt Phoebe looked discomfited, and Jane squeezed Meredith's hand under her bouquet.

"But, really, I cannot think what has gotten into

Mr. Sett to insist that you be married as soon as the banns were called! What people will think I do not know. I only hope it does not hurt his chances to be made vicar one day. Though it won't surprise me if it does. It is simply extraordinary that he could not wait. . . ."

Meredith stole a glance at Jane and saw that she was again on the verge of tears. These past days, Jane had begged her not to go through with this, to write Raceford and let him know, not to throw herself into a hasty marriage.

"Jane, I warn you. If you cry, I shall not be able to stand it!" Meredith said.

Aunt Phoebe fixed Jane with a baleful stare. "Indeed, why should she cry? The very idea is ridiculous. If it were not for this unseemly haste, this is a most suitable match for Meredith, and she is quite lucky to make it. When I think of all the trouble I have gone through to arrange the wedding breakfast, if anyone should be discomposed it is I! Jane, you ought to be grateful that you are at the wedding at all and honored that Meredith has asked you to be her attendant. When I was a girl, such goings-on would never have been countenanced. A servant to stand up at a lady's wedding, and a marriage conducted in such hurry that if he weren't a curate and if you didn't live with me, everyone would say it was a marriage of necessity."

Jane and Meredith looked at each other, neither listening to Aunt Phoebe, and Meredith felt her own tears threaten. But she steeled herself. The time for crying was past. It had been time to cry when she had lost the only man she could ever love. She wondered passionately what he was doing right now, where in all this world he was . . . and if he still thought of her sometimes. If only there was some way she could let him know he was going to be a father. She hoped for a son, a son who would have the same green eyes and black hair his father did, the same wild high courage and reckless nature. She bit back a choke at the fact that Augustus thought the child's breeding to be the lowest, the offspring of a thief, when in fact he was among the highest in the land, nobility. At least her son would comfort her in the days to come. Yes, for his sake, she was doing the right thing.

"And no maid would ever have thought of daring to take a place in her mistress' wedding, and—" Aunt Phoebe was repeating herself, and then she sat up straight. "What was that?"

Hooves. Meredith heard hooves pounding on the dusty road, bearing down on them.

"Wild young bucks, no doubt, come to see the wedding party to the church in boisterous fashion!" Aunt Phoebe exclaimed, incensed. But Meredith found her own heart was beating far too fast with a hope that was ridiculous and impossible. It was as Aunt Phoebe said, just some of the neighborhood's young bloods, and if her heart was beating fast, it was only because twice before her coach had been held up, that was all.

There was a shot, boomingly loud in the English morning.

Aunt Phoebe clutched her hands to her heart and screamed, and Meredith heard the coachman give a shout, then more shouts from alongside the coach. "Stand and deliver!" cried an unfamiliar voice in what sounded like a French accent, and beside her Jane gave a little screech.

The coach rolled to a halt. Meredith was frozen,

unable to move, unable even to hope. Her coach, being held up, again? Oh, could it be coincidence? But she hadn't recognized the voice that had shouted.

"Oh, my dear Lord, we are being robbed by bandits!" wailed Aunt Phoebe at the top of her voice.

And then the coach door swung open and a tall man stood there, a black scarf over his face and a pistol leveled at them.

"You will all climb down from the coach at once," said a voice Meredith had never dared to hope she'd hear again.

Jane was clutching her arms as they stood, while behind them, Aunt Phoebe was screeching a string of invectives and waving her hands. As if in a dream, Meredith climbed down from the coach to find herself looking up into an achingly familiar pair of green eyes.

At his side, also muffled to the eyes in a scarf, stood a man whose hair glinted copper in the sunlight, and beside her, Meredith heard Jane gasp, "Armand!"

"The same," the copper-haired man said with a slight bow. "And now, I have come to do two things. The first is to learn your real name, the second, to marry you, my darling."

"Oh, Armand," breathed Jane, and rushed into the copper-haired man's arms.

Meredith was speechless, unable to look away from those emerald eyes, unable to believe this was really happening. Behind her, she heard the coach creak, then Aunt Phoebe's indignant voice.

"*What* is the meaning of this? Unhand Jane at once! How dare you stop our coach in broad daylight, you rogues! I will see that the magistrate knows about this! I will see that you are thrown into the deepest prison for this outrage! I will—"

"Jane?" smiled Armand, breaking away from kissing her long enough to say her name.

Raceford stepped past Meredith and made a bow to Aunt Phoebe, who was quivering above him on the coach steps. "Never fear, dear lady. I have no intention of robbing you. Indeed, it is myself who was robbed. Something was stolen from me, and I have come here to get it back."

"Stolen . . . from *you!?*" Aunt Phoebe screeched. "What kind of nonsense is this? We are God-fearing English citizens and have never stolen anything in our lives!"

"I would appreciate some silence, madam. It would be regrettable indeed to have to shoot you," Raceford said, and a cowed Aunt Phoebe abruptly closed her mouth.

He turned back to Meredith. "Indeed I have come for the return of something stolen from me. For since I first beheld you, My Lady Angel, my heart has been in your keeping. And only by having you at my side can I ever hope to recover it."

Meredith let her bouquet drop into the roadside dust from nerveless fingers as he advanced on her. "But you are silent, My Lady. Are you not glad to see me?"

"Oh, I am glad!" she breathed at last. "I have never been gladder of anything in my life!"

"Good. Then we have to straighten out this nonsense about a wedding. I told you I'd claimed you as my own. Do you think I'd have let you marry anyone else? It's a good thing I got here before the wedding, or I'd have had to make you a widow."

Breathless, Meredith watched as he led his tall horse up to her, then walked to her side. "I kidnapped you once before, My Lady, and it seems I am going to do it again." With that, his arms came around her and swooped her up, and for a wonderful moment, she was crushed to his chest. Then he set her on the horse and leaped lightly up behind her.

Meredith, through her haze of joy, was dimly aware of Armand putting Jane up on his horse, of the coachman staring at them amazed, of Aunt Phoebe's look of outrage so great it was laughable. Raceford looked down at Phoebe, who still hadn't found her voice.

"Tell this curate," he said, as his fingers tightened on the reins, "that there will be no wedding today. Tell him that her highwayman has come for her, to claim her as his own."

And with that, he put spurs to his horse and galloped away, laughing.

Chapter Thirty-seven

They rode through the summer morning, and Meredith thought she had never known such joy as this. To be held again in the arms where she had always, from the first, felt safe. He had come for her! Against all hope, the man she loved had come to claim her! She leaned back into him, reveling in the feel of his strong arms around her, his lips in her hair.

They rode down the deserted roads where the hedgerows bloomed with poppies, until at last he slowed his horse and turned up a track into a meadow. He turned to wave to Armand and Jane, who cantered past them, Armand with a grin, and Meredith got a good look at the handsome copper-haired man whom Jane loved. She wondered if her own face looked as happy as Jane's did.

The horse slowed to a walk as they followed a faint track up into the hills, until at last they were alone in a high green valley edged with trees. He stopped and for a few moments just sat, his arms around her tightly, content.

Then he said softly in her ear, "Shall we get down, My Lady Angel?"

She nodded and he was off the horse, his strong

hands at her waist, lifting her down. She reached up and pulled off the scarf that hid his face, then stared up at him, dazzled by his looks, blinded by her joy.

He smiled. "And now I think we have some talking to do. But first, it is proper that we be introduced. Deron Redvers, Duke of Raceford, My Lady Angel. And your name?" His eyes danced so that she had to laugh.

"So you know I am not Vivienne?" He nodded. "Then, sir, my name is Meredith. Meredith Westin."

"Meredith." He reached down and gently stroked her cheek with one finger. "A lovely name, as lovely as you are."

"But Deron . . . how did you find me? How did you know where I was and that I was to be married this morning?"

His brows came together threateningly. "As to that, we'll have no more talk of that marriage, My Lady Angel. You must have been mad to even dream of it. How did I know where to find you? But I thought the answer would be obvious. I saw Vivienne."

"You saw Vivienne? Where?"

"I climbed into her bedroom window."

Meredith gaped at him and he laughed, catching her close against him, stroking her hair. "Oh, Meredith, I was mad to let you go—and mad to find you after you'd left! When I came to my senses, I saw that it didn't matter what you'd done before; you were the woman I needed. So I followed you to London. I got there too late to pay a call in the regular way, so there was nothing for it but to climb into the bedroom. I'd done it before and I cherish the memory."

"But what did Vivienne do?" cried Meredith, trying to imagine the scene.

"Well, I regret to say that Gabriel was with her, and since it was dark"—he shrugged—"I knocked him out. It was then that I discovered the woman he'd been kissing wasn't you at all."

"You knocked him out?" Meredith gasped, then laughed. "Oh, Deron, when will you learn?"

"Never, where you are concerned, Angel. Well, then, as you can imagine, it all came out. Vivienne told me who you really were and that you'd pretended to be her in Paris. And she warned me that you intended to marry another this morning. When are you going to get it through your head that I won't allow you to marry anyone but me?" he asked tenderly.

And then he bent his head to kiss her. For a timeless moment, they clung together, kissing each other with all the passion and tenderness and love that had so long been in their hearts. His lips covered her face, her eyelids, her neck, with a thousand kisses, and he was murmuring her name against her heated skin. "Meredith. My Meredith."

He pulled back from her and captured her face in his hands. "Meredith. I love you. Have I told you that?"

"Oh, Deron, I love you, too. So much," she said softly.

"And I pledge my love to you forever. There can be no other woman for me as long as I live." His lips claimed hers again, until they were both breathless with love.

He caught her hard against him and held her to him as if he would never let her go again. "You know," he said against her hair, "though I had made up my mind that your past didn't matter . . . that I was going to marry you anyway, I am damned glad to find that you are not Vivienne after all. I don't know if I could have stood seeing Gabriel again or thinking of another man's hands on you."

"There has been no other. Only you."

He pulled back, and his eyes blazed down at her for a moment with green fire. "Then who the hell was this curate you were running off to marry?"

Meredith almost giggled, wondering what he would think if he could see poor Augustus Sett. "He was an old suitor. I didn't love him. Indeed, I've never kissed him. But . . . I had my reasons to believe I must marry."

"If it was marrying you wanted, why didn't you come to me?"

She dimpled at him. "Because, My Lord Duke, you had not asked me then. As I recall, you told me I was no more than an amusement."

He swore. "And I was a damned fool! But what made you think you had to run off and marry anyone?" he demanded.

She looked down. "Well . . . you had told me you no longer wanted me, had never loved me. And besides, what hope was there for me with you? I am so far beneath you. You are a duke, while I am a penniless nobody."

"Meredith." His voice compelled her to look at him, and she found his tender gaze on her face. "I have never really asked you yet, have I? Will you have me? Will you marry me . . . be my bride? I love you."

She drew in her breath at the love she saw in his face and, for a moment, just gazed at him. Then she spoke. "But, My Lord, there is something I must tell you first. The reason I was in such a hurry to be married. You see, Deron, I—" she paused, suddenly apprehensive, "I am going to have your child."

He stared at her, dumbstruck, then caught her fiercely in his arms and kissed her. "But you weren't going to tell me? You were going to marry another man and let him be the father to my child?" he asked incredulously.

She nodded her head miserably. "I . . . you see, you had told me you didn't love me. And you were so far above me. Besides, you didn't even know who I really was. I had no wish to trap you into a marriage you didn't want, because I loved you too much for that. And besides, I didn't know if you'd be happy. Are you?" she ventured, stealing a glance up at him through her lashes.

"Happy?" He threw back his head and laughed. "My God . . . I'm the happiest man on earth! You . . . the woman I love . . . to bear my child? What more could I ask for? I love you, but I want a family, too! Ten of them someday. Oh, my darling, what you must have been through alone! Thank God, I found you in time!"

He held her tightly, and Meredith wondered if a heart could break from joy. At last he spoke. "But tell me, would you love me just as much if I weren't a rich and powerful duke?"

She looked up at him, wondering. "Of course I would! I loved you even when I believed you to be a highwayman!"

"Then, would it bother you very much if we didn't become Lord and Lady Raceford?"

"But—but Deron, you just asked me to marry you!" she exclaimed.

"I know. But this business of being a duke is bothersome and dead boring. My brother Geoffrey is much better at it than I am, I'm afraid. So I was thinking of letting him take it over. At least, the estates. I'm afraid I'm shackled with the title. And then taking a stake of money and going to the New World. I thought that between us, we could start a decent horsefarm. And it would be much more of an adventure than rotting away on the ancestral lands."

She laughed, throwing her arms around his neck. "Oh, Deron, it sounds wonderful! Much better than being duke and duchess! And a horsefarm! It's what I've always dreamed of doing!"

"I have, too. Though no dream could ever be worth anything without you at my side," he said.

"I love you, Deron," she breathed.

"And I love you, My Lady Angel. Now, as it is your wedding day in any case, do you mind pretending that the priest has just married us? For I find that I can wait not another moment to claim you as my own."

"Neither can I wait," she said, giving herself up to his kiss. As the fire grew between them, they fell as one to the green field and together sealed their pledge of love for the future. And later, a small breeze came over the hill and caught at the garments they had long since shed, picking up Meredith's wedding veil and carrying it light as a feather over the hill.